***Code* **

A N

By Toby Oliver

Cover Design: Spiffing Covers

First published Aug 2013

Republished Sep 2014

Republished Mar 2016

Kindle Edition: ASIN: B00EJOTDUQ

Hard copy/CreateSpace: ISBN 9781492377078

Copyright 2013 Toby Oliver

This is a work of fiction. Names, characters, places and incidents are either the products of the author's imagination or are used fictitiously, and any resemblance to actual persons, business establishments, events or locales are entirely coincidental.

Chapter 1

The chilly autumn night sky was endlessly criss-crossed by the broad beams of searchlights, as the deadly drone of German bombers passed menacingly overhead. The black silhouetted shape of a plane occasionally strayed into the criss-crossing beams, caught like a fly in a trap, as London's anti-aircraft guns sent up a deafening barrage in a desperate bid to bring them down. The resulting blinding flashes mingled with the constant deadly thudding sound of explosions, as the Luftwaffe continued to unleash their lethal cargo.

Driving through the Blackout, two Scotland Yard Detectives, Chief Inspector Luke Garvan and Sergeant Harry Mackenzie drove past the porticoed Haymarket Theatre. Its windows plastered with a diamond pattern of sticky tape, and its walls banked up high with sandbags for protection against bomb blast. The squad car's blackout headlamps pointed feebly on the road ahead.

They cut across Trafalgar Square and drove down toward Parliament Square where they found themselves crawling along behind a large delivery lorry with its rear painted white, to help with visibility in the Blackout. Garvan peered out of the passenger window up at the night sky and guessed that the Luftwaffe would make full use of the clear moonlight reflecting off the River Thames, as they navigated a course to the heart of London. Mackenzie overtook the lorry and then swung left over Westminster Bridge toward Kennington Road.

'Where is Monkton Drive?' Mac asked.

'It's the first on the left after the park.'

As they pulled up outside the Tankard pub in Kennington Road close to Monkton Drive, debris from the bombing raid had already blocked the entrance to the turning.

Mac turned off the ignition. 'We're not going to get down there anytime soon,' he said.

Garvan agreed with him. 'We'll go the rest of the way on foot. The sooner we get this over and done with the better.'

They slowly headed down Monkton Drive. Above the searchlights continued to criss-cross the night sky and the constant sound of anti-aircraft fire gave Londoners some small measure of hope, and a morale boost, that in the midst of all the carnage they were somehow fighting back against the seemingly endless onslaught.

Hot shards of metal began bouncing off the pavements. Garvan darted toward the shelter of a doorway in a nearby terraced house. Crouching down, he looked back as Sergeant Mackenzie suddenly lost his footing and thudded heavily against a lamp post.

'Are you okay?' Garvan called out to him.

'Yes, yes, fine,' Mac said, rubbing his shoulder as he picked himself up off the pavement. 'What's the house number we're looking for?'

'Seventeen, I reckon its half way down.'

A newsagent's shop at the end of the street was already ablaze, and just ahead of them there was a large crater in the middle of the road where an incendiary bomb had exploded moments earlier, fracturing a gas main sending a fierce plume of yellow flames into the night sky.

Garvan instinctively slunk further into the relative safety of the doorway as another wave of incendiary bombs began crashing down around them. The sound was quite unnerving, and with every explosion, there was a strange, weirdly intense bluish light. The highly flammable material started fires that raged with a distinctively, and unmistakable intense orange glow. In Garvan's view, the German incendiaries were a sophisticated version of a Molotov cocktail, and right now on foot in the middle of a raid was the very last place either of them wanted to be.

Sergeant Mackenzie had hoped Garvan might take it into his head that it was simply too dangerous to carry on and call it a day, but as Garvan peered out of the doorway, Mac knew he was out of luck, and the Guv'nor was hell bent on reaching 17 Monkton Drive.

If the incendiary bombs were not already more than enough to cope with, but the larger bombs were causing catastrophic damage to the terraced houses around them. Debris littered the entire road. Garvan silently cursed to himself, wishing to God he hadn't taken the phone call during what was supposed to be a routine visit to West End Central Police Station. They'd been on the point of leaving when the Duty Sergeant had called them back and handed Garvan the phone.

'Assistant Commissioner Harmer says it's important.'

Reluctantly he'd grabbed hold of the receiver. 'Garvan here,' he said, 'you wanted to speak to me, sir.'

The familiar voice of Assistant Commissioner (Crime), Charles Harmer, barked down the line. Luke found himself automatically checking his watch. It was getting late, why on earth was the AC still at his desk, he thought, normally the old man would have long since left the office for the leafy calm of suburbia. There's been a tip-off, Harmer had grunted at him, a girl has been murdered, and he needed Garvan and Mackenzie to get down to Monkton Drive immediately to check it out. He didn't want to chance waiting until the morning in case the house was destroyed during the bombing raid.

Garvan glanced back over his shoulder at the door number behind him. It was 11. At least, they were on the right side of the road; there was no point turning back. He gestured to Mackenzie that he was about to make a move, and slowly began to thread his way along the street, weaving from doorway to doorway. He managed to get about ten yards before Mackenzie shouted at him to take cover. Instinctively he hurled himself over a small wooden gate, and crashed heavily onto the front doorstep only narrowly, avoiding the burning embers from the houses across the road.

Mac took his chances somewhat reluctantly and trailed after his Chief Inspector with the agility of someone driven by both fear and adrenaline. Mackenzie had drawn the short straw this evening as he hadn't meant to be on duty at all. The duty Detective, Sergeant Ticehurst, had been sent home apparently suffering from flu. "More like a bloody cold if you ask me", he'd grumbled to Garvan. It had made no difference, Ticehurst was off sick, and Mac had been ordered to step into his shoes.

In fairness, the evening had started well enough until the call from Harmer. The call had taken Mac by surprise, for Harmer rarely interested himself in routine murder inquiries, especially in an unfashionable area like South London. A swanky society killing in Mayfair or maybe a torrid scandal involving an MP was more to his style. Something high profile, but not too involved, where Harmer could get his name in the papers even if he were not actively involved in the inquiry itself. But for some reason this girl's murder was significant, Mac decided, at least, important enough for Harmer to risk sending two detectives half way across the city during a raid.

On reaching number 17 they were both somewhat relieved to find the house was still standing, albeit a little battered from the raid. The dark green painted front door was blown partially off its hinges, and the window panes were severely damaged.

'Mac, give us a hand,' Garvan shouted, grabbing hold of the front door.

Mackenzie helped him lean the door against the hallway wall. They then gingerly picked their way slowly along the hallway searching for a light switch.

'It's got to be near the front door,' Mac suggested.

Garvan blindly fumbled his way along the wall and found a switch. He flicked it, but the bombing raid had destroyed the electricity supply.

'Sod it,' he swore under his breath. 'Got your torch handy Mac?'

'Yes Guv.'

'Let's crack on then.'

'Shall we start downstairs first?'

'There's no harm. The AC's tip-off reckoned the body's upstairs in the main front bedroom.'

Mac turned on his torch, and they began to search the house methodically. They picked their way slowly through the hallway, and into the living room. The furniture had been upended and smashed into a myriad of pieces. The entire floor was covered with a mixture of glass and debris.

'There's nothing in here Chief.' Mac said, flashing his torch around the room. 'Do you want me to take a look around the kitchen?'

'Might as well.'

Mac peered inside the kitchen and shook his head; he couldn't see anything of interest. So Garvan headed toward the staircase in the hallway.

Flicking his torch toward the stairs, he said. 'The sooner we find if there's a body or not, the sooner we can get ourselves out of here.'

They climbed the narrow, rickety staircase, and hurriedly checked out the bathroom and the small back bedroom. If the house survived the bombing raid, Scotland

Yard's forensic team would at least still be able to carry out a thorough examination of the property; but there were no guarantees the house would survive, which made it imperative that they tried to find the victim.

As they moved through the house the explosions, like so many minor rumbling earthquakes rocked No17 to its foundations. At one point they both stood stock still in their tracks, and exchanged glances, uncertain if the house was about to disintegrate around them.

Garvan puffed out his cheeks and turned his torch toward Mackenzie saying. 'That was a close fucking shave.'

'A bit too bloody close if you ask me, are you still sure about this Guv?'

'We just need to check out the master bedroom, and then we'll call it a day.'

Mackenzie clicked the door open and led the way into the bedroom. The fierce blazing fire from the terraced house on the opposite side of the road cast weirdly distorted shadows across the room. Another gut-wrenching explosion illuminated it just enough for them to see the body of a young woman lying beside a chest of drawers. Garvan knelt and checked for a pulse.

He looked up at Mackenzie and shook his head. 'Dead as a doornail.'

'Has she been dead long?'

'For a while.'

So the old man's tip-off was right,' Mac said, thoughtfully.

They both shone their torches onto her body to get a closer look. The clothes were a little dishevelled, but whether they were the result of some struggle, or merely the result of her falling to the floor, was simply too early to say. As Garvan stared down at the body, a flicker of emotion crossed his otherwise laconic expression. Even in this strange, surreal half-light, they could both see the victim had been quite stunningly beautiful. Mac guessed she had probably been in her mid to late twenties. Garvan reached forward and gently touched her face; she was still partially warm, but only just. On closer inspection the once immaculately coifed blonde hair was hideously stained and matted with congealed blood. Garvan shone his torch directly on her face and noticed a single bullet wound to her forehead just above the bridge of her nose. He flicked the torch light toward the floor. Under her head the carpet was blood-stained, presumably, he thought, the result of an exit wound. He glanced up at Mac blinking against the glare of his Sergeant's torch.

'She's been shot at close range with a handgun, have a look round and see if you can find it.'

Mackenzie nodded and started to rummage about the bedroom. It wasn't easy going with only his torch, and the flickering lights from the fierce fire from across the road to illuminate his way. As he began to grope his way around the room slowly, he stumbled over a chair and dropped the torch just as another blast rocked the house, sending large chunks of plaster crashing down from the ceiling. Mac instinctively ducked down and glanced back over his shoulder noting Garvan hadn't even seemed to notice and was still leaning intently over the girl's body.

Over the years, there'd been so many bodies, so many that he'd lost count. Kneeling beside her, Garvan kept telling himself it was just another crime scene, that it was bread and butter stuff, routine; but for some reason or other, seeing her distinctive light blue eyes frozen in the last moments of her life, he found himself feeling inexplicably emotional. It was such a sad and pointless end. What was her story? Why would anyone have wanted to kill her? There didn't seem to be a sexual motive. Far from it, the gunshot wound to her forehead was clean, professional. Garvan took a quick glance round the room, and couldn't help wondering, what had brought her to this rather shabby rundown old house in a poor area of London. Even by torchlight, he could see the victim was expensively dressed. They didn't quite add up with her surroundings.

'I can't find anything worthwhile in here,' Mackenzie said, in desperation, 'we're just wasting our time, Guv'nor'.

'You're right Mac, it's time we got ourselves out of here there's nothing more we can do. We've found what we came for.' Garvan got to his feet. 'We'll come back in the morning.'

The best case scenario was that if the house survived the night, they might still have a fighting chance of lifting some useful forensics from the crime scene.

They retraced their steps downstairs and tentatively stepped outside. The fire had spread on the opposite side of the street, and three of the terraced houses were by now completely engulfed in flames. Faced with a wall of fire, they recoiled back into the doorway, but even as they did so, they could both feel their hair and eyebrows beginning to singe in the intense heat.

'God Almighty!' Mackenzie gasped, 'what the hell do we do now?'

'Looks like the roads blocked near the Tankard, I don't fancy trying to make it back to the car.'

They noticed a fire tender parked further along Monkton Drive. The crew were attempting to douse the flames from an earlier explosion. Their black helmeted figures were silhouetted against the raging inferno surrounding them. A desperate lack of water pressure was causing them severe problems as several of the hydrants along the street had been badly damaged. From out of the dense smoke an air raid warden emerged and shouted at them to stay well back as the house opposite number 17 was in imminent danger of collapse. Garvan stepped forward and produced his warrant card.

The warden shook his head. 'What the hell's that mate?' he snorted, 'it's too bloody dark to read anything, why aren't you down in the shelter?'

'I'm Detective Chief Inspector Garvan from Scotland Yard, and this is Detective Sergeant Mackenzie.'

The warden narrowed his eyes studying the two men with renewed interest. 'The Yard,' he repeated questioningly, 'Christ almighty what are you two doing round here?'

'Number 17,' Garvan said, gesturing over his shoulder, 'if it's still standing in the morning make sure no-one enters.'

'Why, what's happened?'

'There's been a murder. We'll be back here tomorrow the local police should be here first thing in the morning.'

'Do you know the name of the girl who lived there?' Mackenzie asked him.

'Nah, she was a pretty little thing, though, she'd only just moved in.' The warden hesitated, 'is it her.'

Mac nodded.

'The poor little bugger what kind of nutter would do a thing like that!'

Just at that moment another explosion rocked the street, the ground shuddered beneath their feet, and a house further along the road suddenly collapsed in a huge pall of dust and smoke.

'We can't get back to our car,' Garvan explained, 'where's the nearest shelter?'

'If you carry on walking down the road, past the fire tender, take the first left into East Square, and you'll find a shelter in the gardens,' the warden suggested.

The warden stood rooted to the spot watching them as they disappeared into the dense swirling smoke. He glanced up at the house and shuddered at the thought of the young woman lying dead inside. If it had taken a direct hit, the auxiliary services would have pulled the poor girl's body out of the rubble without a second thought, and assumed she'd died in the blast. Bodies were two a penny these days.

Garvan and Mackenzie carefully picked their way over the snaking fire hoses stretched across the road. They crunched through the broken glass and rubble, and past the gaping holes in the Victorian terraced houses.

They turned left out of Monkton Drive and into East Square. The once elegant Georgian facades were a little battered, and a few of the houses appeared to have been shored up by wooden scaffolding from earlier raids.

Garvan looked up at the sky. Even the moon had taken on a hideous red hue, reflecting the hundreds of fires burning out of control across London. If hell existed he told himself, it was here right now. In these once bustling streets the whole night sky had turned into a flaming inferno.

Although the stench of acrid smoke was not as suffocating as it had been in Monkton Drive, it was still bad enough to catch the back of their throats. The anti-aircraft guns in the nearby park still continued to fire at the enemy bombers. They entered the shelter via a narrow dank staircase and found themselves in a dimly lit subterranean world filled with the families living in East Square. There was also a group of nurses and doctors from Lambeth Infirmary, who'd just come off their evening shift when the raid had started. The shelter had thick walls, and a concrete roof about thirty feet long, with a wooden bench running down the length of both walls, and an opening at either end protected by brick blast walls. There were no internal doors which meant that in the event of a near miss, the blast would go straight through the middle without crushing anyone at a closed-in end. There wasn't much point in worrying about a direct hit. No-one would have survived anyway.

The arrival of the two detectives almost went entirely unnoticed. It wasn't exactly unusual for passers-by to drop in if they were caught out during a raid. The lights inside were dim, and somewhere a radio crackled out live dance music from the Café de Paris in the West End. A baby was crying, his mother was desperately trying to comfort him. A few hardy souls had tucked down on the benches in a bid to catch up on some sleep, but most people appeared happy enough to either chat or play cards.

The air was thick with cigarette smoke. It was certainly one way of trying to calm your nerves Garvan thought. Personally, he wasn't a heavy smoker, but he did find himself envying one of the doctors as he took an occasional swig from a silver hip flask. Right now, a glass of whisky would have gone down a treat.

His gaze drifted across the shelter and settled on an old boy seated all by himself reading a newspaper apparently without a care in the world. Luke couldn't help smiling to himself; he was about the right age to have been in the trenches during the last war, he guessed, that the Blitz probably seemed almost tame in comparison to being ordered over the top into some mud filled hell in no man's land.

Garvan saw a space on a bench and claimed his spot. He eased himself down against the slatted wooden wall.

He wearily closed his eyes, and said, 'I'd kill for a cup of tea right now is there a brew on the go?'

'I wouldn't mind something a bit stronger,' Mac grinned, joining him on the bench.

'Me too, but unless that bastard of a doctor over there is willing to share his whisky, we'd better settle for a cuppa.'

Garvan's eyes came to rest on a smart grey-haired woman. She was talking to a young girl of who was maybe three or four years old. She'd noted their arrival, and after handing the child, a glass of milk approached them with a ready smile of welcome. As they'd hoped a kettle was steaming on a small camping stove nearby, and she offered them sweet tea and a biscuit which they both eagerly accepted.

As they waited for the tea to brew, there was a distinctive whine that swiftly developed into a terrifying high-pitched whistling sound. Christ almighty, Garvan thought to himself, this is going to be a close shave. They braced themselves, waited, unsure if they were about to take a direct hit. There was a deafening explosion and the shelter rocked to its core sending swirling plumes of grey dust into the air. The lights flickered plunging them momentarily into pitch darkness. They sat there shocked, waiting, and hoping for the lights to flicker back into life. There was dryness in their throats, and it was difficult to breathe until the dust began to settle. The dim shelter lights slowly fluttered back into life. The moment had passed, and everyone silently breathed a collective sigh of relief, said their prayers and then carried on as usual.

'Close shave that one, Chief,' Mac said with understated relief.

Garvan idly glanced around the shelter wondering how it was that in such a relatively short space of time, the normality of their pre-war lives had almost been forgotten, in exchange for this strange, surreal world, where life was so precious, and yet so utterly expendable.

'This murder, Guv'nor,' Mackenzie muttered, 'what's so special about it?

Luke gave him a sidelong glance 'Special?' he queried, blankly.

'When was the last time we were ordered out in the middle of a bombing raid to a crime scene, let alone by old man Harmer?'

Garvan gave a shrug. 'I guess we'll both find out soon enough. You've got to give it to the old man his tip-off was spot on. If the house had been destroyed tonight, no-one would have been any the wiser. The rescue services wouldn't have given the girl's body a second glance.'

'I suppose so.' Mac sniffed.

'Let's face it, how many of us these days even bother going down a shelter, at least not in the numbers we used to? We've all been guilty of hiding under the kitchen table or stairs. By the time, they'd dragged her body out it would probably be too mangled to notice even the gunshot wound.'

'Did you ask the AC who tipped him off?'

'Of course, I bloody did, but Harmer wasn't exactly letting on and said he'd go into the details tomorrow morning.' Garvan folded his arms. 'I couldn't argue the point.'

'But what's got him down from his ivory tower?' Mac persisted. 'Either the Commissioner sparked him into life, or that girl is someone important. If she is, I don't understand why she was living in Monkton Drive. The local nick is only just up the road, why didn't he give them a call?'

Garvan blinked wearily at his Sergeant. 'That's your trouble Mac, isn't it? You've been living the high life for far too long now, haven't you?'

'I'm sorry, what do you mean?'

'Would you, have questioned the old man sending us to the Dorchester or the Ritz, bombing raid or not.'

Mac began to laugh in spite of himself. 'Well, at least, you get a decent frigging drink in the West End whatever time of day, but -'

Garvan cut across him. 'Not now Mac, give it a rest until we get back to the Yard. Just try and make the most of it. We're going to be stuck here until morning.' He glanced across the shelter and suggested. 'Why not go and help the lady carry our tea.'

Garvan was feeling tired and wearily closed his eyes, and began drifting off to sleep against a background of aimless chatter, and the crackling music from the radio. But Mackenzie had been right, whoever the girl was, she obviously had contacts or friends in high places, at least, high enough to galvanise the Assistant Commissioner into action, and that in itself was no mean feat.

By daybreak, the sirens sounded the all clear. People gathered up their belongings and started to emerge from their deep, dark subterranean world. They might be tired, but more importantly, they were grateful to have merely survived the ravages of the night before although the cold light of day also brought its own fears. Would they find their homes intact or reduced to a pile of rubble? Would they be homeless? For now, the screaming bombs might have stopped, but the all-pervading stench of smoke clung tenaciously to the air, coupled now with the distinctively sweet, sickly smell of burning flesh.

As they stepped out from the shelter into the stark morning sunlight, there were a few fewer windows in East Square, but by and large, the residents had been comparatively lucky. Just one of the houses had suffered minor structural damage.

Garvan and Mackenzie re-traced their steps and were surprised to find the house had survived the raid. It might be little the worse for wear, but at least, it was still standing. Garvan popped into the ARP Wardens' hut at the end of Monkton Drive. The elderly warden they'd spoken to last night was still on duty eating a well-earned bacon sandwich. Garvan asked him to keep a close eye on the house until the local police arrived. They returned to their squad car and found it was covered in dust, and the bodywork had taken a few hits from flying debris, but otherwise remained pretty unscathed.

'You'll have to fill out a chit for that lot,' Mac nodded, pointing at the scratches and dents on the bodywork.

Garvan shook his head. 'You signed the bloody thing out not me it's your responsibility,' he smirked.

Before heading back to Scotland Yard, they briefly called in at the local police station in Kennington Road and ordered the Duty Sergeant to ensure the murder scene was secured as soon as possible. Garvan then put a call through to the Assistant Commissioner's office at the Yard with a head's up that last night's tip-off had been spot on, and that they'd found a young woman's body at the address.

Driving back over Westminster Bridge the chimes of Big Ben sounded out the quarter hour. It was a strangely reassuring sound. Looking down the Thames toward the dockyards of East London, fires were still burning out of control; in fact, the whole of the City of London seemed to be shrouded in a thick grey and black pall of smoke. Seeing Mackenzie glance anxiously out of the car window toward the smouldering destruction down river, Garvan sensed his unease. He knew exactly what was running through his Sergeant's mind somewhere amidst that burning inferno were his wife and two young daughters. God willing they were safe and well, but they both knew only too well the random nature of survival in the Blitz. The shelter in East Square had provided them with a safe haven last night, but for so many others it would have been a different matter. Emerging from their Anderson Shelters and Tube stations the scene greeting them was often like stepping into the middle of Armageddon.

The trouble was the only way for Mac to check on his family was by phoning the local pub at the end of the street where he lived. Alf Garretty, the publican from the Crown and Cushion, was a good friend and had one of the few phones in the area. Mac's phone line had been destroyed in a bombing raid the week before and hadn't yet been reconnected.

Garvan had often found himself envying Mac's settled family life; his own situation was somewhat different. His was not a happy marriage and hadn't been for some time. After deciding to have their sons' Harry and John evacuated from London to stay with friends in Lyme Regis, they'd rarely seen each other. As it turned out, the boys loved the West Country, and in hindsight, it was probably the best decision they could ever have made. With the boys off her hands, Joan had been left kicking her heels with nothing to do and had decided to volunteer and join the Royal Air Force. Her first posting had been to the War Office in Whitehall, so apart from the long hours, life had continued much along the same lines as before with occasional visits down to Lyme Regis to see the children.

From Garvan's perspective, the only blot on the landscape had been Joan's sudden decision to accept a WAAF posting down to RAF Tangmere in Sussex. It had come as a bolt out of the blue she hadn't even bothered discussing it with him.

He hadn't seen her now for four months, and Joan's increasing reluctance to return to London had left him with a gut wrenching feeling that she'd found someone else. There had been umpteen confrontations, accusations, and endless blazing rows, but as the months passed he found himself preferring his own company, missing Joan less and less; it was easier this way without the emotional turmoil and upheaval. He was even beginning to stop feeling guilty about enjoying his new found freedom and bachelor lifestyle. Since the outbreak of the war, there was certainly no shortage of opportunities to meet women. The nightclubs and pubs were full of women, who'd been called up either for war work or the Armed Services. There had been nothing serious so far he didn't want anything too serious; it was way too soon as his feelings were still raw. The only thing he knew with any degree of certainty was that it was only a matter of time before Joan wouldn't bother coming back to London at all. In his mind, the only issue was how they were going to break the news to their sons.

Leaving Mac to sign the vehicle back into Scotland Yard's car pool, Garvan headed back to the squad's office. He bumped into Sergeant Jack Charteris carrying a large tray of dirty mugs. Jack was always immaculately turned out; he was a tall, wiry man who sported a large grey moustache. His military bearing was the result of many years spent serving with the Indian Army. He'd risen to the rank of company sergeant major, before finally deciding in the mid-1930s' to head back to England and start a new career with the Met. Jack was unfailingly reliable, meticulous, and an ideal uniformed Desk Sergeant. He was the lynchpin of the office and totally trustworthy. If there was ever a problem Charteris was the rock upon which the entire team depended on. Nor did he hold back if he thought one of his colleagues had messed up including Garvan himself. Jack was an excellent administrator, he didn't have a CID background, but even so, Garvan had seconded him to the team, and had come to rely increasingly on his sound common sense and reliability around the office. He also had his nose to the ground at Scotland Yard and little bypassed him. If you needed the latest gossip, or the list of the most recent promotions before they were published, then Charteris was your man.

On seeing Garvan in the corridor, Charteris stopped tray in hand. 'Ah Guv, we've been waiting for you, the Assistant Commissioner wants to see you right away. He's apparently been at his desk since the crack of dawn.'

'Has he?' Garvan smirked. 'I called the Yard earlier and left a message with his sidekick Tait about last night. He didn't bother mentioning the AC was at his desk.'

'I understand he's in a bit of a flap, Guv'nor.'

'The old bugger's always in a flap,' Garvan said flatly.

'Quite,' Charteris answered stiffly, 'I presume this poor woman isn't a run of the mill victim?'

'I guess so.'

'Must be a big job then, even his secretary wasn't expecting him in quite so early.'

'I bet she didn't.' Garvan checked his watch. 'How much time do I have?'

'The AC said right away, Guv'nor.'

Garvan nodded, retraced his steps back along the corridor, and peered round the door of Mac's office to check if he was back from the car pool. He was on the phone trying to contact Alf Garretty at the Crown and Cushion for news of his family. He glanced up at Garvan, judging by the look on his face no-one had so far picked up the phone.

'Upstairs Mac,' he ordered, 'the old man wants to see us in his office right away.'

Mac pulled a face and reluctantly replaced the receiver back onto the cradle. Garvan quickly nipped into the Yard's main reception to check up on last night's charge sheets. No further murders had been reported other than the AC's tip-off in Monkton Drive. The rest was pretty routine stuff umpteen arrests involving the selling of black market goods. The Blackout had brought endless opportunities for criminals, and rationing alone had created an enormous demand for under the counter goods. At the outbreak of the war, rationing laws had been rushed through by Parliament and were consequently riddled with legal loopholes. The Government's intentions had been well-meaning enough, no one could deny that, but the regulations as they stood had resulted in utter chaos. Against this chaotic backdrop, the police were severely overstretched fighting an almost endemic increase in crime.

Mac called to him before heading upstairs to Harmer's office. 'You ready, chief?'

'Sorry,' Garvan apologised handing the charge sheets back to a young PC. 'I got side-tracked.'

Chapter 2

Inside a large panelled office, Assistant Commissioner (Crime), Charles Harmer, sat reading a newspaper. He'd just turned fifty, was a well-built man, with a gravelly voice that was delivered in a deliberately hesitant manner. Harmer scarcely registered the arrival of Garvan and Mackenzie into his office and carried on reading the paper. He had a reputation at Scotland Yard for being immaculately tidy, to the point where it was something of a compulsive obsession. The old Victorian oak desk was geometrically aligned with papers, pens, an inkwell and a large black Bakelite phone, even the green blotting paper was set with meticulous precision centrally in front of him. For a man so addicted to order in his life, Garvan always thought it a rather odd choice of career to join the police, where every single day of his working life brought chaos into his neat, structured world. It was therefore probably hardly surprising Harmer's nerves were frequently at breaking point, and judging by the expression on the old boy's face; this morning appeared to be no exception. Garvan noted there were already a large number of cigarette butts sitting in an ornate cut glass ashtray. With seeming reluctance, Harmer looked up and fixed the two detectives with a steady, rather condescending gaze, and nodded for them to be seated as he neatly folded the newspaper.

Easing himself into one of the high-backed green leather chairs, Garvan suddenly became aware that someone was standing at the window in the far corner of the office. The unfamiliar dark-suited figure remained focused on some far distance point across the Thames. He certainly wasn't from the Yard or West End Central, and to Garvan's mind didn't have the cut of a copper.

Noting Garvan's interest in him, Harmer cleared his throat and with a flourish of his hand announced, 'allow me to introduce you to Spencer Hall, he's from –'

'From the Home Office,' the stranger supplied the answer, dragging himself away from the window. 'I hope you don't mind gentlemen if I remain standing.'

Garvan swivelled round in his chair to get a better look at him. There was the merest hint of a Welsh accent. Hall looked to be in his early thirties, his hair was a black, brown colour and given to a slight wave that had been carefully sleeked down. His was a tough face, the expression uncompromising and direct. The suit was well cut and of Savile Row quality, but however smartly tailored the suit, his whole bearing and attitude reeked of the military and not the Civil Service. After leaving school Garvan had spent some five years working in the rag trade as an apprentice to a tailor off Horseferry Road in Westminster, and he'd never lost his eye for a good cut of cloth. There was no way to Garvan's mind that Spencer Hall was a career civil servant, some nine to five pen-pusher. He exuded an air of innate confidence bordering on the arrogant. The eyes were watchful, but never wary; they were of a light blue colour, not quite cold perhaps, but unwavering in their directness. Garvan couldn't help himself from picturing this smartly suited stranger from the Ministry, dressed as a Commando casually enjoying the act of rearranging someone's face. Over the years, he'd interviewed countless hard men, but sitting in Harmer's office, it struck Garvan, that few of them had seemed more capable of handling themselves than this man Hall. He gave Mackenzie a sidelong glance wondering if he'd come to the same conclusion.

Garvan was beginning to get a nasty feeling about this murder. If Spencer Hall was in the military, then his cover of belonging to the Home Office was merely a euphemism for MI5. It didn't take too long for either of them to realise Harmer was being unusually reticent and polite in Hall's presence, and not his usual irascible self. He appeared to be treading on eggshells for fear of upsetting the man. As Harmer spoke, he kept looking in Hall's direction as if for some reassurance that he was on the right track. The AC's early morning appearance in the office had apparently involved a lengthy Home Office briefing.

'So you found the body in Monkton Drive last night?' Harmer asked.

Garvan nodded. 'Yes, sir.'

The AC held his gaze, his eyes narrowed. Since Garvan's arrival at Scotland Yard, he'd never once addressed him as Guv'nor. Within the Met, it was the ultimate term of respect for a senior officer, the highest accolade, but it had to be earned. The fact Garvan had persistently chosen to address him as sir rankled sorely with Harmer. It was a damning slight that he still hadn't earned his respect.

'It can't have been easy trying to reach the address last night, 'Harmer ventured. 'The local police called me first thing this morning. I understand the crime scene is a little battered but still standing, and they have a PC posted outside.'

Garvan's gaze flickered to Spencer Hall as he started to pace the office. He then looked back toward Harmer, and said 'Whoever tipped you off last night sir was spot on,'

'Did you find her in the main bedroom then?'

Garvan noted there was tension in Hall's expression. He stopped dead where he stood intently waiting for his reply. 'Yes, we found her body in the bedroom. A blast had almost taken off the front door, and the rest of the house was in a pretty bad state. At this stage, the only thing I can say with any degree of certainty is that she was shot in the forehead. Judging by the impact, I'd say the killer fired at point blank range.'

Spencer Hall's expression noticeably hardened.

'Can I ask who gave you the tip-off, sir?'

'It was an anonymous phone call,' Harmer announced stiltedly as if he'd already mentally rehearsed the answer.

'So the caller just happened to have a direct line to your office?'

Harmer looked through him without answering.

'You told me last night you'd taken the call personally.' Garvan pressed.

He still wouldn't be drawn.

Garvan turned to Spencer and stared hard at him. 'Mr Hall, can you tell me why the Home Office is interested in this woman's murder? If the victim was a member of your department, and I would guess a significant one at that, you'd usually instruct Special Branch to have a sniff around the crime scene or failing that, you'd keep it in-house.' Garvan paused, gauging how Hall would react, but his expression remained unreadable. 'To put it bluntly, I'm not too sure what you're playing at.'

'Meaning?' Spencer said, his eyes narrowing questioningly.

'I just need to know whether this is some window dressing exercise. Is it? You know what I mean, just for me to go through the motions.'

When he was either agitated or under stress, the AC developed a twitch in his right eye. Garvan's outburst had hit the right button - the twitch appeared, and his fists were clenched so tightly his knuckles turned white.

'What exactly do you mean by window dressing exercise?' Harmer demanded of him.

Garvan gave a shrug, 'Just wondering whether Mr Hall's Department simply wants a few boxes ticked for appearances sake.'

'Why on earth would they do that?'

'To cover their backs?' he threw in. 'I just don't understand why Special Branch isn't dealing with this caper.' Garvan smiled thinly and added, 'but I guess you have your reasons, Mr Hall.'

'We do Chief Inspector,' he said, coolly.

'So tell me then, do you want a full-blown murder investigation, or is the death of this young lady simply going down as just another unsolved murder?' Garvan folded his arms, decided to play devil's advocate, but he needed to know where he stood. 'Let's face it bodies are cheap in London right now, it's all too easy to cover up a murder. What difference would one more make?'

Harmer started to respond, but Hall raised his hand: 'I think you'll agree that Chief Inspector Garvan and Sergeant Mackenzie deserve an explanation,' he said. 'After all, they risked life and limb last night to reach the murder scene. You're correct in thinking that the victim Sarah Davis worked for the Government. We were colleagues.'

Mackenzie cleared his throat and asked. 'Have the family been informed of her death?'

Spencer nodded. 'That's all been taken care of. Your task is to find out what exactly happened last night. There's no need for you to involve yourself with the family.' He looked to Garvan. 'You can rest assured Chief Inspector that this isn't some fancy game or academic exercise, or whatever you like to call it just to please our lords and masters in Whitehall. We want Sarah's murderer tracked down and brought to justice. As you so rightly say, we could have involved Special Branch, but your profile, your experience and success over the years with the CID, especially in your handling of high-profile murder investigations made you the obvious choice to head up the investigation.'

Garvan looked at him warily.

'What I can tell you Chief Inspector is that the Commissioner, Sir Philip Game, personally put your name forward last night.'

'I don't suppose for one minute your Miss Davis was employed as a typist?' Garvan said, sarcastically.

Spencer allowed the merest flicker of a smile to crease his face, but it vanished as quickly as it had appeared. 'No Chief Inspector, not as a typist,' he answered smoothly.

'And are you at liberty to tell me exactly what kind of work she was engaged in at the Home Office?'

'Sarah was working in a particularly sensitive area of the war effort, which is why I was ordered to attend this morning's meeting. We don't want any details of this tragedy to become common knowledge, not even here at Scotland Yard. I know this isn't going to be easy for either of you, but you have to keep this investigation under wraps. Sarah was working on highly secret material and for security reasons, it's essential that her death isn't openly reported or discussed in public.'

'Will we be able to speak to the girl's parents?' Garvan pressed.

'Perhaps we can discuss that at a later date.'

'Who gave us the tip-off?' Garvan looked questioningly at the AC.

Spencer Hall intervened, 'We genuinely haven't a clue.'

He didn't believe him. 'Male or female, accent, I need something to go on.'

'Male,' Harmer said, thoughtfully. 'The line wasn't at all clear. He mentioned I should call St. James's 1219, and say that Sarah Davis was dead, and that was it, nothing more, nothing less. To be perfectly honest Garvan, I'm as bewildered as you are by the whole bloody thing. I checked with my secretary whether the caller had asked for me personally, which they had, and then phoned 1219.'

'And I answered the call, it's my number,' Spencer explained.

Hall was playing games. What was he up to Garvan wondered. 'Are you always this economical with the truth?' he asked.

Hall wandered back over to the window. 'I will provide you with a brief, a full brief Chief Inspector, but this isn't the right time or place to go into specifics.'

'But you must have some idea who called the AC and asked for him by name?'

Hall shrugged non-committedly. 'Your Assistant Commissioner has appeared in the newspapers recently. Only last week I saw his photo on the front page of the Daily Sketch.' He glanced back over his shoulder and then smiled at Harmer. 'Come to think of it, it wasn't a particularly flattering photo.'

Hall's observation didn't amuse Harmer. He reddened in anger but bit his tongue, and thought twice about crossing him.

'The article was to do with the black-market or something,' Spencer continued, thoughtfully, 'I can't quite remember. But you know how it is, the tabloids keep running stories that you're going to get the top job when Sir Philip Game retires.'

Harmer's face flushed again, this time, flattered that Hall knew about the speculation.

'Can you assure me I have your Department's full cooperation?' Garvan asked.

Hall nodded, his face was expressionless and quite impossible to read. 'We'll assist you in any way we can, Chief Inspector. All her colleagues will sorely miss Miss Davis. We just need her killer to be tracked down and brought to justice as quietly and professionally as possible.'

'And if the murder investigation should lead me back to the Home Office, what then Mr Hall, will I still have your full cooperation?'

'You have my word,' Spencer replied, there was a slight pause before he added, 'but judging by the expression on your face you'll probably take some convincing.'

Harmer intervened. He liked the sound of his own voice, prattling on aimlessly about the inquiry. It was all drivel of course, but he was trying to impress his visitor from the Home Office. For now, Hall was quite content to allow Harmer some slack as it massaged his well-known ego. It also gave Hall time to observe Garvan. The Commissioner had said he was good, his brightest, most promising Chief Inspector, but he needed to reassure himself and to make certain MI5 had made the right choice. Was he really as ruthless and clinical as reported? He knew that Garvan had served with the Met for some fifteen years now, and even his detractors at the Yard admitted his rise through the ranks had been unusually swift. He was seen as a Met high flyer with promotion coming rapidly. By nature, he was reported as being a laconic character, occasionally diffident, but underlined by an innate toughness and blinkered determination to succeed. He was a renowned thief-taker, and since working at the Yard, his reputation had grown even more rapidly.

Having read through the brief from Scotland Yard, Spencer knew that Luke had turned forty this year, almost ten years older than him, taller, about six foot, broad shouldered with short dark hair, greying slightly at the temples. His gaze, Hall noted, was unwavering, almost snake-like; the face was slightly lined but still passably handsome. There was an undeniable air of authority about him, and his contempt for Harmer was barely concealed. There was obviously a long and antagonistic history between the two men. Game had described Garvan as a hard-bitten, no-nonsense copper who was something of a legend at the Yard, renowned both for his thoroughness and dedication, a stickler for accurate reporting. Among the criminal fraternity of London, he was regarded as a ruthless opponent. He was also not averse to confronting senior officers if and when he thought necessary. Judging by his performance in Harmer's office, the Commissioner had not been wrong in his assessment.

On the other hand, Hall was unimpressed by Charles Harmer. No doubt in his day he'd probably been talented enough, but in his view it seemed obvious that Harmer was now just biding his time, trying to keep his nose clean for the top job of Met Commissioner. Spencer guessed the last thing he needed right now was a murder enquiry with security service connections. It could end up scuppering his pitch for Game's post when he eventually retired. Hall suddenly became aware of the on-going conversation between Garvan and the AC.

'This is a special job,' he heard Harmer announce pompously. He was looking directly at Hall now, probably hoping for a reaction, but he waited in vain. 'One of the reasons you were chosen for this case,' Harmer continued to Garvan, 'is that you run a tight ship, you'll just have to make sure it remains water-tight.

'I only have one stipulation', Garvan said, bluntly.

'What's that?'

'If I am to head up this murder investigation I need to handpick my team.'

The AC nodded his approval. 'I'm not interested in how you conduct the investigation; rest assured I'll provide you with the backup you require. We just need you to get the right bloody result!'

Garvan stared at Harmer in stony silence. Despite the outward offer of help, he knew if the inquiry went pear shaped, both he and his team would be hung out to dry. The only consolation was that if he made a hash of everything, by default he'd probably end up ruining Harmer's career as well. The only difference being that while Harmer would be put out grass and pensioned off, Garvan would probably find himself back pounding the beat in some God forsaken, grotty police station in the suburbs.

Garvan couldn't help wondering just how important Sarah Davis had been. The mere fact the Commissioner was involved probably answered the question. But what exactly did Spencer Hall and his cronies already know about her death? Were they genuinely mystified by their colleagues' brutal murder? He somehow doubted it. Garvan's greatest fear was that ultimately, his team would become bit-part players in some shadowy security investigation. He still couldn't help feeling, perhaps unjustly, that Hall's offer of full co-operation was just so much empty rhetoric.

He glanced at Hall then back toward Harmer deciding that there wasn't any point prolonging the meeting, and Harmer was beginning to go round in circles repeating himself. He'd had enough and stood up, shook hands with Hall, and said to him.

'You'll require written reports of course, but let's not get too bogged down by timescales.'

'It's your call Chief Inspector.'

Garvan didn't respond and headed out of the office with Harry Mackenzie dutifully following him.

In the corridor, Mac turned and said. 'What the fuck was that all about, Guv'nor?'

'The only thing we need to know right now is just how important this woman was to The Home Office.'

'And as for that Spencer Hall bloke, he doesn't look like any bleeding career civil servant to me,' Mac smirked.

'Not exactly your average grey admin type is he?' Luke smiled.

'No disrespect to you sir, but why do they want you rather than Special Branch to run the investigation?'

Garvan stopped and swung round to face Mac. 'Do you know Harry I've always thought you were pretty quick on the uptake.'

Mackenzie stared back at him questioningly.

'It's obvious, isn't it?'

'Can't say as it is, no.'

Garvan gave a wry smile, 'I guess it's just that mainstream Chief Inspectors at Scotland Yard are two a penny, and I'm considered expendable.'

'But it doesn't add up. The Home Office, MI5, or whatever you like to call them,' Mac persisted, 'usually only liaise with Special Branch, why bother coming to us?'

'No doubt we'll find out soon enough, they obviously have their reasons.' Garvan headed back to his office, reached into the top drawer of the desk and grabbed a pack of cigarettes. 'Anyway Mac, you ought to be making tracks and going home.'

'I don't suppose the phones lines are back up yet. Are you off to Monkton Drive, Chief?

'Yes, I am. I just need to have a quick shave and freshen up a bit, and then I'll head straight back in about half an hour.' Garvan checked his watched and suggested, 'Why don't you try phoning the Crown and Cushion again?'

Mac nodded and returned to his office.

Garvan disappeared for a wash and shave, and by the time he returned to the outer office, it was obvious Harry still hadn't managed to get through to the pub.

'They'll be all right,' he said, reassuringly. 'It was pretty bad last night; it's no wonder the lines are down. Just get yourself home.'

Without answering Mac reached for his overcoat from the wall rack. 'Jack Charteris said the Tube's still running. I'll go to Tower Hill and walk the rest of the way it isn't too far from there.'

'Let me know how you get on.'

Chapter 3

Having just signed out a Wolsey from the Motor Transport Office, Garvan strode back along a dully painted pale green corridor and down a wide wooden staircase to the ground floor. Clutching the car keys in his right hand, he pushed through the swing doors to the crowded forecourt, lined with neat rows of highly polished black cars. He instinctively pulled up the collar of his overcoat against the icy breeze sweeping off from the river. There was still a distinct lingering smell of acrid smoke in the air left over from the night's bombing. Driving out of Scotland Yard, he turned right along the Embankment and headed back over Westminster Bridge toward Monkton Drive.

The auxiliary services had cleared most of the rubble from last night's raid, but even so Monkton Drive was only passable with care. News of Sarah's murder had soon spread, and Garvan's arrival rapidly caught the attention of a group of women huddled across the road from number 17. A young PC was standing outside and to Garvan's mind, he looked distinctly uneasy in his own skin, not quite sure what he should do. Beside him was a uniformed sergeant from Kennington Road nick, who'd taken control of securing the house. Luke pulled up outside. The constable saluted stiffly as the sergeant stepped toward the curb and opened the door.

'Chief Inspector Garvan, we've been expecting you. The Home Office pathologist arrived about forty-five minutes ago with his assistant. I thought Sir it would be in order for him to start his examination before your arrival. I hope I did the right thing?'

Garvan nodded his approval, not allowing his surprise to register that the pathologist, rather than the Police Divisional surgeon was first on the scene.

'He said it'll be an hour or so before the girl's body could be moved to the morgue for a full post-mortem. The forensic team from Scotland Yard arrived about two hours ago,' the Sergeant said, checking his watch.

'Thank you,' he said, thoughtfully glancing over his shoulder at the women huddled together across the road. 'Have your men started talking to the neighbours yet?' he asked.

'We have a Detective Sergeant working his way down the street. He'll have their statements delivered to your office at the end of play today.'

Garvan slipped through the open door into the hallway. In broad daylight, it could at best, be described as shabby. In spite of the blast damage, there was still no disguising the fact that both the furniture and the décor had seen far better days. He paused briefly at the bottom of the staircase head bowed, listening to the pathologist discussing his findings with a colleague in the main bedroom. It sounded like Sam Menzies. Over the years, their paths had crossed on numerous occasions. Before heading upstairs, Garvan decided to take another look around the living room and retrace his steps from last night. By now every conceivable surface had been daubed with fingerprint powder, the Yard's forensic team were currently working their way around upstairs.

He paused in the doorway trying to read the crime scene. The added effects of the bomb blast were proving at best challenging. If there had been a struggle or a sign of forced entry, the evidence had been entirely obliterated by the bomb blast. He entered the living room casting an eye over the victim's personal effects. A handbag was lying on the sofa, lipstick on the table, and an overcoat slung over the back of a chair. There was something touchingly poignant seeing the victim's belongings scattered quite randomly about the room.

Why was this one starting to get to him? Was it simply because she had been so young and stunningly beautiful? If truth be told, he wasn't quite sure. He began searching through her overcoat pockets and found a key, a bus ticket and a crumpled shopping list before carefully replacing them. There was no way of telling at this stage of the investigation what if anything might prove significant in the way of evidence.

Garvan moved into the kitchen and instantly pulled a face of despair. It was in such an almighty mess there wasn't any point going any further. The entire room was strewn with a variety of broken pots and pans; the ceiling had buckled and was sagging to the point of collapse.

Heading upstairs, Garvan entered the main bedroom where Menzies was kneeling beside the body of Sarah Davis. His young assistant, Ivy Standbridge, was making notes on a clipboard, and occasionally produced little buff envelopes from her jacket pocket as Menzies removed a fragment of evidence from the body. The doctor looked up at Garvan and nodded a silent greeting while continuing to make a seamless running commentary of his observations. They'd known each other for about ten years now. Menzies was high quality, one of the Home Office's leading pathologists. He'd made his name way back in the early twenties with a string of very high profile and infamous murder cases.

Menzies was dedicated to his work and had developed something of a reputation amongst lawyers for his detailed testimonies for the prosecution. He was incisive and spoke with unquestionable authority. He was by now in his early sixties, a man of stocky build and always impeccably dressed. Over the years, Garvan had become convinced that Menzies had grown to enjoy thoroughly the spectacle of his more well-known cases, conducted as they were under the full glare of public interest, with his photograph splattered all over the front pages as he emerged from the Old Bailey. However in fairness, Garvan conceded, Menzies' occasional appearances at the Old Bailey were probably the icing on the cake. He knew from personal experience that Sam's days were usually spent poring over an endless sad litany of suicides or accidental deaths.

Garvan moved closer as Menzies and his assistant clinically worked their way around the young woman's body. The early morning sunlight shone in a shaft of harsh, unforgiving brightness through the broken distorted bedroom window, and somehow only served to exacerbate the victim's plight. The blood that was last night still wet had now congealed and matted her once carefully coifed blonde hair. The faded patterned carpet beneath her head was stained by a crimson patch of blood from the exit wound. The murder scene had been vivid enough last night, but in the cold light of day, the sight of her lying dead with a single bullet hole through her forehead sickened him even more. His gaze wandered across her corpse and set on a trickle of dried blood that had seeped out of the corner of her mouth, that Luke hadn't noticed before. Nor, he decided had he been mistaken last night, even frozen in death it was still clear to see that Sarah Davis had been an outstandingly beautiful young woman. Garvan found himself checking his watch. This time, yesterday morning Sarah had been very much alive, maybe dreaming of her future, much like any other young woman of her age. The only difference was that she connected somehow to Spencer Hall; the man Harmer would have him believe was a civil servant from the Home Office.

He leaned forward and studied the gunshot wound to Sarah's forehead more closely. There was little doubting that she'd been executed with, deadly accuracy. He took his time and checked out the bedroom. The dressing table had been blown clean across the room toward the bed, and two Windsor chairs were upended, but there was simply no way of telling whether they'd been moved by the blast, or were the result of some struggle between Sarah Davis and her killer.

If Spencer Hall, as he suspected was a member of the Security Services, the death of a colleague like Sarah Davis would typically have come under the control of Special Branch, and certainly not the Murder Squad. He still couldn't quite understand why MI5 would want a bunch of nosy mainstream coppers snooping into their affairs, and asking potentially awkward questions. It simply wasn't their style of doing things. Garvan had been half expecting, Norman Kendall, the head of Special Branch, to summon him up to his office and tell him to back off. But for whatever reason Kendall hadn't made contact, and even when they'd bumped into each other in the corridor as Garvan was heading off back to Monkton Drive, he'd seemed very chatty, perhaps overly chatty. So what exactly did Kendall know? And what had forced MI5 to by-pass Special Branch with Kendall's apparent approval to seek help from a Murder Squad CID detective. To Garvan's mind, it just didn't add up, and it was beginning to nag at him. He needed to know what lay behind MI5's decision.

Standing with his back to the window, he couldn't help noticing how long Sarah's red painted fingernails were. Beautifully manicured and bore no sign of her doing any physical work. Luke didn't know of any typist or secretary in his experience who'd ever managed to keep their nails long, hammering away all day on heavy metal typewriter keys took its toll on manicured fingers. It was probably just as well Spencer Hall had already confirmed Sarah hadn't been employed as a typist.

Over the years, Garvan had developed something of a thick-skinned approach to murder cases. It was in many ways no more than a defence mechanism, a way of standing back and not allowing emotions to cloud his judgment, it wasn't that he was devoid of compassion, far from it. One of his very first cases had involved the brutal murder of a four-year-old child. It had not only reduced him to tears but had consumed him with a burning hatred and a need for revenge against the killer. The murderer had never been brought to justice, and that case had haunted him ever since. In no small measure, Garvan had blamed himself for the failure. He'd been so enmeshed, so emotionally caught up and involved, that he'd lost a grip of the investigation and had allowed the killer to slip through the net. From that day forward, Garvan had vowed never to become so emotionally involved again. He simply couldn't afford it, if he wanted to do his job effectively; and from then on, no other murderer had managed to slip through his fingers. That vow had held until Sarah's death, and now for some inexplicable reason his emotions had started to intrude again, but he needed to get a grip, and fast. The case was way too important to allow anything to cloud his judgement.

Sam Menzies slowly removed his surgical gloves and standing back from the body briefly cast an experienced eye over his assistant's notes, before asking Standbridge to pack up the medical equipment and paperwork. It was only now that he turned his attention to Garvan and extended his hand in greeting.

'Chief Inspector, I hope you're keeping well.'

'Good to see you again Doc.'

Menzies smirked at him. 'You weren't expecting me here, were you?

'No,' Garvan said, bluntly, 'I thought the divisional surgeon would have been called in to help.'

Menzies adjusted his half-moon glasses. 'All very hush-hush this caper,' he said, conspiratorially, 'I received a call from the Home Office, the men in grey suits,' he added, with a wink, 'I was ordered to come down here personally, they didn't want the divisional surgeon butting his nose in. They were wittering on about cutting out unnecessary red tape.'

'Well, there's a first time for everything.' Garvan grinned at him.

'Quite,' Menzies grunted. He gestured down at the body, and added, 'it doesn't take half a brain to work out this poor young woman was in some way connected to the security services, does it?

'I guess not.'

Menzies took a sharp intake of breath. 'Pretty little thing wasn't she. I suppose about my youngest daughter's age, I'd say no more than about twenty-six, or seven.'

'Any sign of a struggle?' Garvan asked.

'Nothing overtly violent, there are one or two bruises on her left cheek. They're consistent with her being hit with some force, but not extreme; I'd say it was caused by more of a slap than a punch.'

'So nothing to do with her fall then?'

'I think not,' Menzies mused, thoughtfully as he stared back down at the body. 'What I can tell you is that full rigor mortis has already set in. I presume that ties up with your finding the body?'

'She was barely warm at the time,' Garvan confirmed.

Menzies nodded. 'In my opinion, Miss Davis was probably killed some twelve or more hours ago. I think you'll agree with me Chief Inspector that the gun was held to the forehead at very close quarters.'

Garvan nodded. 'It's a clean, smooth shot. Whoever did it knew what they were doing.'

'If I was of a betting persuasion, which I'm not, I'd say young Sarah Davis knew her killer, but there again,' he grinned, 'what do I know, that's rather more your department than mine. I'll be able to tell you more by the end of the week after the full post-mortem. Do feel free to drop by the morgue if you want to sit in, I'll let you know the time once I've fixed the date.'

Garvan thanked Menzies before checking with the forensic team who were busy finishing off in the main bedroom. So far, they confessed their findings didn't look too promising. Luke then made his way back downstairs and paused in the front porch feeling a sudden sense of relief at being back out in the fresh air. He glanced across the road where the same gaggle of women was still huddled together watching Garvan's every movement; he lit a cigarette. They didn't exactly strike him as promising witness material, but you never knew he might just get lucky. Any clue, no matter how small at this stage of the inquiry would be more than welcome. He crossed the road to join them. The women studied him warily; his tall, imposing figure towered over them. His heavy-lidded eyes were thought of as being cold, and behind his back at the Yard they'd nicknamed him snake eyes, but his natural charm and ready smile melted away any suspicions the women of Monkton Drive might have initially harboured.

He introduced himself. They all appeared suitably impressed he was a Detective Chief Inspector, and even more thrilled discovering he was from Scotland Yard, and not the dreary local nick along the main road. Garvan spoke to them about the bombing raid, and how he and his sergeant had ended up being forced to seek shelter in East Square. He managed to set them at ease; he seemed normal, even if he was some big wig from Scotland Yard. His gaze settled on the badly damaged houses behind them, some were still smouldering, and asked if any of the women had been bombed out. One of them stepped forward, and tearfully recounted how she'd returned from the park's shelter in Kennington Road only to discover the burnt-out shell of her home.

'Up there,' she sobbed, pointing down the road.

She went on to explain her two sons were away in the Army and so her friend, Hazel Saunders, had taken her in, but the only clothes she possessed were the ones she was wearing. There was some talk of her being evacuated to a reception station, but Hazel had said she could stay with her as long as she liked.

'Don't you worry Lily, darling,' Hazel soothed, wrapping a protective arm around her friend, 'we'll look after you.'

Garvan pointed to number 17. 'I suppose you've all heard about the murder across the road.'

A chorus of disbelief rippled through the group as he confirmed their worst fears.

'We weren't too sure if it was true,' Lily explained,' the Chief Warden said the girl had been killed, but we all hoped he'd got it wrong. He can be a silly old bugger at times, gets things a bit muddled, he means well, though.' She took a sharp intake of breath. 'The thing is, Chief Inspector, you never think anything like this is going to happen, at least not on your own doorstep, do you? She was so nice and all.'

The women agreed with Lily, but as they chatted amongst themselves, Garvan picked up an underlying hostility toward the unfortunate Sarah Davis.

'I understand she hadn't lived here for too long,' he interrupted.

'No,' one of the women replied,' only about a month,' she gave a shrug, 'maybe six weeks.'

'Did you see anyone with her yesterday?'

The same woman puffed herself up full of self-righteous indignation. 'I don't like talking ill of the dead, but that girl had more gentleman callers than I've had hot dinners.'

'And your name is?'

'Beverley Wilkes,' she announced proudly.

He'd met Beverley's type before, the local busybody who came to her own conclusions without any basis in fact, but he pressed on. 'So what do you think Miss Davis was up to?'

'I'll tell yer, it's been no better than a bleeding knocking shop over there!' she nodded in disgust. 'We've got a lot of theatrical types lodging round 'ere,' Wilkes huffed, 'it's cheap but handy for the Old Vic up the road and the theatres in the West End. I reckon Sarah Davis was on the stage, got that look about her, hadn't she?'

'Had she?' he queried, blankly.

'Well they're all the same aren't they, that lot!' Wilkes spat at him.

'You mean like those Welsh girls' from the dairy near the hospital,' Lily piped up, 'they're a right flighty bunch.'

Garvan was amused; the dairy was obviously well worth a visit. 'So ladies, let me get this right then, you believe Sarah Davis was on the game. She didn't look much like a Tom to me,' he said.

The group exchanged glances, was he being naive, it's not what they expected from a Scotland Yard Detective, he wasn't some plod from the local nick. Beverley Wilkes continued with renewed vigour.

'She weren't short of nylons that one.'

'Nylons?' he said, quizzically.

'They're in short supply ain't they, but that one never went without! I'll give you she was a classy type, very pretty. Some days she changed her clothes a couple of times, and all the while there'd be these suited and booted men calling morning, noon and night.' Beverley folded her arms. 'Don't know where she got the bleeding energy from. The only thing I'll say about her is she didn't dabble in rough trade; the geezers all looked as if they had money. Wonder how much she charged?'

'Trust you to say that,' Lily snorted.

'Looking at her clothes she must have made a few bob, mind you, she wouldn't be the only actress around 'ere on the game.'

Garvan tossed his cigarette butt into the gutter. 'Ladies,' he sighed, 'do any of you recall seeing anyone visiting her house yesterday, yes or no?'

'I did,' announced an elderly woman standing almost half-hidden by the others. They parted as one as she spoke, leaning heavily on a stick she shuffled forward. 'I'm Martha.'

'How do you do Martha?' Garvan smiled at her.

He found himself gazing down at elderly, hunched woman. She was barely five foot tall, with thinning grey hair swept back into a neatly tied bun. Must be in her eighties, he mused and had what looked like a recent scar over her left eyebrow. Though her face was heavily lined, Martha's eyes had a decidedly youthful twinkle about them; it was almost as if she was somehow trapped inside her tired, distorted body.

'I live next door to the girl, Chief Inspector,' she explained, 'or should I say lived next door to the poor darling, at number 15,' she pointed with her stick.

'Did you see anyone with Sarah yesterday afternoon?'

'At my time of life Chief Inspector,' she continued, 'you tend to watch the world go by, there isn't much else to do,' Martha added, poignantly. 'Sometimes I sit in me downstairs bay window; I think Beverley over there would call me a curtain twitcher.'

It was a barbed comment and for whatever reason it struck home, Beverley Wilkes had the decency to look embarrassed. Garvan decided there was obviously some history between the two women.

'But if the weather's relatively mild like yesterday,' Martha continued seamlessly, 'I take me chair and sit outside the front door. I wasn't there too long, though; it got a bit nippy later on.'

Martha gave a long preamble about the weather and her rheumatism, but eventually, Garvan gently managed to steer the conversation back on track.

'Sarah had a regular visitor,' she explained, 'he was at the house yesterday afternoon. She seemed very fond of him; he was always very polite, he'd say good day to me and doff his hat like a real gent.'

'She was a might too fond of the gentlemen!' Lily chuckled, 'it was like bleeding Clapham Junction over there.'

Martha nodded at her. 'That's as maybe, but the girl was always very kind to me. I speak as I find. Sarah always went out of her way to be helpful, checking if I wanted anything up at the shops. She made me a cup of tea one morning as I was a bit shaken after a raid. I'd spent the night under the stairs and got blown right across the hallway, cut my head open on the corner of the hall table,' she said, pointing to the fresh scar slicing through her left brow. 'Even though Sarah was running late for work bless her, she took me up the road to the hospital and waited while I had the stitches put in, only four of them mind, and then she brought me back home and made sure I was all right before going off to work.'

'Bit early in the day for her kind of work,' Lily grunted, sarcastically.

Martha glared at Lily and added cuttingly. 'You've always been a might too quick to judge others Lily Baker that's always been your bleeding trouble.'

'What's that supposed to mean, I've done nothing to be ashamed of!'

'Well you would say that, wouldn't you!' came the withering response.

Garvan cut across the women. 'What did this regular visitor of Sarah's look like; can you describe him to me?'

'Bit shorter than you,' Martha explained, 'dark haired, usually wore a trilby, very smart, polite as I said, but looked as if he always had a bad smell under his nose, you know the type, bit stuck up.'

Garvan couldn't help himself from smiling, the description could so easily have fitted Spencer Hall; there again, it could have probably fitted half the male population of London. It was still certainly worth checking out if Hall had visited Sarah yesterday afternoon.

'And was he the last visitor of the day?'

'Bet he bloody wasn't,' Beverley Wilkes laughed.

'Behave yourself, Bev,' Martha snapped angrily, 'you're showing yourself up. There were two male visitors during the afternoon. I didn't see the poor luv after about three thirty. Before that she nipped up the road to the newsagents on the corner, I think it was the only time she left the house all day, she looked tired to me. We passed the time of day, we always did. I went in for my tea early before the bombing started and sat listening to the radio. British Relay always just manages to give you a warning of the air raids before the sirens start whining. Not sure how they do it. Those sirens always send a shiver right through me every time they start wailing; I get a knot in the pit of my stomach. I'm rambling now; you ain't interested in that, are you?' She looked away from Garvan toward 17. 'Just to think of that poor girl dying next door to me,' she said, with a shake of her head, 'it doesn't bear thinking about. Sarah was a good, kind and very beautiful girl. I know she hadn't lived here for long, but I liked her a lot.' Her eyes started to glisten, and tears began trickling down her cheeks. 'I'll miss her; she was a good soul. I just can't get over the poor little bugger being scared witless last night, keeps going through my head, was it quick, did the bastard strangle her, or what?'

'You understand I can't go into details Martha, you know that but if it helps I can tell you she died quickly without suffering, she died instantly.'

'Thank God,' she sobbed, cupping a hand over her mouth.

'Do you think the murderer lives round ere?' Beverley asked, warily.

'I don't think you have anything to worry about, it's early days, but so far everything points to the killer being from outside the local area.'

He turned his attention back to Martha, flashed a smile and inclined his head. 'How can I ever thank you, you've been a great help, ma'am'.

'Well,' she said, 'I'll tell you young man, forty years ago you could have done wonders for me, you're not doing too badly now.'

There was that twinkle in her eye again. Garvan instinctively reached out and clasped hold of her hand. 'Martha I assure you the loss is all mine, I was simply born just a little too late.'

Garvan left the women laughing and Martha with a longingly wistful smile on her face. As he headed back toward his car, he caught sight of Sergeant Jack Charteris striding down the centre of the street, his face set in stone.

'What are you doing here, what's wrong?'

'I had a call from the publican at the Crown and Cushion, Mac,' he said, struggling to get the words out, 'there was a direct hit last night; he - he's lost Marie and the girls.'

'Where is he now?'

'Still at the pub, Alf's looking after him.'

Garvan retrieved the car keys from his pocket. 'Take care of this I'll nip over to the Crown.'

Chapter 4

Garvan was tired, dog tired, he gripped the steering wheel tightly, scarcely aware of his surroundings as he drove toward the East End, wondering what the hell he was going to say to Harry Mackenzie. What can you say to a man who's just lost his entire family? Thank God, he and Joan had taken the decision to send their boys to the West Country, away from the endless nights of the Blitz. It hadn't been an easy decision to make at the time, but at least, they were safe and out of harm's way.

As he neared the City of London, it appeared as if there was scarcely a building which had not suffered some degree of bomb damage. He had to make several detours before finally drawing up close to St. Katherine's dock near the Tower of London. The river looked a dull murky grey; even more, flotsam than usual was drifting downstream. Last night's raid had sent cascades of burning embers into the tidal waters below, and buildings had collapsed in a domino effect into the swollen river. All the surrounding streets were littered with debris. Fifty yards up the road a large hole revealed a fractured water main, which was gushing torrents of water down the road. Firemen, their faces heavily blackened, were still damping down the residual fires on either side of the street, and further along, two buildings had totally collapsed.

Garvan decided there was little point trying to drive any further. If the road ahead was anything to go by, he might as well go the rest of the way on foot. As he locked the car door, the distinctive sweet smell of burning human flesh lingered in the cold morning air. A pall of acrid smoke clung over the City; it was cloying, and at times made it hard to breathe.

The going was slow as Garvan picked his way through the narrow side streets. The damage appeared completely random; some roads were entirely untouched by the carnage while others had been covered in raging walls of fire. To his right the top of one of the terraced houses had been destroyed, and yet bizarrely against the only remaining fragment of wall, a Welsh dresser stood inexplicably unscathed by the blast. Two doors down, the local sweet shop, lay in ruins, but miraculously there were various unbroken jars of sweets that had survived the bombing and lay strewn across the road.

Turning the corner beside the sweet shop, Luke stopped dead in his tracks confronted by a scene of utter devastation. He was standing at the end of Reedworth Street where Mac had lived in a neat Victorian terrace. The houses nearest the corner were still relatively intact, but those, further along, had been razed to the ground. The street had been blocked by a hastily erected wooden barrier, a pungent smell of gas clung tenaciously in the air. A small team of soldiers was working around a large crater in the middle of the road. One of them was standing guard at the barrier as Garvan approached.

'Sorry sir, you can't come any closer the street's been evacuated there's an unexploded bomb, we're still working on it,' he gestured toward the team. 'Just as well the bloody thing didn't explode; it would have taken the whole ruddy street with it.' He looked round to check on his colleagues. 'Mind you mate, there ain't much left of the houses', is there?'

'I wouldn't fancy their sodding job,' Luke said, with feeling.

'You get used to it,' the squaddie shrugged.

'I'm just heading up the road; do you know how many casualties there was last night?'

'They're still counting 'em mate. The walking wounded have been taken up to the church hall. Did you hear about the Cantor Street shelter?'

'A direct hit, wasn't it?'

'Yeah, not one poor sodding bugger got out of that one.'

'That's what I heard. Can I get to the Crown and Cushion this way? Garvan said, gesturing down the road.

The squaddie nodded. 'We drove past the pub a couple of hours ago, be a bit careful mate; there's a lot of glass underfoot.'

'Thank you.'

Luke took one last lingering look down along Reedworth Street toward the bomb disposal team as they tried to disarm the device. The Crown and Cushion was far enough away from the unexploded bomb that even if the UXB team failed to disarm it, it wouldn't pose too much of a structural threat to the building. By the time, he managed to reach the pub, a brewery dray pulled by two huge powerfully built grey horses had drawn up outside the main entrance to deliver fresh barrels of beer and collect the empties. The wooden trap doors to the cellar set in the pavement were open; barrels were being loaded swiftly from the cart and rolled down into the dark below.

'Is the landlord down there?' Garvan asked one of the draymen.

The man's eyes narrowed and without answering leaned down toward the cellar and shouted. 'Alf there's a bloke up ere for yer, he looks like Old Bill to me.'

From the gloom below a face peered up blinking against the sudden daylight. 'Yeah,' said Alf, with a grunt, 'you're right Ted he's Old Bill. I'll be up with you in a second, Guv'nor, Mac's still inside, wait just a sec and I'll let you in.'

Alf emerged from the cellar and unbolted the ornate Victorian doors to let Garvan inside. The saloon bar was still pungent with a heady mixture of stale smoke and beer. Alf Garretty was a bear of a man, an ex-professional boxer who sported a twisted broken nose. He was a good friend of Mac's and had also known Luke for about ten years.

Wiping his hands on the leather apron tied around his waist, Alf said. 'Glad you came, Guv, it's been a fucking nightmare, knew I had to tell him, but how do you tell a mate his wife and little'uns are dead. I take it you heard the shelter took a direct hit.'

Luke nodded.

'No-one got out alive, not a bloody soul. I had to physically stop him from going down there.' Alf thoughtfully sucked in his lower lip and slowly shook his head. 'I couldn't let him do that, you see he just wouldn't believe me, thought I'd got it all wrong. The trouble is Guv'nor, his wife didn't always go down there, and the poor bastard was pinning all his hopes Marie and the kids had gone somewhere else.'

'So there's no doubt Marie and the girls' were down there last night?'

'I saw her yesterday afternoon about sixish on the way to Cantor Street with Nancy and Alice. I was outside the pub when she stopped for a natter. Marie was carrying a bag of toys and a bit of food to tide them over until morning. She wanted to be there early and get a decent place for the kids. You see Guv, some evenings Marie took to coming here with the girls. They'd spend the night in our cellar with us.' Alf hesitated, he looked troubled. 'I just wish to God I hadn't let her go to Cantor Street, why the hell didn't I ask her to come and join us, I just don't know!'

'Don't beat yourself up about it Alf, it's not your fault.'

'But I could have stopped her.'

'I doubt it, you know what Marie was like she loved nothing more than to meet up with her friends down the shelter and have a good chinwag.'

Alf remained unconvinced. 'Maybe.'

'So where's Mac now?'

'Upstairs, he's gone to wash. I'm opening in an hour. He needs some peace and quiet. Me wife's sticking to him like glue just to make sure he's all right.' Alf moved behind the bar. 'I know it's early and I wouldn't normally, I don't know about you, but I could do with a sodding drink.' he said, reaching beneath the bar for a bottle of whisky which he kept for special customers.

'I wouldn't say no.'

Alf poured two very generous glasses and took a large swig. 'I went up to the shelter first thing this morning.' He took a sharp intake of breath. 'It's just a pile of bleeding rubble, there's nothing, nothing left at all. The police, Home Guard and every last jack of us were up there clawing with our bare hands until we realised there was no bloody point carrying on.' His grip tightened around the glass. 'There's nothing left to find,' he said, his expression tight with emotion.

Alf Garretty was a hard nut, a hugely successful boxer in his day. He was a welcoming host, and few locals were stupid enough to cause trouble in his pub. When there was the odd fight, he'd quickly intervene and bodily hurl the troublemakers out into the street. He could still handle himself well, but this morning's visit to the shelter picking limbs and other body parts from the rubble had shaken him to the core.

Garvan noticed that his hands were visibly shaking as he held his drink. Garretty's thoughts drifted back to the moment he'd told Mackenzie the awful news, and how Mac had refused to believe Marie and the girls were dead.

Reluctantly, he eventually accepted the news and had shakily sat himself down in a chair, head in hands and slumped across the table.

'No, not the kids - not the girls', I should have been there for them,' he sobbed, eyes brimming with tears, 'I should have been there, not in some poxy sodding house searching for a body!'

He had cried uncontrollably, his shoulders heaving, his entire body wracked with grief. Tears flowed down his cheeks, thoughts reeling, fragmented, like small sharp memories of Marie and the girls. Mac recalled how they had endlessly discussed the idea of having Alice and Nancy evacuated. Marie had never been entirely comfortable with the idea of them living away in the countryside. At Mac's insistence, they had tried for a while; the children were away for three months in Tenterden, Kent. Mac remembered travelling down with Marie by train one weekend and walking along the lane from the station to the farmhouse where the girls were staying. They had spotted them through a window, and the girls had run down the lane screeching for joy at seeing their parents again. Bending down to scoop them up in her arms, Marie's words kept echoing relentlessly inside his head.

'Come on, I'm taking you home with me if the bombs take us they'll take us together.'

If only - if only the girls had remained in Tenterden, at least, they would still be alive. Mac had argued endlessly with Marie about letting them stay in Kent where they were safer than in London. Eventually, he'd been worn down and unable to resist the onslaught of the girls begging him to be allowed home, and his wife's determination to keep the family together. That decision had ultimately cost them their lives, and Mac's life too had ended in the desolation of the Cantor Street shelter.

Slumped forward across the table in the saloon bar, Mac had been only half aware of Alf's vice-like grip on his shoulder. His mind raced forward in fits and starts, snapshots of the family, Marie bustling around the house, the gas-filled mantel lamps spluttering and making a gentle popping sound as they threw strange shadows on the living room walls. He could almost smell the bread baking in the oven and the steaming hot cinnamon cakes on the table. In the background, the crystal radio set crackling on endlessly with Alice and Nancy giggling - happy memories - kids out playing cricket and football in the street. Their neighbourhood had been a closed shop, and even though Mac was a copper, being locally born and bred, he was still classed as one of their own. This was their street, where outsiders were frowned upon. As a child he remembered fancy cars were frequently targeted by the local boys, who'd jump on the running boards for a ride down Reedworth Street honking the car horns.

The memories continued to flood his mind, in short, sharp painful bursts, like a strange out of control montage flashing before his eyes. He wanted them to stop. There was the dustman on his horse drawn cart; one of the horses' broke free causing Mac and the girls to dive for cover behind the wall of someone's front garden. Then there was the ice-cream man on his bicycle riding down Reedworth Street like the pied piper with Alice and Nancy following in his wake; and Prince Monalulu an African man, who was an expert on the horses. All the kids loved him, and followed Monalulu through the streets as he shouted, "Aah gotta horse, aah gotta horse." He would write out betting slips and give the low-down on the horses to anyone willing to pay. Mac guessed he must have been pretty successful; he apparently made a good living from his betting tips.

Mac had sat in the saloon bar for at least an hour lost in a haze of grief before Alf and Renee finally managed to persuade him to take a rest in their flat above the pub. They were still afraid that he might just take it into his head to go to the shelter. The sight of the carnage down in Cantor Street was the very last thing he needed to see right now. Alf was unable to protect his friend from emotional turmoil, but he could shield him from the physical horror of the blast.

'Are you all right?' Garvan asked the publican.

Alf snapped out of his revelry. 'Yes, yes, I'm sorry Guv'nor, I was miles away. I was just thinking about Marie and the girls'.

'Don't apologise,' Luke drained his whisky as Alf's wife Renee came downstairs, her eyes reddened from crying.

'Hello,' she said, pleasantly on seeing Garvan.

'How is he?'

'I've put him in the spare bedroom. Do yer want me to tell Mac you're here?'

Garvan shook his head. 'No - no, not now, just let him get some rest.'

'Probably just as well, you won't get much out of him. The poor darling's huddled in a chair nursing a cup of tea and shaking like a leaf. With any luck he'll be asleep soon,' Renee said, reassuringly, 'I've given him a couple of my sleeping pills; one would be enough to knock out a sodding horse.' She hesitated and dabbed at her eyes with a handkerchief. 'He needs the rest poor luv, it's tearing him apart,' she sobbed, 'it's tearing me apart; I just don't know what to say, what can you say?'

Alf put the bottle of whisky back under the bar and gently placed his arm around Renee. 'We'll get him through it luv.'

'Will we?' she cried, uneasily.

'We have to, the poor bastard's only got us, let's face it, and he's never got on with his mother-in-law, has he?' Alf looked to Garvan and said. 'You know Mac can stay with the wife and me for as long as he likes.'

'I'm grateful; it's very kind of you.'

'It's not out of kindness Guv, he's a good bloke and he'd do the same for us, and so would have Marie, bless her.'

Luke reached into his inside pocket and produced a printed card. 'Call me if either you or Mac needs anything, anything at all. If the phone lines are down, send a telegram for my attention, and I'll make sure Scotland Yard picks up the tabs.' Alf nodded, accepting the card.

*

Back in the cramped squad room, Garvan carefully flicked through a sheaf of notes compiled by the local police based in Kennington Road. He had picked his team two days after Sarah's murder. It was standard practice at Scotland Yard for a murder investigation team to consist of two sergeants: Harry Mackenzie's slot was to be held open until he felt able to return to duty as Luke's number two.

Garvan had seconded Jack Charteris from desk duties; he was old school, a solid type of copper, nearing retirement and not an obvious choice for the squad, his background being strictly uniform and without any previous experience as a detective. His inclusion was greeted with some derision from various old hands around the Yard, but Garvan had chosen him precisely because he was old school, knew how to keep his mouth shut, and ruled the younger squad officers with a rod of iron. Luke needed someone who was professional, but who was outside the almost incestuous culture of Scotland Yard's tight-knit clique. The last thing he could afford right now was to run the risk of Sarah's murder investigation being discussed after work over one too many pints down at the Red Lion in Whitehall.

In addition to Charteris and Mackenzie, he also recruited three junior Detective Constables, John Palmer, Jim Butler and Norm Bartram; all relatively inexperienced, but more importantly not yet worn down or made cynical by the system. They had all been eager to join. Garvan himself had risen rapidly through the ranks, and was renowned for having an excellent rapport with his men and those learning the ropes. Although he was generous with his time, he'd made it clear to them that any sloppiness or leaks would not be tolerated.

'If I so much as get a whiff of the investigation surfacing around the Yard, you'll all be back in uniform before the week's out,' he'd barked at them. 'I know you're new to my ways of working, but I expect detailed briefs of every interview you conduct, and every statement you take. You have to understand that sometimes even the seemingly most insignificant scrap of evidence could end up being crucial to solving the investigation.'

The young officers had already started knocking on doors, visiting the residents of Monkton Drive to try and establish a time of death. They also linked up with the local police who had carried out the initial groundwork immediately after the murder. The three constables were beginning to get to know both the area and the people living there. Following Garvan's orders, they set about trying to identify everyone who had been in the vicinity of number 17 on the day of Sarah's murder. At the moment, the only things they had to work on was that Dr Menzies had confirmed full rigor mortis had set in, and the victim had been shot at close range.

The forensic team noticed the dark green blackout curtains in the main bedroom had not been drawn; indicating Sarah Davis was probably shot before darkness.

Jack Charteris privately expressed his concerns to Garvan, not only about the AC's personal involvement with the murder investigation but also that of Sir Philip Game. Even he realised the Home Office must have requested Game's direct intervention.

'We all know,' Charteris explained, crisply, 'the Assistant Commissioner is only interested in cherry-picking high profile cases. Ultimately, he wants a quiet life, or, at least, nothing that's likely to rock the boat, and spoil his chances of promotion.'

Garvan sat back in his chair. Jack was on a roll, so he allowed him to continue.

'You know the type of Case sir,' Charteris said, with a dismissive wave of his hand. 'Maybe an MP's bit of harmless hanky panky with a tart, or some Duchess, who's lost her jewels in Mayfair, high profile but nothing too serious. Let's face it, it's an open secret he's after a ruddy knighthood, mind you, it'd take more than a bloody title to make Muriel Harmer a lady. Ghastly ruddy woman!' Charteris added, with a shudder. 'I might be talking out of turn sir, but we all know she drinks way too much, and always causes a scene when she's wheeled out to social events. She'll never cut the mustard as Commissioner's wife, and there's talk she's got a gambling problem to boot.'

Luke's expression remained outwardly deadpan. He knew the AC's wife of old, and he couldn't fault Jack's description of Muriel. She was a lush and dominated her husband with a rod of iron. Dear old Muriel, she was renowned for her love of gambling. Charles Harmer had married young, perhaps too young; Muriel was feisty, forthright and loved to party just a little too hard. In Garvan's mind, the only possible reason for Harmer not making Met Commissioner was his wife's rather gauche habits. He recalled there'd been umpteen social events where Mrs Harmer had performed and acutely embarrassed her husband. It had at times been painful to watch, and although not an avid admirer of the AC, Garvan had felt on occasions sympathetic for his senior officer's predicament.

As far as he could work out, there were only two saving graces: firstly, she had not yet managed to upset the Home Secretary and secondly, to date, at least, the National Press had not published any damning stories about her drinking or substantial gambling debts.

He placed a cigarette between his lips and reached into his desk drawer for a lighter. 'Jack,' he said, flicking it on. 'I do apologise.'

'Why, sir?'

'I've just realised that I've dragged you into all this without briefing you properly, my mistake,' he added, holding up his hand. 'I've been under a bit of pressure to get the team sorted out, but that's still not a valid excuse. You're quite right about Harmer, but at the end of the day, you have to understand that it's Spencer Hall and the Home Office who are pulling all the strings, we're little more than stool pigeons. Why do you think Sam Menzies rather than the Divisional Police Surgeon was called to Monkton Drive?

'I'm not sure sir,' Charteris answered.

'It was the Home Office's decision to cut out the red tape, to bypass the surgeon and call in Menzies. The order didn't come from either Harmer or the Commissioner. It came from the Home Office or MI5. They're running the show, certainly not us.' He sucked heavily on the cigarette. 'Jack, you know how the land lies, the Yard will investigate anything from bribery, corruption, crimes relating to Government Departments, but think about it, how often does the Commissioner and his second in command get personally involved? As you said, they're only hands on when our political masters or national security is at stake. The Home Office have their reasons for keeping Sarah's murder out of Special Branch hands. I'll be honest with you; I haven't got the foggiest idea why. But trust me Jack, the only thing you need to remember is that Sarah Davis was somehow vitally important to our lords and masters' in Whitehall. At this stage of the game, I simply don't have a clue how or why. All I can say is that if we mess up the investigation, we'll all be back pounding the beat and the AC will probably be pensioned off for good measure.'

'No wonder the poor old bugger looks jittery,' Jack chuntered, 'he's been waiting for Sir Philip to either pop his clogs or retire for years.'

Garvan grinned. 'What with the Commissioner and the Home Office breathing down his neck, you could say that one way or another poor Sarah Davis has fucked everything up for him.'

'And on top of that sir, you have the whole of the fifth floor and Whitehall breathing down your neck.'

Garvan gave a thin smile. 'Shit happens, Jack. Just keep an eye on Bartram and the others for me. Let's just hope to God they're up to the job. As I've said before, what we need to concentrate on is building up a complete picture of how Sarah spent her last day, her last hours, who she met, who she spoke to, and if she went to work. Just drum it into the three of them that this isn't about personal glory or advancement, it's about the victim and nothing else. We're all under pressure to get results and to get them fast. In fairness,' he added, thoughtfully, 'I guess Sir Philip and the AC will be taking their fair share of the flak from Whitehall as well. In the meantime, I need to contact Spencer Hall and arrange a meeting.'

The following day Garvan was at his desk by 7.30. Jack Charteris already had the kettle on brewing the first cup of the day. He'd hardly sat down when the phone rang. It was the AC asking for an update; there wasn't much to tell him without either the post mortem or pathology reports on his desk. Luke slammed the receiver down into the cradle and glanced at his watch; he'd give it another hour and then take a drive over to Monkton Drive. Charteris knocked and poked his head round the office door.

'Is tea ready?' Luke asked.

'In a bit Guv, Mac's outside at his desk.'

'Are you joking?'

'Wish to God I were.'

'What the hell's he playing at!'

Charteris shrugged. 'He walked in as if nothing's happened.'

'Okay Jack, ask him to pop in.'

'He looks like death warmed up.'

'Just send him in.'

A few minutes later there was another knock on the door.'

'Come in.'

Mac entered, face drawn. He had aged visibly over the last few days. His eyes were puffy, Garvan supposed through a combination of crying and lack of sleep.

'Sit down,' he said, gesturing to the chair in front of his desk.

'If it's, all the same, I'd rather stand, sir.' came the formal response.

Luke reached into the desk drawer and retrieved a pack of cigarettes. 'Want one?' He offered the packet.

'Don't mind if I do,' Mac said, reaching for a cigarette.

Garvan tossed a lighter toward him; he caught it. 'I wasn't expecting you back at work for at least a couple of weeks or more.'

Mac sucked in his lower lip. 'I needed to get back,' he said flatly.

'I just thought you'd be better off giving yourself some breathing space, or at least until after -after the funerals,' he stammered.

Mac stared at him blankly drawing heavily on the cigarette and then said almost mechanically. 'Guv you've got to understand something.' He took a sharp intake of breath. 'There won't be any funerals.'

Garvan looked confused. 'What do you mean no funeral?'

'Did Alf not explain?'

'Obviously not.'

'When he went up to Cantor Street it didn't take him or anyone else long to realise there was nothing left to bury, not a sodding thing,' Mac said, bitterly. 'The local vicar says they'll have a ceremony – a memorial service or whatever you like to call it up at the Church Hall for those who died, and then a blessing at the site, just to give the families some sense of closure.' He paused, flicking ash into a waste bin beside the desk. 'There'll be a memorial plaque with their names on, but that won't be for some time. I guess it'd be pretty pointless anyway at the moment, they'll have to wait until the bombing dies down and they can grass over the site.' Mac briefly closed his eyes. 'It's your decision Guv whether I carry on working or go back to stay with Alf and Renee.'

Garvan wouldn't be drawn.

Seeing he wasn't about to answer, Mac continued, 'I guess I always thought I understood what people were going through, but I didn't, I hadn't a bloody clue. God knows

Guv; we've seen so many poor buggers going through this kind of shit often enough. But I just didn't understand what it's really like to lose everyone you love in one fatal hit,' he said, shaking his head,

Garvan lit a cigarette, not quite sure how to respond.

'I need to keep my mind ticking over,' Mackenzie pleaded, 'believe me, if I stay with Alf and Renee any longer I'll go crazy. I know, I know what you're thinking, it sounds so sodding ungrateful when they've both been so kind.'

'Does Alf know you're here?'

Mac nodded. 'Yes he does, he didn't say much, but Renee thinks I'm not showing enough respect and the mother-in-law, well, she certainly doesn't understand.' He took a drag of the cigarette. 'Grief has a way of swallowing you up whole.' He met Garvan's eyes. 'I'll be honest with you Guv right now I'm just going through the motions. I look around at other people living their lives as best they can, but I feel totally out of it, somehow not quite a part of their world. Do you understand what I'm saying?'

'I do understand.'

'The bottom line is that I need to get back to work and try to get some semblance of normality back into my life.' His face was shrouded now by an expression of total despair.

Garvan stared long and hard at Mac. A sudden thought crossed his mind; there was something about him, a gut instinct that something else had happened. 'You haven't tried doing anything stupid, have you?' he quizzed him.

Mac knew what Garvan was thinking. They had both been at this game too long; you watched for signs when talking to people, it had become second nature. He was reluctant to answer.

'Have you done anything stupid?' Garvan pressed him again.

'Like try to kill myself?' Mac suggested, with an easy off-hand calm. There was no point in lying. 'I've never quite understood suicide, at least not before now I haven't. It always seemed to me such a selfish act, with no thought for those you'd left behind, but you see, I don't have anyone left to hurt, do I.' Mac looked uncomfortable under Garvan's direct gaze. Perhaps by being honest he had blown any chance of returning to duty. 'I'll be frank with you sir, last night I sat in my room above Alf's pub, booze in one hand, a fucking bottle of aspirin in the other - well, let's just say if I hadn't fallen asleep we wouldn't be having this conversation right now.'

Garvan froze. He'd guessed as much, but was still horrified knowing Mac had come so close to taking his own life. It was sometimes a very fine line between life and oblivion. He tried putting himself into his shoes, how would he be feeling right now? How would he be coping? Probably, Garvan conceded much the same way as Mac had felt last night.

'It was just a moment of drunken madness; it's not going to happen again,' Mac hastily, assured him.

Garvan felt helpless. He wanted to reach out, to say he understood, but somehow he couldn't quite find the right words to express his feelings.

'So what's your decision, am I to stay in the office or return to the Crown and Cushion?' Mac pressed.

What was he to do? If he sent Mac back to the East End, God only knows what might happen. He would never forgive himself if Mac had another moment of madness only, this time, he took his life. Better to keep him here Garvan decided, to keep an eye on him. 'There's a backlog of work out there,' he said sharply as if by rote, 'just ask, Jack to bring you up to date.

Mac smiled. Thank you, sir.' He made to leave the office.

'There's one other thing.'

He turned back to face Garvan.

'If you don't want to stay at the pub then you're very welcome to shack up at my place.'

Mac nodded his thanks.

As he closed the office door, Garvan shut his eyes, hoping he'd made the right decision allowing him back into the fold so soon after the death of Marie and the girls. Compassion aside, the last thing he needed right now was a loose cannon on the team.

Chapter 5

Superintendent Frederick Cherill, Head of Scotland Yard's fingerprint division since 1938, submitted the forensic team's report to Garvan's desk as promised by the end of the week. Cherill had already apologised for not attending the murder scene in person, as he'd been required to give evidence in a larceny case at the Old Bailey. He was renowned for his expertise amongst Met colleagues and the legal profession alike. Despite his seniority, Freddie, as he was known to friends, had never lost the thrill of a hands-on approach to forensics. Sarah's possessions had been passed over to Cherill for various tests and analysis. The crime scene itself had provided his team with a myriad of fingerprints, lifted from the powdered smudges found during their visit to number 17.

Cherill noted in his report the results from the master bedroom where the body had been found, provided clear evidence that the murderer had deliberately attempted to wipe clean any possible trace of their prints. Whoever killed Sarah Davis went to some considerable time and effort to conceal their presence. The murder weapon itself had not been discovered at Monkton Drive, but an initial examination of the body provided enough proof that the fatal wound was consistent with a revolver-type calibre of bullet. The post-mortem would, of course, provide conclusive evidence of the weaponry involved in the killing.

Only two viable fingerprints other than Sarah's had been found in the bedroom, one was on the wooden headboard of the bed, and the second on a perfume bottle. The latter print belonged to Sarah; the other was at the time of writing unidentified. In spite of the blast damage to the front door, there were no other visible signs of forced entry to the property. Cherill concluded that the killing had been calculated and pre-planned. His team had discovered the remnant of a discharged bullet in the master bedroom. Dr Menzies, Cherill added, had subsequently confirmed the bullet as being the cause of death; it was a 380/200 Mk I lead bullet, further details will be supplied in the post-mortem report.

Garvan had decided against taking up Menzies' offer of attending the post-mortem. He'd meant well enough, but it was one thing to examine bodies at a crime scene and quite another to experience a full blown autopsy. As a young copper, Garvan distinctly remembered attending his first. The pathologist's junior assistant had been known as "Ed the head." In his innocence he asked why, only to be told that Ed's job was to lop off the cranial cavity and remove the brain. From that day forward he'd never exactly found it an easy experience, and still couldn't quite understand Sam Menzies' enthusiasm for dissection. In the past, there'd been one or two occasions when Menzies had asked Garvan to take a closer look at some particular organ or other. He still wasn't quite sure whether Sam had ever actually realised that he'd always been on the point of throwing up.

The Home Office decision to dispense with the services of the divisional surgeon had kept the investigation tight, and cut back on an extra layer of red tape. In his early career, Menzies had worked mainly for the Metropolitan Police, but had then branched out specialising in pathology, and was now rivalled only by Bernard Spilsbury as the Home Office's leading expert. Spilsbury was famous for being the main medical lead during Crippen's murder trial. Menzies and Spilsbury had both studied at Magdalen College, Oxford. To some extent, there was a professional rivalry between the two men, but it was coupled always with mutual respect.

The pathology report was hand delivered. Menzies had already phoned ahead asking him to call back if he had any questions about his findings. Garvan opened the blue folder, flicked through the usual legal preamble before fixing his attention on the formal clinical report. On initial examination of the body at the crime scene, Menzies observed the extremities were found to be cold, full rigor mortis had already set in supporting death had occurred at least twelve hours before his arrival at the scene. At the post mortem Menzies noted, the victim's body was that to be expected of a young woman in her mid to late twenties, well-nourished, in good health without cause for concern regarding the health of the internal organs; she was five feet six in height and of slim build. There were no traces of powder burns on the hands; therefore, suicide could be discounted, coupled with the calculated distance of the entry wound to the head.

There were no signs of grey or yellow colour powder burns on the cadaver. If present, they would have indicated the victim had already been dead when the shot to the forehead was fired. He went on to explain in the report that powder burns from gunshots were caused by burning particles of powder which are then ejected from the gun and become embedded into the live skin. Although the gunshot wound, in this case, would have been instantaneously incapacitating, it is thought the human body, he wrote, can normally function for up to ten seconds after the heart has completely ceased to function. Until the basal ganglia of the brain dies, which is the lowest central part of the brain situated at the top of the neck, and is responsible for all bodily movement, coordinated movement of the body is still possible, albeit briefly. In this case, he stated Miss Davis would have almost certainly died very shortly after the discharge of the revolver. The bullet entered the victim's head and then exited into the bedroom; this item was retrieved off the carpet. I have formed the opinion the revolver was discharged at no more than two to three feet away from the victim. It was, he confirmed a 380/200 Mk I lead bullet and fired from a Mk I spurless hammer, double action Enfield revolver. This fact was established by Frederick Cherrill's forensic team at Scotland Yard. My understanding, Menzies continued, is that this type of weapon is a standard British Forces issue.

As he turned the page, Garvan's attention was drawn to Menzies next paragraph. The post-mortem revealed that sexual intercourse had taken place at some point before the victim's death; Menzies confirmed that this may have occurred several hours before the point of actual death. There were a few relatively minor abrasions and bruising on the left side of the face. In my opinion, he observed, they were most probably caused by either a blow or slap of the hand, but certainly not a fist. The skin was broken, but was, he concluded caused by contact with a fingernail. This abrasion was caused before death. In summary, the fatal gunshot wound did not occur as a result of a struggle, and could not have been self-inflicted by the victim.

Garvan sat back in his chair holding the report in his hands churning over the snippets of information from Menzies report. So who'd made love to Sarah Davis before her death? The killer or perhaps someone else, someone entirely unrelated to her murder. The fact the murder weapon was a standard British Forces issue revolver opened up endless avenues for the inquiry. He needed to call Spencer Hall sooner rather than later. Sarah Davis was killed with deadly precision, by a professional, perhaps a colleague, but he needed to know why. So far this girl's death had involved the Home Office, MI5 and the Met Commissioner. If Sarah was so vital to the war effort, what was really at stake, Garvan asked himself, and why would the murderer have taken such a risk? As thing things stood, he was merely scratching the tip of the iceberg. He closed the file; his thoughts cast back to finding Sarah Davis lying dead on the floor of that cheerless, run-down terraced house. It haunted him still; she'd appeared so indescribably beautiful and so at odds with her surroundings. Why had she been there, Garvan asked himself, was Spencer Hall being truthful?

On his second visit to Monkton Drive, the one thing that had immediately struck him was the lack of personal effects around the house. He accepted the master bedroom was full of clothes and make-up, the usual kind of paraphernalia he expected to find. From that perspective, there was nothing unusual. Admittedly, she hadn't lived there long, but in Garvan's experience personal effects, the emotional and material baggage that accompany your entire life, the things that make people feel at home were normally among the very first items to be displayed when moving into a new property. At number 17, he'd noted there were no books, photographs, personal letters or any other signs of Sarah's life. It didn't feel like home.

Luke wandered over to the office window hands thrust deep into his trouser pockets, and stared down at the car park as the Assistant Commissioner's car arrived to collect him for some meeting or other. Having read Cherrill's and Menzies reports Garvan decided to make two phone calls.

The first was to Spencer Hall. He walked back to his desk and dialled St. James' 1219. The receiver was picked up almost immediately, Hall's Welsh tones instantly recognisable.

'Luke Garvan Scotland Yard,' came the response.

'Good to hear from you. I'd already pencilled in my diary to give you a bell by the end of the week. Any news?'

'I've received the forensic and post-mortem reports, I'll send you copies.'

'No need,' Hall replied, 'I'll get someone to walk over and collect them if that's all right with you, say in an hour or two?'

'That's fine; we need to meet up once you've read them let's say sometime on Friday, late morning would be best for me.'

There was a pause as Hall rifled through his diary. 'I can make 11.30, what about the Lyons Corner House, the one in Lower Regent Street, is that okay with you?'

'Yes, see you Friday.'

Garvan made a note in his diary then picked up the phone again and dialled Len Dunmore in Fleet Street. He was a respected political newspaper reporter and had been Garvan's primary source of information in a number of highly sensitive cases. They arranged to meet the following day at the Chester Club in the West End.

Len had his finger on the pulse of Whitehall thinking, not exactly an easy task since the war started. Over the years, Dunmore had built up a reputation for cultivating leading political and criminal contacts. He formed close friendships with both, without ever abusing his position. It was a delicate balancing act, but the result had led to various spectacular editorial scoops and front page headlines. From time to time Scotland Yard had also benefitted from his insider knowledge.

Len had always managed to skilfully weave his way through any potential pitfalls caused by his close ties with Whitehall and criminals alike. He'd never lost sight of a good story, and perhaps, more importantly, he'd never lost the trust of his various contacts.

Garvan realised that by phoning Dunmore about Sarah's murder investigation he was taking a calculated risk, but ultimately, he needed to sound out Len's contacts across Government. From his perspective, Spencer Hall was an entirely unknown quantity. How important was he? Where did Sarah Davis fit into the equation, what kind of work was she involved in? Garvan needed to know as much as possible.

Dunmore's contacts were in the very highest echelons of the political world and West End society: their social and sexual skeletons, be it a politician, jaded BBC director, a debauched aristocrat, or a London gang leader, it really didn't matter. He was the lynchpin, the oracle of all the latest intrigue and gossip. Len's newspaper columns very much reflected his insider knowledge, and while he'd made some enemies, no-one could afford to ignore his articles. He was usually spot-on.

*

The Chester Club was in what had once been a large Georgian House in Berkley Square. Over the years, it had been drastically altered and extended to reflect its reincarnation and changing needs as a top West End club. The place had become a Mecca for the fashionable, and for those hell bent on forgetting their fears in war-torn London. The Chester was, in fact, a healthy mix of a society levelled nightly with the prospect of possible imminent death. Every evening without fail the party continued unabated through even the worse bombing raids.

Inside, the music was in full swing. A large dance band that was fronted by an attractive brunette singer blasting out popular dance tunes. The music was loud and if the occasional bomb landed a little too close the glasses, and bottles might rattle, the floor might shudder, but for the Chester's customers, it was only a minor glitch. The seething mass was still hell bent on continuing to party.

Garvan paused momentarily taking in the scene, before threading his way through the packed crowd toward the main bar at the far end of the club. Here the lighting was even more subdued, and a number of young couples had found somewhere more private, in secluded alcoves away from too many prying eyes.

As he neared the bar, Luke caught sight of Dunmore perched on a stool downing a large shot of whisky. He was in his mid-fifties and was wearing a pair of round-lensed glasses perched on his nose. He had greying hair and a decidedly rotund figure, which owed much to his love of fine food and drink. Like most Fleet Street journalists, Len lived life to excess, working hard and playing even harder. He had a reputation for pub constipation - he just couldn't pass one without stopping for a drink. From Garvan's recollection, Dunmore had three ex-wives, two children and a dog to support. By his own admission, all three marriages ended in divorce, a result of his infidelity. He loved women just a little too much for his own good and that of his various ex-wives and his bank balance.

Sensing he was being watched, Len swivelled around on the bar stool and clapped eyes on Garvan. 'Hello me old darling,' he called out with a theatrical wave of his hand, 'pull up a pew. What d'ye want, whisky, gin?'

Illicit booze was crammed behind the bar on mirror-backed shelves. It was the same all over the West End, places like the Ritz and the Savoy hadn't been seriously affected by the rationing laws. Despite the legislation, most London clubs and hotels operated a bottle party night. It was in effect a semi-legal way of circumventing the law. There were, of course, flagrant abuses of the system as well. At the lower end of the market, customers were asked to sign their names on forms requesting their order, local retailers then delivered the booze, the loophole being that the alcohol had never actually belonged to the club or bar in the first place.

Celebrated clubs like the Chester were rarely if ever troubled by the law. The clientele included the leading lights of society, the police, and members of Parliament. It had developed a reputation as something of a refuge for the disaffected and the affluent, a smokey world of subdued lighting and a magnet for every level of London society. Whatever your particular persuasion, the social mores of the outside world was enthusiastically forgotten inside the Club.

Len smiled, as Garvan carefully scrutinised the neatly stacked shelves of spirits behind the bar. 'It's all black-market you know!'

Luke faced him with a steady, unwavering gaze. Dunmore let out a deep, chesty smoker's chuckle. 'Lord above,' he guffawed for the barman's benefit, 'I never know when to keep me trap shut, do I? Fancy admitting in front of a Detective Chief Inspector from Scotland Yard its black market booze! Are you going to shut us down Garvan?' Dunmore demanded, with a broad smile. He knew the answer already.

'I'm Murder Squad these days Len you know that I'm not interested in chasing some ruddy spiv selling black market booze. It's been a long day, and I just need a bloody drink.'

Dunmore raised his empty glass with a flourish. 'Last week, Herbert Morrison announced in Parliament that the clubs and hotels of the West End are now firmly under legislative control, that rationing applies to every establishment right across Britain.' Len paused, gesturing across the dance floor. 'Fucking crap, or what?'

Garvan perched himself on a stool beside Dunmore, pointed to an Irish malt and asked for a double.

'I heard about Harry Mackenzie's family, how is he?' Len asked with genuine concern.

'Struggling,' Luke said reaching for his wallet.

'So what brings you out on a night like this, me old darling?'

'You might be able to help me.'

'How exactly?'

'With a murder investigation.'

Dunmore started a heaving; racking cough, then lit a cigarette, swearing as he did so, that smoking helped ease his chest. Garvan shook his head in disbelief.

'It does,' Len pleaded with him. 'My help, you say?'

Luke nodded. Dunmore narrowed his eyes, and said, 'Requests from the Met for my help since the outbreak of the war have become pretty thin on the ground, almost as rare as hen's teeth.'

'Have they?' Garvan said, blankly.

'You know they have,' Len said. 'Don't play games with me, me old darling. We are all aware that since Herr Hitler started playing soldiers across Europe if political journalists so much as break wind these days it's covered by the Official Secrets Act, or,' he added with a wave, 'National Security, whatever you like to call it.'

Garvan smiled thinly. 'I just need some information that's all, a bit of background stuff, nothing too serious. Shall we say it's more like bending the Official Secrets Act than actually breaking it?'

'My dear boy,' Len quizzed, 'what sordid grubby little crime are you investigating?'

'The murder of a young woman in South London.'

'South London,' Dunmore repeated registering surprise, 'and just how exactly is this unfortunate woman's death connected with the men with no names? That's what we're saying, aren't we?' he asked, pointedly. 'These days I only get dragged in by Scotland Yard when some bloody MP or other has been playing a bit too fast and loose and has got himself caught with his trousers round his ankles.'

'At the moment, believe it or not, the victim isn't my top priority.'

Dunmore rested his arm on the bar 'Tell me more.'

'I want you to sniff out as much information as you can about a colleague of hers, Spencer Hall. Apparently he's from the Home Office.'

Len let out a chesty cackle. 'Well, that generally covers a multitude of sins, doesn't it? So what exactly do you want from me?'

'I need to know what Hall's role is, and I want his home address.'

'Ah,' Dunmore laughed with an airy wave, 'a mere bagatelle me old darling. Is that all?' he asked, sarcastically.

'More or less,' Garvan shrugged.

Len drew heavily on his cigarette and abruptly ordered another whisky. 'It certainly isn't going to be easy, not even with my contacts. If this Spencer Hall of yours is doing something a bit hush-hush, I'll probably find myself opening a complete can of worms. I have to watch my back these days; it's not as it was before the war.' Dunmore sucked heavily on the cigarette. 'And I'm sure you wouldn't be asking for my help if this Hall character was some bog standard civil servant.'

Garvan offered to pay for the drink.

'If you're paying, then make it a double,' he said, with a flourish to the barman. 'And the fact you're paying Chief Inspector, means you've found yourself in the shit with this one. What was the girl's name?'

'Probably better you don't know.'

'Like that, is it?'

'As I said, at this stage I'm only interested in Spencer Hall, and if push comes to shove, I guess you can always call in a few favours from your political mates. Let's face it, Len, you could blackmail half of bloody Whitehall if you wanted to.'

Len shrugged. 'More than half,' he smirked. 'Don't worry I'll get your information,'

'Just be careful otherwise, we'll both be in the shit.'

As they chatted, a young girl sashayed over toward them carrying a tray of cigarettes. There hadn't been any acute shortage since the outbreak of war, just as long as you knew what shops, pubs or clubs supplied them. The girl was dressed in a short pink water silk effect dress with puff sleeves and wore heavily applied make-up. Her nails were painted a deep red to match her lipstick.

'Pack of twenty Players please,' Luke said, searching for some change in his pocket.

'Are you on the late shift tonight, Bella?' Dunmore asked her.

'Yeah, been here since opening,' she pouted handing Luke the cigarettes. 'Not seen you here before,' Bella said, coolly appraising him from head to foot. 'We could do with a few more like you at the Chester.'

Garvan gave her a forced smile. 'I wouldn't want to steal Len's thunder now, would I?'

Bella let out a giggle. 'He's lovely aren't you, my darling,' she said, tapping Dunmore's shoulder. 'You're no trouble at all, well, not like some of 'em here,' she snorted.

As Bella began to thread her way back through the nearby tables, Luke said. 'Was that bad timing on my part? Does she fancy you?'

Len threw up his hands in mock horror. 'Only in my dreams, Garvan. Look at me for Christ's sake!'

'I wasn't sure if I'd stepped on your toes, or not?'

'Not a chance!' Len grunted, emphatically.

Garvan raised his glass, took a large swig and said, 'I've been following your campaign in the Times.'

Dunmore looked surprised. 'Have you?'

'It's made for an interesting read.'

'Where are you going with this?' he asked, suspiciously.

'You've accused various MPs of double standards.'

Len's eyes narrowed. 'What if I have?'

'You've highlighted their illegal champagne lifestyle.'

'It's no more than the truth.'

'But I can't help thinking Len, isn't it a bit hypocritical of you?'

'What do you mean?' Len snapped, at him.

Luke set his glass on the bar. 'Look at you Len, caviar at the Ritz one night, salmon at the Savoy the next.' He gestured around the club, 'and here we are, knocking back whisky after sodding whisky. We know it's not legit.'

'Can't argue with that one me old darling,' Dunmore smiled, disarmingly, 'but I'm not the one, am I who stands up in Parliament arguing the toss about rationing, and how we've all got to tighten our belts. And I'm not one of the bastards legislating in the Commons, who then comes down here to the West End every night and gets pissed on black market booze while the vast majority of people are going without and joining fucking queues to get bread and groceries. Money speaks - I guess it always has. Take last night for example. I was at the Ritz, and they served up venison, supplied by the customer from his country estate, all legal and quite above board. I guess it's the equivalent of someone going out and bagging a few rabbits, but all of this,' he said, with an expansive gesture, 'there's a lot of people growing rich on this war, me old darling. I accept it's morally wrong, but war is also a great leveller Just look around you Garvan, everyone feels free to act as they please in here, yet once the war's over, we'll retreat again behind some misguided moral façade of respectability.' Dunmore drained his whisky. 'We live in uncertain times, and I sometimes wonder if I'm doing the right thing, running a campaign against the hypocrisy of the rationing laws. Am I being a killjoy?'

'I don't think so,' Garvan assured him, 'you are only highlighting double standards.'

'Just remember one thing: life's no longer a valued commodity. If the Chester gets a direct hit tonight, come the morning we'll be nothing more than another Government statistic.'

Garvan nursed the whisky glass between his hands and said seriously. 'Tell me something, am I asking too much of you?'

'Too much?' he queried, pulling a face.

'You're already out on a limb with your campaign. If my asking you to check up on Spencer Hall is a step too far, you must tell me.'

Len gave a shrug. 'I guess we'll only know for certain once I've put out a few feelers.'

Garvan set a five-pound note on the bar. 'Have another one or two on me'.

'That's mighty generous of you.'

Garvan felt a hand grip hold of his shoulder and found himself faced with the unsteady figure of an expensively dressed Chester Club hostess. The girls were all attractive, but getting pissed at work meant it was unlikely she'd still be employed by the end of the week. The rules governing hostesses were strict, whatever private business a hostess might drum up was her affair, but it was forbidden to solicit during opening hours.

'I've been watching you,' she slurred at him.

'Good for you darling.'

'You look like you'd be up for a good time.'

The very last thing the Chester Club's owner needed was a legitimate reason for the Met to close the place down, and one sure way of doing so was having a hostess openly plying for trade. The barman's expression froze. If it wasn't already bad enough with Dunmore discussing the Chester's black market booze, a hostess propositioning the same Scotland Yard copper was tantamount to professional suicide. He was having a bad evening.

Garvan coolly looked her up and down. 'Not tonight darling, try your luck somewhere else.'

'Oh fuck off you bastard,' she spat and staggered away.

'Bloody typical,' Len chuckled chestily between coughs, 'I'm here every sodding night and not once has anyone asked me for a bit of hanky-panky.'

'At your age and weight I'm not surprised,' Luke grinned, 'five minutes with that one and she'd see you off for good!'

Len laughed. 'Too true, too true me old darling, the spirit's willing but the body, well that's quite another matter.'

Shaking hands with Dunmore, Garvan stood up and said. 'Give me a bell.'

At that moment, the whole building shuddered from its foundations as if struck by an earthquake. As a shock wave ripped through the club, everyone on the dance floor was swept clean off their feet in a chaos of tables, chairs, and broken bottles. There followed a nervous, uneasy silence, broken only by the odd muffled sob. Once the dust had settled, people breathed a sigh of relief. They'd escaped with only a few relatively minor cuts and abrasions.

The blast had blown Garvan against the bar, its sheer force sucking his breath away. Dunmore was knocked off his stool and had landed in a dishevelled heap on the floor. With the dust and smoke still swirling through the club, there was a strange, unnerving, whistling noise. Instinctively, everyone dived for cover. Garvan fell to his knees beside Dunmore, bracing himself for what was to come.

Closing his eyes, Garvan thought they'd be lucky to escape this one; it was too bloody close for comfort. The club shook even more violently than before. The bomb crashed into a building to the rear of Berkley Square, but even so, the blast wave seemed as if it would suck out every wall of the Chester. There was, even more, dust this time as plaster crashed from the ceiling.

When the choking, clogging dust began to settle, the building itself appeared to be largely intact, minus a few windows and the odd unhinged door. Garvan dusted himself down, his thoughts with those poor souls under the full force of the explosion, and helped Dunmore back to his feet, then checked to see if the barman and those around them needed help. The band members dusted themselves down and started to play again while the staff put the tables and chairs back in order. No-one was killed, so there was no reason not to continue with the party.

'I thought we were goners there,' Dunmore grumbled, straightening his jacket.

'They say it's the one you don't hear which kills you.'

'The trouble with that theory, me old darling, is that generally no-one survives a direct hit to tell the tale. Am I to contact you at the Yard?'

Luke scribbled his telephone number down on a scrap of paper. 'Don't go into any detail over the phone. If you feel you're getting too much flack, just back off and forget it. At the end of the day, it's my problem and not yours.'

'Bless you me old darling but I wasn't born yesterday. If I find anything on your man I'll let you know.'

'Thanks, Len.' He turned and caught sight of Charlie Price. He knew Charlie of old, a gangland boss whose reputation for ruthlessness was unsurpassed.

Garvan acknowledged that Price's brutality was matched in equal measure with a good business brain. Even before the war, he'd amassed a small fortune by creating a two-tier empire - one quite legitimate, in which he paid taxes, employed the very best accountants and ran restaurants and wholesale businesses. Then there were his extortion rackets, the robberies and clubs like the Chester, which didn't officially belong to him. If Charlie's fellow cons crossed the line and strayed into his manor, or behaved recklessly by attracting the unwanted attention of the Met, then they were taught a severe lesson by his 'Firm'. In extreme cases, this often meant their life expectancy was somewhat limited, but more often than not offenders were merely given a heavy-handed warning.

Price was a snappy dresser with a penchant for fine wine and glitzy women, all of which were very much in evidence this evening. Not overly tall in build, Charlie was in his late fifties, with a closely cropped head of greying hair, and despite his age, still retained a powerfully muscular frame. Charlie was a smooth talking villain, leading a crack team who spent their time planning some of the biggest cash thefts across the capital. As far as Price was concerned, the Blitz was nothing more than a Godsend and had only served to increase the gang's success.

As cons went, Garvan conceded, he was likeable, with a ready sense of humour and an almost old world sense of values. As a young rooky copper, Luke had learnt never to underestimate him. He'd given him the run around in his early career, but those days had long passed, and there was a grudging respect between them. Garvan took his leave of Dunmore and weaved his way across the club, unable to resist paying a visit to Price's table. On either side of the gangland boss sat two peroxide blondes. They were attractive in an overt, rather than classy way. Seated beside them were two, smart dark-suited minders.

Over the last year or so, Maisie, Charlie's wife, was rarely seen in his company. She'd taken a back seat, preferring to lead a quiet life in the sleepy suburbs of Weybridge, where Charlie had bought a palatial family home. Their children had all been educated privately and for their sake, Maisie desperately wanted to distance herself from Charlie's criminal activities.

As he made his way across the club, Price's gaze locked hard onto Garvan. It crossed Luke's mind that in the subdued lighting of the Chester, Charlie somehow looked even more menacing than usual. Their paths had crossed many times and although Price had on occasion ended up in prison; he'd always managed to escape a lengthy stretch. He was too clever by half; Garvan accepted, could afford the very best lawyers and his acolytes usually ended up serving long sentences instead.

'Hello Charlie,' Garvan said on reaching the table.

'Bit of a close shave earlier,' Price said, casually lighting up a large cigar.

'I guess our time wasn't up.'

'Just think of it, Mr Garvan,' Price said, blowing out a cloud of blue smoke, 'we could have ended up sharing the same obituary page in the Telegraph. I wonder what people would have made of that. So what brings you to the Chester tonight?'

'A bit of business Pricey, that's all.'

'So nothing to do with me then?'

'I'm always interested in you Charlie; you know that. Let's face it half the fucking Met would be unemployed without you and your boys!'

Charlie smirked. 'Never thought of it that way, but you're right, guess in me own way I'm doing a bit of a public service. You still at the Yard?'

Luke nodded.

'Since you left West End Central and your number two Mike Venables stepped up; it's not been the same. If truth be told he hasn't bothered me too much.' Price smiled smugly. 'It's all getting a bit too easy now Mr Garvan. You sent me down a few times, but Venables hasn't got a cat in hell's chance, he's a second rate plodder.'

'Is that a compliment?'

Price shrugged. 'Respect, Mr Garvan, it's all about respect.'

'So how's business, good is it?'

'Can't grumble, just enough to keep the wolf from the door, but we've all got to tighten our belts, there's a war on you know,' Charlie grinned.

'You tighten your belt?' Luke laughed. 'This place alone brings in a bundle every week.'

Charlie paused, looked around the club, and said almost convincingly. 'I'd love to own the Chester I really would, but whatever rumour you've heard this isn't my gaff. I thought you of all people would have sussed that out by now.'

'It's me you're talking to Charlie, not fucking Venables. I know the Chester isn't on your books, at least not officially, but -.'

'But prove it,' Price interrupted sharply. He clicked his fingers at a waitress and ordered another round of drinks for his table.

'Give my regards to Maisie,' Luke said.

'That's very good of you Mr Garvan. At the end of the day, like you, I just want me, kids, to have a good education, a better life. In that respect, I guess we're not that different, are we?'

'We're poles apart Charlie,' Garvan said, 'but I know what you mean.'

Price gestured toward Dunmore, who was still propping up the bar. 'Doing a bit of business over there, were you?'

Luke instinctively glanced back over his shoulder. 'You could say that.'

'These days Mr Garvan political reporters' like old Len have had their wings clipped. Watch yourself otherwise they'll ave you banged to rights before you know it. You'd be far better off keeping me company than old Dunmore. I'm a safer bet.'

Garvan couldn't help but laugh. 'You know what Pricey, you're probably right. If you do hear I've been banged to rights in Dartmoor, put in a good word in for me, won't you.'

'Trust me,' Charlie grinned broadly and winked, 'I'd make sure my boys took care of you, very good care.'

'I bet you fucking would.' Garvan made to leave, but paused, turned back again to face Price. 'Just one word of advice.'

Price narrowed his eyes. 'Advice?' he repeated.

'It's about one of your hostesses'.

Charlie's expression tightened.

85

Garvan looked around the club and pointed to the expensively dressed woman who had propositioned him earlier. 'That one,' he said.

'What about her?'

'She's touting for business.' Price nodded. 'You don't want West End Central poking their noses around the Chester, do you?'

'You know me, Mr Garvan, I don't employ pros'. Charlie leaned forward across the table and spoke to one of his minders. 'Get rid of her, tonight!' He raised his glass in salute to Garvan. 'As I said before compared to you Mike Venables is a second rate plodder. Respect Garvan, it's all about respect.'

'It's mutual, Pricey, see you around.'

*

Two days after their meeting at the Chester Club, Luke and Dunmore caught up in Bird Cage Walk near St. James's Park. It was one of those cold, bright autumnal mornings where the leaves had turned to the colour of burnished copper and the sunlight glistened on the still waters of the park's lake. As Garvan headed over the metal bridge, he caught sight of Dunmore slumped on a wooden bench overlooking the lake. He looked even more red-faced, and out of breath than usual. On catching sight of Garvan, he waved in greeting.

'I'm getting too old for this kind of game!' he wheezed.

'Let's face it Len you've been out of condition for years.'

Dunmore coughed wheezily. 'Got a fag?' he spluttered.

Luke lit one for him. 'You're going to kill yourself one of these days.'

Len shrugged. 'I don't mind admitting to you Garvan I've called in more than a few favours over the last few days. This Spencer Hall of yours is in a league of his own.'

'I didn't think it'd be easy.'

'I've been a political journalist now for thirty-odd years. I've lost count of the number of stories I've investigated during that time. You know the type, the juicy ones that make for a good story, and keep me in business.' He swivelled around on the bench to face Garvan. 'I've never actually worried about my personal safety before; it's never been an issue, that is, until now.' He drew heavily on his cigarette and said. 'I spoke to one or two of my tame MPs and a few close friends from the Home Office. Your, Mr Hall or Major Hall, is highly respected in security circles. When I asked what type of work he was involved in my sources clammed up so completely it was as if someone or something had put the fear of God up their arse.'

'What's so strange about that?'

'Fear old boy, abject bloody fear. They knew far more than they were either willing or able to tell. All they would say is that it's rumoured Hall's section is working on the direct orders of Churchill. Now me old darling, Churchill giving direct orders is like God personally stepping down from his throne. Do you understand what I'm saying? Whatever secret war operation this Spencer Hall of yours is involved in, is way, way above my league and come to think of it way above yours as well. A word of warning,' he said, discarding his cigarette. 'Now, I'm not a hundred per cent certain whether Hall's outfit is working on Churchill's direct orders or not, but my sources were scared witless. For some reason, I'd overstepped the mark.' He held his cigarette lightly between his fingers staring thoughtfully across the lake. 'Tread very, very carefully Luke. In wartime, the law exists only to protect the country at large, national security and all that. The minnows like us are entirely expendable. If you have a choice Luke, I'm telling you to walk away from the whole damn business!'

'If only it was that simple Len, Sir Philip Game and the Assistant Commissioner are involved already, I can't just bale out.'

Dunmore puffed out his cheeks. He was more worried than he cared to admit. 'Think seriously Luke is finding this girl's killer worth ruining your career? Or for that matter your life? My sources are usually pretty calm customers, but as I said, Hall's name set the alarms bells ringing.'

'I do appreciate what you've done for me.'

'Why on earth did the security services involve you and not Special Branch?' Dunmore quizzed him. He shook his head. 'No, there's something else going on here, the trouble is I can't quite put my finger on it. The only thing I know for certain is that you're up to your neck in shit and still drowning.'

Luke threw back his head and laughed. 'Thanks for that Len - I think.'

'Well me old darling, can't say as I haven't warned you,' Dunmore came to his feet and dusted the liberal sprinkling of cigarette ash off his jacket. 'If your murder victim was involved in the same kind of operation as Major Hall, then I'm still not quite sure why they thought to involve you or the Yard at all, but one thing is for certain.'

'What's that?'

'The security services or the Government, perhaps both, will be playing some elaborate game of cat and mouse with you stuck firmly in the sodding middle as bait.'

Dunmore shook Garvan's hand. 'Shall we call it quits? You've now called in every sodding debt I ever owed you. Old codgers like me don't get easily spooked, but I'm backing off, this one's too deep, too bloody deep for me. Whatever they're paying you at the Yard, it's not enough.'

As he let go of Garvan's hand, he passed him a folded piece of paper. 'Just take care and watch your back. And if you need any more help – well,' he said, waving his hands in the air, 'just don't call me!' Dunmore chuckled, and with a brief salute set off back through the Park toward St. James's tube station.

Luke unfolded the paper and scanned Dunmore's untidy scrawl with Hall's home address on it. He slumped back on the wooden bench and sighed. The fact that Dunmore's normally talkative sources were starting to run scared, and diving for cover was sobering enough, but the mention of Churchill's name had cranked the whole investigation up even higher. Spencer Hall was obviously at the heart of the security world's inner sanctum. But that didn't answer why Special Branch had been bypassed, and why the enquiry had landed on his desk and not theirs. It just didn't add up.

Luke remained on the park bench for some considerable time lost in thought idly watching the world pass by, office workers on their lunch break, lovers walking hand in hand, oblivious to those around them. No-one seemed to have a care in the world. Right now he'd have given his right arm to swap places with any one of them. Hall was obviously the lynchpin between Scotland Yard and the Home Office, or perhaps more correctly MI5, but that didn't automatically eliminate him as a suspect in the case, at least not to Garvan's mind.

He tried figuring out the ramifications of placing surveillance on Hall. It might be worth the gamble, but at the same time, it might well backfire on him. No doubt Dunmore's ferreting around had evidently caused ripples across Whitehall, in which case Luke's reputation was firmly on the line. Even so, it might well be worth pushing things a bit further, he decided, just to test the waters, and to test Hall's commitment to the inquiry.

Chapter 6

Garvan stood at his office window looking at the traffic crossing over Westminster Bridge when something caught his eye. He glanced down toward the Yard's car park and saw Charles Harmer's sleek black car pull up outside the main entrance. The AC emerged with a bundle of papers tucked under his arm. Luke wondered how much breathing space he'd be allowed before the inevitable summons to the fifth floor to report his initial findings. There was a knock on the door.

'Sir, you wanted to see us,' he heard Jack Charteris say.

Luke swung away from the window as Mac closed the door, a cup of tea in his hand.

'Sit down,' Garvan said, gesturing to the two chairs in front of his desk. He chose to remain to stand. There was no preamble, he briefed them about his initial meeting with Dunmore at the Chester Club, and then about yesterday morning's encounter in St. James's Park. Mackenzie shot him an expression approaching despair. Of all the people to involve in a case with security overtones, Dunmore was probably the very last person he'd have trusted.

With difficulty, Mac kept his temper in check until Garvan had finished.

'I'm sorry but what the hell were you doing talking to Dunmore about the case?'

Jack looked genuinely horrified at Mac's outburst. 'The Guv'nor's only doing his job, and if Dunmore can give us a steer -.'

Mac cut Charteris dead. 'Don't you sodding understand?'

Jack looked affronted and said. 'I guess I don't, so tell me then, what's wrong with calling in a few favours?' Where's the harm if it helps with the investigation?'

'Len Dunmore is no ordinary bloody journalist!' Mackenzie continued. 'He's a political journalist with enough clout and insider knowledge to blackmail half the bloody House of Commons.'

Jack eased himself back into his chair and countered. 'That's as maybe, but surely we have to know exactly where we stand. I admit unlike you I don't have years of CID experience under my belt, but even I know this isn't a run of the mill murder case. We've got the fifth floor and Whitehall breathing down our necks, so are you saying we should just sit back and do nothing? Right now it seems the Home Office are pulling all the strings and expecting us to dance to their tune. Let's face it Mac, the Yard has a long history of using the Press to our advantage, and if Dunmore manages to gives us some insider information, then surely that's all that counts.'

'Yes,' Mac said, irritably, 'of course we use certain journalists. We all know of cases where it's paid off in the past, where cons have gone down as a direct result of the Press passing us information, or by us placing headlines in the newspapers' about an investigation to put the fear of God into some criminal or other. It's often been just enough of a scare to make 'em break cover. I accept all that entirely Jack, of course, I do, but contacting Dunmore right now amounts to little more than suicide!'

Garvan's steady gaze didn't waver. Any other Detective Sergeant at Scotland Yard would have backed off by now, kept his mouth shut. In the normal run of events Luke would have come down hard on them, but he allowed Mac a certain leeway. His number two wasn't just talking as a junior officer, but perhaps far more importantly as a close friend. He could see the value of what Harry was saying, and yet he'd never have considered changing his decision to contact Dunmore. Admittedly, it had been somewhat of a calculated risk, but ultimately, Garvan had wanted to force the issue out into the open and see just how committed Spencer and MI5 were to tracking down Sarah's murderer.

Garvan felt Mac had completely missed the point. Outwardly, he accepted his decision to meet with Len appeared unwise, but he was also disappointed that Harry couldn't see the wider picture. If Sarah was a prominent member of the Security Services, then it was a given Luke was already under surveillance by Hall and his shadowy colleagues. He really wouldn't have expected anything else. In effect, he'd ruthlessly used Dunmore as a distraction, a conduit, nothing more, and nothing less than as a means of hopefully ruffling a few feathers around Whitehall.

Garvan drew an end to their bickering and raised his hand to silence them. 'Mac, I understand what you're saying, but I think you're missing the point.'

'How exactly am I?'

'If Spencer Hall wasn't from the Home Office you really wouldn't think twice about carrying out usual routine background checks on him, would you?

Mac pulled a face. 'I guess not.'

'And that includes making good use of your contacts in the Press, or whoever else you might think helpful to the inquiry. Do you honestly believe for one second Spencer's cohorts haven't already checked us out, or placed us under surveillance? I'd almost be disappointed if I hadn't been followed to the Chester Club.' Garvan wandered back over to the window, his gaze briefly setting on a barge sailing slowly down the river. 'We have a description of a suspect resembling Hall placing him at Miss Davis' address on the afternoon of the killing. At this stage, I'm not going to eliminate anyone from the inquiry, not even Spencer Hall.'

'So what's next?'

'I was thinking of having him placed under surveillance, at least until such time as I can confirm he's out of the equation.'

Mac shook his head still unconvinced about Garvan's tactics. 'If old man Harmer or Sir Philip Game get wind of this we'll all be strung up and left out to dry. The AC will never agree to it.'

'It's on a need to know basis. I know there's no way Harmer would sanction us nosing around, but if Hall's as clean as a whistle, then there's no point worrying him about it. Besides, I don't want the old man's blood pressure to get any worse than it already is,' he grinned, opening his desk to retrieve a pack of cigarettes.

'And what if Harmer or Spencer Hall gets wind of the surveillance?'

'Stop worrying, Mac, it's my neck on the line.'

'That's why I'm worried. Why take unnecessary risks?'

'I'm following a lead, that's all, just give it a rest, one way or another we'll find out exactly how many feathers Dunmore's ruffled after ferreting around Whitehall!'

Mac stood up. 'If this goes tits up you'll be back on the beat within a fortnight, the old man will go through the roof, and for once I'd have to agree with him. In his shoes, I'd want my Chief Inspector keeping me fully briefed, especially if it meant placing surveillance on some bloke from the Security Services.'

'It might not come to placing surveillance on the good Major. I'm meeting Hall tomorrow morning, so let's just wait and see how that goes, and what his reaction is to my involving Dunmore.' A smile crossed Garvan's face.

'Stop looking so worried Mac, if they do mean for us to find Sarah's murderer, it'll take more than ruffling a few feathers to seriously upset the apple cart. And as for Harmer, the only real thing on his agenda at the moment is an eye on the future. He wants the top job, and to get there he needs to keep his nose clean. Cases like this unsettle the old bastard. I think he'd perjure himself in court to save his own neck, rather than run the risk of blotting his copy book. I appreciate your concerns Mac, but trust me.'

*

As arranged over the phone Garvan made his way to the Lyon's Corner House in Lower Regent Street. By the time Luke arrived Hall was seated already close to the front door, incongruously beside a large potted palm. He had a cigarette balanced between his fingers and was reading the Times; sensing Garvan's arrival, he looked up and nodded briefly in greeting. As Luke pulled up a chair, a waitress appeared smartly dressed in her trademark black dress, crisp white linen apron and matching mop cap, a notepad clutched in her hands. He ordered tea.

Spencer folded the newspaper. Since their initial meeting in Harmer's office, it was Garvan's first real chance to observe him. What first came to mind, was an overt stillness about him, a stillness he'd often found in gangland bosses like Charlie Price, that same aura of a tough and hardened man. They were no doubt qualities in high demand during wartime, and never more so than in certain secretive, shadowy Government Departments, where his talents had probably made him indispensable. Spencer was confident, urbane and with a natural charismatic charm. His smile transformed and softened his rugged, angular face. It occurred to Garvan that talking to Hall was akin to playing poker. Few emotions intruded. He was at times probing, then reticent, but always quietly testing the waters.

'Thank you for the forensic and post-mortem reports, it's much appreciated,' Hall said, 'at least we now know Sarah didn't suffer too much in her final moments.'

'I'll be perfectly frank with you,' Garvan said, toying with a teaspoon, 'I need to know where I stand.'

Hall raised an eyebrow questioningly.

'Unless my team have the full co-operation of your department, it's not going to be very long before we hit a brick wall.' He met Hall's steady, almost curious gaze. 'You do want me to solve this case, don't you?'

'Why wouldn't I?' came the short, sharp reply.

'Was the girl expendable?'

He raised his hand in an airy gesture 'Chief Inspector; we're all expendable until the war's over.'

'Stop playing fucking games with me,' Garvan said, sharply, 'there's any number of cases on my desk right now I'd rather be investigating, but I was collared to take on Miss Davis's murder by the fifth floor, it certainly wasn't by choice. As I see it we can either play it with a straight bat or simply go through the motions; there's no point in either of us wasting our time.'

Hall stubbed out his cigarette and promptly lit another with slow, studied deliberation. There was a slight smile on his face. 'I guess we need to clear the air Chief Inspector, after all, trust is a two-way street.' He sat back and drew heavily on the cigarette, before adding.' So let's start with you, shall we.'

Garvan's eyes narrowed questioningly. 'Meaning'

'You contacted Len Dunmore the other night at the Chester Club. It was a mistake, and if I may say so, a rather sloppy mistake.'

'Hardly sloppy, I'd prefer to call it a calculated risk,' Garvan shot back at him.

'How so?'

'I needed to test the water, most of all I needed to know where exactly I stood with you. That pretence in the AC's office about you being a Civil Servant was at best naive. I've been a copper long enough to know when I'm being fed a load of bullshit. I could have decided to wait until we met up today and accepted everything you said at face value, but I guess you always had a gut instinct that wasn't going to happen. And I'm also certain you know I haven't made a career of accepting information at face value.' Luke poured his tea. 'So where does that leave us?'

Spencer was interested, but he wouldn't be drawn, not just yet. He liked Garvan's forthright attitude. They'd get on, he decided.

'At the mere mention of your name,' Garvan said, 'Dunmore's contact was scared witless.' He held Hall's cool stare. 'That speaks volumes, doesn't it?'

'Does it?'

'I'd have been more surprised if you hadn't placed me under surveillance, and the fact we're now having this conversation has proved the point. But I still haven't got the foggiest idea what exactly you do in Whitehall.' Garvan raised the flat of his hand. 'Just don't insult me by saying you're some bloody pen pusher or other.'

'As you say Chief Inspector placing you under surveillance was a matter of routine,' came the slow, measured response. 'In all fairness, I was under few illusions that you wouldn't return the compliment. After all, why wouldn't you consider me to be a suspect, I accept that.'

Garvan didn't respond.

'I guess I didn't give you enough credit for using Dunmore, on the surface it seemed to be a pretty reckless move.' Spencer thoughtfully toyed with the cigarette between his fingers. 'Forgive me, I didn't think it through properly, call it the pressure of work. In your shoes, I'd probably have contacted Dunmore as well, after all, why the hell should you trust anything I say? We all know Len's a debauched old so and so, but his contacts are second to none. Fortunately, in this instance, his tame MP holds only a junior appointment at the Home Office, or at least a part of it, the Ministry of Home Security. Minor or not, the fact he was willing to discuss any aspect of his role has had inevitable repercussions.'

'What repercussions?'

'Let's just say The Right Honourable Gentleman has been medically advised to take early retirement through sudden health issues. It'll be formally announced in the Press next week. Ironically we've decided to go to print in Len's newspaper.'

'Tell me something, will you, why was Sarah Davis living in Monkton Drive?' Garvan asked.

'It's one of the several properties we have dotted around London and the suburbs; they're safe houses.' The irony wasn't lost on Hall. 'I guess in hindsight it wasn't that safe, was it?' Spencer went on to explain Sarah's role as a Desk Officer in his Section, 'I guess you could say we're a bit of a mixed bag really, mainly military diverted from regular duties'.

Sarah, he explained was the only civilian female Desk Officer drafted in to join the team primarily on account of her fluency in German. When war broke out she had initially been co-opted to work for the Foreign Office, but her talents were soon recognised, and it was only a matter of time before she was recommended to the head of Spencer's section, who promptly recruited her at the end of 1939. In the 1930s' Sarah's father had worked as a diplomat in Germany, she'd grown up to be bi-lingual, and part of her education was spent at an International School in Berlin.

By the time the family left the British Embassy in early 1939, her father, Sir Louis Davis was by now a renowned expert on German politics and political thinking. His in-depth knowledge had rubbed off on his daughter. She too had been brought into close contact with members of the regime and had developed a profound understanding of German culture and its people. Sir Louis was currently working as a Government adviser in London. Sarah's death had affected him deeply, and he was on extended compassionate leave to be with his family until after her funeral.

'She was quite simply a Godsend to us, 'Spencer explained, before adding reflectively, 'I was a language student in the 1930s, and for a couple of terms went on an exchange visit to Germany. It gave me an insight into what was going on, to be honest, you really couldn't miss it, but my knowledge and understanding was nothing in comparison to Sarah's. Her analysis of the intelligence we received from Hamburg and Berlin was way out of my league. She possessed an almost encyclopaedic knowledge of Nazism, from the political structure to an in-depth understanding of their intelligence services.' He smiled slightly. 'She also had a way of keeping us in order. There were times when the team would sometimes head off at a tangent, and completely miss an intrinsic point embedded in the intelligence transcripts. But she always managed to drag us back onto the straight and narrow. Sarah analysed everything right down to the minutest detail at an entirely different level to that of our own outstanding. You could say her eye for detail was almost photographic.' Spencer paused thoughtfully before adding. 'In short, Sarah was quite stunning in every single way, there was nothing of her really, and yet she was bloody tough with a razor sharp mind.'

'So her role was to analyse information?'

'In essence yes, incoming messages to German agents based here. Sarah was under a great deal of stress. Her work - our work - is high pressured and emotionally demanding, we simply can't afford to make even the slightest mistake.'

Spencer proffered Luke a cigarette, he accepted.

'So let me get this right, you monitor messages between Germany and Britain?'

'It's a little more complicated than that. British Intelligence has successfully turned the agents we control. In effect, they're double agents, and yet to all intents and purposes, they're still outwardly, at least, under the control of their Abwehr commanders.' Hall handed over his lighter to Garvan. 'I'm sorry Chief Inspector, but that's as far as I'm permitted to take it until the CO briefs you.'

'Then I'll call you this afternoon to confirm a date in our diaries. So is that it for now?'

'There's something else you ought to be aware of.'

'What's that?'

'Before Sarah was murdered at Monkton Drive there had been two earlier attempts on her life, the first outside her flat in Westminster, and the second when she was leaving a bar in Mayfair a month later.'

'What happened?'

'Gunshot on the first occasion, the second occurred when a car mounted the pavement as Sarah left the bar. She was with a girlfriend at the time, but with the Blackout, it was impossible for either of them to identify the driver or the vehicle. You have to understand the decision to contact Scotland Yard hasn't been one we've taken lightly. I'll be perfectly honest with you, there's been a great deal of soul searching on our part whether to keep things completely under wraps, but the stakes are so high we couldn't afford to take any chances. Quite simply we needed professional help. The reasoning is that whoever killed Sarah wanted to silence her before she managed to expose them. We have a rogue agent on the loose. At best we're playing a deadly game of shadows, and at the moment, the entire network is at risk and in danger of crashing down around us as we speak. If it does, the ramifications will jeopardise the whole future conduct of the war against Germany. One of our double agents has broken cover, and we believe Sarah managed to either decipher or receive a report from a foreign contact, which could potentially have blown the agent's cover. God knows we've been through her notes time and again. If something is staring us in the face, we haven't yet managed to find it.' Spencer breathed deeply; there was a sense of a man burning up inside, fired up with emotion and determination. He said at length. 'Sarah was under no illusions about the risks. Placing her in South London was simply a way to lessen the chances of further attempts on her life.' He stared unseeingly at some far distant point across the café completely lost in thought. When he spoke again, there was a certain edge to his voice. 'We minimised the risks as best we could …' his words trailed off, and his expression shut down like a mask.

'The neighbours mentioned a number of male callers to number 17. Presumably, you'll be able to supply me with a list of her visitors?'

'That's easy enough to answer; the only official visitors to the house were colleagues, sometimes in civvies, sometimes in uniform. But there were only ever four male callers. The agents under her control were never allowed access to the house.' Spencer looked questioningly at Garvan. 'You look surprised, Chief Inspector.'

'The neighbours have made formal statements that there were rather more than four male callers.'

'I'm sure they may have done, but whatever the good neighbours of Monkton Drive believed was going on, I can tell you was very much wide of the mark. As I said it was a safe house, access was very much restricted and controlled by the office in St. James'.'

Garvan decided to play devil's advocate. 'Is there any chance Sarah's killer might be a colleague rather than your rogue agent?'

Spencer was unfazed and answered smoothly. 'After the murder, we underwent an urgent internal investigation. We checked the whereabouts of the entire team. Everyone could be accounted for on the night of the killing. Believe me, the investigation was thorough and not some vague academic exercise.'

'My team discovered some headed notepaper at Sarah's address, from a firm called Carrington Insurance based in Leicester Square. Sergeant Mackenzie has made a few inquiries since then, and it seems Carrington's doesn't appear to exist. You wouldn't happen to know anything about the Firm, would you? Is it a bogus setup?'

Spencer gave a dismissive shrug. 'Don't trouble yourself Chief Inspector. Carrington Insurance is a red herring and nothing to do with Sarah's murder. The place is a cover and on occasions, we use the address for administration purposes. We also have some background staff based there in rented offices.'

'If only we'd known we were on a wild goose chase, it'd have saved us all a great deal of time and effort.'

'I apologise.'

'If I do manage to track down Miss Davis's murderer,' Luke said, 'will they stand trial?'

Hall gave a slight nod. 'We can't afford a public trial. Provide the evidence Chief Inspector and we'll provide the solution.'

Garvan drained his tea. 'Any thoughts about the type of weapon used to kill Miss Davis?'

'It's a bog standard issue. Just about anyone can lay their hands on that type of Enfield these days.'

'Including your own agents?'

'Well only through the black market, certainly not through our hands.'

Garvan pressed on, pointing out that the pathology report indicated Sarah had sexual intercourse in the preceding hours leading up to her death. 'Did that come as a surprise to you? Or did your internal inquiry shed any light about Sarah having a lover?'

The sarcastic edge in Garvan's voice was not lost on Spencer, and without missing a beat, he replied. 'That's an easy one to answer Chief Inspector it was me. I had sex with Sarah Davis that afternoon, and apart from her murderer I must have been the very last person to see her alive.' His face seemed suddenly drawn as if struggling with his emotions, but when he spoke his voice was controlled. 'The killer made their move under the cover of the bombing raid, and my deepest regret is that I wasn't there for her.' He leaned forward and stubbed out his cigarette, and said abruptly. 'Let's get out of here, I need some fresh air.'

Chapter 7

The two men walked together through Piccadilly in uneasy silence. For Garvan, the case had now taken on an entirely different slant this was no longer just about the loss of a work colleague. However important Sarah Davis was to the security services, there was now another intriguing layer to the investigation. When Hall momentarily faltered, revealing his feelings for Sarah, Garvan had felt an almost selfish sense of relief, knowing that his involvement in the investigation wasn't just an empty sham, conjured up by the security services in some shady Machiavellian scheme.

Spencer suddenly turned right into the Haymarket.

'Maybe I ought to be getting back to Scotland Yard,' Garvan suggested. 'I'll give you a call to fix up a meeting with your CO.'

'Why not come back now,' Spencer said bluntly.

'To your office, you mean?'

Hall didn't immediately respond but shot him a penetrating look. 'Yes, so why waste time, the sooner we get things moving, the better it'll be for all of us.'

His reply when it came was short, sharp and to the point as if he hadn't said anything out of the ordinary. On the surface, Garvan appeared to accept Hall's announcement with indifference, but in truth, it took him completely by surprise. Things were moving much faster than he imagined and he found himself wrong-footed. He hadn't prepared for any meeting, let alone in MI5's inner sanctum without any prior warning.

Garvan had already convinced himself that his meeting with Spencer at the Lyons Corner House had merely been a prelude, an academic exercise almost while Hall sounded him out and tested the ground. Garvan had resigned himself to a long, drawn-out campaign of resistance from the security services before they eventually allowed him into their confidence. But he'd completely misread the situation, and more to the point, completely misread exactly how important Sarah Davis was to Spencer Hall's organisation.

They ended up outside MI5's HQ at 58 St. James's Street, it was a rather unprepossessing, but elegant dark bricked former house. In Regency times, it had been the site of the Jordan Hotel and was now conveniently situated just round the corner from the SIS counter-intelligence team, who worked out of Ryder Street. The entrance, like many buildings in London, was protected by sandbags. The windows had been crossed with sticky tape to prevent the windows imploding on bomb blast. There was certainly no outward sign of the secretive and dangerous occupation of those working within its solid Georgian walls. Garvan followed Spencer up the shallow stepped entrance which led directly into a cavernous black and white tiled hallway. Inside were two armed Royal Marines who sprang to attention. Spencer acknowledged their salute with the slightest of nods and headed across the hallway toward the reception desk where a smart-suited, grey-haired, middle-aged man stood up in greeting. Hall exchanged a few cursory pleasantries with him before introducing Luke. The man consulted a list on his desk and ticked off the Chief Inspector's name.

'That's okay sir; the Colonel is expecting you both.'

So this was certainly no spur of the moment decision on Spencer's part. The visit had obviously been pre-arranged. Rather than take the broad sweeping staircase to the first floor, Spencer headed off toward an old-fashioned lift on the right-hand side of the reception area. With a judder, they lurched up to the first floor and stepped out of the lift into a long high-ceilinged corridor. Other smaller corridors were leading off on either side.

Spencer led the way to the end and into a surprisingly small compact office filled with a swirling fog of cigarette smoke. The desks were crowded together, and all of them were piled up high with reams of paperwork. Hall's colleagues were busily sifting through the constant incoming radio transmissions from Germany. Their task was to analyse the intelligence, and then concoct suitable responses to the Abwehr. The team kept meticulous, cross-referenced records, to avoid any possible slip-ups when drafting their double agents' messages to their Nazi controllers.

In one corner, Garvan noticed four uniformed men huddled around a desk deep in conversation. They barely acknowledged their arrival in the office, being far too engrossed in what they were doing actually to take much notice.

As Spencer strode through the office and knocked on the door at the far end, and waited until a muffled voice from within gave permission to enter. Garvan followed and found himself in a surprisingly spacious room that had apparently once served as a library. The walls were still lined from floor to ceiling with beautiful leather bound books interspersed by a series of maps covering every conceivable corner of the world. Near a sash window stood a large Victorian desk allowing the occupant to benefit from the extra light. As Garvan entered, he stopped dead in his tracks confronted by the all too familiar figure of Tommy Argyll Robertson, or Tar as he was known on account of his initials. He stood up from behind the desk, his tall, lean, wiry figure dressed in a khaki jacket coupled with the tartan trousers of the Seaforth Highlander's Regiment. He was clasping a Meerschaum pipe in his right hand.

'Christ almighty,' Garvan grinned in disbelief, 'I thought I'd seen the last of you!'

Robertson smiled warmly. '1933 or was it 34 - Chelsea Barracks?'

'Is it really that long ago? I think it was 33.'

Spencer quietly closed the door. 'What's this,' he said, intrigued, 'so you two already know each other. Don't tell me the good Chief Inspector had cause to arrest you, sir?'

'Not quite,' Tar chuckled, 'We met in the lead-up to the court-martial of an officer called Norman Baillie-Stewart, you might remember the case,' he said airily, 'it was all over the newspapers at the time. He was a subaltern in my regiment and after falling desperately in love with some German woman or other, developed Nazi sympathies. Mind you, I'd always found him a little bit odd myself,' he smiled. 'The bugger took himself off to Germany and went absent without leave, and ended up offering his services to the Nazis. He had a chip on his shoulder the size of the Grand Canyon, and for some damned reason or other, believed his senior officers looked down on him. God knows why, his credentials were far better than mine and for that matter most of us in the regiment, including the senior officers.'

Garvan cast his mind to the case, thoughts flooding back, as he recalled Baillie-Stewart had borrowed documents from the Aldershot Military Library on the pretext that he was studying for the Staff College exams. His aim all along had been to pass photographs and specifications of an experimental tank, an automatic rifle, and various other related confidential notes to German Intelligence. Garvan had been part of a Special Branch team who'd been ordered to carry out surveillance duties, and they ended up tracking down Baillie-Stewart's movements to the Netherlands where he'd met up with his German handlers.

Robertson was called as a witness for the prosecution in the courts martial, and Sir Vernon Kell, the then Head of MI5, had been so impressed by his performance in the witness box during the trial, that shortly afterwards he was approached by the Security Service and subsequently recruited. With some relish, Robertson recalled having to don a copper's uniform as a police constable in Birmingham. Garvan smiled to himself. It was common knowledge the Police Training School in Birmingham was an intrinsic part of the MI5 induction course. All potential agents were trained or put through their paces for a few weeks in Birmingham, alongside both military police and local trainees.

'It all seems like a lifetime ago,' Robertson said, with an expansive wave. 'If memory serves me, dear old Baillie-Stewart was sent down for five years for his sins. Didn't he spend them all at the Tower of London?'

'I believe he did,' Garvan replied.

'So where is he now?' Spencer asked.

'In 1939 he made a few radio propaganda broadcasts from Berlin for the Reichs-Rundfunk-Gesellschaft,' Robertson explained, 'I guess you'd describe them as the equivalent of the BBC. He's been sidelined now and is working as a translator at their Foreign Ministry.'

Robertson wandered over to an ornate mahogany cabinet and opened the doors to reveal a drinks cupboard crammed with a large variety of spirits. 'Whisky anyone?' He didn't bother waiting for a reply and poured three generous glasses. 'I recall you were a Detective Sergeant back in those days, and a bloody good one at that,' he said, handing Garvan his drink.

He met Robertson's eyes. From Luke's perspective things were beginning to fall slowly into place, to make sense, at least, he now realised why he'd been singled out to head up the murder investigation into Sarah Davis's death. It must have been Robertson's decision, his input to the Commissioner that had sealed the deal. Tar beckoned him to take a seat in front of his desk. Spencer eased himself into the identical small Chesterfield style chair beside Garvan.

'Welcome Chief Inspector to the Twenty Committee,' Robertson said, raising his glass in salute.

'The Twenty Committee?' he repeated, quizzically.

'It's just a play on words,' the Colonel explained, 'we were set up at the outset of the war with a very specific remit.' His words trailed off, leaving Garvan wondering whether he was calculating how much more he should divulge.

'So what is your remit exactly?'

'To capture and interrogate German agents with the view of turning them into double agents, and ensure they end up working for us, for British Intelligence. The committee, along with other interested parties across Whitehall, ultimately decides what manner of intelligence we need to spoon feed over to the Germans via our double-agents.'

'So let me get this right, you give the Abwehr or whoever classified information?' Garvan asked not quite sure if he'd heard Tar correctly.

Robertson let out an amused chuckle. 'Well dear boy, I do admit it does sound rather absurd, but that's how things stand, it's all harmless stuff, but the Germans aren't to know that, are they.'

Tar explained in detail how the committee had decided to use the Roman numerals XX or twenty as their motto; after that, it became popularly known in Government circles as the Double Cross Club. The organisation was made up of the three Armed Services, with additional representatives from MI5, MI6 and Home Defence. The chairman of the committee, John Masterman, was a renowned academic. The newly formed set-up didn't stand on ceremony, and, as a result, rank within the group was regarded as wholly irrelevant, results and ability were the only things that counted or mattered.

'I'm not sure how much Spencer has told you already?' he mused shooting his operative a questioning look.

'As we agreed on nothing too in-depth, only broad brush strokes.'

'Then you've probably guessed circumstance has forced our hand,' Tar said, offering both men cigarettes from a silver case before snapping it shut.

He continued to hold the case lightly between his fingers, waving it occasionally as he made some particular point. Robertson confessed that immediately after his department's internal investigation into Sarah's death had begun to stall, and they failed to track the killer down, with the endorsement of the Twenty Committee, he'd flagged up Garvan's name to Sir Philip Game to head up the murder investigation.

Tar admitted that over the years he'd kept an eye on Garvan's progress through the ranks and his rapid promotion. Robertson's contacts at Scotland Yard had marked him out as one of their most talented detectives. He'd also followed Garvan's career through various newspapers articles reporting his assistance to provincial forces to investigate murders, and, of course, his success against some of London's notorious gangland bosses. The fact that Robertson had been impressed by Garvan's professionalism, and had also worked with him during the Baillie-Stewart case sealed the endorsement of the entire XX Committee. Quite simply they needed his expertise to help track down or flush out the murderer of Sarah Davis.

Over the intervening years, Robertson had become a slick Whitehall operator and a renowned specialist in clandestine wireless communications. Relations between

MI5 and the Special Operations Executive could at best be described as prickly. The SOE had refused to part with signals traffic from their own agents based on the Continent and had initially refused all requests to share their intelligence. Robertson, for his part, had desperately needed sight of them to gain a sense of their content, and without sight of the SOE signals traffic, it would have severely hampered his Desk Officers' ability to both draft and interpret material for their double agents' Germans handlers. Without his renowned easy charm and diplomacy, the internal petty jealousies and inter-departmental turf wars would have endangered the entire future of the Twenty Committee's Double Cross team.

'I need to be as open as possible with you Chief Inspector,' Robertson explained, toying thoughtfully with his whisky glass, his attention drawn fixedly to an open file on the desk. 'I guess you could describe my Section as the blunt instrument of our political masters in Whitehall.' The words trailed off, a crease suddenly furrowing his brow. 'Who was it who said war is the continuation of politics by other means?'

'God knows,' Spencer shrugged.

Robertson smiled at Hall. 'Well, whoever it was, they were quite correct.' He leaned back in his large swivel chair occasionally moving it from side to side as he spoke. 'Where do I begin to explain this whole sorry saga?'

When he spoke it was in a measured, thoughtful manner, explaining how the war against Germany was being fought in many different ways. Each in itself was fundamental in preventing the imminent invasion of Britain, and ultimately, in defeating the Nazi regime. At the outbreak of war in 1939, a collective decision by both the security services, and the Prime Minister was made that almost all German spies sent into Britain should be left in place and allowed to operate under controlled conditions. They were picked up, of course, arrested, and those turned under interrogation by MI5 provided Britain with invaluable information from the heart of the Third Reich. Garvan found himself increasingly intrigued as Tar opened a window on to a world he scarcely knew existed.

Robertson openly confessed that there had been many times over the last year or so when he'd felt a little like King Canute trying to battle a tidal wave of hostile agents landing on British shores. In spite of the odds the Twenty Committee's team remained confident that ninety-nine per cent of the German agents parachuted or landed by sea had been captured. Once British Intelligence had successfully turned an Abwehr spy, Tar explained, they were then subdivided into two main groups.

The Colonel paused slowly inhaling on his pipe. 'Arguably,' he mused, 'the most important group are those sending wireless communications to the German secret service in Hamburg. The second group communicate by various other means, sometimes personal contact, and air mail or by letter, mainly to the Abwehr operation based in Lisbon.' He placed the pipe down into an ashtray. 'The information we provide our double agents could best be described as chicken feed.'

'What do you term chicken feed?' Garvan queried.

'Snippets nothing major, run of the mill stuff about air raid damage, military movements, the location of some factory or other, but it's all very much controlled. If Hamburg HQ repeats the information to Berlin, then it's a given we have them hooked,' he said placing his hands together as if in prayer.

'You make it all sound so easy,' Garvan shot back at him.

'Do I in what way?' he asked, with a slight bemused smiled playing about his mouth.

'How on earth do you set about getting agents to change their allegiance from the Reich?'

'Ah, well you have to start by being a good judge of human nature and a ready listener, much like yourself,' he smiled, warmly. 'You also have to penetrate the mindset of their German controllers.'

Garvan met Tar's steady, watchful gaze. 'I might be a good judge of character and a good listener, Colonel, but as you know, it takes a great deal more than that to put villains behind bars.'

Robertson's eyes glistened mischievously 'We have many methods at our disposal Chief Inspector, a few more than you are permitted within the constraints of the law. To put it simply, we use whatever it takes. Blackmail, bribery, there's no set pattern. We treat each case depending on the circumstance. Ultimately, we make them offers that are, shall I say, difficult to refuse, especially when you consider the alternative.' Tar took a swig of whisky. 'In my experience, Chief Inspector, people tend to respond rather positively when faced with either the prospect of a firing squad, or a dawn appointment with the hangman. It tends to focus the mind.'

The remark wasn't made at all glibly; it was just a matter of fact. The morality of the Twenty Committee's decisions was often blurred, the stakes were so high; it was a struggle of life or death. Both British Intelligence and the Abwehr were playing a deadly game of counter-espionage. For either side, the prospect of failure would be catastrophic. Robertson went on to describe in detail how the system of actually converting spies operated. One of the first German agents MI5 discovered was a man named Arthur Owens, to all intents and purposes a respectable businessman, but as an extreme Welsh Nationalist, with little, if any loyalty to Britain.

In the 1930s, his company had made batteries for the Royal Navy. Arthur also had close contacts with the Kriegsmarine in Kiel, who were to become one of the largest and most important builders of U-boats. Owens was by nature a complex character, recruited in Germany by the Abwehr. Monetary gain appeared to have been outweighed by his love for the number of women his German handlers could readily supply. For some reason or other, he was given the Abwehr codename of Johnny; but on Arthur's return to Britain, he started to have second thoughts about his recruitment to German Intelligence. Robertson could only surmise that he finally realised the enormity of his betrayal, and for whatever reason Owens had a change of heart. He subsequently made contact with the British authorities and admitted he was due to receive a radio transmitter from the Abwehr. At the same time, he volunteered his services to MI5.

The transmitter was duly delivered and placed in the left luggage at Victoria Station. This all happened Robertson explained at the beginning of 1939. Over the following months, MI5 came to the conclusion that Owens had the makings of a useful double agent. He was given the Codename SNOW. All the transactions between German agents and their handlers in Hamburg and Berlin were monitored by the Radio Security Service based at Hanslope Park, just north of Bletchley. Owens' subsequent value to the Twenty Committee could not be overestimated; he'd helped deliver numerous German spies into the hands of MI5, and had become an important point of contact for new agents arriving in Britain.

The Colonel paused. 'Am I going too fast for you, Chief Inspector?'

Garvan pulled a face. 'I guess normally I'd be taking notes by now, but I assumed you wouldn't take too kindly to my walking away from St. James's with this lot in my notebook.'

'It's merely background information,' Robertson assured him, 'and not strictly relevant to Sarah's murder.'

'I have a question, sir. Are you absolutely sure Sarah Davis's killer is one of your double agents?'

Robertson leaned forward on his desk clasping his hands together tightly. 'We're playing a dangerous game here Chief Inspector, we're vulnerable, and the system itself is vulnerable. It'd take just one rotten egg, a German, British-based triple agent, to bring the whole system crashing down around our ears. Day in day out we play, we act out this deadly balancing act with the Abwehr and Sicherheitsdienst; you might know them as the SD. If they ever manage to get wind that we've turned half, let alone all their British-based agents the game would be well and truly up not only for MI5 but the country itself. You have to understand Chief Inspector that we actively run and control the entire German espionage system in this country.'

Garvan was impressed, and didn't quite know how to respond, so kept his peace.

'The information we're receiving,' - Robertson's words momentarily trailed off as he reached for his whisky, and drained the glass. 'The information we're receiving and transmitting will ultimately determine whether we either win or lose this war; our work is as important as that.' He placed the empty glass back on the desk; his expression was thoughtful. 'We do know that Sarah's killer has become a triple agent, and unless we can successfully flush them out, and quickly, the whole Double Cross system is in jeopardy. As things stand at the moment, our internal investigation has managed to narrow the search to two operatives, both of whom were controlled by Sarah Davis.'

Garvan began to believe that ignorance was bliss. Robertson's story was a tangled web of intrigue, and one he could scarcely understand, or for that matter wanted to. There was a lot to take on board, and right now, he was feeling more than slightly out of his depth. It was an entirely alien world, governed by a maelstrom of deceit and he was a complete outsider, reluctantly drawn into Sarah's world, which he found at the same time both utterly fascinating and yet deadly in equal measure. For Garvan, Robertson's work with the Twenty Committee put into perspective the day to day grind at Scotland Yard, which in the grand scheme of things, now seemed to pale into insignificance.

The war had, of course, impinged on Garvan's life. The kids had been evacuated, his wife, had found another life somewhere down at RAF Tangmere. Sergeant Mackenzie had tragically lost his entire family in a bombing raid; but his experience of the war had been personal, affecting both friends and colleagues alike. Sitting here in St. James's with Robertson and Spencer Hall, he suddenly realised, that Sarah's War had functioned on an altogether different level to that of his own.

Her colleagues had placed their private lives on hold, and their personal needs firmly in the background. If he'd understood it correctly if the Twenty Committee failed, and the Abwehr or SD gained the upper hand, then Britain's fight against Hitler was at serious risk, and the prospect of Nazi troops marching down Whitehall was a real possibility.

Robertson for his part, carried on seamlessly with an almost cold detachment, as if he were describing nothing more mundane than the weather forecast. Garvan gathered himself and listened to Tar describing how British Intelligence had managed to decipher medium grade hand cyphers, known as ISOS. The subsequent blank questioning look on Garvan's face prompted a fuller explanation. ISOS, Robertson smiled, stood for Intelligence Service Oliver Stanley, after the man responsible for breaking the Abwehr codes. The breakthrough had subsequently enabled MI5 to keep a complete track of messages from their double agents and had also given them the ability to pick up on new German spies as and when they arrived in Britain.

'In effect,' Robertson finished, 'all their German agents are under my direct command.'

For the first time, Garvan noticed that Robertson looked almost grey with tiredness, his searing blue eyes burning through him.

'All of them?' he asked incredulously.

The Colonel nodded. 'We may, of course, have missed someone new, but we currently run forty-seven spies. By breaking the German codes, we've managed so far to round every single agent up in Britain. Some of them are very skilled, others, shall I say are somewhat less talented, and we can spot them a mile off. Once they're taken into custody, we send them to Latchmere House near Richmond. It's MI5's main interrogation centre. We try to weed out those we can't make use of, and those we think suitable to become double agents are then fed into the system.'

'And what happens to the failures?'

'Mostly imprisoned, some have been tried and executed for spying. At the end of the day, it's a fairly stark choice. You could say they're culled. It sounds a little harsh I know. There's no escaping the fact that some of them are executed if only to convince the Germans that we're being proactive. MI5 has a say in their fate of course. We conduct the interviews and write up the reports, but ultimately, the final decision rests with the lawyers' and the Home Office. Those chosen to become double agents have communications with their German handlers carefully monitored. Here at the Twenty Committee,' Robertson added with an expansive gesture, 'we decide which strand of intelligence we feed back to Germany. It's a balancing act and a very dangerous balancing act at that. We intercept all our agents' correspondence; bug their telephones and also their homes. You'll understand better than most that it takes a great deal of expertise to juggle so many balls all at once. My Desk Officers immerse themselves entirely in the lives of their controlled agents, but they also have to understand the psyche of their German counterparts in Hamburg and Berlin. You see that's where Sarah was so brilliant. Having been brought up in Germany, she always had that edge over us, that profound insight into the regime's thinking and strategy.' Robertson breathed deeply, his thoughts lingering on his much-missed colleague. 'She was such a strong character, opinionated, so very funny, and so very beautiful.'

A silence fell between them, in the background the ticking of the long case clock in the corner of the office seemed to grow louder by the second, filling the empty void. Robertson poured himself another drink, and resumed his seat, twisting the glass thoughtfully between his hands before breaking the silence in a measured tone.

'The prospect of a rogue agent, a triple agent, has caused us to divert a great deal of time and effort we can ill afford. As I said to you earlier, our internal investigation has managed to narrow the field down to two spies under Sarah's direct control. Our understanding is that Sarah received information from France regarding one of her agents, from a contact called Louis Durand, he's an influential member of the Interallie network.'

'What's the Interallie network?' Garvan repeated questioningly.

'It's a French Resistance network, the creation of Roman Czerniawski, a Pole, and a quite brilliant spy. As you can imagine like many of his fellow countrymen, he has a somewhat profound hatred of the Third Reich and all it stands for. He created the Interallie network in Paris and employed mainly French agents. Until recently he has been very successful in supplying us with various high-grade reports about the German set-up in France. The quality of the information from Czerniawski's network has been second to none. The Germans have been angling to make a move against Roman and his outfit for some time now. A few months ago two of the Abwehr's most trusted British-based female agents, Joyce Leader and Maggie Hamilton, were instructed by their German handler to travel to France and infiltrate the Interallie. They were the ideal choice. Both agents have French mothers, and speak the language fluently, but more importantly, one of them was an acquaintance of Louis Durand. Before the war, he was a well-known nightclub owner and still owns several venues in Paris and the South of France.'

Garvan looked confused. 'I'm sorry you've lost me.'

'What is it you don't understand?' Robertson asked, with a smile.

'Just let me get this straight. Why would you risk sending these women into France knowing full well their handlers wanted them to infiltrate the Interallie? It simply doesn't make sense at least not to me it doesn't.'

'Two reasons,' Spencer said. 'Firstly, if we hadn't allowed them to obey their instructions the German's would have immediately realised we were pulling their strings. Secondly, and perhaps more importantly, the girls were ordered to France on the personal instruction of Captain Nikolaus Ritter or Dr Rantzau as he likes to call himself these days. Through their transmissions to Hamburg, we discovered Ritter was going to travel to Paris to meet up with them.'

'What's so bloody important about this Captain Ritter that you'd risk jeopardising the entire Interallie network? It still doesn't make sense.'

'Captain Ritter is my opposite number,' Robertson told him, 'he's based permanently in Hamburg. The mere fact he intended travelling to France to meet up with them was an important move in itself, and too important for us to ignore.'

'I think what you have to do sir, is to put everything into context for the Chief Inspector,' Spencer said, cutting across Robertson. 'The Abwehr had already been circling the Interallie network like vultures for some time. They've had one or two minor successes, but in reality, Roman's organisation had been living on borrowed time for the last six months. No matter what we did or didn't do, the outcome was always going to be the same. Ritter's presence in Paris was simply too much of a golden opportunity to pass up. For starters, it was obvious he viewed Leader and Hamilton highly. Otherwise, he'd never have bothered travelling all the way from Hamburg to Paris just to meet up with them. Our main objective was for them to bring back valuable information, to get an even better understanding of Ritter's intentions. It was also a one-off chance for the women to get themselves acquainted with Hugo Bleicher; he's the top Abwehr officer in Paris. Bleicher has a reputation for being utterly ruthless. He's certainly the most feared Nazi counter-intelligence officer operating in the entire city. He was the man ultimately placed in charge of disabling the Interallie network. I assure you Chief Inspector that both Louis Durand and Czerniawski were well aware of our plans, and albeit reluctantly, they both understood the wider picture.'

'How did you get Leader and Hamilton over to France?' Garvan asked.

'We didn't,' Spencer explained, 'they were picked up by a specially converted German bomber used for spying missions. It was painted black with no visible markings. It's standard practice to rip out the bomb release mechanisms to reduce the overall weight. The RAF does much the same thing when we drop SOE agents into France or Holland. We knew the exact time the plane was due to arrive over the Kent coast, so we didn't take any chances and ensured the airspace was clear just long enough to so that some trigger-happy Spitfire pilot didn't blast them out of the sky. The plane flew back low over the Channel without incident, and the only thing our agents reported was that the pilot didn't seem old enough to fly the ruddy thing.'

'And did the mission go according to plan?' Garvan questioned him.

'Not quite.' Spencer said, lighting a cigarette. 'We got a great deal of information on Ritter and rather more than we were expecting on Hugo Bleicher but it wasn't entirely without cost.'

'How big a cost was it?'

'As I said, it was only a matter of time before the Interallie network was destroyed but it happened rather sooner than we were expecting.'

Robertson explained to Garvan that while Joyce Leader and Maggie Hamilton were still in France, Roman Czerniawski was arrested by the Gestapo. They'd burst into his bedroom late one night, and dragged him out of bed by Bleicher. A week or so earlier the Gestapo had taken into custody one of Roman's agents and not surprisingly, he'd caved in under torture. The Interallie then started to implode. Agents ran for cover, closed down their wireless operations, and either moved across Paris or out of the capital altogether.

'The only useful clue we have so far is from Louis Durand. He managed to tell us the Germans had nicknamed our rogue agent Nicolette. We also found the name scribbled amongst Sarah's notes.'

Both of Sarah's female agents had initially gone to ground after the arrests in Paris. Tar explained sporadic messages had subsequently passed between London and their agents. The only sign that something had gone drastically wrong came from the scant transactions they'd received from what remained of Czerniawski's organisation. From Durand's message it soon became apparent one of the women had become a triple agent and was now jeopardising the Double Cross system itself.

As their Desk Officer, Sarah knew her agents far better than either Robertson or Hall did; with Czerniawski firmly in the clutches of Bleicher, it still wasn't entirely clear how much information Sarah had received from Louis Durand before her death. But it had obviously been enough to place her life in immediate danger. A month before Sarah's murder Hamilton and Leader returned to England using a French fishing vessel courtesy of Bleicher.

'Why return them to Britain?' Garvan asked.

'With the Interallie on its knees,' Spencer replied, 'there was no longer a reason for either Bleicher or Ritter to keep them in France. They'd served their purpose, the mission was accomplished, and quite rightly the Abwehr wanted them back in London where they'd be far more useful.'

'So let me get this right, they infiltrated the Interallie and then ended up helping to destroy the network?'

'It isn't that clean cut,' Spencer replied, 'they were kept deliberately on the periphery of the organisation, neither of them had enough information for the system to crack that quickly.'

Garvan needed time to take stock. Sarah's murder was far more complicated and far more dangerous than he'd initially suspected. Spencer and Robertson had opened a window onto a scary world of bluff and counter bluff. He'd dabbled briefly with the security services in the past with the Stewart-Baillie Case, but that was trivial in comparison with what he was facing now. Garvan's growing incredulity was mixed with the realisation that he was way, way out of his depth.

Robertson glanced at his wrist watch and then double checked the time against the long case clock. 'I'm sorry gentleman,' he apologised with a broad smile. 'I have an appointment at the Savoy in half an hour. Spencer will give you any additional information you need; we've already prepared a written brief about our internal investigation.' He shoved a packet of pipe tobacco into his trouser pocket and made to leave, but hesitated as he neared the door. 'By the way, if you have any problems with your Assistant Commissioner just give me a call, and I'll deal with him.' He gave a rather thin smile and shot Garvan a look. 'Failure isn't an option Chief Inspector. If we don't find Sarah's killer, I cannot emphasise enough that the ramifications will be nothing short of catastrophic for the war effort.'

As Robertson closed the door, Hall said, 'Come on, I might as well give you the paperwork now.'

In the smoke-filled outer office, Spencer moved over to a large grey tumbler lock safe which was ajar. He reached inside and pulled out a manila covered file with a large red cross printed on the outside. He placed the file down on a nearby desk, pushed the chair aside and reached into the corner for a well-worn black leather briefcase.

'You'd better take this; we can't have you walking back to Scotland Yard with a Top Secret file stuffed under your arm.' He handed the briefcase over to Garvan. 'You have permission to show the contents to Charteris and Mackenzie, but not to your PCs. The information is on a strictly need to know basis. I'll leave it up to you how much you feel they should be told, but please keep it to the bare minimum. Does that cause you a problem?'

Garvan placed the file in the briefcase. 'Not particularly, I know we need to keep a tight lid on things, and depending on what your report says I may have to entirely re-think whether I need anyone other than Mac and Charteris on board.'

'Once you've read the file, give me a call me, and we'll take things from there. I have to escort you back downstairs to sign you out of the building.'

Chapter 8

Garvan had hardly sat down at his desk before being summoned to the Assistant Commissioner's office. He strolled into the outer office, glanced at his watch and perched himself down on the corner of Martha Northcote's desk. The AC's long-suffering secretary emerged from Harmer's office, smiled briefly at Garvan, and said: 'Sorry about that, but the old bugger's in a foul mood today.'

'Got out of the wrong side of the bed, has he?'

Martha started to usher him into the office, saying in a dull, flat voice, 'God knows why he's spitting rivets, but something's upset him. What have you been up to?'

'Nothing, at least, nothing I'm aware of.'

Once inside Garvan was sharply invited to take a seat. Harmer's face had taken on a decidedly florid hue. The AC had always possessed a dogged mindset and a seemingly unflagging belief in his own innate abilities; unfortunately, it wasn't a belief that was shared by his colleagues. He wasn't held in high esteem, and although he had once commanded respect, over the last few years, his reputation had taken a nosedive after several noticeable blunders after meddling unnecessarily in various high profile investigations.

Garvan knew only too well that some senior officers deliberately baited the old man. It wasn't exactly malicious, but the trouble was, the few friends and allies Harmer had, had long since been alienated by his bombastic blustering and arrogance. His rare charm offences tended only to gravitate upwards to the Commissioner, the Home Office, or whoever he felt might be useful in his mission to step into Sir Philip Game's shoes when he eventually retired. Harmer was renowned for flying off the handle at the slightest provocation and had something of a reputation for brow beating junior officers into submission. Garvan had long suspected the explosions of rage were signs that Harmer was losing the plot, and couldn't handle high levels of stress without cracking up.

Garvan had never taken to keeping his head down below the parapet in his dealings with the AC. It was sometimes a high-risk strategy, but his willingness to lock horns elicited a grudging admiration from Harmer. It wasn't too often someone had the balls to stand their ground against him. It was often said that his leadership skills had all the hallmarks of a modern day Genghis Khan. What amused Garvan more than anything else was that at weekends the old man was a lay preacher at his local church; it seemed a complete mystery to him why he was unable to transfer his deeply held Christian beliefs to Scotland Yard during the working week.

Garvan suspected today's summons to the fifth floor was nothing more than a fishing trip for information. Since the outset of the murder investigation, Garvan had given nothing away and played his cards close to his chest. He also assumed that Harmer may well have got wind of his meeting with Tar Robertson from the Commissioner; who'd probably received a courtesy call from MI5.

Harmer snatched two forms from his in-tray and thrust them toward Garvan; he could see at once they were the expense slips for his get together with Len Dunmore at the Chester Club. 'I trust this bloody hack of yours was worth the fortune you spent pouring whisky down his ruddy throat all night. Haven't they heard of rationing at the Chester Club?'

'They've certainly heard of it Sir,' Garvan responded, calmly.

'Well, we'll see about that!' Harmer snorted, slamming the expense claims down on the desk. 'I'm not prepared to have the Chester or any other fancy Mayfair club breaking the law. I've a good mind to ask West End Central to take a closer look at the ruddy place.'

Garvan folded his arms, and said, 'A word of caution sir, half the Cabinet enjoy the odd drink or two at the Chester, and so does Sir Philip for that matter. I do think you might have a bit of a fight on your hands if you try closing the place down.'

Harmer wouldn't be drawn, and with some measure of satisfaction, Garvan noticed an involuntary twitch under the AC's left eye. It was always a good sign that Harmer was irritated - whenever he was under extreme stress or angry, the tell-tale twitch appeared, and always under his left eye.

Harmer leaned forward resting his elbows on the desk. 'I understand from Sir Philip Game, that you're effectively out of Scotland Yard's control.'

'It would appear so sir.'

'Then I guess Garvan, these expenses are probably the very least of your concerns.' He grabbed hold of the claim forms again and tossed them into a pending tray. 'I presume you know why I wanted to see you.'

'No sir.'

'The Commissioner informed me earlier today that it appears Sarah Davis's murder investigation is a case of national security - sensitive is how he described it. So I've no choice other than to back down and accept the status quo,' he said, with barely suppressed irritation. Perhaps he felt slighted; Garvan wasn't entirely sure.

'I understand you've drawn a .45 from the armoury?' Harmer barked at him.

'Yes, I took a call from Spencer Hall earlier this week advising me to take one out.'

'I don't mind telling you Garvan; I've had my doubts about this case right from the very start. You were their choice to head up the investigation, MI5's choice for this job, if you thought you were already out on a limb, then it's nothing compared to where you are now. I only pray God this caper goes well for you. If it doesn't,' he gave a shrug, 'then neither Sir Philip nor I will be able to save your career.'

It hadn't occurred to Garvan before now that either of them would ever have busted a gut to save him if the investigation went belly up. He'd assumed right from the outset that if he cocked everything up, then he'd find himself back in uniform pounding the beat in some God forsaken hole in the suburbs.

'That'll be all for now,' Harmer said, dismissively.

'What a waste of fucking time that was,' Garvan said under his breath as he closed the door.

Returning to his office, he lit a much-needed cigarette and opened the briefcase Spencer had given him. He was eager to get on with things, to start some serious reading, and hopefully get a better insight into both the double-cross network, and the two spies, Joyce Leader and Maggie Hamilton.

The report written by Hall began by providing Garvan with background information about MI5's German counterparts. The first name he came across was Hugo Bleicher whom Robertson had mentioned at St. James's. From what Robertson had said he knew Bleicher was responsible for arresting Roman Czerniawski the head of the French Interallie spy network.

Other names, new names, started to spring up from the pages. Under the heading Chief of the Abwehr was Admiral Wilhelm Canaris. Hall described Canaris as a shrewd, brilliant spymaster, and much admired by his British counterparts. His position in the hierarchy of the Reich would have been described as complex. He was in many respects an unknown quantity and his loyalty to Hitler remained difficult to assess fully. While Canaris was thought of highly by Hitler, he was completely mistrusted by Himmler. Even so, Canaris appeared to have little difficulty outwitting the ruthless Himmler.

Spencer explained the Admiral's Achilles heel was that he was often accused of running the Abwehr as his personal fiefdom, with little or no reference to the high command in Berlin which remained a somewhat constant irritation to Himmler. Many of the German General Staff were openly scathing of the Abwehr, calling it, 'The Canaris Family Limited', on account of the number of the Admiral's family working for the organisation. Hall confirmed that it was a valid criticism. Canaris had also been known to employ the sons of family and close friends, thus ensuring they avoided any possibility of fighting on the frontline. All the latest intelligence reports indicated that he appeared increasingly out of step with Berlin. As early as the invasion of Poland when the Admiral had personally witnessed the killing of civilians in Poland by SS troops, he had been completely appalled by the wanton brutality that had followed Poland's defeat. The only certainty was that Canaris was certainly no hard-line Nazi party member.

Sarah Davis, Spencer explained, had met the Admiral on numerous occasions when her father had been a leading British diplomat in Germany. She'd described Canaris as a quiet erudite man of very few words. Sarah had found him charming, the perfect gentleman, and an old school type, caught in a world torn apart by war. MI6 had verified reports that Canaris had saved the lives of seven Jews who were to be transported to a concentration camp. He had personally complained directly to Himmler that the Gestapo were arresting his agents; it was an outright lie of course, but a very brave one. In the end, his audacity saved their lives. The Jews were subsequently handed over by the Gestapo to the Abwehr and taught a few secret codes. It was just a cover of course, but all that mattered was that they were safe and out of Himmler's reach and certain death.

Spencer concluded the notes about the Admiral by saying there were times when he appeared to be totally at odds with the doctrine of the Third Reich. He was first and foremost loyal to his country and not necessarily to its warped leadership. At this stage, it was impossible to second guess either his motives or intentions regarding the future conduct of the war.

The final section concerned Captain Nikolaus Ritter, Robertson's opposite number. His formal title was Chief of Air Intelligence, of the Abwehr's espionage section. Spencer described him with some considerable understatement as being a somewhat interesting character. Nikolaus was in his early forties and had spent some ten years or more working in New York in the textile industry. His background in America made him an ideal candidate for the Abwehr, and he was recruited during the 1930s. He spoke English with a broad New York accent and fronted a company based in Hamburg. Admiral Canaris had placed Ritter in charge of the spy offensive against Britain in what became known in Germany as Operation Lena.

Interestingly, Spencer wrote, their Double Cross agents had indicated that Ritter was interested in pinpointing the reservoirs supplying London with fresh water, their ultimate aim was assumed to target them with bacteria-laden bombs. Whether or not that was the Reich's real intention until the theory could be discredited British Intelligence had to take the threat seriously.

Garvan decided to take a ten-minute break. He made himself a cup of tea and had a fag. He needed time to think and gather his thoughts together.

Returning to the office he carried on reading the Brief. He turned over the page. It was titled "Twenty

Committee Agents". This was the bit he needed to get a handle on. He found himself skimming over the initial preamble about how German agents captured in Britain underwent intense interrogation. Robertson had briefly covered the process. The only line Garvan found himself stumbling over was that the British Government paid Double Cross agents a monthly salary. That can't be right; he said to himself, the bastards are spies! According to Hall, MI5 ensured their salaries were paid at a rate, at least, equivalent to the one they received from the Abwehr.

Garvan re-read the line again still not quite sure if he'd misread it the first time round. Financially, some of them were probably doing quite well for themselves, considering both the British and German Governments were in effect paying for their services. So just how much money were agents raking in every month? Before now the financial aspect hadn't occurred to him. He'd naturally assumed that political ideology drove the majority of Abwehr agents. He was now beginning to realise their reasons for jumping ship were far from clear cut.

Garvan stubbed out his cigarette and turned another page. The heading was titled Joyce Leader. This was what he had been waiting for: the nuts and bolts of the case.

Born 1916 in London, her mother Bridget was French, her father Kurt, was of Anglo-Austrian origin. Spencer had annotated the margin in black ink. "Bit of a mongrel our Joyce, she has dual nationality both British and Austrian". Kurt Leader came from a prosperous family of engineering manufacturers and had inherited vast wealth from his late mother's family. He had never worked a day in his life and had enjoyed a somewhat enviable playboy lifestyle before the outbreak of the war. He had married Bridget Artois in Monte-Carlo apparently between bouts at the gaming tables. Garvan smiled to himself; he could almost hear Spencer delivering the lines in his rich caramel-like Welsh tone.

Joyce Leader finished her education at the Sorbonne and was fluent in French, German and English. Pre-war, she was a member of the cosmopolitan smart set, spending her time flitting aimlessly around Europe. By all accounts, her father was not known to be an ardent Nazi, quite the reverse in fact and since the outbreak of the war had kept a deliberately low profile in Austria.

Since 1939, Kurt Leader had successfully managed to transfer a large slice of his fortune out of Austria and Germany. With the invaluable assistance or bribery of several influential Swiss bankers, he continued to fund his daughter's lavish lifestyle. Joyce's younger sister, Elisabeth, was married to a senior officer of the Wehrmacht.

It was still unclear why Joyce had decided to remain in France after the outbreak of the war, but her somewhat complicated love life may have had some influence on her decision. After the Nazi occupation, Leader had been swiftly recruited by the Abwehr. Being highly intelligent, attractive and multi-lingual, she was prime agent material. Nikolaus Ritter had personally recruited Joyce. Colonel Robertson was of the opinion that Ritter had desperately wanted to ingratiate himself with the fabulously wealthy heiress as a lever into fashionable society. By all reports Ritter was amused when Joyce disdainfully rejected his offer that she should be placed on the Abwehr's payroll, stating that she'd never held down a paid job in her entire life, and certainly had no intention of doing so now not even for the Third Reich.

On Leader's eventual recruitment to the Double Cross Robertson had given her the codename Borgia, after Lucrezia Borgia whose wealthy family had dominated the ruthless Machiavellian politics and sexual corruption of the

Renaissance Papacy in Italy. To Robertson's mind, both the name and her family background fitted Joyce to perfection.

Leader was parachuted into a remote part of the Norfolk coast by a unit of the Luftwaffe dedicated for undercover operations. Her German handlers had been totally confident that following the fall of France, it was only a matter of time before Britain would be invaded. In Norfolk Joyce was met by a fellow agent, Arthur Owens, who unknown to her had already been turned by British Intelligence.

Wishing to retain her pampered lifestyle, Joyce had arrived with £10,000 in ready cash, and a wad of expensive jewellery stuffed into her pockets. After her arrival in England, the security services monitored her progress. She was allowed to continue her mission, albeit under close surveillance. The delay in picking her up allowed MI5 enough time to check out whether there were any other active agents they might have missed, who might try to make contact with her.

On her arrival, Joyce had been struck by the fact that Britain was not on its knees, and at the point of capitulation. The people were still carrying on with their daily lives much as they had before the war. The bomb damage and the resulting devastation had made a huge impact of course; but the reality of what she saw and what she witnessed, was that the endless propaganda churned out on the radio in occupied Europe, was a complete, and utter lie.

On being interrogated by Lt. Col Stephens, the Commandant of Latchmere House, where she was imprisoned, Joyce Leader had referred to her recruitment by the Abwehr and her subsequent arrival in England as a suicide mission on a hiding to nowhere. Whether she said it on the spur of the moment or genuinely believed her mission was futile, was still very much open to conjecture, but it appeared to marry up with her apparent disillusionment when she had first arrived in Britain.

Spencer described Joyce as efficient, dependable, and had been greatly valued by Sarah Davis. She was adroit at assimilating the information Sarah provided her to pass onto her German controllers. The Abwehr had never once doubted the veracity of her transmissions, believing the intelligence had been picked up from her various society acquaintances and conquests – of which, Spencer annotated in the margin, "there were many!"

Joyce had inherited her father's great love of gambling and spent most evenings at Crockford's the Mayfair Casino. She frequently lost vast sums at the tables, but with a substantial private income from her father, could easily afford to do so. Her losses had never seriously concerned Colonel Robertson, although one or two members of the Twenty Committee had expressed their unease. Robertson was content to let things ride. It kept her happy, and there was little harm to be gained by her losing the odd fortune at the tables if it wasn't affecting the quality of her work for St. James's. Tar's view, was that, however, significant her losses, she was never likely to be vulnerable to blackmail, she was completely immune and cushioned by her family's enormous wealth. He was also equally content to allow the flow of cash from Switzerland to continue as long as she remained a useful asset to MI5.

Hall described her as an exceptional personality. She made friends easily, knew how to make and establish useful contacts. She dressed expensively and had an army of admirers. Joyce enjoyed the nightlife London provided, and was a creature of habit; she always started off the evening at the Ritz Bar before usually heading off either to a club or Crockford's. Her conquests were somewhat legendary; there was a whole raft of politicians, senior military officers 'and industrialists', and it all continued unabated under the scrutiny of the security services. For the most part, Robertson remained relatively indulgent toward her. Ritter had expected Joyce to sleep with society contacts, to either compromise or elicit information from them. There had been one or two occasions when either Robertson or Sarah Davis had felt the need to remind Joyce to wind her neck in. It was only if they thought her liaisons were likely to compromise security. Spencer had again annotated in the margin: "There's no doubting Leader's enthusiasm for the job in hand – if you get my drift". Garvan smiled and flicked over the page.

The initial report and analysis of Joyce Leader had been raised by Camp 020, at Latchmere House, near Richmond, the interrogation centre for all captured German agents in Britain. The officer in charge, Lieutenant Colonel Robin Stephens, was nicknamed 'Tin Eye' so called because of the thick monocle always wedged firmly in his right eye; with swept-back dark hair, he was an imposing figure with a rather fierce expression.

Anyone deemed unsuitable for use by British Intelligence faced either the firing squad or the hangman, although a few German spies' ended up imprisoned on the Isle of Man. On arrival at Camp 020, prisoners were stripped of their clothes and kitted out with a flannel prison uniform. The routine never varied, they were escorted to a cell and left entirely alone without any hope of outside contact. After a suitable period in isolation, they were then photographed, and given their first formal interview. According to the records, Joyce Leader found the entire process utterly degrading, and still professed to have recurring nightmares about being forced to wear "a fucking baggy prison uniform".

Lt. Col Stephens primary aim, Hall wrote was to achieve a signed confession from his inmates. Preliminary reports were typed up on yellow paper to make them readily visible in the buff coloured folders. The report contained an agent's codename plus the date of their mission to Britain. The Security Services nick-named the forms yellow perils, as they could ultimately seal an agent's fate. Stephens also provided St. James's with a detailed psychological analysis to help determine their viability to work for the double-cross system.

From the outset, Stephens had been emphatic that violence was a complete taboo amongst his team, for he believed it only served to produce an answer to please the interrogator rather than the actual truth. In his opinion, there was absolutely no reliability under torture, and he couldn't afford to make mistakes and jeopardise the Twenty Committee's work. Spencer described Stephens as a formidable character with an extraordinary ability to break even the most hardened of spies.

In 'Tin Eye's opinion, Joyce Leader wasn't a particularly hard nut to crack and had readily agreed to become a double agent for MI5. He suggested she was nothing more than a socialite caught up in a maelstrom of events, which had been entirely outside of her control. Leader's linguistic skills and important connections were enhanced significantly through her sister, Elisabeth's, marriage to a senior Wehrmacht officer, and had by default made Joyce an even more desirable catch for the Abwehr. Leader's decision to accept Nikolaus Ritter's approach was in 'Tin Eye's view, partly driven by political expediency, and partly from a perceived threat, real or imaginary to imprison her wealthy parents. She told Stephens that Ritter had said to her. "We know where your parents are, and we can arrest them at any time of our choosing." The threat Stephens concluded couldn't be dismissed, although he advised caution as her version of events could not be verified.

Leader had apparently met up with Ritter a week after their initial meeting when he again repeated the threat against her parents. However affable might Ritter appear she was only too aware that it wasn't an idle threat, and that he'd meant every word. She was only too aware that some years ago the Gestapo had raised files on her parents. Before the war, a local party official had visited the family and told them that their reluctance to join the Nazi Party had placed them in a high-risk category with the State. It was a warning, and one they couldn't ignore. Her sister Elisabeth's marriage to a Wehrmacht officer had given them breathing space, but certainly not enough to save their lives if they crossed the line with local Party officials. The family had always moved in the highest echelons of society, and with her father's well-documented ambivalence to the Reich, he was already a marked man.

Joyce knew, as her father had done, the only way to survive was to conform and appear, at least outwardly, to be a true Nazi. In the report, she stated it had been a calculated decision to accept Ritter's offer. Ultimately, it was a matter of self-preservation, and a means to protect her parents. In summing up, Stephens had come to the conclusion that Leader's only real loyalty was to herself and no-one else.

However, his advice to the Twenty Committee had been that Joyce Leader was not to be underestimated. Her moral compass, he admitted, might often be suspect, but if handled correctly she would be a formidable opponent. Under interrogation, she mentioned being disillusioned with the regime even before her arrest. It was a stock answer and at this stage, Stephens had decided should be treated lightly and not given too much credence.

Garvan slowly found himself building up a mental picture of the woman. The report so far probably served to raise more questions than answers, but he supposed that was the point of it. Was she the victim of Ritter's threats against her family, or had she simply been right from the start a confirmed Nazi? There was simply no way of telling at least not without interviewing her.

The final Section of the Top Secret File was headed Margaret Hamilton, known as Maggie. Born 1914 in London, her mother Marianne Auton was French; while growing up, she'd spent every summer and Christmas holiday with her maternal grandparents in France. Languages: She was fluent in French, German and Italian. Maggie's father James Hamilton was a successful lawyer and came from a well-connected aristocratic family. Maggie's politics had been influenced heavily by her father's right wing extremism.

Throughout the 1930s as war loomed James Hamilton had pushed for appeasement to accept peace with Hitler, no matter what the long-term cost to Britain might be. Maggie's own forthright and very public views exactly mirrored those of her father, and by default had brought her to the attention of the Abwehr. As an ideological recruit to the Nazi cause, Spencer wrote that Maggie had not been placed on their payroll.

Garvan could recall reading about her father in the newspapers, and seeing his picture plastered all over the front pages. Without exception, they'd branded him a dangerous anti-Semitic politician, a firebrand and renowned for his powerful oratory. Spencer wrote that James Hamilton belonged to a secret organisation called the Right Club. Their mission, according to its founder Archibald Ramsay, a Scottish Unionist Member of Parliament, was to oppose the activities of the so-called organised Jewry and their supposed influence on public life. The exclusive Right Club included the Duke of Westminster, Lord Redesdale, and a host of the great and not so good right wing sections of British society. Unknown to its members the club had successfully been infiltrated by an MI5 agent called Joan Miller.

When war was declared the Right Club had to all intents and purposes disbanded. In fact, it had only gone underground and was planning on ways to aid Germany. The Club's activities, therefore, came under even closer scrutiny by the Security Services. MI5's plant Joan Miller proved more than efficient at wheedling her way into the heart of the organisation. It didn't take her long before she managed to stumble across vital documentation regarding certain individuals who'd supplied state secrets to the Nazis.

Spencer wrote that MI8, the wireless interception arm of the Security Services, had successfully picked up various messages indicating that Admiral Canaris had personally read direct correspondence between Churchill and Roosevelt. Joan Miller's initial evidence had pointed the finger at a man called Tyler Kent, an American cipher clerk, who was working at the US Embassy in London. In effect, Tyler had passed the information to a woman called Anna Wolkoff, a Russian fascist living in England. MI5 later discovered she was a member of James Hamilton's pro-fascist Right Club.

Although James Hamilton had not been directly implicated in the Tyler/Wolkoff plot his previous activities, and membership of the Club had not only meant him being placed under close surveillance, but he'd also been called in for questioning on several occasions by Special Branch and MI5.

As a successful lawyer, Hamilton had always managed to hold his own under intense interrogation and had skillfully distanced himself, from what he termed the rogue faction that had adhered themselves to the Right Club. In Spencer's opinion, although it was unlikely that Hamilton had known of Wolkoff's activities it couldn't be discounted.

The next paragraph was sub-titled: Recruitment of Maggie Hamilton to the Abwehr. Christmas 1938 and, as usual, the Hamilton family had spent the holidays with their French relatives. It was during this particular trip that Maggie was recruited by an Abwehr talent scout called Walter Patreaus, whom she'd met some years earlier when he was in London. It was certainly no secret that her father had influenced her political views. Maggie was, in essence, a Fascist, but for whatever reason had never felt inclined to join her father's Right Club.

When Maggie first met Walter Patreaus, he was studying at Southampton University, improving his English on a student exchange from Berlin. At this point in his life, Patreaus was not a member of the Nazi Party, nor had he developed any keen political allegiance, that was to come later. His maternal grandfather had been a Scottish flax merchant, and by all accounts, he was inordinately proud of his Clan connections. After his studies had finished at Southampton, Walter decided to take himself off and cycle round Britain. His trip ended in London where he first met Maggie Hamilton at a dinner party.

They were young and by all accounts enjoyed a brief but none too serious relationship. It perhaps wasn't too surprising, Spencer wrote, as they had a great deal in common - their shared Scottish heritage, both were intellectuals and tended to be deeply impressionable. By the time Patreaus returned to Germany his mother had become an ardent Nazi. Just as her father had influenced Maggie, so Walter was influenced by his mother's newfound political views. He subsequently joined the Nazi youth movement and rose rapidly through its ranks. He was to be snapped up by the Abwehr, and due to his friendship with Maggie was deemed to be the ideal choice to recruit her to the Nazi cause.

In 1939, Hamilton was encouraged by Nikolaus Ritter to try to get herself a job at the BBC. Her language skills were an obvious asset, and with the help of a family acquaintance, she managed to land a job as a translator. Following Ritter's instructions to the letter, Maggie set out to make as many useful contacts as she could across both the media and Whitehall. The BBC had developed something of a reputation for being a haven for theatrical types, Spencer wrote, a louche world of which Maggie wholeheartedly disapproved of.

She also found herself increasingly at odds with the Government propaganda she was expected to help broadcast and made disparaging comments in her radio transmissions to Ritter. He'd made light of her complaints: he wasn't interested in her personal opinions, only results and ordered her to knuckle down, and remember that her role was to provide high-grade information to the Reich.

By November 1939, Maggie was transferred to the BBC German Service. The Abwehr now had everything they wanted. It was an ideal opportunity for her to obtain insider knowledge of the Government's political aims and strategy. Spencer had annotated, that in Germany, people faced arrest for merely listening to the BBC broadcasts. Although the programmes were routinely jammed by the Germans, to hear the broadcasts, listeners' were forced to press their ears against the radio, but by doing so, they risked arrest as traitors.

It was during this period that Ritter instructed Maggie to embed herself closely with her colleagues at the BBC Monitoring Service. "You can imagine," Spencer wrote, "that Ritter was more than pleased with the reports provided by Hamilton, and had marked her down as one of his most efficient and professional agents." It was a long way from her original initiation test when he'd asked her for a timetable of all UK mainline stations. It wasn't exactly high-grade material, but as the Germans had a habit of shooting up everything in sight on the railways in occupied territory, MI5 had assumed they probably intended to carry out the same strategy in Britain.

British Intelligence had been monitoring her radio transmissions right from the outset. A decision had been made to leave her in-situ until such time as they needed to bring her into custody. At the time, Robertson had wanted not only to ensure there were no other Abwehr agents embedded within the BBC, but with the Twenty Committee's endorsement he wanted to hold back, and allow her some leeway while MI5 continued to investigate her father to see if he was also spying for the Abwehr.

Maggie, Spencer noted was an intelligent woman, and when she chose could be good company, but she was by nature moody and given to bouts of sulking if ordered to do something which wasn't quite to her liking, as both the double-cross and Ritter had found to their cost. "Is the word for her petulant, or spoilt?" He'd scribbled in the margin. "I'm not sure probably both." Just like Joyce Leader, she also appeared completely devoid of any serious moral outlook on life.

Before Maggie's eventual arrest, the only blip St. James's had faced came from the unlikely source of Hugh Carleton-Greene, the Head of the BBC's German Service, who was becoming increasingly uneasy about Maggie's employment within his department. With her well-known extreme right wing views, and family background he'd long harboured doubts about her suitability. The German Service was now beginning to play an increasingly pivotal role in the war effort, and this had only served to increase his anxiety about her role at the BBC.

Carleton-Greene had taken the opportunity to raise his concerns with a close friend from the Home Office. A week later, MI5 was informed of Hugh's doubts, and word soon spread that he was angling to sack her from the German Service. Alarms bells started ringing across Whitehall. Tar Robertson simply couldn't afford her to lose the job, there was too much at stake, it was vital she remain at the BBC. The Twenty Committee convened and decided it was time to move in. They'd deal with Carleton-Greene in due course, but first they decided to move in and take control of Maggie, so to some extent, it was a high-risk strategy as there was no guarantee that she would jump ship and become a double agent.

Waiting until Maggie returned from work one evening, Special Branch officers accompanied by MI5 operatives arrived at her flat. During their search, they found some incriminating documents and a radio transmitter concealed in a linen cupboard.

She was caught red-handed, and that's all they wanted to maximise the effect on her. Special Branch arrested Maggie immediately and placed her in custody. A week later she found herself being interrogated by 'Tin Eye' at Latchmere House. Hamilton claimed that since being recruited by the Abwehr, she'd had a change of heart, and had finally come to realise that her own, and her father's right wing beliefs had at best been naive. At this point, Spencer included an extract from the interrogation carried out by Stephens.

"I've grown up, I was a bloody fool," and she'd pleaded to Stephens, "I was flattered to be asked by Walter Patreaus to become a spy. Why had they picked on me? It had all seemed so glamorous, so exciting back then."

"But you're a fascist!" Stephens had said, bluntly, "Are you saying that wasn't the real reason for your willingness to become a German spy against your own country, a country at war fighting the very Fascism in which you believed?"

"I didn't think it through," she'd sobbed. "I didn't fully understand what I was getting myself into."

'Tin Eye' had concluded his assumption of the interview by saying that given time Hamilton could prove a useful asset to Double Cross. She was amenable and outwardly repentant at becoming an enemy agent. At this point, Spencer added his personal thoughts about Stephens' decision. Right from the outset he had remained wary of her joining Double Cross, but was overruled by both Robertson and the chairman of the Twenty Committee, John Masterman. Spencer still maintained that if it hadn't been for Maggie's arrest, it was doubtful if she would ever have shown the slightest remorse about her espionage activities for Germany. He also had to concede the same could be said of any number of the double agents now under their control. As an afterthought, he'd scribbled in the margin: "In fairness both Leader and Hamilton have proved their worth time and again, on occasion by literally placing their lives on the line."

Maggie Hamilton had been rattled severely by the experience at Latchmere House. But at least, the system had proved it was working, that was the whole point of the exercise - to test, to gauge her responses, and take her to the edge, to see if she'd buckle under the strain of interrogation. The prospect of being tried for espionage and the sheer humiliation of being dragged to the Old Bailey, even in a closed court, had also played a crucial role in Maggie's reasoning, the entire process had scared her witless.

The only thing Maggie had in common with Joyce Leader was their shared experience of Stephens' interrogation techniques. Familiarity was discouraged at every stage, and prisoners were kept standing at attention throughout their interviews. It was a long grinding process where they were made to feel that their actions for the Abwehr were indefensible. They were told that British Intelligence had intercepted their transmissions to Germany, and there was nowhere left to hide. Each cell was bugged, there was simply no escape - MI5 more often than not planted even their cell-mate.

On the recommendation of Stephens' Report, the Twenty Committee sanctioned Maggie's recruitment to the Double Cross. Robertson gave Maggie the Codename Joan of Arc. To his mind, there were certain parallels between the two women. Joan of Arc had become a passionately religious woman in her teens, blinkered in her beliefs, and at an equally tender age through her father's Fascism, Maggie had also developed a keen sense of political awareness. With characteristic understatement Stephens recorded that after Hamilton's arrest, the bleak reality of her situation had somewhat served to concentrate Maggie's thoughts, knowing that as a traitor she could very well end up either on the gallows or facing a firing squad. Not unnaturally the prospect scared the girl witless. 'Tin-Eye's' interrogation techniques had quickly worn her down. She'd become vulnerable, open to suggestions, and was willing to do or say anything to save her own neck. Maggie had supplied MI5 with valuable information about her recruitment in France, and her subsequent dealings with Hamburg. "The Double Cross system," Stephens insisted, "could and should use her in the future." Morally he accepted Hamilton was as twisted as a corkscrew but pointed out she was certainly no different from any of their previous recruits to the network. He also noted that during this period Robertson had allowed her to operate unhindered by MI5. She'd proved to be an effective and efficient spy for the Abwehr.

After release from Latchmere House, Maggie like Joyce Leader was formally interviewed by Robertson and John Masterman. It was only then after their final endorsement that she was accepted officially into the fold. At this point, Hugh Carleton-Greene, Maggie's boss at the BBC, was summoned to a meeting with the Home Secretary, Sir John Anderson, and given the bare bones of Maggie's situation. He thanked Hugh profusely for raising his concerns about her suitability working on the BBC's propaganda broadcasts to Germany but was told in no uncertain terms that in the interests of the war effort, Maggie would be returning to her old job and once more placed under his direct control. The matter was now closed.

Garvan's attention was drawn to Spencer's handwritten scrawl at the bottom of the page: "Carleton-Greene isn't anyone's fool and must have known Anderson was being economical with the truth. At the end of the day, he didn't have a choice other than accept Maggie back into the fold. The Twenty Committee needs her to remain at the BBC, for her to retain her legitimacy with Nikolaus Ritter in Hamburg."

Spencer thought it important to explain the background to the turf wars faced by Robertson and his team. He started by explaining that the Interallie network headed by Roman Czerniawski was an asset of the British Secret Intelligence Service (SIS) rather than the SOE. Garvan sat back and reached for his desk drawer and retrieved a pack of cigarettes. He needed to take a break again. He'd been making his notes while reading the file but guessed that even by Scotland Yard's standards the turf wars of the Security Services probably paled into insignificance, compared to the shadowy world of Spencer Hall's bitter inter-departmental rivalries. What were they expecting from him?

Garvan almost physically braced himself before flicking over the page. Some of the stuff he decided to read and digest at a later date, but something about Tar Robertson suddenly caught his eye. Hall noted that Robertson was one of the few MI5 operatives trusted by both the SOE and SIS, and unbeknown to each organisation, he was playing a slick game with both of them. Neither had any inkling about his remit to turn German operatives into double agents. It was said that Tar's charm could melt an iceberg, and he needed it to as he skilfully negotiated his way around the endless inter-security wars across Whitehall. Without the knowledge of the SIS, Robertson had managed to cultivate personal contacts within the Interallie, and especially Roman Czerniawski; which in turn, had then led to high-grade intelligence reports landing on his desk in St. James's. The SIS, Hall explained, would have been incandescent had they ever got wind of Robertson's sleight of hand as he carefully muscled his way in on their territory.

During this period, the BBC had sent a coded message to the Interallie congratulating them on their first birthday. Garvan scanned the page, his eyes locking on the name of an agent named Keiffer. Yes, he remembered that one, Robertson had mentioned he was taken into custody by the Gestapo and that the Abwehr had discovered four wireless sets belonging to the Interallie. It wasn't just a case of the Abwehr getting lucky; they were beginning to pick up agents and their equipment with pinpoint accuracy. A steady pattern was starting to emerge, and alarms bells began ringing simultaneously in both Paris and London. It had now seemed only a matter of time before Keiffer buckled under torture, but he alone certainly didn't know enough to bring down the entire network. The sudden implosion of the Interallie wasn't the result of a single arrest.

With the Interallie in its final death throes, Ritter had decided that both Hamilton and Leader would be more useful back in London, their mission in France was no longer viable. At the time, there'd been just one Interallie wireless set still operable in the whole of Paris.

The girls managed to make contact with St. James's and let them know Ritter's decision. They then both returned to England via a fishing vessel.

Six weeks later Sarah Davis was shot dead in cold blood, assassinated by one of her agents, a rogue agent. The internal investigation conducted by the Twenty Committee had thrown up a notepad on which Sarah had underscored the words 'Codename Nicolette – contact Louis Durand immediately.' Durand was a leading member of the Interallie; he'd left Paris and gone to ground after Roman's arrest started to tear the organisation apart. Louis had eventually managed to link up with a smaller Résistance network in the provinces, which provided him with a temporary safe haven. By the time St. James's had re-established contact with Louis, Sarah was already lying dead in a morgue. His eventual warning came just too late.

What Durand did manage to confirm was that at some point during Leader and Hamilton's mission to France, one of them had changed sides. In effect, they'd become a triple agent. The traitor was given a new codename, the codename Nicolette by Ritter. Durand had promised Robertson that given time if he managed to make contact again with his colleagues in Paris, they'd be able to supply him with the identity of the traitor.

The prospect of a triple agent in their midst meant that they needed to act fast before it was too late. Durand had gone to ground since his last transmission. The Abwehr were hard on his heels, and it was simply too dangerous for him to remain in one place for any length of time. He was the lynchpin to the entire enquiry, but as things stood there was no way of telling whether Durand had been arrested by the Gestapo or was still in hiding. St. James's enquiry had also failed to flush out the killer, and without Durand they'd been forced to bring in Scotland Yard to take on the investigation.

Chapter 9

Garvan picked up the phone to Spencer Hall. 'I've read the file.'

'It's an interesting read, isn't it?'

'I presume Hamilton and Leader have probably guessed they're the main suspects for Sarah's murder?'

'At the end of the day, they're not bloody fools, far from it. We've drip fed them snippets to see how they respond we need to keep them on their toes. We've obviously rattled them. To be perfectly honest with you at this stage we'd rather there wasn't anything too formal. It's just a suggestion of course. At the end of the day, it's entirely up to you.'

Spencer's reply was loaded, like a double-edged sword. MI5 needed him, but only on their terms. 'Is it up to me?' was Garvan's deadpan reply.

'I'm sorry?'

'Just cut the crap Major I think we have to come to an understanding.'

'Do we?'

'MI5's internal investigation failed to flush out Sarah's killer, and while I'm more than willing to listen to your suggestions, I'm not prepared to toe the line. You've failed once already after all.'

A slow smile crossed Spencer's face. 'I guess Chief Inspector you have my measure.'

'Just as long, as we understand each other.'

'I think we probably do.'

'So let's get back to your rogue agents then shall we? You don't want anything too formal, what does that mean precisely?'

'We don't want either of them to be spooked too soon.' Spencer waited, half expecting Garvan to challenge his reasoning, but silence greeted him. 'What I was trying to suggest,' Spencer persisted, 'was that both you and Sergeant Mackenzie should meet them, but at this stage, I'd rather it didn't take place at Scotland Yard. From their point of view, it will make things appear normal, you know, routine, if you get my drift. Or do you think I'm on the wrong track?'

'No, that's fine.'

'I'll get back to you and set everything up, and make all the necessary introductions. And if you don't mind Chief Inspector, I thought that I might make my excuses part way through the meeting.'

'Why?

'So you can have some time alone with them. They'll certainly feel a more at ease without me hanging around. Just let me know how things turn out.'

Garvan agreed Spencer's terms. The unlikely rendezvous turned out to be a pub nestled under the railway arches of Waterloo Station. Spencer's diary was crammed full, and there hadn't been too many opportunities available to fix up a date. Late Wednesday afternoon appeared to provide a small convenient window as he was due to attend a meeting in Aldershot earlier in the day and was expecting to be back in London about five in the afternoon.

Heading over Waterloo Bridge toward the pub, Garvan and Mac passed St. John's Church on the south bank which had taken a direct hit only a fortnight ago. The resulting explosion had killed at least a hundred people sheltering in the deep crypt. The destruction had been so devastating that the rescue services and the local authority had come to the conclusion the only way to deal with the carnage was to seal the crypt. Their plan was to consecrate the entire area as a formal mass grave for those who'd perished. The once splendid church was now a blackened skeletal shell.

As they neared the church, Mac stopped to stare up at the dark silhouetted shape, his thoughts lingering on his family who'd died in the bomb shelter in Cantor Street. How many more families had perished here, he wondered? How many other people were feeling as if their whole life was in an endless limbo? As Mac gazed up at the ruins, he couldn't think of a single reason he wanted to carry on, consumed as he was by an overwhelming numbness of grief and emptiness.

Garvan instinctively knew what his friend was thinking. He had wanted to chivvy him along past the burnt-out shell but had thought better of it. Instead, he waited, not quite sure what to do or say until Mac was prepared to move on.

Garvan recalled reading a London County Council report at the beginning of the war that due to the number of anticipated casualties there might be a shortage of wood for coffins. So far it hadn't quite come to that, but as with the Cantor Street shelter, the blast at St. John's had been so great there were simply no bodies left to bury.

Garvan kept a respectful distance as he followed Mackenzie past St. John's toward the run down pub nestled beneath the old railway arches of Waterloo Station. Inside there was an eclectic mix of commuters, servicemen in transit and stall holders from the nearby market in the Cut, a street that runs between Waterloo Road and Blackfriars Road. The pub was a popular meeting point, its main drawback being that conversation was often drowned out by the sounds of trains rumbling overhead.

Seated toward the rear of the bar Garvan saw Spencer Hall, accompanied by two young attractive women. Garvan didn't allow his face to register surprise, having read Hall's brief he'd already built up a somewhat sketchy mental picture of the two double agents. He was pleasantly surprised they were far more attractive than he'd imagined from the clinically written appraisal.

'Pull up a chair,' Spencer called out catching sight of them. He stood up shook Mackenzie's hand and introduced himself, then gestured toward one of the women, a blonde with neatly coifed wavy hair, pencil slim, elegant and sophisticated with a ready infectious smile. She wore blood red lipstick with long matching fingernails.

'This is Joyce Leader,' Hall announced. There was a reserved air to her demeanour, the grey-blue eyes watchful as she coldly appraised the two policemen with a sharp and direct shrewdness, coupled with an innate self-assurance. Garvan had a gut feeling that very little was likely to faze her. The prospect of being questioned by two Scotland Yard Detectives was probably something of a welcome relief after being interrogated by the severe 'Tin Eye' Stephens at Camp 020.

'And this is Maggie Hamilton,' Spencer added, gesturing toward the girl on his right.

The two women were strikingly different. Maggie was auburn-haired, her eyes a dark brown with an attractively open face. Whereas Joyce Leader had an impenetrable, almost deadpan expression, Hamilton's gaze was merely quizzical with a ready, warm smile. Garvan couldn't help thinking that espionage, dangerous as it was, certainly had its compensations for Spencer being surrounded by incredibly attractive women. It was an undeniable perk.

'Let me get the drinks in,' Spencer offered.

'A pint of bitter, please,' Mac said.

'Make it two.' Garvan added.

As Spencer got up to get the drinks in they joined the women at the table. Joyce leaned down to pick up her handbag for a pack of cigarettes and produced a slender, expensive solid gold lighter. She deftly placed a cigarette into an elegant ebony holder. Garvan guessed it was probably something of a fashion accessory, an affectation, but it also prevented her fingers from being stained with unsightly nicotine stains. Joyce lit the cigarette and flirtatiously locked her eyes onto Garvan's. He couldn't help smiling to himself - what kind of game was she hoping to play?

In stark contrast, Maggie Hamilton appeared almost diffident with a dreamy, almost wistful smile. Occasionally she'd check her watch as if pre-occupied about missing an appointment or perhaps a date.

When Hall returned with the drinks, it didn't take Garvan long to realise that Hamilton was watching him with a wary intensity and seemed overly eager to please. She was suddenly bubbly, coquettish even while Joyce Leader's expression had closed down the instant Spencer re-joined them. There was no longer any hint of flirtatiousness only a cool unreadable, steely glint in her eyes.

Spencer chatted idly about his afternoon meeting in Aldershot. He seemed perfectly relaxed and superficially at least very friendly toward his two agents. Garvan wondered if Hall's veneer of amiability had perhaps lulled them into a false sense of security, perhaps even into believing they were no longer in the frame for murdering Sarah Davis. The situation was quite difficult to read. They both seemed very guarded in their responses to Spencer. They laughed at his jokes, were pleasant enough to one another, but Garvan had a feeling that Hall was toying with them, skilfully manipulating, playing to their strengths and weaknesses.

Hall drained his beer and as pre-arranged made his excuses to leave early. He set the empty glass down on the table and winked at Garvan apologising profusely for not being able to stay, but that he needed to make tracks for a meeting with Tar Robertson. Joyce coolly watched after

Spencer as he weaved his way through the crowded bar, all the while playing with her gold cigarette lighter before snapping the lid shut.

'Well gentlemen,' she announced setting her gaze on the two detectives, 'shall we get on with this? I understand you need to ask us some questions about Miss Davis.'

Since arriving at the pub, one of the first things Garvan noticed was that Joyce Leader spoke with a perfectly cut glass English accent without even the slightest intonation of a foreign accent. No doubt her wealthy Anglo-Austrian origins and expensive education accounted for her fluency. With Spencer out of the way she became flirtatious again, self-assured and bordering on being arrogant, almost dismissive of them as if their investigation into Sarah's murder was some minor blip in her busy schedule. As she spoke, Garvan found himself becoming increasingly irritated. She was, after all, a German spy, admittedly one who was now working for MI5, but she was still only one small step away from the gallows.

'I need to be at Crockford's in an hour,' Joyce announced, with a broad fixed smile.

'Crockford's,' Garvan smirked at her, 'what for a game of poker?'

'Well poker or Baccarat, it doesn't matter much,' she shrugged indifferently.

Garvan could tell that Mackenzie was having difficulty keeping his temper in check. He met his gaze, and held it for a moment; it proved just enough to prevent Mac from completely losing his cool.

'If you don't mind,' Maggie piped up, once again checking her watch, 'I have a meeting at 7.30 with Colonel Martin Douglas he's a colleague of Major Hall. Martin's taking me to the Beouf sure le Toit in Orange Street. Do you know it?'

They both nodded. It was just off the Haymarket, and like the Pink Sink at the Ritz was a well-known haunt of the West End's homosexual community. Since the outbreak of the war, the clubs were magnets not only for homosexuals but for anyone wanting to enjoy a hedonistic night out, places where you could forget the bombing raids, the death and the destruction. In so many ways the war had proved to be both a leveller and a catalyst for social change. There was now a definite underlying sense of sexual equality, and what Garvan feared, was that once the war was over the new-found freedoms would disappear as rapidly as they'd emerged and society would return to its normal peacetime, bigoted rigidity.

Mackenzie gave Garvan a side-long glance. He could tell by Garvan's expression that he was struggling to keep the conversation light. He was also trying hard to suppress his anger at their seemingly dismissive attitude toward a formal murder investigation. What the hell was the boss playing at? He'd expected Garvan to come down hard on them, but for some reason, he was holding back. Maggie was still seamlessly nattering away in her artless manner.

'Colonel Douglas and I have arranged to meet an agent at the club. I don't wish to appear rude, Chief Inspector, but all hell will break loose if I miss it. Besides,' she sighed, 'Colonel Martin said he'd meet me here just before seven.'

Garvan gave nothing away and didn't respond.

'This is only a preliminary meeting,' Mackenzie felt compelled to explain to them, 'we intend interviewing you both separately at a later date.'

Maggie flashed him a brief, perfunctory smile. 'Yes, I understand completely. Of course, I'll do anything to help you find Sarah's murderer. My - I mean our situation,' she stammered shooting a hesitant look toward Joyce, 'isn't at all easy.'

'I don't suppose it is,' Garvan mused.

'No, quite,' Maggie said, suddenly looking a little uneasy.

'My understanding is that Miss Davis was your Desk Officer?' Garvan pressed.

Maggie pursed her lips thoughtfully considering her answer. 'I'll be perfectly honest with you, Chief Inspector, there were times when I found Sarah rather off-hand.' She gave a shrug, 'dismissive even, but I'll say this for her, Sarah was fair, and you always knew exactly where you stood.'

'So you didn't find it easy working for her?'

'That's not what I meant!' Maggie snapped back at him defensively. 'There were bound to be frictions. My own situation didn't exactly help. I always felt she came down on me harder than the other agents under her control.'

'Why do you think she treated you differently?'

'Unlike most of the others, I'm British born and bred. I'm certain Sarah and everyone else for that matter at St. James's viewed my spying as a far greater crime than for the foreign nationals under their control.'

Garvan gave her a deliberately blank expression as if he didn't quite understand what she was saying. Her cheeks flushed slightly. 'You know, Sarah took a dimmer view of me. I couldn't blame her really.'

'So tell me, was Miss Davis your London Controller from the outset?'

'Yes, she was. I'll admit that at first things were a little tricky between us, but over time, I grew to respect her.' Maggie took a deep breath and reached for her drink. 'I still can't quite bring myself to believe she's dead. I mean Sarah could look after herself. I just don't understand why she wasn't able to defend herself.'

'Did Miss Davis always carry a firearm with her?' Garvan asked.

'I don't know whether she'd always carried one, but at the office a few weeks ago I saw her place a weapon in her handbag.' Maggie's fingers tightened around the stem of her glass. 'Maybe it all happened so quickly that Sarah simply didn't have time to- to-,' the words died on her lips.

'To defend herself,' Garvan suggested.

Maggie nodded.' Yes,' she said, with another deep intake of breath.

Spencer Hall hadn't mentioned Sarah Davis had been carrying a firearm on the night of her murder. There again it probably shouldn't have come as much of a surprise, as he'd advised Garvan to protect his team by drawing firearms from Scotland Yard's armoury. The Home Office had already sanctioned their being armed even before the paperwork had hit the Commissioner's desk. In hindsight, it was probably a moot point, but one Garvan would prefer to have been pre-warned about rather than hear from one of the two potential murder suspects.

'We didn't find any trace of a weapon at the murder scene,' Mac said to them, 'do either of you think it possible Sarah was perhaps killed by her own gun?'

Maggie gave a shrug. 'I suppose there's always a possibility. I guess you can't rule it out altogether, at least, not until the forensic report is published, but to be perfectly honest with you I haven't given it too much thought either way.'

Joyce interceded. 'If the killer had an ounce of common sense they'd have removed Sarah's weapon from the house. I would have done.'

'Would you?' Mac asked.

Leader calmly returned his gaze; her nostrils flared as if enforcing her derision for what she considered his stupidity. Wasn't it obvious the killer would have removed the weapon? 'Without Sarah's pistol as evidence,' she said, 'there's no way forensics can compare the ballistics from the crime scene.'

Mackenzie stared through Leader. 'Once we know the exact type of weapon Miss Davis was issued, we can compare it with the calibre of the bullet which killed her. We'll then know if we can discount her firearm from the investigation. Mackenzie had checkmated her, and she didn't like it. She sucked heavily on her cigarette holder and calmly turned her attention toward Garvan. 'I might have misread the situation, Chief Inspector, but judging, by the way, you both looked at one another when Maggie mentioned Sarah was armed, I couldn't help thinking that Major Hall hadn't mentioned it to you, am I right?' She'd thrown the question at him almost as a challenge.

Garvan met her cold expression and lied in a deadpan voice. 'You've misread the situation.'

Maggie cut across them. 'I think you have to understand that for some weeks before Sarah died things had started to become a bit awkward for us. Our contact with her was becoming increasingly sporadic. Colonel Robertson eventually called us in for a formal meeting and told us there'd been two attempts on Sarah's life. At that point I don't think either of us knew what to do or say, it came as a bolt out of the blue.'

'There wasn't any point in doing or saying anything,' Joyce sniffed condescendingly.

'Why was that?' Garvan asked, again feeling irritated by her arrogance.

'Sarah was one of Colonel Robertson's most trusted desk officers, and from day one it was obvious the finger of suspicion would naturally point toward one of her agents.' Who else would have had a motive for wanting Sarah dead?'

Garvan couldn't fault her logic.

'So after the two failed attempts on Sarah's life,' Mac queried, 'why do you believe the Colonel didn't have her removed from London?'

'We didn't know where she was living,' Maggie explained, 'the only thing I knew with any degree of certainty was that Sarah was supposed to be under Spencer Hall's protection.'

Joyce deftly fiddled with her ebony cigarette holder, before flicking a long trail of ash into a metal ashtray. 'It was surely a sprat to catch a mackerel.'

'What do you mean?' Mackenzie pressed her.

'If the Colonel and Major Hall had seriously intended protecting Sarah, as you say they'd have moved her out of harm's way down to some safe house or other in the countryside. Let's face it; it wouldn't have been that difficult.' Joyce paused, drawing heavily on her cigarette. 'We're not fools Chief Inspector, Maggie, and I know exactly where we stand.'

'And where exactly do you stand?' Garvan shot back at her.

'We're both expendable,' Joyce said without any visible trace of emotion. 'Our lives are controlled by Colonel Robertson. It's he and his committee who decide whether we continue to be of use to MI5. Sarah, on the other hand, was an indispensable member of the Colonel's team.' Joyce leaned back in her chair crossing her long shapely legs. There was the merest hint of a challenge in her eyes, as she said: 'Surely you must have asked yourself, Chief Inspector, why the Colonel and Spencer took such a chance, such a high risk of placing Sarah's life on the line at that house in Monkton Drive?'

'I'm new to this game Miss Leader,' Garvan smiled with disarming modesty, he wanted to draw her out, they were playing cat and mouse with each other. This was not going to be easy he decided. 'So why do you think they didn't whisk Sarah off to some God forsaken place in the countryside? By keeping her in London as you say they must have realised, they were putting her life on the line.'

Joyce pulled a face. 'There's only one possible reason at least as far as I can I tell. Keeping Sarah in London was nothing more than a ruse to force the rotten apple among us out into the open. Why else would they have kept her here after the earlier attempts on her life?'

Garvan picked up his beer and said. 'You appear to know all the answers Miss Leader. A rotten apple what's that all about?'

'A triple agent,' Joyce replied stiltedly. 'Nothing else would ever have forced them to risk Sarah's life. She was way, way too valuable for there to be any other reason.'

'And the rotten apple killed Sarah, is that what you're saying?' Mac queried.

Maggie leaned forward resting her arms on the table hands clasped together. 'I guess there's always an outside chance that it was some local cretin who killed her, but realistically from what Spencer has told us, the murder had all the hallmarks of a professional killing. Neat, clean cut and the icing on the cake, they did it under the cover of a bombing raid. Perfect really,' she added, thoughtfully.

'So do you think the killer took Sarah by surprise?' Garvan asked.

Joyce answered with her usual sangfroid. 'I doubt it.'

'So what do you think happened?'

'I think she probably knew her killer. I might be wrong of course, but doesn't it seem obvious?'

'At this stage of the investigation Miss Leader nothing seems obvious to me, that's why we're here trying to gather together anything that might help us track down her killer.'

'From all I know,' Joyce continued, 'Sarah was an experienced operative she certainly didn't take chances. She was pleasant enough, straightforward, but ruled us with a rod of iron. Step out of place and all hell broke loose. You didn't cross Sarah, well, if you did, you soon learnt not to do so again.' Joyce breathed deeply clasping the ebony cigarette holder thoughtfully between her thumb and forefinger, before adding. 'She was a very beautiful woman.' Joyce hesitated, and for the first time looked slightly uneasy. 'I have to admit that I misjudged her completely.'

'How did you misjudge her?'

Joyce momentarily lowered her eyes. 'I wrongly assumed Sarah was just some bottle blonde who'd made good, and had probably slept her way up the ladder.' Joyce smiled, almost to herself. 'How wrong I was Chief Inspector,' she said softly, 'Sarah was good, bloody good at what she did. That's why I can't believe anyone could get that close without her knowing them; it just doesn't add up.'

'I agree,' said Maggie, 'the only other option is that maybe during the bombing raid someone managed to take her by surprise, but even then they'd have to be damn good.'

'Do either of you have any idea who might have killed her?' Garvan asked.

They both seemed uncertain how to respond.

'No ideas at all, then?' he pressed.

It was Joyce who spoke up. 'In this line of work we're constantly looking over our shoulders Chief Inspector. Trust and betrayal walk hand in hand.'

'You're spot on Miss Leader, somewhere along the line betrayal cost Miss Davis her life.'

'How exactly was she betrayed?' Joyce asked, curiously.

'You both said earlier that whoever managed to get close enough to Sarah would have to be very good, professional at what they did.' He coolly looked at each of them in turn and said. 'It sounds to me as if you think one of your colleagues, a Double Cross agent, murdered Sarah'.

Joyce shrugged. 'That's anyone's guess Chief Inspector. The rotten apple might not be one of us, in Sarah's line of work she must have made a few enemies, and not just within the Double Cross.'

Garvan didn't pursue the matter further. He changed direction and said: 'At the moment we're trying to establish who saw Sarah on the day she died, did either of you perhaps see her?'

'I'm sure Spencer would have checked her diary by now and told you precisely what she was doing,' Maggie said, almost flippantly.

'I saw her in the morning,' Joyce announced, 'it was early, about eight. She popped into the office in Leicester Square.'

'Isn't it an insurance firm?' said Garvan, remembering the headed paper they'd discovered in Monkton Drive.

'Yes, I think there was a Carrington's Insurance in the office block at the beginning of the war, but they've long since moved out or gone bust. Colonel Robertson retained the signage; no-one gives the place a second glance.'

'So did you have a meeting?'

'No, no nothing like that, we passed the time of day; if anything she seemed a bit evasive why we hadn't seen much of her over the past few weeks. I came away with the distinct impression that she wouldn't be back in the office for a while. Then Spencer turned up, I received my instructions from him and returned home.'

Garvan hesitated slightly before asking. 'Do you believe that Major Hall and Miss Davis were close, I mean, not just work colleagues?'

'Well,' Maggie gushed, animatedly; 'we all thought something was going on between them, you can always tell, can't you?' she giggled. 'She'd never have let on at least certainly not to us. Why on earth would she? And as for Spencer, well, he's such a hard bastard that one,' she said, with feeling. 'I grant he can be charming at times, but beneath it all, he's totally ruthless. I don't mind admitting to you, Chief Inspector, he scares the hell out of me, and since Sarah's died and he's become our desk officer you could say things have changed, he's changed -,' her words slowly trailed off.

Mackenzie said to Maggie: 'You didn't say whether you saw Miss Davis on the day she died.'

Maggie shook her head. 'No, I hadn't seen her for about a week or so. I've not long returned from -,' she paused, 'am I allowed to say?'

'Spencer said it was okay,' Joyce said.

'I mean we've just returned from France, we were on the same mission together. When we got back I went down with a severe bout of bronchitis; I was laid low for a few weeks, so our paths didn't cross too much before she died. I suppose the last time I saw her was at the Savoy. Colonel Robertson had arranged a meeting at the Hotel with Captain Eldridge; he's on the Colonel's team.'

'So you can't think of a reason Sarah was singled out by her killer,' Mac pressed.

Maggie reached down for her handbag, pulled out a compact mirror and quickly reapplied her red lipstick. 'That's anyone's guess sergeant,' she muttered, distractedly, 'we might all work for the Colonel and Major Hall, but our remits are usually entirely separate. Otherwise, we'd compromise security, and quite possibly each other's lives; to be perfectly honest with you I simply do as I'm ordered and keep my head down. It's much safer that way.'

By now Maggie was busy powdering her face. Garvan wondered whether she wanted to impress Colonel Douglas or their contact at the Beouf sure le Toit. Joyce coolly glanced in the direction of her colleague; it didn't take much to see there was no love lost between the two women. It was evident Maggie had lost interest in proceedings and was more intent on her rendezvous on Orange Street.

Turning his attention back toward Joyce, Garvan asked: 'Do you keep your head down as well Miss Leader?' He somehow doubted that she would.

She gave him a non-committal smile. 'By and large, we tend to work in isolation from each other, but, of course, I've got to know other Abwehr spies since being here in England. As I said before I admired Sarah Davis, she was tough, but you always knew where you stood.' Her face softened momentarily. 'Since her death things have not changed for the better. Having Major Hall as a desk officer is rather like having the grim reaper perched on your shoulder.'

'I guess that probably makes things a bit difficult at times,' Mac suggested.

Maggie peered up from her compact mirror and said sharply. 'You try working for the Major for any length time, and you'd know exactly what we mean. To be perfectly honest, I think Spencer would love nothing more than to line us up against a wall and shoot the lot of us. I'm sure he just sees us as some embuggerance.'

Joyce cut across her colleague. 'I expect you've been told already how the system works, well of course you have,' she said, stubbing out her cigarette in an ashtray. 'I'm in a position of my own making, my stupidity, whatever you like to call it. I have to accept that. There's simply no escape, at least, not until the wars over, but until then if I end up upsetting either MI5 or the Abwehr, I won't live long enough to see things through. Emotionally and physically the cost is high, sometimes too high Chief Inspector.'

Maggie checked her reflection again before snapping her powder compact shut. She'd finally finished her make-up, but had obviously been listening to her colleague. 'I couldn't agree with you more.' Her gaze suddenly shot toward the door of the pub as Colonel Douglas arrived. Following her gaze, Garvan swivelled round in his chair, and clapped eyes on a tall uniformed figure framed in the doorway holding a brown leather briefcase; he inclined his head in recognition toward Maggie.

'Now gentlemen,' she announced, 'I'm sorry, but I'll have to make my excuses otherwise I'll miss my 7.30 appointment.'

Garvan nodded. 'We'll be in touch to arrange another meeting.'

'I look forward to it,' she said with a perfunctory smile, stooping to pick up her handbag off the floor.

As another train rumbled overhead, Maggie sashayed out of the pub trailing her distinctive perfume. Garvan detected a flicker of annoyance cross Joyce Leader's face as she watched Hamilton leaving the pub, but the moment soon passed, exchanged for her usual impenetrable expression.

Chapter 10

In Garvan's view, the meeting with Maggie Hamilton and Joyce Leader had thrown up more questions than answers. The following morning he phoned St. James's and told Spencer that he needed to discuss the case in greater detail with him. He'd half expected to be fobbed off, for Hall to make some excuse or other, but he seemed amenable enough to the idea, that rich Welsh voice assuring Garvan over the phone he could meet up with him later that morning.

'How about eleven, I'll take a stroll down from St. James's, and meet you on the Embankment outside Scotland Yard,' he suggested.

'Fine by me,' Garvan said, replacing the receiver.

Good to his word Hall was already waiting for Garvan as he crossed the road as Big Ben struck out the hour. They shook hands.

'Shall we walk down toward Charing Cross?' Spencer said, gesturing toward the railway bridge.

Hall led the way, the collar of his raincoat pulled up against the biting wind coming off the Thames, hands thrust deep into his coat pockets as he set off down the shallow steps toward the river.

'At least, it's not raining,' Garvan smiled, discarding a cigarette butt into the murky grey water lapping the dark granite Embankment wall.

'The air will probably do us some good' Hall grunted, pausing to look toward the South Bank.'

There was a high tide sweeping in from the estuary to almost within a foot of lapping over the Embankment walls. The flotsam and jetsam from last night's bombing raid bobbed and floated in the swirling, murky tidal waters.

'I really ought to try and get out of the office more often,' Hall continued.

'Silly question I suppose, but do you have a lot on at the moment?'

'I guess like you, there's never a day when my desk isn't piled high with a mountain of bloody paperwork.' With his gaze remaining set on the South Bank, it was almost as if he was thinking aloud. 'Every file, every sodding piece of information is cross-referenced. It takes time and patience. Sadly, I don't appear blessed with either of them.' He leaned forward, resting his arms on the parapet. 'I'm not a natural administrator, Chief Inspector, and I'm certainly not an intellectual.' He glanced at Garvan. 'I'm surrounded by all these people with brains the size of planets. There are times,' the words died slowly on his lips.

Spencer lit a cigarette and carried on walking toward Charing Cross. As they strolled in silence along the river bank, it struck Garvan that few people he'd met, so effortlessly dominated their surroundings, be it in Robertson's office, at their meeting with the Assistant Commissioner, or at the pub with Leader and Hamilton.

Garvan gave him a side-long look. There was something intriguing, something controlled, almost dangerous about the man, but it was all rounded off by an easy, infectious charisma. Garvan needed to know more about the man; he needed to get his measure if they were to work successfully together. He might clam up on him of course, but at the moment, Hall had the upper hand, and knew Garvan's background inside out, whereas he knew next to nothing about him.

'If you don't mind me saying so,' Garvan said, casually, 'you've never exactly struck me as being someone who'd be entirely comfortable stuck in an office all day.'

Hall's eyes locked onto Garvan's, his expression questioning. 'Don't I, Chief Inspector?'

'Let's face it you don't quite fit the mould of a grey Whitehall pen-pusher, do you? I've spent most of my career observing people, appraising them, it comes with the territory, and after a while, you develop a gut instinct for how things are, for peoples' characters, their lives. I could, of course, be entirely wrong Major, but you strike me like a square peg in a round hole. But if I'm right it begs the question, why did Colonel Robertson recruit you?'

'That transparent am I?' Hall smirked at him. 'If you must know Tar initially recruited me for a six-month secondment from the Special Operations Executive. My brief was to help him set up the Double-Cross team, to get things up and running. He'd been having countless inter-departmental turf wars with the SOE and SIS. The spats within the Intelligence Service are probably even more ruthless than they are at Scotland Yard.'

'We have our moments,' Garvan smiled.

'Tar thought I'd be able to smooth things over with them. I knew the way they worked, I had all the right contacts, allowing him to carry on with the serious stuff organising the team without getting too bogged down by internal rivalries.' Spencer sucked heavily on his cigarette. 'Collectively, the Twenty Committee is a rather odd bunch. I think Tar may have told you already, that it's made up of the military, civilians and academics. Outside the usual mix, he needed someone with an in-depth knowledge of how agents work in the field and the mindset of their German controllers. I guess that was the real reason Tar wanted me on board.' Spencer allowed the merest flicker of a smile to cross his face. 'When push came to shove I didn't have any choice in the matter; the decision was made on high. I'll be perfectly honest with you, Chief Inspector, Sarah's death has somewhat delayed my leaving St. James's. I can't see any prospect of my secondment coming to an end until her killer is tracked down, and even then I won't be holding my breath.'

'What exactly is the Special Operations Executive?' Garvan asked him.'

'The SOE is an amalgamation of umpteen different pre-war departments. At a very basic level we carry out sabotage, espionage, help organizations like the Interallie, and in fact, do anything that's a bit underhand. I guess it all adds up as to why Robertson thought I'd be ideal for the Double Cross.' He stopped dead on the pavement and turned to face Garvan. 'Enough of me, what did you think of Joyce Leader and Maggie Hamilton? Lovely, aren't they?' he said, sarcastically.

'Let's just say it was interesting, I needed more time of course.'

Spencer's gaze was intense, watchful. 'Spit it out, Chief Inspector, what's on your mind?'

'I think we both need to be completely straight with one another.'

'I thought we'd already sorted that one out.' Spencer said, and carried on walking along the Embankment.

Garvan fell once more in at his side. 'But are you?'

'I am being completely frank with you. Robertson wouldn't have it any other way. Something or someone has sown a seed of doubt in your mind. What on earth did the bitches say to you?'

'They're clever, everything and more that you described in the file.'

'I'm glad you thought so.'

'The safe house Sarah was living in at the time of her death.'

'What about it? I told you before it's one of our properties, one of many'.

'You also told me that by the time Sarah moved to Monkton Drive, there'd already been two attempts on her life. So why exactly did you decide to keep her in London, and not send her out of harm's way to the countryside? Hamilton and Leader suggested you were using Sarah as a sitting target to draw out your rogue agent. Is that right?'

'One way or another we're all expendable, Chief Inspector,' he shrugged dismissively. 'Sarah knew the risks, we'd had countless meetings at St. James's about the situation, and to the best of our ability we tried to limit the risks to her. We discussed all the options, but at the end of the day we all agreed, Sarah included, that the most important thing was, and still is, to flush out the triple agent and prevent the Double Cross system from imploding.'

He gave Garvan a long, hard look. 'You have to understand there's simply too much at stake here for the future conduct of the war, not to have risked everything in our power to track them down. You can think what you like, but placing Sarah's life on the line wasn't an easy decision for any of us.' Spencer stopped, cupped his hands, and lit another cigarette. 'In hindsight was it the wrong decision.' He paused and then said, simply, 'Of course it was. Sarah ended up on a ruddy slab in the morgue, and we're no nearer to outing our rogue agent.' He blew a cloud of grey smoke into the chill morning air. 'You don't have to tell me that I let her down; I wasn't there for Sarah when she most needed my protection.' He took a sharp intake of breath. 'I have to live with that, Chief Inspector, with the guilt of the decisions I took that day. During the last few weeks, I've been to hell and back every single day.' He shot an almost questioning look at Garvan. 'I guess your Sergeant Mackenzie must be going through the same absolute hell right now.'

Garvan nodded in agreement. 'Sometimes the only answer is to lose yourself in your work.'

'Perhaps you're right.'

'Who found Sarah's body?'

'After I left Monkton Drive I returned to St. James's and worked late; I couldn't stay with her any longer there was a flap on. As usual she reported in every hour by phone to our office, there's always someone there to take calls. Everything was normal right up until eight o'clock when she didn't call. I tried calling. The phone was ringing so I knew the landlines weren't down. Colonel Douglas Martin, you may have seen him when he met up with Maggie, was going off duty and volunteered to drop by Monkton Drive to check on her.' He hesitated, his mouth set firm. 'The rest, as you know is history.'

'There's something I don't understand?'

'What's that?'

'How did your rogue agent manage to slip the net long enough to get themselves over to Monkton Drive, and back again without being missed? From what I understand, they've been placed under close surveillance since the first attack on Sarah.'

'I only wish to God I knew. There were no gaps in the monitoring as far as we're concerned. It's patently wrong of course, but that's where you come into the equation. We must have missed something, but I'm not sure where or how. You can read all the surveillance notes until you're blue in the face, but I'm damned if we've missed anything. Hopefully, your team might spot something we've missed.'

'So where were your agents' on the night of Sarah's murder?'

'Joyce was at Crockford's gambling as usual. Maggie was working an evening shift at Bush House in the Aldwych helping with some broadcast or other to Germany.'

'There's something else that's been bothering me.'
Hall looked at him questioningly.

'They told me last night that Sarah was issued with a firearm.'

'Yes – yes, of course.'

'But why didn't you mention it earlier?'

'It wasn't relevant to the inquiry,' he said, blankly.

'The pathology report mentioned the calibre of bullet that killed Sarah was from an Enfield revolver.'

He shrugged dismissively. 'It's a bog standard issue firearm'.

'But we haven't' found any trace of the murder weapon at the house. Is there any possibility that Sarah's own gun was used to kill her?' Garvan queried.

'No, not at all. Sarah had a Smith and Wesson, she'd probably watched too many American movies,' he smiled, 'it wasn't exactly suitable for your average handbag, but she loved it, adored the bloody thing. That's what she wanted, demanded it and the Colonel pandered to her every whim. I guess the murderer decided to remove it from the house.'

'So we have to assume that apart from the killer you were the very last person to see Sarah alive.'

Hall stopped dead in his tracks and swung round to face Garvan; he looked right through him. 'And your point is?' he demanded.

'Major, if this was some run of the mill investigation you'd be the prime suspect right now and under close surveillance before I decided to haul you in for questioning'.

'Are you playing devil's advocate?' Spencer questioned, challengingly.

'Not necessarily.'

'Don't ever lose sight of the fact that while Hamilton and Leader might be astute, they're certainly twisted. Why else would they be working for us? They're very good at what they do, and they've obviously sown seeds of doubt in your mind, made you question everything Tar and I have told you.' His face broke into a fleeting smile. 'There again if they hadn't I might well have been disappointed in them.'

'You obviously know them so much better than I do,' Garvan conceded. 'Joyce struck me as being very intense. I could well be wrong, but my gut instinct is that she's probably the deadlier of the two.'

'She'd kill you at twenty paces with a single withering glance, let alone with a pistol in her hand. Jo is fiery and has a vicious temper on her. She now claims to hate the Nazi regime, and all it stands for, and apparently believes that Hitler has to be defeated at all costs. But God knows what she's really thinking or believes in. Jo is as hard as nails, but to be honest, with you I'd be hard pressed to trust either of them.'

'Last night you appeared to get on very well with them.'

'Did I?' Spencer mused, 'you see, Chief Inspector, I'm learning to play the game, it's taken me quite a while, but I've learnt from the master.'

'Robertson?' Garvan surmised.

'Yes, utterly charming and deadly at the same time, but I've too many rough edges to be that good.'

'What I found interesting is that it was quite marked they both visibly relaxed once you'd left the pub.'

'That's why I made my excuses. You'll always get more out of them when I'm not around. It's as it should be. Tar, on the other hand, could charm the birds from the trees. The girls are relaxed in his company, but he's no less playing a game than I am, we just have different strengths for different occasions. I always end up pulling Jo's leg that if she'd remained in Austria with her Aryan blonde hair and blue eyes, she'd have ended up in one of Himmler's breeding farms.'

'What on earth are you talking about?' Garvan said, unsure if Hall was joking.

He wasn't, in fact, joking at all and carried on seamlessly. 'The breeding farms are one of Herr Himmler's madcap schemes to create a so-called master race. He calls it the Lebensborn Programme, the literal translation means fountain of life. Let's just say he encourages SS and Wehrmacht officers to have children with pure Aryan women, the idea being the children will one day lead a Nazi-Aryan nation.'

'You are joking!

'If only I were. I suppose if you take a step back there's a certain irony about it all.'

'What are you on about?'

'Think of it, there's Hitler, Himmler and Goebbels trying to create this superhuman master race, and yet when it comes down to it, they wouldn't actually qualify for the breeding programme themselves. To a man, they're malcontents, the flawed products of human nature. Himmler with his insane desire to create some distorted valiant SS knighthood and his apocalyptic idealism. Goebbels has a club foot, and as for Hitler, he makes Stalin look some bloody kindergarten teacher. You have to ask yourself how so many dangerous misfits managed to seduce the German people.'

Spencer allowed his cigarette butt to drop into the river and sat himself down on one of the benches dotted along the footpath. Garvan thought he seemed distracted, troubled.

'Why was a call placed to Harmer's office on the night of the murder?' he queried.

The question dragged Hall back from his revelry. 'We couldn't contact Sir Philip Game,' he explained. 'The decision was made at St. James's to call Harmer instead, but not to get bogged down in too much detail about Sarah, and our involvement. We obviously touched base with Special Branch, and asked them to contact Sir Philip, but there wasn't any time to waste, and Tar wanted you to be first on the crime scene.'

'It must be a bit of a juggling act trying to keep things on an even keel with Leader and Hamilton.'

'We're keeping things as normal as we possibly can. We can't afford to allow the Abwehr to suspect anything is wrong; they're both still sending their messages to Hamburg. I've also been re-checking Sarah's notes again. I'll pass everything across to you shortly. As I said, we may well have missed something.'

'And is there any news of Louis Durand in France?'

Hall shook his head. 'Unfortunately not, we're still trying of course, and we've asked the SOE to help us track him down with their contacts.'

'As far as I can see everything that could go wrong, has gone wrong.'

Spencer shot him a glacial look. 'From an outsider's perspective, then yes, I guess it does look that way. The risks were high, extremely high in agreeing Leader and Hamilton were to be sent to France, but we had to play the game, to play along with Hamburg's orders to infiltrate the Interallie. Otherwise, we'd have risked not only their covers being blown back in London, but the whole Double Cross system itself. And from our point of view, the mere fact Nikolaus Ritter would be in Paris at the same time was nothing less than manna from heaven. In all fairness to them, it wasn't exactly risk-free for either Hamilton or Leader. I do understand what they were going through. It's never easy having the risk of discovery constantly hanging over your head like the sword of Damocles. At any moment, your luck might run out.'

'Before you joined Colonel Robertson's team did you serve abroad with the SOE?'

'I speak fluent German, Chief Inspector I leave it to your imagination where the SOE decided I should spend my time. Looking back now, in some ways I viewed the secondment to St. James's as a bit of a breather.'

'So were you sent to Germany?'

'Berlin.'

Garvan stared at Hall in disbelief. 'Berlin?' he repeated.

'What better way to find out what's happening than in the eagle's lair.'

'What did you do there?'

'It's complicated,' he answered, with a slight wave of his hand. 'Certain handlers in Hamburg and Berlin believed I was - how shall I say, one of their own, even Nikolaus Ritter thought highly of me.' He turned and smirked. 'Believe it or not, I'm quite good at what I do.'

'So you're a double agent?' Garvan asked incredulously.

Spencer let out a laugh like rapid gunfire. 'Well that's one way of putting it I suppose, I was a mole, a plant at the heart of the Abwehr. If you'd been in Berlin,' the words trailed off, 'but that's another matter.'

'Why not use your Abwehr connections to discover the identity of Sarah's killer?'

He shook his head. 'It's no longer possible, but even if things had been different, and I'd started digging around or showing too much interest trying to discover the identity of a supposed colleague of Nicolette, I'd have blown my cover sky high.'

Garvan was taken aback, didn't quite know how to respond, he was still trying to take on board Hall's bombshell. One of the first things that had struck him about Spencer was his overt stillness, an almost quiet explosive aura of a tough and hardened man. Those qualities, coupled with a rare kind of courage had placed him at the epicentre of the Third Reich, where he'd walked a tightrope of bluff and counter-bluff, where capture, torture and certain death were ever present, where every day might well be your last. He admired Spencer's courage, his nerve, and his bravery; it was the type of courage that few possessed.

'You have to understand,' Hall said, breaking the silence between them. 'Through our double agents, we give Ritter the impression that Britain's Home Defences are strong and well-fortified.' He leaned back on the bench and folded his arms. 'It's patently untrue of course, at the moment our Home Defences are scarily vulnerable, but you have to understand that misinformation is a potent weapon in itself, and at times, such as now, it's our only viable weapon.'

'Are things really that bad?' Garvan quizzed him.

'If Hitler invaded tomorrow, we'd not have a cat in hell's chance; that's the reality. We need to play for time, need the Double Cross to develop until we're able to move against the Third Reich. One loose cannon could destroy everything we've worked for; that's why Sarah agreed to lay her life on the line.'

Spencer fell silent, recalling the first time he'd met Sarah in the team's cramped St. James's office. She'd quite taken his breath away with her dazzling beauty. Despite her initial aloofness and coolness toward him, six months down the line they were deeply in love, they'd even discussed marriage. He felt a gnawing, gut wrenching guilt for not being there when she'd needed him most. On that last day, the last time they met at Monkton Drive, she'd been so vibrant, so alive, they'd made love. The time had passed so quickly; he'd had to leave, return to St. James's. He'd desperately wanted to stay, God he never wanted to leave her, but there was a flap on at the office, and Sarah understood why she always understood.

Spencer closed his eyes. And now, he thought, he'd never hold her in his arms again, or see that warm twinkling glint in her eyes as she laughed. He might well love again but never so deeply. If only there were some way of turning back time, if only he hadn't headed back to the office, if only there hadn't been a flap on, Sarah, his Sarah, would still be alive and at the centre of his world.

Garvan sensed that beneath the toughened exterior Hall was desperately struggling with his emotions. He decided to hold back. It was a gut feeling and allowed Hall to break the silence between them. He needed to understand their relationship, where it fitted into the murder inquiry, and whether Spencer's internal investigation had been affected by his obvious grief for Sarah.

'When I was a kid,' Spencer said at length, 'every Saturday morning I'd go to the cinema and watch all those beautiful Hollywood movie stars up on the screen. I'd sit there fantasising that one day I'd marry one of them. It was just a kid's fantasy of course. And then I met Sarah. She was quite just as fascinatingly beautiful as any of my childhood idols. With her,' he said, wistfully, 'the dream became a reality.'

Discovering her body at Monkton Drive, the single bullet wound to Sarah's forehead certainly hadn't destroyed her beauty; even in death it was quite magnetic, her distinctive light blue eyes frozen in the last moments of life. Having knelt beside her in Monkton Drive, Garvan understood Spencer's turmoil, his grief, and although he hadn't known her in life, he'd found himself inexplicably drawn to the pointless end of this young woman's life.

Spencer drew heavily on his cigarette, almost desperately. 'She was often weighed down by her workload, but she was always kind, always charming and yet somehow remote. The entire office at St. James's was in her thrall. Sarah, my Sarah, possessed a razor-sharp intellect, and managed to wrong foot us most of the time, even Tar.'

Garvan couldn't help noticing the strain on Hall's face. He looked drawn there were dark shadows beneath his eyes. 'You obviously adored her,' he said tentatively, but with genuine envy.

Spencer continued to gaze unseeingly across the river; his thoughts locked somewhere in the past. 'I'll love her until my very last breath.' He glanced at Garvan, meeting his eyes with a steady, uncompromising gaze. He smiled briefly. 'We might have burnt each other out – but what a way to go!' he chuckled.

Garvan laughed with him. 'I could probably think of worse ways to go.'

'Do you fancy a cuppa?'

'I wouldn't mind one.'

'There's a cheap and cheerful café in John Adam Street, but they make a decent cuppa.' As they crossed the road, Hall asked. 'Did you draw a pistol out of the Yard's armoury?'

'Yes,' Garvan found himself answering hesitantly, 'and also for Mac and Charteris.'

Spencer nodded. 'You needed to.'

'I've re-assigned the three PCs to another squad.'

'Good - good,' Spencer said, and added casually, 'I thought you ought to know that someone took a pot shot at me last night. They obviously missed,' he grinned.

'Did you get a good look at them?'

He shook his head.

'Where were you?'

'I had a meeting with two of our agents in Brook Street near Park Lane. We had the meeting and afterwards went our separate ways. I went to pick up my car when suddenly all hell broke loose.'

By the time Spence stepped back out into Brook Street after his meeting, the clouds had cleared, and the moonlight pierced the oppressive darkness of the Blackout, leaving a trail of elongated shadows on the glistening wet pavements from an earlier downpour. Illuminated by the stark white moonlight, Hall recalled fumbling for the car keys inside his suit pocket and hearing the unmistakable thud of a muzzled pistol ringing out from across the street, followed by the sharp ping of a bullet hitting against the bodywork of the car.

Instinctively, he'd ducked down behind the vehicle and drew his revolver. He waited, crouched behind the car, listening for the sound of footsteps. Hearing nothing, he edged his way toward the rear of the vehicle. Another shot suddenly pranged the bodywork, this time only narrowly missing the petrol tank. Whoever was firing the weapon, knew what they were doing, it was sheer luck the bullet bounced off the bodywork rather than penetrate the tank.

Looking desperately around for cover, Spencer scrambled down the basement steps of a nearby house, eyes still straining for the slightest sign of movement convinced he could just make out a figure crouching in a shop doorway, he decided to take aim, but hesitated, fearing he might end up shooting an innocent bystander. From the relative safety of the basement, he saw a young couple walking along the street hand in hand, and blissfully unaware of what had just happened. Spencer shoved the pistol back inside his suit jacket; he needed to make certain they were not involved, and the girl wasn't one of his agents. Emerging from the basement, he crossed the road and walked straight past them. Fortunately, as it turned out, they were entirely innocent, and the would-be assassin disappeared back into the darkness.

By the time Hall had finished recounting his close shave they had reached John Adam Street. Office workers on their lunch break crowded the cafe. They ordered tea and found a table wedged in an alcove. It was just far enough away from the other tables for them to carry on their conversation without being overheard.

Spencer toyed with a teaspoon, the hint of a smile hovering about his mouth. 'It was almost murder number two for you last night.'

'Christ almighty, please don't say that I've enough on my plate already. But what if that couple had turned out to be your would-be assassins?'

'It was a calculated risk, but I'd have taken at least one of them out with me. I just needed to discount them'.

'Was it meant as a warning?'

'No, whoever it was messed up, as simple as that. It was sloppy, but at least, we have a result,' he added, with a self-satisfied smile.

'Do we?' Garvan queried. 'I'm not sure I'd call being shot at much of a result.'

'But it is, Chief Inspector, don't you see, we now know for certain we're on the right track.'

'And we didn't before?'

'We did of course, but last night just confirmed everything. You coming on board would appear to have unsettled the killer even more. We're still pulling out all the stops to track Louis Durand down, and if there's a way of lifting him out of France, we'll do it. In the meantime, we don't have any option other than to rely on your investigation.'

'At the moment, I don't have very much to offer you.'

'To be honest with you, we weren't expecting that much, its early days.' Spencer glanced down at his watch. 'God is that the time already? 'I'm sorry, I don't mean to be rude, but I need to get back to the office, I'm afraid I'm running late.' He drained his cup, stood up and shook Garvan's hand. 'Take care, Chief Inspector, and watch your back.'

Chapter 11

They'd already had a long day at the office, reading through the notes Sarah had written in the preceding weeks leading up to her death. It was getting late, and they'd arranged to meet Joyce Leader at the Sesame Club in Mayfair. It was their first opportunity to catch up with her since their initial meeting near Waterloo Station. Garvan didn't know the Sesame well at all, it had always been a rather discreet place, its clientele tended to be select, and membership was at the strict discretion of the owner.

His only previous visit was way back in the late 1930s' when he turned up at the club to arrest a wealthy antique dealer for theft from a local gallery. At the time, it had caused quite a stir and managed to gain a few column inches in the newspapers.

Inside, the club was in full swing. Joyce had pre-booked a table for the three of them. They checked in at reception and were escorted by a young waitress to their table. Weaving their way through the crowd they became aware of a striking young woman singing on the stage, and to their amazement, the woman belting out a ballad was none other than Joyce Leader.

She was wearing an expensive black dress and matching suede high heels shoes with a double choker of pearls draped around her neck. Her voice was good, easily good enough to be professional. Neither of them could quite bring themselves to believe the ice maiden was actually up on stage belting out a love ballad with a strong, sexy, silky voice. Her performance transfixed them. The distant hauteur and untouchable aura had temporarily vanished as she held the entire audience in the palm of her hand.

'Bloody hell,' Mac said sitting down at the table, 'who'd have thought it.'

'She's good.'

'Better than most professionals I've heard.'

She'd managed to bring the entire dance floor to a complete standstill. Everyone gathered around the stage. At the end of her song they stood as one, cheering and clapping. They whistled and called for another song, but Joyce merely shook her head, flashed a broad smile and hurried down from the stage accepting the admiration of those around her with an unassuming charm. Still flushed with the excitement of performing, she threaded her way through the crowd to join them.

Extending her hand in greeting, she said. 'Hello Chief Inspector, hello Sergeant Mackenzie.' She sat herself down and reached for a half-finished glass of martini.

'Do you sing professionally?' Garvan felt compelled to ask her.

'Good Lord no,' she grinned. 'Some time ago my friends over there,' she added, gesturing toward a group of men and women standing at the bar, 'persuaded me to have a go. It was a few months back now; we were having a party when I mentioned the lead singer sounded pretty awful.'

Joyce drained the martini. 'At least, I thought she was pretty awful. To be honest, with you I'd had a few drinks and jokingly said I could do better, the trouble was they threw down the gauntlet and literally pushed me up on stage. I felt like a frightened rabbit staring into the headlights; it could have gone disastrously wrong, but fortunately, I somehow managed to pull it off. It's not something I do on a regular basis, only when I'm in the mood.'

'I'd have thought the owners' would want you up on stage every evening,' Garvan said.

'That's very kind of you. Let's just say that after my drunken debut I still somehow managed to impress the club's owner, and he kindly indulges me when I'm here, he allows me to sing whenever I like.'

'I'm surprised Major Hall didn't mention your talent for singing.'

She threw back her head and laughed. 'I don't think Spence is that interested in my singing abilities. Colonel Robertson has been here once or twice. He was apparently impressed.' She gave a dismissive shrug, 'But who knows, he could have been lying, there's no way of telling.'

Joyce seemed outwardly at least, unaware of just how good she was. It was little wonder the club's owner had given her carte blanche to take to the stage whenever she wanted. Joyce produced her cigarette holder and lighter from her handbag and tapped a cocktail cigarette into the holder. She suddenly shot Garvan a quizzical look. 'Why are you staring at me like that?'

'I think I'm probably still in shock after seeing you up on stage, that's all.'

'So just what were you expecting of me, Chief Inspector, some uptight cold hearted bitch? First impressions can be wrong you know.'

'Well, since you mentioned it.'

Joyce giggled. 'I'd have thought you of all people would know you can't always judge a book by its cover.'

A waitress came over to their table with a round of drinks.

'Thanks, honey,' Joyce said to her before adding, 'Don't worry gentlemen, the drinks are on my tab.'

'That's very kind of you,' Mac said.

'Not at all, I wouldn't want you to getting into trouble, the drinks here are exorbitant.'

Seated casually in her chair, a fresh glass of martini lightly held in her hand, Garvan thought she looked tired, but tiredness or not she was an attractive woman, and even in those rare moments when she raise the glacial shutters, there remained the perception of someone who was both calculating and driven. Spencer had called her exacting; Joyce preferred to call herself a perfectionist. Garvan guessed that patience probably wasn't her greatest virtue, and didn't doubt she was a handful to control.

Joyce met their gaze with an assured candour. 'I was half expecting a summons to Scotland Yard. All things considered, you're keeping this pretty low key.'

'We're still at a preliminary stage,' he lied.

'Don't bother playing games with me Chief Inspector, there's no point,' she said, blowing out a cloud of smoke. 'You and I both know I'm under suspicion of murdering Sarah Davis. Otherwise, we wouldn't be having this conversation, and you're here for one reason and one reason only.' Her attention strayed as a male singer took to the stage.

'Let's cut through the crap then, shall we.' Garvan suggested.

Joyce swivelled round in her chair to face him, and as her eyes locked onto his, a sudden thought crossed her mind. She hadn't noticed before, but the Chief Inspector was quite good looking in a rugged, unconventional sort of way. She'd flirted with him at the pub, but then, she flirted with everyone. Under different circumstances maybe they might have got together, he looked like he could be a bit of a challenge, and she loved a challenge! Garvan was talking, oh God she hadn't heard a single word, he'd said.

'Sorry, what did you say?'

'Sarah's murder, it must have come as a shock to you.'

'Yes of course it did. I knew the spotlight would fall on the agents under her control. Let's face it who else would have wanted her dead?' Leader cupped her hands around the long-stemmed martini glass. 'Even so I can't understand why anyone would have risked killing her.'

Although Leader's expression was difficult to gauge, Garvan knew she was holding back, knew far more than she was willing to let on. 'You must have discussed it amongst yourselves?'

'You mean with Maggie Hamilton?'

He nodded.

'Of course, we discussed it; from a selfish point of view, we wondered how it would affect us.'

'How did you think it might affect you?'

'Whether we'd still be allowed the same amount of freedom, or whether they'd batten down the hatches and keep us under lock and key. There was simply no way of knowing how St. James's would react. But whatever we may, or may not have discussed falls way short of knowing what happened to Sarah.

'Do you believe the killing was a one off?' Mac asked her.

Joyce looked at him, a crease furrowing her brow. 'What do you mean?'

'Do you think other desk officers might be at risk?'

'Lord I don't know, that surely depends on the killer's motive doesn't it? I assumed Sarah came across some piece of intelligence which put her life in danger, and maybe her killer got wind of it.' Leader gave a shrug, 'or perhaps it was simply a grudge, there's simply no way of knowing. Let's face it there could be any number of reasons.'

'So you don't think it was a random killing then?' Mac queried.

'I don't believe in coincidences, at least not in our game. As I said when we met before she was highly trained. I can't imagine she'd have been caught out by a random nutter off the street.'

'And it was after the failed attempts on her life that Miss Davis was placed under Spencer Hall's protection?' Garvan mused.

Joyce flicked ash from her cigarette into an ashtray and shot him a penetrating look. 'You know that already, Chief Inspector.'

'But I'm asking you.'

'Yes, she was under his protection, well, protection of sorts - Sarah wasn't a bloody fool, she must have realised just how vulnerable she was. In my mind, there's absolutely no doubt she was kept as a sitting target to draw out the killer.' She breathed deeply. 'And by God didn't it work, with disastrous results for poor Sarah.'

'Do you think Major Hall should have kept her out of harm's way?' Mac inquired.

She narrowed her eyes. 'I'm really not sure where you're going with this.'

'Aren't you?'

'I thought we went over all this at the pub.' She paused, before adding diplomatically: 'Hindsight, Sergeant is a luxury we can ill-afford. I think you have to remember it wasn't Spence's decision alone. Colonel Robertson and the rest of the committee must have been involved in the decision making. I'm quite sure they all acted for the best; it could have worked out differently, but unfortunately, Sarah ended up paying with her life. My understanding is that Spence had to work late that night, there was some big flap on or other, and he couldn't provide extra cover for her. It can't have been the first time; there's always a flap on at St. James's. Who knows how Spence is feeling, but it really can't be an easy time for him.'

'No, I don't suppose it is,' Garvan said.

'We all make mistakes, Chief Inspector, God alone knows look at me. I've made an utter mess of my life, trapped in an endless spiral of deceit with no hope of escape until the war's over.'

'But aren't you sitting pretty whatever the outcome of the war?'

'How so?' she snapped at him.

'As a member of the Double Cross, if we defeat Germany you'll be released from your duties and allowed free to go as you, please. On the other hand as an Abwehr agent, if Nazi storm troopers goose step their way down Whitehall you'll still be on the winning side.'

'I wouldn't survive a Nazi occupation,' she said, with conviction, her expression set in stone.

'Why wouldn't you?'

'I think before any storm troopers got the chance to march their way down Whitehall, I'd either have been liquidated by MI5 or exposed to the Nazi's as a double agent. British Intelligence would go down fighting and make damned sure they brought us down as well.'

'Did you get to know Miss Davis well?'

'In some ways,' was her non-committal response.

'I've been informed that your desk officers immerse themselves in their agent's lives, is that correct?'

She set her grey-blue eyes on Garvan in a direct, unblinking gaze. 'War creates intense relationships. In another world, another time, maybe Sarah and I could have been friends, she was good company. I'd also heard a whisper she and Spence were an item. He certainly seems to have become even harder since her death, even more, unforgiving than before. He's tough, uncompromising and there's no room for manoeuvre when you're working for him.' She crossed her legs and calmly waited for the next question.

'I understand you've enjoyed quite a few close relationships since you've been operating in London,' Garvan said, it wasn't a question, but a statement of fact.

'I suppose,' Joyce said, meeting his gaze with the merest of smiles, 'you could say the war makes for strange bedfellows. Most of the relationships have been business, nothing more, nothing less,' came the calm, unruffled reply. 'I bed them, you see, Ritter my German controller expects it.'

'What's he hoping to gain?'

'Herr Ritter believes that my well-placed contacts provide me not only with aimless tittle tattle but information that is vital to the Reich's war effort. He's unaware of course my radio transmissions are the creation of Robertson's team. There's always just enough tantalising tidbits to keep the Abwehr hooked. Up until now I've been granted a certain amount of freedom. Let's just say I still manage to enjoy myself,' she said with a wink.

'Did Sarah help write your transmissions to Germany?'

Joyce nodded. 'Sarah was brilliant at drafting; she'd put in the odd personal line. Some were quite funny, you know it made it all the more convincing, we often had a good laugh about it, and I'd add a few personal lines just to make it sound even more convincing. The rest of the stuff, the misinformation part, is based on various policy directives, I assume from Whitehall. By and large, it doesn't mean that much to me, but for some reason, Herr Ritter thinks its good quality stuff. My standing with him is apparently quite high,' she added, and suddenly laughed. 'That doesn't mean to say that I don't get some real juicy nuggets myself. Usually, it's from some drunken, chatty General or the odd War Office civil servant. When I do get snippets like that I pass the information over to Spence or the Colonel, they take it on board and then -,' her words trailed off.

'And then what happens?'

'I guess they get rid of people who can't keep their mouths shut. The trouble is Spence thinks I have the morals of a tomcat.' Joyce giggled at her own expense. 'I guess he has a point, but ninety percent of the time I'm only following orders. As for the rest it gets a little complicated, the trouble is I could easily compromise someone who's entirely innocent. There have been one or two particular occasions when it's become a little bit out of control; the first time was with an MP, and the second with an industrialist. Spence and Tar warned me off and then I guess the good Major scared the hell out of them. They certainly weren't business, just enjoyable fucks,' she emphasised, waiting to see if there was a reaction from them, but none was forthcoming. 'Since the war started we live out our lives with intensity. I guess it's all to do with never knowing if every day might be your last.'

Garvan found himself increasingly drawn to her. She was intriguing, dangerous. He hoped to God she hadn't noticed that he found her strangely attractive, to her that really would have been the icing on the cake. Steering the conversation back to Sarah's murder, he asked: 'I think you said the other day that you didn't know about the safe house in Monkton Drive?'

'I'm only the hired help, why on earth would they tell me about the place?'

'That's not what I asked.'

Joyce stubbed out her cigarette and returned the holder to her handbag. 'No, I didn't have a clue where she was living. You may also find this hard to believe, Chief Inspector, but I was worried about the attempts on Sarah's life. One way or another it was making our lives difficult, the security was getting tighter, to the point where it was becoming stifling. Even here,' she said, gesturing toward the dance floor, 'I'm under surveillance.'

'If security is that tight, how do you think Sarah's killer escaped the net?' Mac queried.

'Nothing is ever fool proof, is it, no system's a hundred per cent, agents can and do give their minders the slip.'

Garvan caught the attention of a waitress and ordered another round of drinks. As the girl headed off back toward the bar, he asked 'Did you hear that an attempt was made on Major Hall's life last night?'

He waited for a reaction. For the first time Leader appeared to be wrong-footed, she seemed ruffled. He was undecided whether she was a consummate actress, or genuinely taken aback.

'What happened?' she asked, her face outwardly etched with concern.

'Major Hall was shot at when he was returning to his car,' Garvan explained. 'By all accounts, he was lucky to have escaped with his life. If he hadn't managed to dive behind his car, I'd have been investigating murder number two.'

The waitress returned and handed out the drinks. Leader toyed with her martini glass; wariness had crept into her usual unreadable expression.

'As you've guessed we can only assume,' he continued, 'that one of your colleagues has turned rogue, and has become a triple agent. The Double Cross has already lost one desk officer, and Major Hall only narrowly escaped with his life. The whole fabric of the system appears to be in danger of collapse.'

'Did Spence see who fired at him?' Joyce asked.

'No, it was too dark.'

For a while, she looked pensive, almost distracted before the shutters came down leaving her expression impenetrable. He was undecided whether her distraction stemmed from concern for Spencer's safety, or fear that he might have managed to recognise his would-be assassin.

'Taking pot shots at Spence smacks of sheer bloody desperation to me,' she said, as if by rote. 'They've upped the stakes. Trust me crossing Spence is like writing your own death warrant.' She leaned forward on the table; hands clasped. 'Don't you see this investigation was already personal to him because of Sarah, but now this?' She shook her head. 'It beggars belief they'd go this far.' She paused, her gaze locked on Garvan. 'He has this ruthless streak; it's totally ingrained. The charm, the sophistication permeates to the surface, but it's a thin veneer. God help us all,' she added with feeling.

Garvan began to sense he'd managed to plant just enough doubt in Leader's mind to keep her on edge. He'd rattled the ice maiden just sufficient to start winding up the pressure. Finishing his drink, Garvan made his excuses to leave; it had been a long day. As they politely shook hands, he couldn't help wondering whether this self-assured woman was Sarah Davis's killer, the Twenty Committee's rogue triple agent.

As they stepped outside the Sesame Club, Mac turned and said: 'I don't know about you, Guv'nor, but I wouldn't trust either of the buggers.'

Garvan pulled up his collar against the chill night air. 'My bet is on Joyce Leader.'

They walked the short distance to their squad car; the blackout was all pervasive. In the pitch darkness, Mac bumped into a rubbish bin sending it crashing to the pavement. They were approached twenty yards further on by a girl standing in a doorway; she flashed a pencil torch into their faces. She was a prostitute waiting for passing trade. Before she managed to speak, Mac raised his hand and said. 'We're not punters darling we're coppers', better luck next time.'

She turned off the pencil light and hurriedly slunk back into the doorway.

'Have we fixed up a meeting with the Hamilton girl?' Mac asked.

'Tomorrow morning. I've just got to confirm where with Spencer Hall.'

'I've only one problem,' Mac said, pulling the car keys out of his pocket. 'You're playing with fire.'

'What do you mean?'

'It's fucking obvious you fancy her.'

'Who are you talking about?'

'Joyce Leader.'

'Good God,' Garvan lied, 'She's not only a murder suspect but a German spy to boot. Give me some credit, Mac!'

Mackenzie unlocked the car door. 'She can't have failed to notice the way you were gawping at her. The woman's dangerous, Guv.'

'Just get in and drive,' Luke said, 'it's freezing out here.'

Chapter 12

The day after their meeting with Joyce Leader at the Sesame Club, Mac and Garvan found themselves climbing the rickety staircase of an old dank-smelling office building near Victoria Station. The lighting inside was poor even in broad daylight, and at night, it must have been little short of a death trap.

As Mac followed Garvan up the stairs, he called out. 'Are you sure this is the right place, Guv'nor?'

'Spencer gave me the address first thing this morning.'

'Christ almighty,' Mac grumbled, 'you'd think MI5 could have found somewhere bit better than this bleeding dump!'

'Don't knock it, Mac, it's a brilliant cover.'

On the first floor landing, they heard the noisy rattle of a typewriter. There was little natural light in the corridor, save for a small dirty window overlooking an inner courtyard. They followed the direction of the rapid tap-tap of the typewriter, toward a shaft of light coming through a half-open door along the dingy corridor, and into a dilapidated office lined with green metal filing cabinets. Paint peeled off the walls and ceiling hanging like Christmas paper chains. The brown badly stained lino floor had a large jagged rip just inside the doorway.

The room led directly through to another office, where they came across the source of the rapid tap-tap of the typewriter, an elderly, grey-haired woman. She didn't acknowledge their entry. A fag was clenched tightly between her lips, and ash fell sporadically from the cigarette onto both her cardigan and desk. Occasionally she'd glance down at the neatly handwritten document from which she was typing. Garvan cleared his throat to attract her attention; she didn't respond, perhaps the old girl was hard of hearing he decided, he changed tact and slammed the door shut. She suddenly looked up, stopped typing, removed her glasses, and swivelled around in her chair to face the door. She folded her arms and calmly appraised the two strangers with complete indifference. There was a noticeable flicker of irritation on her face.

'We have an appointment.' Mac announced.

'Ave yer,' she replied in a broad cockney accent, arms still folded, and the fag remaining gripped tightly between her lips. 'Who sent yer?'

'We're from Scotland Yard; Major Hall asked us to meet him here.'

There was a moment's hesitation then she reached for a large well-thumbed diary. 'Names?' the elderly Valkyrie barked at them.

'Detective Chief Inspector Garvan and Detective Sergeant Mackenzie,' Garvan answered.

She traced her finger along the page, sniffed slightly on seeing their names, and snapped the diary shut.

'Ave a seat,' she said, gesturing in a short, sharp stabbing motion toward two battered Windsor chairs set against the wall.

Both men exchanged glances and silently sat down. She promptly began typing again on her large black Imperial typewriter, muttering something or other about constant bloody interruptions with the fag wriggling between her lips. They sat in stony silence listening with growing irritation to the constant, rapid clatter of the typewriter. In the corner of the office, a young girl was seated at a desk. She looked up and smiled nervously, before continuing to unpick a file held together with metal tagged purple string. She was transferring the papers to a new file, and re-threading them again, carefully checking the documents against a detailed minute sheet. Occasionally she'd consult a small metal box on her desk stuffed with cross-referenced card indices.

'Looks like a boring job,' Mac said quietly and nodded in her direction.

They heard voices in the corridor, and then footsteps getting nearer, and then a click as Spencer peered round the door, took in the scene and instantly began to laugh.

'I see you've met Lil, I hope she's been keeping you entertained,' he smirked, 'have you, Lil?'

Lil stopped typing; there was nothing wrong with her hearing now. 'Not bloody likely, I'm too fucking busy,' she grunted puffing on her fag.

Her nickname at the Twenty Committee was fag ash Lil; her trademark cigarette never seemed to leave her lips, and, in fact, Spencer was convinced it'd have to be surgically removed. She was loved and feared in equal measure and didn't suffer fools gladly, whether a junior clerk or some high-handed visiting General. If they crossed her, Lil would erupt, effing and blinding at them until they beat a hasty retreat. At the end of the day "fag ash" was a bloody good typist, as tough as old boots, trustworthy, and the fact she'd put the fear of God into numerous senior officers for not following procedure only served to endear her all the more to Spencer and Robertson.

Garvan watched on in amusement as she rushed across the office and retrieved Hall's overcoat from an old wooden coat stand. The old battle axe obviously had her favourites.

'Major Hall,' she gushed, 'not going already are yer?' Spencer took his overcoat and with a flourish gently kissed the elderly lady's hand.

'You know how it is Lil. We've all been so busy since Sarah died. But they're not working you too hard, are they?' he queried buttoning up his coat.

'Don't pay any fucking overtime do they, its bleeding wartime?'

Spencer leant forward and gave her a hug. 'I really ought to try and get over here more often.'

'You've already got enough on yer plate, Major,' she said, cupping his face in her hands. 'Tell Colonel Robertson that he's got to give you some leave, he's working you far too hard.'

At face value fag ash Lil was just a typist, but sitting in the outer office, Garvan formed the opinion she probably had a greater in-depth relationship with the leading members' of the Committee than most of their high ranking colleagues across Whitehall. In the grand scheme of things Lil wasn't an especially important cog in the machine, but she was a sounding board, a sponge of information that both Spencer and Tar could totally rely upon. Lil smiled at Hall like some love struck schoolgirl rather than a woman who looked well past retirement age.

'I've just been to a Briefing,' Spencer explained to them, 'Maggie's free now.'

'Not quite St. James's is it,' Garvan said, staring up at the peeling paint and wallpaper.

'I hope it's only temporary,' Hall said, following his gaze. 'We were bombed out of our other office in Kingsway about four months ago; this is all we could find at short notice - but what a cover,' he added with a chuckle.

'You can say that again,' Mac said.

'Thankfully St. James's is still standing. By the way, how did your meeting with Joyce Leader go last night?'

'Interesting,' Mac replied, 'when we arrived at the Sesame Club she was up on stage singing.'

'Yes,' he smiled, 'quite a voice, but there again she's quite a girl.' He looked to Garvan. 'Give me a call in the morning.' Garvan nodded.

After Spencer left Lil ushered her visitors along the corridor to another equally dingy office. Inside, they found Maggie perched on a desk, feet resting on a chair reading a thick A4 folder. On the desk beside her was a small perfume bottle. Garvan recalled how on leaving the pub at Waterloo she'd trailed the distinctive scent in her wake.

'Visitors,' Lil announced gruffly at her.

'Yes,' Maggie murmured, reluctantly setting the paperwork down on the desk. 'Do be seated,' she said, gesturing toward a couple of faded red leather armchairs in front of the desk.

Lil closed the door. They shook hands with Hamilton and sat down. Maggie seemed anxious, in fact, just as she had on their first meeting, she was distracted. Sensing she was under scrutiny, Maggie felt obliged to explain that Spencer had set a tight deadline for a radio transmission to her Abwehr controller in Hamburg and that he was placing her under a great deal of pressure.

'I've got to sift through this lot,' she said patting the folder, 'I need to get tonight's wireless message spot on.' She smiled at them thoughtfully and asked. 'I'm sorry how can I help you?

'We just need to ask you a few questions,' Garvan said.

'I guess the sooner you manage to track down Sarah's murderer the sooner things will start to settle down again. At the moment, none of us quite know where we stand.'

'When we first met you, you implied that you believe Sarah knew her killer.'

'Lord yes,' Maggie answered, 'she was far too professional to be caught out by some chancer or amateur. I'm convinced she knew her killer.'

'The same person who tried to kill her before you mean?' Garvan asked.

'Of course, there's no doubt in my mind it was the same person.'

'Why would anyone have wanted her dead?'

Maggie shrugged. 'That's anyone's guess Chief Inspector. I imagine only Major Hall or Colonel Robertson can answer that question with any real degree of certainty. They know every one of their agents and desk officers inside out. Every move Sarah had made since working for them was well-documented. They must have some idea who pulled the trigger.'

'If they did,' Garvan mused, 'why would they have bothered calling in Scotland Yard?'

She pulled a face. 'They're always selective with the truth; it's part and parcel of who they are. I can't second guess what they're playing at, or how much they know.'

'I genuinely believe they haven't any idea who might have killed her,' he lied.

Maggie hesitated as if trying to find the right phrase. She hadn't expected such apparent naivety from a senior Scotland Yard Detective.

'Believe me,' she said, thoughtfully, 'they'll be running rings around you if you're not careful.'

'Thank you for the warning, Miss Hamilton,' he said, evenly giving nothing away.

'For God's sake Chief Inspector,' she groaned in exasperation, 'you don't understand, do you? Spencer knows more about me than I do myself. It's un-nerving never quite knowing whether I've quite passed muster, he's not exactly an open book.' She took a sharp intake of breath before adding, 'when he took control of Sarah's agents, he came down like a ton of bricks on us, not that there was ever much room for manoeuvre, it's just that now …,' the words slowly died on her lips. Maggie began fiddling distractedly with her necklace, twisting and untwisting the gold chain between her fingers. 'I might have misjudged the situation, but if they don't already know the killer's identity, then I reckon it's only a matter of time before they catch up with them.'

'That's not what they've told me.'

'They'll use Scotland Yard as they use everyone else, Chief Inspector. Misinformation is their speciality, why bother making an exception in your case, unless of course it's to their advantage in some way?'

'Tell me,' Garvan said, flipping open his notebook. 'Did you hear about the attempt on Major Hall's life the other evening?'

Maggie's expression faltered, she folded her arms. 'No, no I hadn't. What happened?' She listened intently as Garvan retold Hall's account of the shooting. By the time he had finished talking she had appeared visibly shaken, the colour had drained from her face.

'They must have a death wish,' she said, barely above a whisper, 'why else would they risk it, he's the last person you'd want to cross.'

Her response almost entirely echoed Joyce Leader's. Hamilton seemed plausible enough, but then so had her colleague. The trouble was that they'd both probably forgotten where the truth ended and the lies began. It had become a way of life for them, caught firmly in the vice-like grip of both the Abwehr and the British Intelligence.'

'When was the last time you saw Miss Davis?' Garvan asked her.

Maggie stretched across the desk and retrieved a diary from her handbag. 'I'll check,' she answered rifling through the pages. 'Ah here we are, it was back on the 14th, there was a meeting,' she tapped the page with her index finger, 'it was here actually, in this building. I remember now, it was just a bog standard briefing, nothing out of the ordinary'. Maggie snapped the diary shut. 'But I do recall there was a bit of a clash after the meeting.'

'What do you mean by a bit of a clash?' Garvan repeated questioningly.

Maggie slid off the desk and moved over to the window; she seemed suddenly anxious. 'It was about three weeks after Joyce, and I returned from France, we'd gone through umpteen debriefs, to be honest, we'd lost count of how many. With the Interallie on its knees, everything was up in the air.' She turned to face them. 'I'm probably talking out of turn it may be nothing at all.'

'There's no harm in telling us what's on your mind, we'll decide if it's important or not,' Mac said, soothingly.

She puffed out her cheeks, took up pacing the room with her arms folded. 'After the meeting, there was a bit of an argument between Joyce and Sarah Davis.'

'Do you know what about?' Mac pressed her.

'Lord I don't know Sergeant I heard raised voices and just the odd snippet. I couldn't honestly tell you what it was about. You could try asking Spencer; he might be able to tell you, from my experience not much slips him by. He seems to have his finger in every pie. He was certainly there when it kicked off between them.'

It hadn't gone unnoticed that whenever she mentioned Hall's name, there was a barbed edge to her voice.

'Tell me something.' Garvan said to her.

She raised her brows questioningly.

'Has Major Hall ever done or said anything to upset you?'

She burst into laughter.

'What's so funny?'

'Make no mistake at one time or another he's crossed swords with every single one of us. You could say it's something of an occupational hazard.' She looked at him quizzically, 'But why do you ask?'

'It's just that every time you mention his name I can't help noticing there's a certain edge to your voice, a particular hostility, am I right?'

'Am I that transparent?' she smiled in mock surprise.

'I guess you are.'

'Forgive me,' Maggie replied, 'it's just that he gave me a bit of a roasting earlier. I made a couple of errors during my last transmission to Hamburg, nothing too serious, but the mistakes were picked up by St. James's. Let's just say he wasn't in the best of moods. I'm just having a bad day; that's all.'

Maggie dutifully answered the rest of their questions as if by rote. As she spoke, her thoughts flashed back to her arrest and being caught red-handed with a radio transmitter concealed in her flat. At the time of the raid, she'd been living in a flat in Chelsea owned by her father, James. In spite of his well-publicised right wing views, she'd been advised by Nikolaus Ritter not to divulge any information about her activities to him or to anyone else for that matter. Maggie had blindly obeyed his instructions without question. She'd firmly believed Britain would be far better off under a Government who shared the values and the aspirations of the Third Reich; it hadn't been a difficult decision to join the Abwehr. In fact, she felt it was almost a duty.

As the Special Branch officer had drawn at the main gates of Latchmere House, she'd peered through the passenger window. Her heart was pounding it looked just like a fortress surrounded by vast interlocking piles of barbed wire. Her overriding memories of Latchmere were of a strange, eerie quietness and an overwhelming sense of isolation. The guards wore tennis shoes to muffle the sound of their steps along the corridors, there were no cigarettes, and sleep deprivation was the order of the day; by that point, she was frightened of her own shadow.

The initial interrogation had been carried out by Lt. Col. Robin Stephens or old 'Tin Eye' as he was known. He appeared for her interview wearing Gurkha uniform. When he spoke, his words had come out like a machine gun. She shuddered, recalling how the thick monocle over his right eye had glinted menacingly in the shafts of light shining through the barred windows. Stephens was, she discovered, half German himself and fluent in several languages. She'd sat before him, intimidated, scared for her life, and uncertain what was going to happen next. Within twenty-four hours Maggie knew exactly where she stood. If she refused to cooperate the only outcome would be a firing squad. Stephens and his team never laid a hand on her; they were too astute and skilfully manipulating for that. Tin Eye always told his staff. "We are here to crush a spy psychologically, crush their mind into small pieces, examine those pieces and then if they reveal qualities useful to the war effort - like becoming double agents - they must be mentally rebuilt. Those who do not have the qualities we require will end up on the gallows or before a firing squad in the Tower of London."

When Tin Eye arrived to announce his decision about her future, he appeared in the doorway of the interrogation room flanked by two intimidating uniformed Army officers. Maggie had stood up. The room was bare under the glare of a single bare light bulb. It was time to know their decision and she was terrified, uncertain if she was about to face a firing squad at the Tower. Perhaps her execution would appear in the national newspapers, or on the newsreels; her name plastered all over the front pages.

At the beginning of the war, life had seemed so black and white, but since then the hours, the days all seemed to pass in a hazy blur, and both her political beliefs and ideology had been quashed. 'Tin Eye' and his team had grilled her for hours on end. They'd broken her. Self-preservation, survival, was now her only real concern. "I'm not threatening you," Stephens had said to her, "but you're here in a British Secret Service prison and at the present time, it's our job to see that we get your whole story from you. Do you see?" His words had hung menacingly in the air.

Maggie was suddenly aware of Garvan's voice again. 'Sorry, what did you say?' she said apologetically.

'Do you have any regrets, any second thoughts about joining the Abwehr? I know your father was a member of the Right Club, I guess his politics must have influenced you.'

'It's true I was idealistic,' Maggie confessed. 'You see I adored my father, I still do.' She hesitated, her eyes beginning to glisten with tears. 'As a child your only yardstick, your only moral compass comes from your parents, how else do you learn?' She looked at them almost pleadingly. 'My father tried so hard to avoid another war - another war with Germany. He'd survived the trenches whereas most of his friends had been slaughtered or hideously maimed on the battlefields of France and Belgium.' She brushed away the tears. 'Papa was gassed,' Maggie sobbed, 'he was sent back to England to convalesce since then he's never enjoyed the best of health. He simply didn't want to see another generation decimated as his own had been, buried in the name of politics. During the 30s when I was growing up, and there was talk of another war, another Armageddon, my father stood up against Churchill, he viewed him as nothing more than a warmonger.' She paused, casting her mind back to those pre-war years. 'You have to understand Chief Inspector, he meant well, tried his best, but didn't fully understand what the Third Reich stood for.'

'Are you sure he didn't?' Garvan asked, unable to avoid sounding sarcastic.

'What do you mean?' she snapped back at him.

'I understand all the reasons why your father would have wanted to avoid Britain plunging into another war, who wouldn't? But let's face it, he didn't merely oppose Churchill and his condemnation of the Nazis regime, he became a member of the Right Club. Even back in the 30s', the organisation was under surveillance and considered to be a threat to national security. That wasn't anything to do with Churchill, far from it, he wasn't even Prime Minister then, but the Government of the day still thought your father was a security risk!'

He waited for a reaction. Hamilton folded her arms again and looked through him defiantly, but wouldn't be drawn.

'Your father's views Miss Hamilton are anti-Semitic, so right wing, in fact, he's a Fascist in all but name.' There was still no response. Perhaps she didn't know how to respond. 'Colonel Stephens spared you,' he continued, 'given a lifeline to work for the Security Services, but where do your loyalties lay Miss Hamilton - Berlin, Hamburg or London?'

Maggie pursed her lips, and when she spoke it was slowly, considered. 'I hold my hand up, I made mistakes, Chief Inspector, you're right I was totally idealistic, I can't exactly deny it. I wanted to do my bit, but my ideals were at best skewed. You have to understand that it wasn't an easy decision to join the Abwehr,' she lied, 'I accept my politics were extreme, but even so,' Hamilton's words trailed off, as she reached for her handbag to retrieve a pack of cigarettes. 'To begin with it seemed so exciting, an almost addictive way to live your life, the transmissions to Hamburg, my instructions from Ritter.' She lit the cigarette. 'Believe it or not, it took a little time before I realised that I was way, way above my head, completely out of my league, and that I hadn't a clue what I was letting myself in for.'

'But was that after your arrest?' Garvan said.

'Yes, it was,' she answered candidly. 'As you know I was taken to Latchmere House - God I was such a bloody little fool,' she said, laughing at the memory. 'It was only then that I finally realised this wasn't some bloody game. I'd been playing with fire, and I simply hadn't a sodding clue.' Hamilton smiled lamely at them. 'You could say I grew up overnight, and began to question everything I'd ever believed in, or thought I believed in. I can't deny it was a tough time for me.'

'And if we lose, if Britain loses the fight against Germany, won't you still be sitting pretty whatever the outcome of the War?' He wondered if she would react the same way as Joyce Leader had to the same question.

'Will I?' she said, curiously.

'Isn't it obvious?'

She looked at him blankly.

'Surely if Germany wins the War, then as a member of the Abwehr you'll be given preferential treatment. On the other hand, if the Allies win, MI5 will no longer have any need for your services, and you'll be free to go.'

'Do you really think it'll be that cut and dry?' Maggie scoffed.

'Yes, I do Miss Hamilton.'

'If Germany wins then my life will be forfeit, there's no way on earth I'd get off Scot free. Spencer, or whoever, would make sure I was either exposed as a spy or put a bullet through me before German troops ever got a foothold on British soil. Whatever you may think Chief Inspector, I do not want Britain to lose this war.' She sucked in her lower lip and added thoughtfully: 'After my interrogation at Latchmere House, believe me meeting Sarah Davis was like a breath of fresh air. She gave me hope that if I toed the line, and obeyed her instructions, I'd live long enough to see out the war.' Hamilton stubbed out her barely smoked cigarette into an ashtray. 'After Sarah died, everything changed, as you know Spencer stepped into the breach, and took over control of her agents.'

'I guess he doesn't suffer fools gladly.'

She raised her eyes heavenward and said. 'When I went to Latchmere House, I don't mind telling you I was frightened out of my life, but even so, in comparison with old 'Tin Eye Stephens and his team, Spencer Hall is in a different league altogether. I'll be honest with you Chief Inspector; he puts the fear of God into me in a way that Stephens never could.'

Garvan decided to end the meeting. He stood up and shook her hand. 'Thank you for your time Miss Hamilton.'

She said: 'Do you know what I think the hardest thing will be once the war is over?'

'Tell me.' He smiled.

'If I'm lucky enough to survive, it's difficult imagining what it'll be like slipping back into the normal hum-drum of daily life.' She looked at each of them in turn. 'Can either of you imagine what it'll be like?

'I think I'll be bloody grateful it's all over.' Mac smirked at her.

She smiled almost wistfully. 'Perhaps I've lived on the edge for far too long, but I don't personally think it'll be easy adapting to peacetime.'

Garvan made to leave but turned back. 'One last question, Miss Hamilton, that perfume,' he said, gesturing to the bottle on the desk, 'it's very distinctive.'

Maggie visibly relaxed and picked up the squat rectangular bottle with a mushroom-shaped stopper. 'I couldn't resist; I brought half a dozen back from Paris. It's called Shalimar, do you like it?'

He nodded. 'Yes I do,' he said, ''I'll put it on my Christmas list.'

She smiled. 'Your wife might just have to wait until the war's over.'

'I guess she might,' he answered.

Maggie had put up a very convincing performance, but there again so had Joyce Leader. Whereas Joyce had mainly kept a tight lid on her feelings, there'd been moments during the interview with Maggie when she'd apparently struggled to keep a grip. It could have been a charade, of course; it was difficult to decide. What he had found interesting was that each of them had spoken highly of Sarah Davis. They'd obviously genuinely respected her. But the reality was that he still hadn't any clearer idea who pulled the trigger.

Chapter 13

The day after his meeting with Maggie Hamilton, Garvan headed off to meet Spencer Hall at his office in St. James's Street. He was duly signed in at reception and escorted to the outer office of the Double Cross team by a young typist. As she opened the door onto the cramp, smoke-filled room, Spencer was seated at his desk, phone in hand. He smiled and gestured to Garvan to take a seat.

'Just get it sorted,' Hall barked down the phone, 'and stop fucking me about!' He slammed the receiver into the cradle. 'Good to see you again Chief Inspector, so how did it go yesterday afternoon?'

Garvan opened his briefcase and produced a buff coloured folder. 'Read the report. Everything's in there, including my thoughts on Joyce Leader,' he said, placing it on the desk.

'So where are we, any further forward?'

Garvan closed the briefcase. 'I hope you're not expecting miracles.'

'Hardly,' Spencer said, opening the folder.

'To be perfectly honest, I wasn't expecting a great deal from either of them, were you?' Garvan queried.

Spencer looked up from the folder and shot Garvan a look of understanding. 'I'd be lying if I said that I was.'

'Let's start with Joyce Leader.'

'How did she strike you?'

'Calculating and totally in command. That is, right up to the point when I mentioned someone tried to kill you the other evening.'

'Rattled her, did it?' Hall said, thoughtfully.

'It rattled her all right, but whether because she was genuinely horrified or because she'd pulled the trigger is anyone's guess.'

'And Maggie Hamilton?' he asked, 'did she blub?'

'Yes, she broke down.'

'She always does,' Spencer said, with a shake of his head. 'She turns on the waterworks like a sodding tap. She was probably hoping to get some sympathy from you.'

'Well, she wasted her time.'

'So what sob story was she trying to sell you?'

'That Daddy had meant well by being a member of the Right Club, and only did so because he wanted to avoid another war with Germany.'

'So there were no surprises then?'

Garvan shook his head. 'At a superficial level neither appears to have any Nazi sympathies, but then again, they would, wouldn't they?'

Spencer casually flicked through the folder.

'Can you explain something to me?' Garvan asked him.

Hall looked up. 'Fire away Chief Inspector.'

'When agents pass through the interrogation process at Latchmere House, who has the final say about their recruitment to the Double Cross system?'

'Stephens gives his initial report to the Twenty Committee for approval. I guess you could say we act as a kind of clearing house. John Masterman, the chairman, then forwards our recommendation to Whitehall. In my experience, it's rare for MI5's advice not to be endorsed.'

'I have to confess we haven't made much progress, and we're not likely to unless we begin to crank up the pressure on them.'

'What were you thinking of doing?'

'Drag them in for formal interview.'

Hall closed the folder and paused before answering. 'Personally, I think just by talking to them you've rattled their cages. It's your call, but I really wouldn't worry too much about dragging them into Scotland Yard, at least not just yet.'

'Are you sure, you know them better than I do?' he asked, doubtfully.

'Think of it, one of the buggers tried to kill me the other evening, they panicked.' He smiled slightly. 'Rest assured, Chief Inspector, you've rattled them, and that's exactly what we hoped your investigation would achieve.'

Hall's phone rang. Garvan made to leave, but Spencer raised his hand and gestured for him to remain seated. Everyone in the office seemed to be either on the phone or talking very loudly. Hall closed his eyes, cupping a hand over his ear as he listened to the diatribe down the line with an increasingly pained expression on his face.

'For God's sake,' he groaned in despair, 'stop pissing me around, and just get it right!' He slammed the receiver down. 'Come on,' he said, pushing his chair back. 'Let's get out of here, fancy a drink at the Red Lion in Whitehall? I've a meeting at half two at the War Office down the road.'

The small pub nestling midway between the House of Commons and Downing Street consisted of a rabbit warren of bars over several floors. It was still early by the time they arrived, but customers were starting to drift in. The lunchtime mix mainly consisted of Civil Servants, officers from the War Office and MPs in need of urgent liquid refreshment and a bite to eat. The owners had thoughtfully installed a division bell for the MPs in case they needed to make a quick dash back to the Commons to vote on some Bill or other, but since the outbreak of war it had rarely been used.

Garvan and Hall sat themselves down on one of the long wooden stalls overlooking a side turning leading to Derby Gate, the main entrance to Canon Row police station.

Garvan raised his glass checking the cloudiness of the bitter. It was surprisingly clear. He guessed that being this close to the Commons the publican had managed to secure some decent quality beer from the nearby brewery in Wandsworth. He lit a cigarette. Unusually, Hall declined the offer.

'I'm not sure where to go from here,' Garvan said honestly. 'And I'm damned if I know which one of them is lying.'

'Don't worry yourself too much, you're certainly not alone.'

'From a police perspective there isn't any forensic evidence to speak of, let alone eyewitness accounts to give us a lead.'

'I'm convinced everything we need is in Sarah's notes,' Spencer said. 'Unless we can make contact with Louis Durand, we've nothing else to go on.'

'Then let's hope the Germans don't get to him first.' Garvan drew heavily on his cigarette, before resting it on the side of a dirty metal ashtray piled high with discarded dog ends. 'Maggie mentioned there was an argument between Joyce and Sarah when they last met.'

'Really,' Spencer said, curiously, 'you mean at our office near Victoria Station?'

Garvan nodded. 'She said you were there.'

'It wasn't an argument as such. Joyce was miffed; she's volatile at the best of times - so was Sarah for that matter.' He picked up his beer. 'It could get quite explosive between them.'

'So what had happened?'

'We had a problem. Joyce stepped out of line.'

'What did she do?'

'She ended up in bed with someone who was strictly off limits. He's an engineer working on Blenheim Bombers. She got friendly with him at the Savoy. Sarah had already warned her off once before. For some reason, Joyce ignored us and bedded him again. She was hauled in after the meeting and given a dressing down by Sarah and told to keep her fucking legs closed unless on Double Cross business.'

'I bet that went down well.'

'Like a ton of fucking bricks.'

'Do you think she was up to mischief?'

Spencer smiled and shook his head. 'My gut instinct is that Jo wouldn't risk everything for a Blenheim boffin, they'd have to be a bit more high profile.'

'What makes you say that?'

'Berlin certainly wouldn't have gained any new technical data. That doesn't mean to say we didn't need to warn her off. I think it was simply a case of her fancying the poor sod, lust won over common sense. It's not the first occasion; it happens from time to time. She behaves herself for a while until the next good looking mug catches her eye.' Spencer's attention was drawn suddenly to a slight, scruffily dressed man, leaning on the bar. He was wearing a creased raincoat and a rather weather-beaten trilby hat. Hall's expression hardened as he quickly glanced around the pub as if looking for somebody else.

'We have company,' he said.

Garvan followed his gaze. 'Who is he?'

'An Abwehr agent called Henryk Nowak. He's Polish by birth. It's a bit of a long story how he ended up being with the Abwehr.'

'Is there a problem?'

Spencer blanked the question. 'I have a proposition,' he said reaching into his jacket to retrieve a heavy gold clasped leather notebook. He passed it across the table. 'Here's a present for you.'

Garvan opened the notebook and began to look through. There were columns of names inside. He looked up and asked. 'So what exactly do you want me to do with this lot?'

'It's a list of active agents, like our young friend over there at the bar.'

A name was crossed through. 'And this?' he said pointing to the entry

Hall leaned forward to check the entry. 'They were removed from the active list.'

'And then what happens?'

'Spencer pulled a face. 'We don't exactly run a repatriation service back to Germany.'

'And the ones on the newsreels, the spies at the Tower of London, are there many?' Garvan asked.

'Not that many. The spies who make the news usually end up being shot,' was the measured response. 'We show a selected few, you know those we're unable to use. If we paraded more than a handful, people might start getting alarmed that we're overrun with German spies.'

Hall's gaze drifted back to the slight figure of Henryk Nowak as he moved away from the bar and sat down. Puffing nervously on a cigarette, Nowak seemed ill at ease. Observing Spencer at close quarters, there was an almost chilling quality about him. Whereas Robertson was the suave Whitehall operator, it was obvious that Hall served a double purpose, not only as a buffer against the inter Intelligence turf wars, but he was very much the blunt instrument to tackle difficult agents head on. There was little doubt to Garvan's mind that Henryk Nowak had somehow already tried Hall's patience to breaking point and that he was probably living on borrowed time.

Garvan stubbed out his cigarette. 'Returning to this notebook of yours, what do you want me to do with it?'

'At the back you'll find some notes written by Sarah, I've highlighted them. The codename Nicolette appears on a couple of pages. I might have missed something, something important.' He leaned forward resting his elbows on the table. 'If we can't rescue Louis Durand then we're back to square one.'

Garvan closed the book and asked. 'Meaning what precisely?'

'If push comes to shove and Durand is picked up by the Gestapo, our only real hope is to fool Sarah's killer into thinking we know Nicolette's identity.' He drained his beer. 'Hopefully, it'll force them to break cover.'

'So why on earth bother waiting, why not just do it now?'

'Caution, timing or whatever you like to call it. Until we know for certain what's happened to Durand, we think it best to hold back. God willing if the SOE can track him down, and if we can get him back safe and sound to London, then the game will be up, and we'll have Nicolette's identity delivered to us on a plate.'

It struck Garvan that without Durand Sarah's killer would never give herself up voluntarily. 'Working alongside you Major,' he said, 'feels a bit like being a pawn on a chessboard.'

'A pawn,' Hall repeated, and then broke into laughter, 'a rook perhaps, not a pawn, Chief Inspector, I assure you.'

Garvan bought a round of drinks, and as he set the glasses down, he noticed that Spencer's attention was drawn again to the young, scruffily dressed agent. As he followed Hall's unblinking gaze, it struck Garvan that Nowak was probably the last person in the entire pub you'd have picked out as a spy. He was nondescript and blended seamlessly into the background. Perhaps that was why he'd been chosen by the Abwehr in the first place; no-one would have given him a second glance. Spencer's expression was set in stone and without another word he set his glass down on the table and strode across the pub. As he placed a hand on Nowak's shoulder, the young man visibly jumped at his touch and spun round.

'Major,' he exclaimed expansively, 'you frightened the life out of me.' His English was good with only the slightest intonation of a foreign accent.

'Where's Captain Eldridge?' Hall barked at him.

'At the tobacconist's next door.'

'How long does it take to buy a pack of fags?'

'He told me to wait here and get the drinks,' Nowak pleaded,

Hall checked his watch; by now Nowak should have been en-route to 300 Polish Bomber Squadron at RAF Bramcote, near Nuneaton in Warwickshire. Henryk's controller in Hamburg had asked for specific information about the base. They'd wanted him to test security, and also to test his ability. Over the past month or so there'd been one or two problems with the quality of his transmissions to the Abwehr. British Intelligence had already picked up on Ritter's growing uneasiness with Nowak's performance, and at the same time, MI5 were becoming increasingly aware that Nowak's drinking was spiralling out of control.

'Why aren't you in Warwickshire?' Spencer asked him.

'A last minute change of plan, Captain Eldridge told me the trip was off.'

Hall gripped the agent's shoulder tightly. 'Not been making a nuisance of yourself again are you Henryk? Not been getting yourself paralytic?'

'No Major, I swear, I've cut right back just as you ordered.'

At that moment, Captain John Eldridge strolled into the pub without an apparent care in the world until he caught sight of Spencer standing beside Nowak.

'My office- seven thirty sharp! Hall barked at Eldridge.

'Yes sir,' he spluttered.

Spencer shot his junior officer a withering look, before brushing past him out of the Red Lion into the bright, cold autumnal sunshine. Garvan followed in his wake.

'What the hell was that all about?'

Hall buttoned up his overcoat. 'Nowak, Agent Tad, has a drink problem he missed a wireless message the other evening to Hamburg. The stupid sod was pissed out of his brain. He's on his last warning. Henryk isn't the brightest thing on two legs, but even so he has had his uses, or did have certain uses.' Spencer gestured over his shoulder. 'And I can't think what the hell Eldridge was thinking about bringing Nowak to a pub. He's supposed to be on the bloody wagon! Eldridge needs a fucking boot up his sodding backside.'

'What are you going to do with Nowak?'

'That's anyone's guess. It's up to Colonel Robertson and the Twenty Committee to decide his fate.' As he thrust his hands into his coat pockets, Hall's face visibly hardened half in anger with Nowak, and half in grief as he thought of Sarah.

'Is Tad, Nowak's codename?' Garvan asked.

'Y-yes,' Spencer answered distractedly. 'It's short for Tadpole. He's small fry compared to some of his colleagues. I'm afraid it's not very original; we must have been having a bad day when we named him.'

A street vendor was standing on the corner selling the Evening News. Garvan fumbled in his pocket for the right change and glanced at the headlines. It was something or other about the increase in munitions manufacture. He guessed it was the usual propaganda-based editorial leader. There was probably an essence of truth in the article, but at the end of the day, it was aimed at keeping up public morale.

Garvan and Hall parted company in Whitehall near the elegant stone edifice of the Cenotaph. They shook hands and agreed to arrange a suitable rendezvous to meet up with Joyce Leader and Maggie Hamilton. Garvan headed off down Derby Gate toward the dark red-bricked turrets of Scotland Yard leaving Spencer to carry on up Whitehall for his afternoon meeting at the War Office.

Chapter 14

Garvan strolled along Millbank toward his flat. The night was drawing in, and the shadows were beginning to lengthen in the fading autumnal sunshine. Leaves from the tall London Plane trees lining either side of the road had fallen, thickly carpeting the pavements. He turned into John Islip Street and continued past the rear of the Tate Gallery, and the pretty little gardens on the opposite side of the road. He decided to stop at the corner shop to buy a packet of cigarettes and a pint of milk. He checked his watch. The local café would still be open he hadn't eaten since breakfast and was starving. He grabbed a bite to eat, left the café an hour later, and headed toward his flat in one of the large red brick Victorian mansion blocks opposite the Royal Army Medical College. He'd lived there since 1930. His sons had both been born there, but now it seemed strangely empty, and no longer like a family home. It was just a base, somewhere to eat and sleep.

Garvan was still thinking about his children as he climbed the granite staircase to the first floor. He turned left on the landing and headed along the familiar corridor. He placed the key in the lock, opened the door and entered the large airy hallway. Garvan entered the living room and threw his raincoat onto the couch. He rubbed his hands together and hurriedly lit the fire with a gas poker. For some reason, the flat seemed icily cold, unusually so. He waited until the fire flickered to life before heading off to the bedroom.

Then Garvan saw why the flat was so cold. The window was wide open, and the curtains were billowing into the room like sails. Every drawer and every cupboard were ransacked. Clothes, the bedding, his personal effects were strewn across the floor. There'd been no sign of forced entry at the front door, and it seemed unlikely anyone had climbed the drainpipe to gain access - it would have been all but impossible to reach the window.

Garvan looked at the mess on the floor and wondered why the rest of the flat had been left untouched. As he turned to go back into the hallway, somebody stepped out from behind the bedroom door and connected a heavy blow to the side of his face. He clutched his head, feeling a sharp, excruciating pain before crumpling to the floor into an all-consuming darkness.

It was 9.30 in the morning and Jack Charteris checked the office clock, lifted up the receiver and dialled Garvan's home telephone number for the umpteenth time. The Guv'nor was never late, at least not without checking in first. Mac poked his head round the door.

'Still not answering the phone?'

'It just keeps ringing,' Jack said, anxiously.

'Come on,' Mac said to him, 'get your coat on there's no point sitting around here wasting time and worrying.'

Charteris smacked the receiver down. 'Something's wrong; I know it is.'

'Just get your coat and I'll sign out a car. Meet me downstairs.'

Back at the flat in Millbank, Garvan had started to rouse. The darkness began to clear, fragmented at first, and then followed by a bright, unforgiving light which hurt his eyes. In his confusion, he reached up blindly in search of a light switch until it slowly dawned on him that the blinding light was sunshine blazing through the window.

As he lay there, Garvan began to wonder why he couldn't move. What the hell had happened? He couldn't think straight, and the wild pounding inside his head felt like he could hear his own heartbeat.

Then he began to sense that someone else was in the flat. He heard something, indistinct at first and slowly started hearing low urgent voices.

Where were they, he asked himself, why didn't they speak up, why were they whispering? Garvan opened his eyes. The world seemed strangely fuzzy and unfocused, and the room was circling him at an alarming rate. He still couldn't quite grasp what he was doing lying on the floor. Then he felt a firm hand placed on his arm and became suddenly aware of someone leaning over him, a man in a belted raincoat and trilby hat. The face slowly began to take shape, and the hazy mass developed features, the voice, indistinct at first finally became recognisable.

'Luke for Christ's sake, are you all right? We thought you were fucking dead,' Mackenzie said, anxiously.

Garvan rolled on his back, still squinting against the harsh light. 'Get me up,' he begged, 'just get me up off the floor.'

Charteris helped Mackenzie to haul him to his feet. He was a dead weight, and his legs were so shaky that he was unable to support his weight. Maybe they should have left him on the floor; Garvan thought to himself. His head not only felt like a ton weight, but he was now struck by an overpowering urge to be sick. Fearing the Guv'nor was about to collapse on them, not daring to loosen their grip they carefully sat him down on the edge of the bed.

After a while, his nausea began to subside. Garvan gingerly felt the open wound on the side of his head, and immediately felt an instant, searing pain. He winced and was hit by yet another wave of nausea.

'What the hell happened to you?' Mac said, crouching down beside him.

'I'm - I'm not sure,' he gasped, 'some - some bastard knocked me senseless, God knows why they didn't finish me off, they could have done.'

'Did you see who did it?'

'No, it happened too quickly.' He closed his eyes as the room started to spin again. It was almost like having a severe hangover without the benefit of the booze.

Charteris closed the windows. 'Were you followed home last night, sir?'

Luke desperately tried to remember. 'Yes - I mean, I'm not sure, it's all a bit of a blur.'

'Is anything missing?' Charteris asked.

Garvan managed to open one bleary eye and gave a cursory glance around the room. 'Lord knows!'

'Mind you,' Mac interrupted, 'it didn't look that much different before the break-in, Jack.'

Garvan silently accepted that Mac was right. Since Joan had left he'd let things slip, there hadn't seemed much point. He worked long hours and used the flat more like a hotel than a home. He half-heartedly tried to scan the mess left by the intruder. What were they looking for? There was certainly nothing of intrinsic value; Joan had long since taken all her jewellery. The only possible motive for the break-in must be Sarah's murder; perhaps they'd hoped to find something connected to the investigation. If so, they were unlucky. The case notes were safely under lock and key at Scotland Yard.

He felt Mac place a steadying hand on his shoulder. Garvan's mind was racing. He couldn't understand why the intruder hadn't killed him; it would have been easy enough. Why not finish the job, or had it merely been a warning? But why, why now? Had the interviews with Leader and Hamilton thrown something up? But what had he missed, there must be something?

Mackenzie gently checked the wound. 'We've got to get you to the hospital, Guv.'

'Just leave me here,' he begged them, 'I'll be okay where I am.'

'You're going to the hospital; there's no way we're leaving you here. That blow could have killed you.'

'Just don't call a bloody ambulance, please!'

'We'll drive you; it won't take a minute,' Charteris assured him, 'it'll be quicker than waiting for an ambulance Westminster Hospital is only round the corner.'

'You've got a squad car?' Garvan asked.

'Of course, we have, Guv.'

'You'll have to help me down the fucking stairs!'

As they started to haul him out of the flat, Garvan felt weaker than he cared to admit to them. He'd never have managed to support his weight without help. The movement and the exertion made him feel sick again, so much so, that in the foyer he began to retch. To his relief he wasn't physically sick, and when the retching eventually subsided they carried him the short distance to the car.

Just as Charteris opened the rear passenger door, Mackenzie blurted out. 'For Christ's sake Jack, maybe we should have waited for an ambulance, after all, we might end up killing him.'

'Too late now,' Charteris said, helping to bundle Garvan into the car.

With some difficulty, they managed to prop him up in the corner of the back seat Mac then climbed in the other side and wedged himself against Garvan to support him.

The world seemed strangely detached as if he was seeing and hearing everything from a great distance; it was almost like being trapped in a long dark tunnel. He was vaguely aware of their concern, but couldn't always quite catch what they were saying. The car started, Jack floored the accelerator, and they hurtled down John Islip Street. With his head still pounding, Garvan decided it was probably only the pain that was keeping him conscious.

Jack turned left out of John Islip Street into Horseferry Road; they only needed to drive a few hundred yards before they drew up at the main entrance of the Westminster Hospital. They carried Garvan from the car into the crowded Casualty, but they flashed their identity cards at Reception and swept through to a side ward. The next thing Garvan recalled was waking up and being propelled on a hard, uncomfortable trolley along a corridor. Above him were large circular ceiling lights which started to hurt his eyes. It was all still a bit of a haze. He remembered there was a battery of tests, and a great deal of prodding and probing by a series of nurses and doctors.

Three hours later the Registrar announced: 'You're a very lucky man, Chief Inspector.'

He supposed it was one way of looking at it. But lying on a hospital trolley feeling like shit; lucky wasn't the first word that had sprung to his mind.

'You're suffering from a concussion, and that's about all,' the Registrar continued, 'we'll give you some stitches for that head wound of yours, and to be on the safe side, we'll have you in overnight for observation. We don't want to be taking any chances now, do we?'

Another wave of sickness came over him, and he closed his eyes in the hope the room might stop spinning. He just wanted to be left alone, but the Registrar was the talkative type, and prattled on endlessly about x-rays, and made a few banal jokes about Garvan having an especially tough skull to crack, he really didn't need it, at least not right now. If he'd had the strength to haul himself off the trolley, he'd have floored the bugger.

'Someone else,' the Registrar laughed, 'would've had their head stoved in with a blow like that. It's a wonder you didn't end up on a mortuary slab!'

'Try swapping fucking places with me mate, and see how you feel!' Garvan spat at him. He hated sarcastic, smart arse bloody doctors, he'd come across more than his fair share in his time, and the last thing he needed right now was another one.

The Registrar smirked at him. 'As I said, you'll need some stitches but otherwise, given some rest, you'll be just fine.'

Mac and Charteris stayed at the hospital with him until his admission to a ward on the first floor. Once back at Scotland Yard, Mac contacted St. James's. Luckily Spencer Hall was at his desk. Hall thanked him and asked to be informed of his progress if they needed anything he was at their disposal.

Mac guessed that at best, news of the attack on Garvan would go down like a lead balloon at St. James's. In Garvan's absence, he was uncertain how to take things forward with St. James's. Spencer had told him that he'd let Colonel Robertson know of the attack, but as far as Mac was concerned the Major was an entirely closed book and way out of his league. It was beginning to make him nervous. All things being well, Garvan would soon be on the mend, but in the meantime, Mac feared things might just get a little bit tricky liaising with St. James's.

Mackenzie returned the next morning after he was assured that Garvan would be discharged. He went to the sideward only to find the same chatty Registrar was back on duty. He explained that Garvan's dizziness would pass after a few days.

'Just make certain he takes things easy for the next few weeks.'

'That might be easier said than done.'

'He doesn't have a choice if he wants to make a speedy recovery. Otherwise, he'll end up back on the ward.' The Registrar smiled, 'and I somehow don't think your Chief Inspector would relish the thought of our paths crossing again, at least not that soon.'

Mac imagined that Garvan probably hadn't proved to be the easiest of patients to deal with. Jack Charteris was waiting for them in the flat. Having negotiated the stairs with Mac's help Garvan slumped on the couch exhausted. They made him a cup of tea, but he began to feel irritated by all the fuss; they meant well enough and were genuinely concerned if he'd be able to cope on his own.

Garvan didn't want to offend by asking them to leave him alone, but his head was still pounding, and he couldn't concentrate on what they were saying. He kept reassuring them that he was fine, but his deathly pallor and inability to hold a conversation beyond a couple of syllables had given the game away that he was feeling far from well. Without being too abrupt or rude after about half an hour, he finally managed to persuade them to leave.

In hindsight it was probably just as well, they left when they did, he was desperately tired and slept like a log for a solid sixteen hours. When he finally awoke, that same annoying drumbeat was still hammering away inside his head like a migraine, only a thousand times worse.

The following afternoon Charles Harmer phoned him at home to check on his progress. He said how sorry he was to hear of the attack. It was a short, stilted conversation, and nothing more than a duty call.

By Wednesday of the same week, Spencer called and asked if he was feeling up to a visit. Garvan readily agreed, he was still feeling unwell but was starting to become bored stuck in the flat all day without anything to do. Spencer told him he'd be there at 10.30 sharp.

Just before Spencer had called he'd managed to venture out of the flat for the first time since the attack to check in his mailbox in the foyer. There were only two letters. The first was a bill which he couldn't be bothered to open, and the second had the familiar neat scrawl of his wife's handwriting. Back upstairs he opened Joan's letter. It was short, sharp and to the point. They needed to talk, to discuss their divorce and decide between them how best to let the boys know their marriage was over. He turned over the page, his eyes instantly locking on the line about her lover. She'd finally given the name of her Squadron Leader. The words leapt up off the page. It was the final, gut-wrenching blow.

In disbelief, Garvan found himself re-reading the line, not quite sure if he'd read it correctly the first time. God, her timing was out, he thought to himself, he didn't need to read this and didn't want to know the gory details about her lover, at least not right now. He'd been prepared to read about some handsome young RAF pilot that she'd taken up with. Perhaps he could even have understood her wishing to move on, but no, this was something else entirely. Joan was about to throw their marriage away because she'd fallen in love with a female Squadron Leader.

Garvan couldn't quite bring himself to finish the letter. His thoughts were reeling. How on earth could they possibly begin to tell the boys what had happened? It was never going to be an easy thing to do, but this had completely wrong-footed him. He just couldn't think straight or take it all in. Joan had always been the headstrong type, but how could she do this to them, to him? Had she married merely for appearances' sake, just because her family had expected it? Perhaps she'd always preferred women. There was just no way of knowing.

He was still reeling from Joan's letter when good to his word Spencer Hall arrived promptly at 10.30. Garvan opened the door, his expression at once registering surprise. He hadn't expected him to turn up with Joyce Leader in tow.

Spencer grasped his hand noting the bruising and stitches on his forehead. 'Christ almighty, they did take a swing at you, didn't they?'

'Please come in.'

'Sorry,' Spencer apologised, gesturing toward Joyce. 'I should have mentioned I was bringing Jo along, it completely slipped my mind. I'd pencilled in a meeting with her this morning down in Kent, but Tar wanted me to catch up with you first before we left. So tell me, how are you doing?'

Garvan closed the door. 'I'm taking enough painkillers to floor a ruddy elephant, but I've still got a thumping bloody headache.'

Joyce trailed after Spencer into the living room and sat down beside him on the couch. Spencer asked him about the assault. It was still a little hazy he explained. All he knew for certain was that he'd been very lucky to escape with only superficial bruising and a few stitches. It could have been a whole lot worse. Having been knocked senseless Garvan didn't understand why his assailant hadn't bothered to finish the job off.

'My gut instinct is that you probably took the intruder by surprise,' Hall said.

'So why not break into my flat earlier in the day when they knew I'd still be at work?'

'What time did you get home?'

'At about half eight, I guess.'

'Is that earlier than usual?'

Garvan gave the question some thought before answering. 'I don't usually get home until about ten.'

'So you've not been varying your routine as I told you to?'

Garvan held up his hand. 'I know, you warned me. I did for the first week or so, and then -,'

Hall cut across him. 'If they kept tabs on you I guess half eight in the evening probably didn't seem that much of a risk.'

'So why not finish me off?'

'Do you mind if I smoke?' Hall said to him.

'Go ahead.'

'Don't take this as an insult, Chief, but I guess your intruder didn't think there was anything to gain by killing you. Sarah, on the other hand, was a different matter altogether; she was one step away from knowing the identity of Nicolette.'

Garvan was surprised Spencer had opened up so much in front of Joyce Leader. He wondered what she was thinking, but as usual, she was giving nothing away.

'Maybe they thought I knew their identity?'

Hall stood up and winked at Garvan. 'I doubt it Chief Inspector. Otherwise, you'd be dead by now.'

Apart from the obvious physical scars of the assault, Garvan looked drawn and painfully frail. In fact, Spencer was surprised he'd agreed to see him at all. There was no doubt in Hall's mind that it was Sarah's killer who'd broken into the flat, possibly in a bid to find the black leather notebook he'd passed to Garvan at the Red Lion in Whitehall. If that was the motive for the break-in, then there was only one person who could have tipped off the murderer Henryk Nowak, who'd been present in the pub when Spencer handed it over to him.

There was a knock at the front door. Garvan answered it was Hall's driver needing to speak with the Major urgently.

'What's wrong Simpson?' Spencer asked him.

'Lieutenant Carrington's outside sir, he's got an urgent hand delivery from Colonel Robertson.'

'I'm sorry,' Hall apologised before following his driver downstairs.

Joyce waited until Spencer had left the flat before placing a cigarette in her now familiar ebony holder. 'Do you mind if I light up?' she asked.

'Feel free.'

'I wonder what that was all about?' she mused.

'I suppose we're probably both in the same boat, in some respects.' Garvan said to her.

'How so?' she asked, lighting the cigarette.

'We'll only ever find out why Carrington's here if MI5 and Spencer want us to know.'

Joyce smiled, she visibly relaxed, but wouldn't be drawn. She sat with the cigarette holder poised lightly between her fingers, without an apparent care in the world. Garvan found himself wondering if it had been Joyce who'd knocked him senseless. There was simply no way of telling, she was as always, her usual rather flirtatious self. She glanced toward the side table beside the couch and picked up a silver-framed photograph of two smiling boys.

'Yours?' she asked, waving it in the air.

'Yes, they were evacuated to Lyme Regis at the outbreak of the war. John's the eldest; Harry is eighteen months younger. They've taken to living on the coast like ducks to water, to be perfectly honest with you; I'm not sure they'll want to come back to London.'

'They're good looking boys,' she observed.

'Thank you.'

'Is your wife with them?'

'No, after they were evacuated she found herself a nice little number working at the War Office, and then managed to wangle herself a posting to RAF Tangmere.'

Joyce carefully set the photograph back on the side table. 'Where's Tangmere?'

'Sussex, it's not too far from Chichester.'

She pulled a face. 'Not too far then. It could have been a whole lot worse. Your wife could have been posted to the other end of the country.'

Garvan held her gaze and said. 'To be honest with you, I haven't seen her for about three or four months now.' He glanced fleetingly at the picture. 'I guess things haven't been right between us for a while now. Joan's found someone else.'

'Do you mean a good looking pilot?'

'If only it were.' He hesitated before saying 'I'd almost have forgiven her if she'd fallen in love with some dashing fighter pilot or other, but no, my wife's fallen in love with a woman, a WAAF Officer.'

For Christ's sake he thought to himself, why on earth am I telling Joyce Leader of all people, what the hell's up with me? Another thought suddenly crossed his mind. Spencer Hall must have known all along the identity of Joan's lover, yes, yes, of course, he must have. The Security Services would have carried out the usual background checks to ensure his suitability before entrusting him with access to top secret material. In fact, the whole of the bloody Twenty Committee must also have known about Joan's love life.

To give her credit, Joyce's expression didn't falter. She stood up and instinctively brushed the back of her hand against his cheek. 'I'm so sorry. It really can't be easy for you, but then it never is,' she said, tenderly.

Garvan turned away, almost flinched at her touch. He didn't want her to see that he was struggling to control his emotions. He was all over the place, it must be that sodding blow to the head, or so he chose to believe. Why hadn't he just kept his fucking mouth shut? He needed to keep a level head, and more importantly, keep Joyce Leader at arm's length. She was clever, manipulative, and one of only two possible suspects for the murder of Sarah Davis. So why in spite of everything, did he still find himself strangely attracted to her? I'm acting like a bloody fool; he said to himself and headed off to the kitchen.

'Do you want something to drink, some tea?' he called to her over his shoulder.

'Thank you I wouldn't say no.'

Sugar?'

'No, just as it comes.'

Following Garvan into the kitchen, she watched him put the kettle on. Whereas Hall was as hard as nails, with few, if any discernible chinks in his armour Joyce found herself intrigued, and attracted to Garvan. There was a certain vulnerability about him, and never more so than right now. It was an attractive quality, she decided. He was her type, she mused. It just such was a pity he was strictly off limits.

Garvan opened a kitchen cupboard. 'All I can offer you is a digestive biscuit or a tin of corned beef.'

Joyce peered inside and giggled. 'Aren't you taking rationing a bit too far, there's nothing but a dozen tins of corned beef and what looks like a half-eaten pack of biscuits, and I guess they're probably stale!'

He shrugged. 'I think you're probably right,' and promptly dumped the biscuits in the waste bin. 'My only excuse is that I eat out most evenings. I get home late, and I don't have time to shop.' He smiled, a crease furrowing his brow. 'I'm not sure why I'm bothering to tell you all this, what the hell do you know about standing in a queue at the shops? You practically live at the Ritz.'

'I like the Rivoli Bar,' she said, 'it's a handy for business. My German handler, Nikolaus Ritter, believes the bar is - how shall I say a good hunting ground.'

'For punters you mean'?'

'Punter isn't a word I'd use,' she said sharply. Joyce pursed her lips thoughtfully. 'At the end of the day, Chief Inspector, the Abwehr expect me to befriend politicians, and bed the odd crusty old General or Admiral.' She paused, her gaze locking steadily onto Garvan. 'I'm sure you know exactly how things stand with me. I'm a small cog, a very small cog in Colonel Robertson's master plan for providing misinformation to Hamburg and Berlin.'

He didn't respond and set out two cups on the small kitchen table. 'Tell me, don't you ever get sick and tired of sleeping around with old men?' he shot back at her.

Her expression was suddenly glacial. 'For the record Chief Inspector, they're not all old or on their last legs, some of them are quite young and attractive. Her face relaxed slightly. 'And on the odd occasion, I've also been known to do it for pleasure.'

The hint of sarcasm in her voice was not lost on him, but if she was hoping to elicit some response, she was wide of the mark.

'I don't expect you to understand, why should you?' she continued, almost feeling obliged to explain herself. 'My life here in London is like being on a roller coaster, the highs and lows come in equal measure, one moment it's sheer exhilaration followed the next by abject bloody fear.' She hesitated, before adding: 'but, all things considered, things could be worse, far worse. Perhaps one day, one day I'll escape all this crap,' she said it almost wistfully.

The kettle boiled, he made the tea. Her next question stopped him in his tracks. 'Why didn't your intruder finish you off?'

'I think Major Hall might have got it right, maybe they didn't think there was anything to gain it was probably just a warning.'

He handed her a cup and returned to the living room and sat down. Joyce wandered over to the window and moved the net curtain to check on Spencer in the street below. He was standing by his staff car talking to a uniformed Navy officer that she didn't recognise.

'I guess you must be wondering if it was me that clobbered you,' she said, with disarming candour.

'It crossed my mind,' he shot back at her.

Joyce took a sip of the tea. 'The thing is Chief Inspector I'd have made sure I finished you off.'

'But would you?' Garvan quizzed her.

'What do you mean?'

'Personally, I think you're far too calculating for that.'

She was intrigued. What was he getting at? He could see the questioning look in her eyes.

'Why create even more trouble for yourself? Far better to leave me unconscious than add another murder to your tally.'

'I didn't murder Sarah Davis if that's what you're thinking!' she snapped back at him.

'I wasn't expecting a confession.'

'But you think I might have pulled the trigger?'

'Until I can prove otherwise then, yes, why wouldn't I?'

Joyce didn't respond. She moved away from the window and noticed a pewter framed photograph on the mantelpiece. It was an opportunity for her to change the subject, Garvan thought.

'Is that your wife?' she said, pointing to the picture.

'Yes,' he said, tersely.

Joyce picked it up to get a better look at the smiling brunette. 'Such a dumme schlampe,' she said breaking into German.

'What the hell does that mean?'

Joyce replaced the picture back on the mantelpiece. 'It means your wife's a stupid little bitch!' By now she was staring down at him, the back of her hand once again brushing against his cheek.

The front door opened. Spencer let himself in, and without missing a beat said.

'Put the Chief Inspector down Jo, there's a good girl.'

Garvan was embarrassed. He'd misread the situation. For her part, Joyce merely smirked at Spencer, and eased herself back down on the couch, and casually retrieved her cigarette holder from the ashtray on the side table.

'Sorry about that,' Hall apologised to Garvan. 'I'll let Colonel Robertson know that you're on the mend. It mortified him that you ended up in the hospital. Sarah dying was bad enough, but the icing on the cake would have been losing a senior Scotland Yard Detective as well. It really wouldn't have gone down too well in Whitehall.'

'I'm sorry to have put you to so much trouble,' Garvan smiled.

'We just don't want any more bloody disasters, at least not just yet.' He looked at his watch. 'Right Jo, we're running late get a wriggle on! I'll be in touch Chief. When are you expecting to get back to the office?'

'Next week.'
'Good, I'll give you a bell

Chapter 15

Garvan was running late for a meeting with Robertson and Hall at the Savoy. He'd started off in plenty of time from Scotland Yard, but half way along The Strand the heavens had opened, and he'd been forced to take shelter in a shop doorway. Driven by an increasingly strong wind, the sheets of rain came down so hard they bounced off the pavements and caused rivulets of water to gush along the gutters as the drains struggled to cope with the sudden deluge. Garvan waited until the rain began to lessen, and by the time he arrived at the Savoy he was ten minutes late.

Spencer was loitering in the foyer, and on spotting Garvan bedraggled and soaked to the skin, he couldn't stop himself grinning. Garvan's umbrella had blown inside out and broken two of its spokes. The rain darkened his light coloured raincoat, and the rim of his trilby was dripping with droplets of water.

'You should have taken a car,' Hall said in greeting.

He pulled a face. 'It was still sunny when I left the Yard.'

The hotel doorman stepped forward and relieved Garvan of his broken umbrella and sodden raincoat, assuring him it would be dried off by the time he'd finished lunch.

'You might as well forget the umbrella,' Garvan said to him.

The doorman smiled and headed off back across the foyer.

'Do you want to freshen up first?' Spencer asked.

'No, no I'll be fine,' Garvan said, making an attempt to smooth down his hair. 'What's this all about? Bit short notice, isn't it?'

'I'm sorry; I didn't get a chance to explain what's going on.'

A member of the hotel staff escorted them to a small private oak-panelled dining room on the ground floor. On first impression, the room appeared almost overpowered by a large crystal chandelier. The dining table had been dressed with a pristine white linen cloth and set for four people. The ornate crystal wine glasses and silver cutlery glistened under the twinkling lights of the chandelier. Standing before the white marble fireplace was the familiar figure of Robertson; he was wearing his favoured tartan trousers and khaki army jacket. He leaned toward to the hearth to empty out his pipe. Beside him was a slightly built man, whom Garvan guessed to be no more than about five feet five in height, his hands thrust deep into the pockets of a grey charcoal suit jacket. It fleetingly crossed Garvan's mind that he looked like an insurance or bank clerk. The stranger was smiling at him; his face was thin, almost gaunt in appearance, but with a pleasant, open and kindly expression.

Robertson turned away from the hearth. 'Chief Inspector, I trust you're feeling a little better now, by all accounts you took quite a knock. It's good to see you up and about, you're looking remarkably well.'

'Thank you, sir.'

'Allow me to introduce you to Louis Durand.' His softly spoken voice carried lingeringly across the dining room.'

Garvan's eyes narrowed as he extended his hand in welcome to the Frenchman. How wrong first impressions can be. He certainly wasn't a bank clerk.

'Louis arrived at the weekend from Paris,' Robertson explained, 'after a great deal of hard work we finally managed to pluck him to safety in the early hours of Saturday morning.'

Garvan nodded.

'You'll know he's a close friend and colleague of Roman Czerniawski, a leading member of the Interallie, and a very successful one at that.'

Durand inclined his head, thanking Robertson for the compliment.

Tar pressed the buzzer beside the hearth. 'Let's order lunch, shall we gentlemen?'

Louis Durand sat down and picked up the menu card. He held it at arm's length - perhaps he'd forgotten to bring his glasses, Garvan wondered. He was still finding it difficult to imagine this slight, and rather unprepossessing man was a successful spy. The waiters took their orders for lunch and when it was served they left four bottles of red wine in the centre of the table.

'Now gentleman, 'Robertson said as the door closed, 'let's get down to business, shall we.' Toying with a fork between his fingers, he addressed Garvan. 'We've already explained to you that Monsieur Durand was the last person to meet Czerniawski before being arrested by Hugo Bleicher. It was a stroke of sheer luck that he wasn't arrested himself, a few minutes later and –.'

Durand cut across him: 'Or I wouldn't be enjoying lunch at the Savoy. I was very lucky.' He spoke quickly, in accented but quite fluent English, with only the occasional hesitation when he searched for the correct words.

'Before Roman's arrest, we'd spent the evening talking about the increasing number of arrests of our members by the Gestapo.' Durand paused, looked across the table, and coolly held Garvan's gaze. 'My apartment is around the corner from Roman's you see, Chief Inspector. We often met up of an evening to talk things through.' He raised his wine glass and sniffed the bouquet. 'It's probably a bit rich to call my home an apartment. I rent a couple of rooms near Montmartre.' He took a sip of the wine. 'After our meeting I went across the road to a bar, for- for how do you say - last drink?'

'Nightcap,' Spencer intervened.

'Yes, thank you, Major,' he nodded, 'nightcap - I was sitting in a window seat and saw the Gestapo draw up in two Mercedes. All I could do was sit there and watch, there was simply no time, no time at all to warn him.'

As Durand savoured his wine he recalled how he'd sat in the cafe, his mouth had dried, and his hands had trembled uncontrollably around the stem of the glass, as he watched on helplessly as the Gestapo entered Roman's apartment block.

Shortly after a shot had rung out from the building, Louis explained. He had a bird's eye view and sat tight in the comparative safety of the bar as his friend was manhandled out of the building, and roughly bundled into one of the waiting cars. There was just enough light from the gas lamps lining either side of the street, for Louis to recognise the dark spectacled figure of Hugo Bleicher emerge from the building. The cars had turned left at the end of the road; he assumed they were heading to the secret military police HQ based in the Hotel Edward VIII. With Czerniawski under arrest, the network was now sure to implode, no-one was safe.

Louis waited in the bar until he was sure the coast was clear. He had to move quickly, to warn as many of their agents as possible. It was a race against time, and one Durand always knew he was going to lose; it was just a matter of trying to limit the damage. He spoke almost without drawing breath, his thoughts racing ahead. Everyone had scattered, gone to ground, the network was in disarray, wireless sets moved, and agents fled Paris. Garvan listened intently as Durand described the domino-like collapse of the Interallie organisation.

He interrupted the Frenchman. 'But what about Sarah Davis, what happened, why was she killed?'

Louis paused, his eyes weary, his expression strained. 'Because of Nicolette,' he said, scarcely above a whisper. 'Sarah received a message, a garbled message from me. My wireless transmission was rushed. I didn't have a choice; it was simply too dangerous to stay in one place for any length of time.' Durand pushed his plate away; he'd barely touched the meal. 'You see I was careless Chief Inspector.'

'Not careless,' Robertson insisted, 'the Gestapo were hard on your heels, you really cannot blame yourself.'

It was evident Durand wasn't convinced. He still believed that he'd let Sarah down, and exposed her to unnecessary danger. 'Part of the message,' he continued, 'was intercepted by the Abwehr, enough of it, at least, to place Sarah's life in jeopardy.'

'And is it true you know Agent Nicolette's identity,' Garvan pressed him.

'He does,' Spencer said his expression taut as he lit a cigarette. 'We have our killer, Chief Inspector.'

Garvan looked to Durand. 'So who is it?'

Louis wouldn't be drawn. He wanted to explain how they managed to track Nicolette down before revealing her identity.

'Rumours spread like wildfire through the entire network,' he said, with studied deliberation, his voice etched with emotion. 'Most were wide of the mark, but the Gestapo had successfully scattered our agents, although for some weeks to come we still had just enough people on the ground to operate a limited operation. It was during this time we managed to discover Agent Nicolette had become the lover of Hugo Bleicher, and that her pillow talk had led to the direct arrest of six Interallie agents. I'm not saying she was directly responsible for Roman's arrest by the Gestapo, but without a doubt, she helped place the final nail in the Interallie's coffin.' Louis paused to accept a cigarette from Spencer. 'If it hadn't been for a chance sighting by one of our agents, who saw Nicolette dining with Bleicher at an expensive restaurant, we'd never have suspected her. Let's just say it was obvious to anyone who saw them, that they were close, they were lovers. My agent followed the happy couple to a hotel nearby where they spent the night together.' He stared unseeingly down at the cigarette as he rolled it thoughtfully between his fingers. 'At the time many of our agents were caving in under torture, the network, Chief Inspector, was quite literally on its knees. Things were moving fast, but until the restaurant incident with Bleicher we had no reason to suspect that either Leader or Hamilton had become a triple agent.' He drew heavily on the cigarette. 'Several weeks passed before they could get word to me of the sighting, but by that time I was in hiding, and had left Paris. You have to understand communications were very difficult, almost impossible. At the same time as I discovered Nicolette's identity, I also heard that Nikolaus Ritter wanted them to return to England. You know,' Louis said, raising his hand to emphasise the point. 'There was simply no reason for them to remain in France. They were far more useful to Ritter this side of the Channel.' He looked to Spencer, and held his gaze for a moment, before adding: 'When the Abwehr intercepted my wireless transmission it all but signed Sarah's death warrant. Nicolette was ordered to eliminate her; neither Bleicher nor Ritter wanted the risk of British Intelligence discovering the truth.'

   Seeing Garvan's increasing frustration that Louis still hadn't revealed the killer's identity, Spencer cut across him. 'Our triple agent, your murderer, Chief Inspector, is Maggie Hamilton.'

'Hamilton!' Garvan repeated in disbelief. He'd already made up his mind up that Joyce Leader had pulled the trigger on Sarah, not Maggie. When Durand mentioned that Agent Nicolette had taken Hugo Bleicher as a lover, he'd automatically assumed that with Leader's track record she was their rogue agent.

'But why, why did Hamilton turn, do we know?' he asked.

Robertson refilled his glass. 'I guess,' he said coolly, 'there were a number of reasons.' He shot Hall a long hard look. 'I know Spencer harboured grave doubts about her right from the beginning, but in reality, she was no more of a risk than Joyce Leader, or for that matter any other member of the Double Cross.' He passed the bottle of wine to Garvan. 'Bleicher was attracted to Maggie, there again why wouldn't he be, she's an attractive woman, and to all intents and purposes outwardly one of their own. We wanted them to get close to Ritter and Bleicher, but unfortunately, in Maggie's case, it got entirely out of hand.'

'Surely to God,' Garvan said to him, 'Maggie knew you'd eventually discover her betrayal.'

'I suppose you have to place yourself in her shoes,' Tar said. 'Here was a woman who proved to be completely out of her depth, and probably scared to death that either Bleicher or his Gestapo colleagues might at any given moment discover her involvement with British Intelligence. Quite simply she couldn't take the pressure. The upshot is that somewhere along the line she panicked, and sang like a canary, and in no small measure helped to bring down the Interallie network before finally murdering Sarah Davis to save her own neck.' He fell silent for a moment. 'In the long run, she'll realise it's better to keep your mouth sealed rather than your coffin.'

'But how can you be sure that before Maggie was parachuted into France, she wasn't already a triple agent?' Garvan queried.

'We are,' Robertson responded smoothly, 'otherwise, we'd never have agreed to the drop. We'd have picked up on any unauthorised transmissions with Hamburg. As I've already explained to you dropping them into France was considered to be an essential move. Otherwise, we'd have exposed the Double Cross to German Intelligence. We simply couldn't afford that to happen. There was also the matter of Ritter's presence in Paris. It sealed the deal as far as we were concerned; we really couldn't pass up such a golden opportunity.'

'So even though you're left with God knows how many agents behind bars in France, including Czerniawski, and, your own desk officer murdered in cold blood here in London, you still think it was worth the risk?' Garvan asked, incredulously.

Tar calmly lit his pipe considering how best to reply. 'It never was going to be an easy decision, Chief Inspector,' he said softly, with characteristic understatement. 'In this line of work, there will always be victims. My remit, the Twenty Committees remit, is to help Britain and her Allies win the war against Nazi Germany. Our involvement using the Double Cross has allowed us to run and control the entire German espionage system in this country.' Robertson puffed on his pipe and blew out a large bluish cloud of smoke. 'I accept all the doubts, and the arguments against the decisions we made. It was very much a calculated risk, and admittedly a dangerous one at that, but it was one we simply had to take. As Louis will tell you, we briefed both him and Czerniawski well in advance. Leader and Hamilton's activities with the Interallie were kept deliberately to a minimum. In many ways the gamble paid off, although it might not seem that way to you,' Tar smiled at Garvan. 'But we now have a much better understanding of Ritter's mindset and his plans over the coming months. The cost has been high, some might well argue way too high, but the Twenty Committee has to take decisions with a long-term view regarding the future of the war. You must never lose sight of the fact that our counter-espionage methods are very successful with a proven track record for deceiving the Nazi regime. It works, but if we were to fail, if we faltered, quite simply we'd end up losing the entire war.' He cupped the pipe in his hand, and added smoothly, 'so to answer your question Chief Inspector, the risk was certainly worth taking.'

'But you still have a rogue agent on your hands.'

'Yes, yes, we do,' he said, thoughtfully.

'So why was Hamilton given the Codename Nicolette?'

'It was Bleicher's idea,' Tar explained, 'a reward if you like for her betrayal of the Interallie. He thought it faintly amusing to give her a pretty French nom de plume.'

'And what now, do you want me to arrest her?'

'Not immediately.'

Garvan looked perplexed.

'We'd like to arrange another meeting with them. We still feel even at this late stage of the game that it's important not to spook her. Remember a lot is riding on this, and we can't run the risk of her getting word to Ritter that we've discovered her identity as Nicolette.' Robertson placed a hand on Durand's shoulder. 'And if I'm not mistaken I believe Louis would also like the opportunity of meeting up with Agent Nicolette again to reminisce, and perhaps to tie up a few loose ends.'

A smile flickered briefly across Durand's face. He wanted to ensure Nicolette paid the ultimate price for the betrayal of his agents and the cold-blooded murder of Sarah Davis, but needed to do so in a calm, calculated manner, and not served up in the heat of the moment. More than anything he needed closure.

Chapter 16

Spencer paced Garvan's office, hands thrust in his trouser pockets waiting anxiously for Luke to finish reading his notes. He'd proposed a meeting with Joyce and Maggie the following evening at the Union Jack Club, for no other reason than it was situated conveniently close to Waterloo Station, but he needed Garvan's agreement.

Hamilton had a long-standing visit arranged to Gosport, and Robertson had been reluctant to cancel it without just cause. About a month ago now Ritter had asked Maggie to make use of her naval friends and contacts, to see if she could manage to visit as many military installations along the south coast as reasonably possible. The Twenty Committee had analysed the request, and Robertson and the other committee members had agreed to play along with the Abwehr's request.

It was common practice for Double Cross agents to be allowed to visit the actual places they were meant to be spying on. This often meant taking them to major ports, military bases and industrial sites. The committee thought this would enhance the authenticity of both their written reports and radio transmissions. It also meant they were less likely to be caught out when the Abwehr posed tricky questions to verify their reports.

Hall was growing increasingly impatient for a response. It was time to put Sarah's murder investigation to bed. Tar still wanted to retain a semblance of normality to Maggie's routine commitments, but perhaps more importantly, allow her just enough rope to believe she'd managed to outwit St. James's.

Garvan finished reading Hall's notes.

'So what do you think?' Spencer asked him.

Garvan scratched his head. 'Let me get this straight: At 18.25 tomorrow afternoon, we meet Joyce Leader at Waterloo Station.

Spencer nodded his agreement.

'And then Maggie's train arrives at approximately 18.35. Mac and I then take them to the Union Jack Club in Waterloo Road ostensibly for a meeting over dinner.'

'That's correct.'

Garvan tossed his pen down on the desk. 'But why not just get it over and done with and arrest Hamilton now? What's the point of going through with this fucking charade?'

Hall sucked in his lower lip thoughtfully before answering. 'Tar has his reasons.'

'What reasons?'

'Before we make a move we need to settle,' he hesitated before adding, 'we need to settle a turf war.'

'You mean in British Intelligence?'

'Yes,' Spencer sighed, 'I do.'

Garvan's expression was questioning.

'The SOE,' Spencer explained,' view Louis Durand as one of their own. Let's just say there's been a lot of infighting since his arrival in London. For good reason, they were kept out of the loop about Hamilton and Leader's mission to France.' He pulled a face. 'Let's just say they're none too happy with Robertson at the moment.'

'So why weren't they informed?'

'They didn't need to know. In fact, they've no idea about the scope of the Twenty Committee's work.'

'And I thought it was bad enough at Scotland Yard.'

'It's all about wheels within wheels.'

'It's just an observation, Major, but wouldn't life be easier all round if your team picked Maggie up rather than getting Scotland Yard involved?'

Spencer's attention was drawn fleetingly to the traffic flowing over Westminster Bridge. 'If I had my way Chief Inspector,' he said, distractedly, 'I'd love nothing more than be able to pull the trigger on the bitch and forget all the legal niceties.' He turned round to face Garvan. 'But the Colonel plays it strictly by the book. He has to take in the wider picture, the politics, the games of cat and mouse across Whitehall. At the end of the day, we're constantly being judged by our peers. He has enough on his plate at the moment without complicating matters. Let's just say he wants you on board to keep things neat and tidy.'

Any hope Garvan may have harboured of avoiding the meeting at the Union Jack Club had just been well and truly scuppered.

Spencer added. 'I know you think we're just wasting time delaying the inevitable, but if we move in too soon, and make a hash of it, there's a real risk Maggie might have time to warn Ritter off.'

'But I thought you monitored all their messages.'

'There's a possibility that when she was in France, Ritter might have issued her with an agreed check sequence.'

'Check sequence?'

'An embedded check within a given message, you know,' he tried explaining 'a slight variation in the transmission.'

'I'm sorry Major, I don't understand what you're on about,' Garvan said sharply.

'A check sequence is a means of alerting the Abwehr she's in trouble with MI5. As things stand, we can't be sure Maggie wasn't handed a check sequence. If she was, then we might not be able to pick it up until it was too late, and right now that's the last thing we bloody need.'

'But surely that doesn't just apply to Maggie, what about Joyce Leader, how sure are you about her?'

Spencer considered his answer. 'Well, for a start Jo knows which side her bread's buttered. Remember at the moment Maggie's living life on the edge, and our top priority is to close her down without any further risk to the Double Cross.'

'Will she face trial for murder?'

'We can't afford the publicity, not this time round. There's simply too much at stake. A trial would only serve to bring up Sarah's role at St. James's; it's just not going to happen even in a closed courtroom.'

'Do you want me to arrest her tomorrow evening?'

'Yes, we do.'

'So what are you going to do with her?'

'The plan is to take her into custody, and hold her initially at Latchmere House.'

'And then?'

Spencer shrugged. 'I guess she'll be placed in the Internment Camp on the Isle of Man for the duration of the war, but that's for the Home Office to decide.'

'And what about Ritter, how are you going to explain her disappearance to him?'

'We'll get Joyce to transmit a message to Hamburg saying Scotland Yard has arrested Maggie on charges of espionage.'

'And will they swallow that?'

'There's no reason they shouldn't, and, more importantly, they'll be none the wiser of her ever having been a double-agent. Ritter won't even blink at her passing, and in the meantime Leader will go up even higher in his estimation, and so the game of bluff and counter-bluff will continue as before without any discernible interruption.'

Garvan leaned back in his chair. 'This whole business can't have been easy for you,' he said.

Hall didn't immediately respond. By nature a closed book, unable or unwilling to share his innermost feelings, he found there was something about Garvan that made him comfortable, that he felt able to share the kind of emotions that he instinctively kept buried.

Sarah had pierced that same armour, and had made him vulnerable, and for the first time in his life, he'd willingly laid himself open. Their relationship had been all-consuming. Maybe the intensity had been heightened by circumstance, but there was only one certainty in his life he'd never again experience such an intensity of all-consuming love. Perhaps it was a mark of Garvan's professionalism that he felt able to share his feelings, or perhaps it was a shared empathy because Garvan's life was in such turmoil after the break-up of his marriage.

Spencer breathed deeply, wrestling with his emotions. 'Sarah was someone who allowed me to pour out my feelings without regret, or embarrassment.' He hesitated, 'Quite simply she was the most stunningly beautiful, and kindest woman I'd ever met in my entire life.' He hesitated again, his expression set in stone, and only the tenderness in his voice gave any hint to his feelings. 'I came to the conclusion that my whole life rested on her existence and now without her -' his words trailed off. He turned his back and faced the window as his eyes burnt with tears.

Garvan didn't quite know how best to respond, he found himself feeling a frisson of envy for Spencer's deep-rooted love for Sarah. He even began to wonder if that type of all-consuming love only ever happened once in a lifetime, and then only if you were perhaps very lucky, it wasn't something he'd personally experienced.

Garvan had once imagined himself in love with Joan, even besotted, but those feelings had withered even before the boys were born. Joan turned out to be controlling, openly criticising his every move and had nagged him constantly. In truth, he hadn't exactly been easy to live with either. In hindsight, it had probably been nothing more than a marriage of convenience. At the time, he'd needed stability in his life, a yardstick for his career, a way forward for future promotion. For her part, Joan had wanted security, the social respectability of marriage, children, in fact, everything that goes with it. They both played the game and ultimately paid the price. Thinking about it, they were probably incompatible right from the very start.

The trouble was it hadn't dawned on him until he'd spent an evening with Mackenzie drowning his sorrows about his marriage. Having listened to him long enough, Mac had piped up: "Let's face it, you fell out of love with Joan years ago. Did you stay together for the kids? There can't be any other reason, surely?" Strange as it sounded he hadn't given it much thought before, they were a couple, they were married, life was what it was, an existence of sorts. But Mac's words had struck home hard. He'd been unable to deny it. The only saving grace was that they had two adored sons. For that reason alone he didn't regret marrying Joan, only that they should have parted years ago before she'd felt the need to find somebody else. They'd both wasted too many unhappy years together.

It was Spencer who broke the silence between them catching Garvan completely off guard, as he blurted out 'You're attracted to Joyce Leader, aren't you?'

He narrowed his eyes questioningly, what on earth had made him come out with that? Looking at the expression on Hall's face there didn't seem to be any point prevaricating. 'That obvious is it?' he answered coolly, still not quite sure where the conversation was heading. Was Hall uncertain about his ability to see the job through to the end?

'I first noticed at your flat when you two were standing so close,' Spencer explained, 'and then again yesterday, your reaction on finding out that Maggie Hamilton was the murderer rather than Joyce only confirmed my suspicions.'

'S-Sorry?' Garvan stammered.

'You looked so fucking relieved.' It wasn't quite a smile on Hall's face as he asked, 'am I wrong?'

It wasn't often someone could make Garvan feel uncomfortable, but he couldn't exactly deny it. 'No, you're not wrong, but nothing has happened between us.'

'Oh I know nothing's happened Chief Inspector,' Hall said, almost reassuringly, 'if it had I'd have known about it. All I'll say is tread carefully, very carefully with that one. Just remember when you look at the package, Jo has the sensuality of Greta Garbo and the eyes of Caligula. It's not necessarily a good combination,' he grinned.

Garvan had to agree it was probably a pretty fair description of her. 'Are you talking to me professionally, Major?'

'Not entirely. Once the investigation has been wound up, you'll be a free agent to do as you please, but free or not, you'd be playing with fire if you decided to take things further. You may or may not have realised that Jo is one of our most successful double agents. All I can say is that having a relationship with her would be like playing Russian roulette.'

'Major, I'm not about to dive headlong into any relationship.'

Spencer smiled thinly at him. 'I'll be getting along. If you have any more questions about the meeting, tomorrow just give me a call.' He handed Garvan a card. 'If you can't reach me at the office that's my home number. I'll be there this evening from about eight onwards.'

As Hall closed the door, Garvan reached into the top drawer of his desk, pulled out a bottle of whisky and poured himself a large tot. Tomorrow was going to be a long day; he needed to play it carefully. His main concern was how Maggie would react once she realised the game was up. He picked up the phone. He needed to let Mac and Charteris in on the plan.

The following afternoon Garvan put a .45 revolver in his overcoat pocket.

'You ready?' Mackenzie called from along the corridor.

'Are you armed?' he shouted back.

'Christ yes Guv, I'm not taking any fucking chances tonight.'

Garvan joined him in the corridor. 'Let's get going.' He checked his watch. 'We'll meet up with Leader on the concourse and wait for Maggie's train to arrive and then head for the club. Where's Charteris?'

'He should be at St. James's by now with the Major's men and Bill Lewis from Special Branch. By the time we get to the Union Jack Club, they should be in position.'

'Good, are you ready?' Garvan asked, stuffing a pack of cigarettes in his pocket.

'Ready as I'll ever be,' Mac said, instinctively feeling the pistol was secured safely inside his jacket. 'I do hope Major Hall's thought this through,' he grumbled. 'If Hamilton panics we could be in all sorts of shit in the club.'

The light was already fading by the time they left Scotland Yard and headed along the Embankment. There was a hint of rain in the air, the pavements and cobbled side streets were glistening under the glow of the spluttering gaslights lining the river's edge. The Blackout would soon be in force blanketing London in a deep dark shroud against the Luftwaffe. They walked briskly over Westminster Bridge and fell into an uneasy silence. They turned left into York

Road, then crossed to the other side and headed in the direction of the local market.

'Sad that,' Garvan nodded, in the direction of the severely damaged remains of the Trocadero Theatre.

'Yeah,' Mac said, 'I once saw Max Miller there. He was bloody funny.' The once grand theatre was now little more than a burned-out shell awaiting demolition.

On climbing the main entrance steps leading into Waterloo Station, Garvan glanced up at the impressive stone carving commemorating the First World War. The massive great white figures stared down at the crowds below hurrying through its great portals to catch their early evening commuter trains. On the concourse, Garvan checked his watch against the large station clock suspended from a cavernous glass roof with its distinctive four circular dials.

'Five minutes to spare,' Garvan said, gesturing toward the clock.

Mac scanned the arrivals board. 'Portsmouth Harbour train wasn't it? It's on time, due in at platform 1.'

'There's Leader over there,' Garvan said, pointing toward a small coffee stall.

Mac followed his gaze and saw her sitting on a hard wooden bench. Joyce appeared agitated as she rummaged through a leather handbag. They hung back as she leaned forward to scoop up a canvas gas mask bag from the floor. At the outset of the war, gas masks had been issued to the entire population because the Government believed there was a very real threat that the Luftwaffe might drop poison gas bombs on Britain. Even now there was still an official requirement to carry one, but these days it seemed to happen less than less. The threat of poisonous gas, for now, at least, appeared to have slipped from public consciousness.

Joyce opened the canvas bag, there was certainly no sign of a gas mask inside, it was crammed full of cosmetics and assorted miniature bottles of perfume. Garvan smiled to himself; it hadn't taken women very long to discard their masks and re-invent them as handbags. Joyce dipped her hand inside and retrieved a compact mirror. She clicked it open to re-apply her red lipstick, before suddenly becoming aware of being watched, and instinctively looked around, her eyes searching the crowded concourse. Catching sight of them she allowed a slight smile of recognition to cross her lips. She drained the last dregs of her coffee, gathered up her bags and joined them beneath the clock.

'Good evening gentlemen.'

Mac mentioned to her that she looked tired.

'Too many late nights' Sergeant,' she confessed disarmingly. Trying to burn the candle at both ends catches up with you eventually. It's entirely my own fault.'

It seemed everyone kept unsocial hours during the war; there were countless volunteer Air Raid Wardens, Police and Auxiliary Services who carried out their duties after a full hard day's work. Sleep was often a rare and priceless commodity. On the other hand, Joyce Leader's sleep deprivation was self-inflicted after spending night after night in the heady atmosphere of numerous cocktail bars, nightclubs and Crockford's. But Garvan guessed it probably wasn't just the late nights that were taking their toll on her. Since Sarah's murder, her life had changed out of all recognition. For a start, Joyce knew she was a prime suspect, and the pressure was beginning to build. Spencer had ordered her to attend this evening's meeting, but she knew better than to ask why. It was much safer to keep a low profile and try not to ruffle too many feathers, especially Spencer's.

The Portsmouth Harbour train duly arrived on time at 6.35 sharp; great plumes of smoke and steam spiralled up toward the glass roof. The huge train slowly and noisily chugged to a creaking, grinding halt at the buffers. The sight of the sleek black steam engine transported Garvan to his childhood; when his mother had told him that the hissing beast standing at the platform was a disgruntled dragon spitting fire and steam. To a five-year-old boy, her story had been pure magic, and even now decades later the memory lingered fondly.

The heavy iron gate leading from the platform was pulled open by the uniformed ticket collector, and the passengers began surging through the gate and spilled out onto the concourse. The old engine continued to belch steam as they waited for Hamilton, who must have been sitting in one of the rear carriages as she was one of the last to pass through the barrier. When she did emerge, she was carrying a small black leather briefcase flanked by two uniformed Navy officers.

Garvan observed there was a rather bemused smile playing around Joyce Leader's mouth as she watched Maggie blatantly flirting with her companions. There was no great love lost between them. Maggie handed over her ticket at the barrier and said farewell to the officers. She tip-toed up to kiss each of them in turn on the cheek, waved her goodbyes and hurried across the concourse toward the station clock.

'Sorry,' she called out breathlessly to them, 'I hope I haven't kept you waiting?'

'No, not at all,' Garvan said, 'how was your journey?'

'Fine,' Maggie smiled, 'I stayed near the naval base last night, it had the most spectacular sea views,' she gushed excitedly. 'Well, it would have if there hadn't been this great bloody dirty battleship moored just outside my window.'

'We have a table reservation at the club,' Garvan said, and led the way towards a side exit.

As they threaded their way through the crowded station, there was a tannoy announcement warning commuters the Blackout would be coming into effect in thirty minutes time. They slipped out of the station and crossed Waterloo Bridge Road to the Union Jack Club. The club was a popular venue with servicemen. It was situated conveniently for the fleshpots of the West End, but also gave them somewhere to eat and sleep relatively cheaply. Spencer had pre-booked a table for them in Garvan's name.

Having ordered dinner both detectives kept the conversation light, and the mood relaxed. Mackenzie surreptitiously felt for his pistol needing reassurance that it was still there. As the conversation flowed, Mac settled back in his chair slowly scanning the crowded dining room. He didn't recognise anyone and wondered just how many of Spencer's operatives were designated to keep watch over them. If Maggie suddenly panicked and took flight, things could soon become quite hairy.

'I suppose you must be wondering,' Garvan said, after the main course, 'why we asked to meet up this evening.'

'It crossed my mind,' Joyce said. She lit a cigarette with studied deliberation and blew out a cloud of smoke, her eyes set in a hard, direct gaze.

'This case,' he continued, 'hasn't been the easiest to solve.'

Maggie waved her hand declining Joyce's offer of a cigarette, and said: 'So Chief Inspector do tell us, have you managed to solve Sarah's murder?'

Garvan didn't respond. He reached into his jacket pocket and retrieved the leather-bound notebook that had once belonged to Sarah Davis. Both women instantly recognised the ornate gold clasp. They'd seen her with the book often enough, and since Sarah's death, Spencer had occasionally referred to her notes at meetings. To the best of their knowledge, it contained a list of agents working for St. James's.

They merely exchanged glances but said nothing. Their impassive expressions were completely unreadable. He opened the notebook and placed it down on his placemat.

'Major Hall gave me Sarah's notebook a few weeks ago.' He brushed his fingers over the gold clasp. 'Do you recognise it?'

'We've seen it often enough but what's it to do with Sarah's murder? Joyce quizzed him. 'I was under the impression it contains a list of Double Cross agents.' She toyed thoughtfully with her cigarette holder. 'I guess by now there are probably a few names scored through.' Joyce met Garvan's gaze. She made to speak, but ended up deciding to remain silent; she'd probably said enough for now.

'Sarah's notebook initially provided us with our only tangible clue to her murder, our only real piece of evidence.' Garvan placed the palm of his right hand on the open book. 'You see, not long before Sarah died she received a somewhat garbled message from a close colleague of Roman Czerniawski. I think you both know him very well.'

'Who is it?' Maggie asked.

'Louis Durand.' Garvan said, looking steadily at them. 'You do know him, don't you?' The challenging edge to his voice wasn't lost on either woman.

'Of course, we do,' Maggie said her expression unreadable. If she was feeling uneasy, it certainly wasn't showing. 'So what was so important about the message from Louis?' she pressed.

Garvan raised his hand from the notebook. 'We now know that Sarah was murdered for one reason and one reason only.'

'For God's sake,' Joyce snapped at him impatiently, 'put us out of our misery and tells us!'

'Quite by chance the Interallie stumbled across the identity of a triple agent called Nicolette. As soon as he was able, Durand passed the information over to London for Sarah's personal attention. The only problem was the message wasn't only incomplete, but was intercepted by the Abwehr, and in effect signed Sarah's death warrant.' He allowed them enough time to digest the information. 'You have to understand that the Gestapo were hard on Durand's heels. When Sarah was murdered, MI5 still hadn't been able to identify Nicolette positively.' He paused thoughtfully, allowing his words to sink in, before adding. 'After her death Major Hall went through Sarah's notes with a fine toothcomb, piecing together every last scrap of Intelligence from Paris, Berlin and Hamburg. In fact, he read everything she'd written in the weeks leading up to her death. He eventually found the message from Durand.' Garvan drummed his fingers on the notebook. 'It was short on details, but nevertheless provided us with the one vital clue we had to the killer's identity.

'Agent Nicolette,' Maggie said. 'Is that it? To be honest with you Chief Inspector, it doesn't seem to be an awful lot to go on. There were any number of double agents on the ground in France at the time, there always are.' Maggie was playing it cool, and to his mind still confident that he didn't have enough evidence to prove her guilt.

'Nicolette,' Joyce mused, drawing heavily on her cigarette, 'why did they call her that, is it significant?'

'My understanding is that Captain Ritter or should I call him Dr Rantzau thought it amusing to give his agent a pretty French name in honour of her betrayal of the Interallie.'

'So we're going back now some three, or four months,' Joyce said, curiously. A furrow creasing her brow as she slowly turned to face Maggie. Her eyes set icily on her colleague. 'So what do you think?'

Garvan was curious. Leader's glacial expression appeared to make Hamilton uneasy.

'I think,' Maggie said at length, 'that if the Chief Inspector had concrete proof of Nicolette's identity, he'd have made an arrest by now.'

Maggie was unaware that Louis Durand was threading his way across the dining room to their table.

As he placed his hand on her shoulder, she spun around and looked startled. She faltered, the tension around the table now was almost tangible, you could almost taste it, smell it. The slightly built Durand was smiling down at her, his thin, gaunt face still outwardly, at least, retaining an open kindly expression. But it was edged with a hint of self-satisfaction. He nodded briefly in greeting to Joyce, and then pulled up a chair from a neighbouring table.

'Hello Maggie,' he said to her in a deceptively soft voice.

Eying him nervously, she reached down for her handbag and retrieved a cigarette. When she lit it, her hands were visibly shaking under his steady, watchful gaze.

'Oh my God, what have you done?' Joyce snarled venomously and leaned toward her rattled fellow agent, their faces almost touching. 'You've not only endangered the Interallie but our lives as well, you stupid fucking little bitch!' Joyce was seething with anger. Renowned for having a short fuse at the best of times, she was now bubbling with a mixture of emotions, a red mist had descended upon the normally ice-cold blonde. 'How could you murder Sarah, tell me, how could you do it?' she demanded angrily.

Maggie tried to retain, at least outwardly a display of sangfroid and looked away from Joyce quite unable to hold her gaze. Durand folded his arms. Vengeance was a dish best served cold. He took his time, but when he spoke his voice was quiet, his tone calculating.

'Tell me one thing Mademoiselle, have you ever wondered how many people have been tortured or killed as a result of your treachery? More to the point do you even care? He fell silent. Was it pity or disgust in his eyes, Garvan wasn't quite sure which. 'Do you sleep easy at night, Mademoiselle?'

Hamilton's mouth was already dry, her heart pounding so heavily that it was echoing in her ears. She started to feel light-headed and wanted nothing more than the ground to swallow her whole. Louis with his feigned softly spoken gentleness made her feel uneasy. This small, intelligent Frenchman had finally sealed her fate. There was now no escaping the catastrophe that her betrayal had caused, and perhaps worse of all at some point she'd have to explain herself to Spencer Hall - now that did frighten her.

'The game's up,' Durand smiled thinly, 'but I'm curious about one thing.' She was tense, irritable and tired.

'About what?' she snapped back at him.

'As one of Colonel Robertson's Double Cross agents you were already living on borrowed time, the noose was tightening around that pretty little neck of yours, so what made you risk everything, what did Hugo Bleicher offer you other than his bed?'

'My life,' Maggie replied in a breathless whisper.

'Then it was too cheap, too cheap by half!' Durand said sharply, and shaking his head in disgust. 'I know for a fact that neither Ritter nor Bleicher suspected you of anything, let alone of having been turned by British Intelligence.'

She looked at Louis, her eyes consumed by fear. 'Hugo lied,' she explained rapidly, if unconvincingly, 'he said I'd been accused by an Interallie Agent the Gestapo had picked up.'

'Accused you of what exactly?'

'Of being a British Agent.' Maggie sobbed tearfully. 'What was I to do?'

'But there were only two members of the Interallie, who knew of your involvement with British Intelligence, apart from Roman Czerniawski, I was the only other person.'

'Precisely, after Roman's arrest, he must have buckled under the Gestapo's interrogation.'

'But you were seen wining and dining with Hugo Bleicher long before Roman's arrest. So why was that? Your trysts weren't exactly business meetings; we know that much. No, it had gone way beyond your remit from St. James's. You turned, you reverted to kind, a traitor not only to the Interallie but perhaps worse of all, to your own country.' He looked at her with utter contempt.

Tears began trickling down Maggie's face; she didn't respond to his accusations.

'Don't waste your tears on me!' Durand sighed wearily.

She reached into her handbag and retrieved a handkerchief, dabbed at her eyes and then screwed it up tightly in her fist.

'You see at first we weren't entirely sure what had happened,' Louis went on, 'we knew the network was in turmoil, of course, we did, but there again it had been for a little while even before your arrival. But now things were moving fast, much faster than we'd expected. You were spotted at Maxims.' He bestowed an almost pitiful look on her. 'I think that was very careless of you.'

'Why?' she pouted, almost petulantly.

'Since your Third Reich friends marched down the Champs-Elysees they've made Maxim's their favourite watering hole. For us, the Interallie it was also a golden opportunity to place agents in the restaurant, waiters, bar staff, it didn't matter as long as they supplied us with information. Under the circumstances, you were naive to believe we wouldn't keep you under close surveillance.'

'But aren't you missing a point,' she argued fiercely.

'What's that Mademoiselle?'

'Why wouldn't I be invited to Maxim's? As far as Hugo was concerned I was an Abwehr agent!'

Louis threw up his hands in despair. 'Sacré Bleu, your mission was to infiltrate the Interallie not to fuck your Nazi bosses. Miss Leader played by the script, kept to the remit. But you were all over Bleicher, like how do I say, éruption.' Durand placed his head in his hands, desperately searching for the right words. 'Yes- yes you were over him like a rash, I'm not sure how you say it in English, is that correct? Garvan nodded with a slight smile.

'The head waiter was one of our agents. He said you were very affectionate with one another, kissing, touching that, you were obviously lovers. You cannot deny it.'

Garvan tried gauging Maggie's reaction to Durand's quietly-spoken onslaught. She shakily wiped the tears from her face. There didn't seem any point in prolonging the inevitable, Durand was quietly, and systematically destroying her. Maggie picked up her handbag fumbling for a clean handkerchief. Her mind was racing in panic, she felt claustrophobic, almost as if the room was somehow closing in on her. She needed to get out of the club.

'Are you going to arrest me?' she asked, almost pleadingly of Garvan, and blowing her nose into the handkerchief.

'Major Hall has a car waiting for us in Mepham Street. It's just over the road from here.'

Maggie was tense. 'So you're not arresting me then?' she persisted.

It was obvious that she would much rather be placed under formal arrest than the prospect of being handed over to Spencer's custody.

'All in good time Miss Hamilton,' Garvan tried assuring her, 'we'll complete the formalities' but not here.'

She was looking at him warily, uncertain if he was lying. 'I just assumed you'd rather not be arrested in the middle of a crowded dining room.'

Joyce met Garvan's eyes and said bluntly 'I think we should stay here, or, at least, wait in the foyer until Spencer arrives. What do you think Louis?'

Durand wasn't about to be drawn. 'I think that decision must rest with the Chief Inspector.'

Joyce had been hoping for some moral support from Durand. She was uneasy, sensing that Maggie might be planning one last-ditch bid for freedom, for right now she had nothing else to lose.

In fact, the only thing Maggie wanted to do was buy herself a little more time before being handed over into Spencer's care. Right from the beginning of his secondment from the SOE to the Twenty Committee, he'd proved to be her nemesis, the one person who'd seen right through her, the one person who'd dared question Lieutenant Colonel Stephens report and the decision of the committee to endorse 'Tin Eyes' findings.

He alone had cast doubts about her commitment and reliability as a double agent. Hall had always been the consummate professional, gifted, highly articulate, and toughened soldier who longed to return to the Special Operations Executive, and to active service rather than confined to a desk in St. James's. She also knew full well how much he'd loved Sarah Davis. Maggie was terrified that

Spencer might just take it into his head to hang the consequences and kill her outright. He had little enough respect for red tape or convention at the best of times. And if he did choose to shoot her dead in revenge for taking Sarah's life what would the Twenty Committee do in response? They might perhaps give his knuckles a rap, but that would be an end to the matter.

Maggie nervously glanced around the dining table and decided she'd rather endure the shame of arrest in public than be handed over to Hall and his MI5 cohorts.

'Where is Spencer?' She asked Garvan.

If only, he knew. He scanned the dining room, but there was still no sign of him. Where the hell he had got to?

'He's outside,' Garvan lied, disguising his unease. Coming to his feet, he shook Durand's hand and said. 'Thank you so much for all your help Monsieur.'

Louis smiled but remained seated. Joyce insisted on joining them, and there was no time to argue with her. He just wanted to escort Maggie out of the dining room as quickly as possible. He'd half expected to find Spencer waiting for them in the foyer, but there was still no sign of him. Garvan was now getting agitated; this wasn't going to plan. He'd promised to keep an eye on things in the dining room, but had apparently failed to put in an appearance; something must have gone wrong, but what?

They stepped out of the club into the cool night air and were greeted by a steady drizzle of fine rain. The sky was an eerie flaming red as fires burned all along the waterfront. Bombs screamed and exploded, rumbling like rolling thunder in an electrical storm, interspersed by the monotonous drone of the bombers. By the look of things, the Luftwaffe were concentrating their efforts on the nearby Surrey Docks.

Garvan stayed close to Maggie as they crossed Waterloo Road and down Mepham Street, a dreary, narrow side turning flanked by railway arches that were now used for storage. The rain had left the narrow cobbled street slippery underfoot. Seeing a black saloon car parked up ahead Garvan felt a sudden wave of relief; grateful that things might get finally back on track.

His relief was somewhat short-lived. Mepham Street seemed strangely quiet, and apart from the waiting vehicle, there was no other visible sign of Spencer's men. They were out on a limb, where the fuck was he? Garvan thought to himself, desperately hoping that someone would step out from the shadows to meet them.

Spencer had in fact positioned himself in the dining room an hour before their arrival at the Union Jack Club. He'd deliberately kept his distance, and at one point had even toyed with the idea of intervening sooner than planned, that is, right up until the point Maggie had retrieved a fresh handkerchief from her handbag to supposedly blow her nose. From his vantage point near the head waiter, he'd noticed her check out the revolver inside the bag. Spencer had immediately gestured his agents to remain seated, he couldn't run the risk of Maggie panicking and shooting her way out of the club.

Since Durand's arrival, she'd taken on the look of someone who was torn between fight and flight, unable to move or think properly. Hall kept out of sight not wishing to spook her any more than was necessary.

As they neared the parked saloon, Maggie was slightly ahead of them; on reaching the car, she stopped dead in the middle of the road, reached into her handbag, and spun round to face them.

Garvan braced himself and called out. 'What's wrong?' As he spoke, he saw the revolver gripped in her right hand. He stood stock still staring down the barrel of the gun.

'You can't escape,' Mac found himself saying as if by rote.

'What's the alternative,' she spat at him waving the pistol in the air, 'I've nothing to lose, have I, Sergeant?'

'What about your life?' Garvan suggested to her evenly.

She let out a strangled laugh. 'Don't you understand Chief Inspector you can't honestly believe they'll allow me to walk away from this lot, do you?'

Garvan needed to buy time and needed to keep her talking. 'Why not just give me the gun, there's been enough bloodshed already?'

Maggie raised the pistol. Garvan's heart was pounding, his mouth dried up. Where the fuck was the bastard, where was Spencer, he promised to be here? He needed to pacify her, to think on his feet, but knew that nothing short of a miracle was going to work; that is apart from making some suicidal lunge for the gun. He was rapidly running out of ideas.

'So was it you who broke into my flat? His voice sounded deceptively calm. 'What were you hoping to find?'

'I was looking for the notebook.'

'Sarah's notebook. How did you know I had it?'

'Henryk Nowak mentioned it to me.'

'Why would he be that damned stupid?'

'He was drunk. He's always drunk these days. His drinking is getting way out of hand; he wasn't thinking straight otherwise he'd never have told me.'

'So was that the only reason you broke into my flat?'

'The fact Spencer had passed you the notebook meant it was important. I didn't know why, so I decided to see if I could find out.'

'But why did you think I'd take it home?'

'It was an outside chance, but I needed to know.'

'How did you break in?' he pressed.

'Learning how to use a radio wireless wasn't the only thing the Abwehr taught us, I picked the lock.'

'So why did you open the windows in the bedroom?'

'My perfume,' she said, quietly.

'Perfume?'

'When you interviewed me at the office in Victoria, you mentioned that my perfume was distinctive, you asked me what it was. Do you remember?'

'Shalimar,' he recalled.

'I couldn't run the risk of leaving any trace of it behind.'

'What the hell did you hit me with?'

'I panicked,' she said, 'when you came back earlier than expected, I hit you with the butt of my gun.'

Joyce took a step forward and angrily yelled at her. 'You stupid fucking little bitch!'

Garvan closed his eyes in despair. All hope of trying to keep things on an even keel were blown out of the water by Leader's angry outburst. Maggie nervously pointed the revolver toward her colleague and took aim. Without thinking Mackenzie made a lunge to grab the weapon, but he wasn't fast enough. There was a bright flash followed by a chillingly loud report, her right hand jerking up with the force of the kickback. Mac froze to the spot; his adrenaline took hold, and everything around him seemed as if it was moving in slow-motion. He felt a sharp, searing pain, and collapsed onto the damp cobbles with a sickening thud. For a split second, Maggie hesitated, then turned on her heels and started running for her life along Mepham Street toward York Road.

As Garvan knelt down beside his stricken colleague two men ran past them after Hamilton. He gently turned his friend over onto his back.

'For Christ's sake whatever you do, don't fucking die on me? Where did she get you?' he asked, anxiously.

Mac gasped. 'My shoulder, the bitch shot me in the shoulder.'

'Thank God,' Joyce said sinking to her knees.

'What d'ye mean thank God?' he spluttered.

'She didn't mean to kill you.'

'You could have fucking fooled me!' he grimaced as Garvan carefully opened his shirt to expose the wound. Even in the darkness, the crimson blood stain showed clearly against the white shirt. He set about trying to stem the flow of blood with his handkerchief and a scarf that Joyce handed him.

'She wanted to kill me,' Joyce said, softly. 'If you hadn't made a grab for the gun I'd be dead by now.'

'I've always been a bit ham-fisted luv,' Mac gasped, his breathing becoming increasingly erratic, 'f-fancy stepping in the way of a sodding bullet.'

'I've called for an ambulance.'

Hearing the calm, familiar voice of Spencer Hall Garvan glanced over his shoulder. Jack Charteris was standing beside him.

'Where the hell have you been?'

'Believe it or not, I've been trying to keep you alive. I was in two minds whether to step in at the club.'

'So what stopped you?'

'The moment Maggie reached into her handbag and I saw her loosen the clip on her gun. If we'd rushed into the dining room, she'd have ended up taking pot shots. It was a calculated risk.'

'Yes, you calculated, and we took the risks!' Garvan snorted. He knew Hall's hands were tied, but he needed to blame someone for what had happened, and right now Spencer was the obvious choice.

'What about me!' Joyce said, rounding on Hall as well. She was back on her feet by now. 'I may be many things, but to think that you believed I killed Sarah!'

'Jo,' Spencer replied smoothly, 'not now, I've no time for self-pity, stay here with Sergeant Charteris and look after Mackenzie until the ambulance arrives.'

She backed down; he was right, without another word she returned to Mac's side and took over from Garvan to apply pressure to the wound.

'Let's get going,' Hall barked at Garvan.

'Where are we going?'

'Get in the car I'll drive, we have radio contact with St. James's, it works in the same way as the Met system, the only difference being that your cars are linked to – to.' Spencer couldn't quite remember.

'They're linked to the Information Room on Victoria Embankment.'

'Yes, well, whatever. We had a car already positioned in York Road, so hopefully she can't have got too far. With a bit of luck, they may have picked her up already.'

As Garvan opened the door of the saloon, he heard Mac grumbling to Joyce. 'You know what's going to happen luv, they're gonna make me lie bare arsed on some bleeding hospital trolley all night.'

He smiled to himself and clicked the door shut. By the time they'd reached the end of the road, one of Spencer's operatives was running back along Mepham Street; he darted over to the car. Hall wound down the window.

273

'Did you get her?' he barked.

'No sir, she was ruddy lucky, though, when she ran out into York Road there was a tram hurtling along the tracks heading toward the terminus at Kingsway. How she didn't get herself killed God only knows, she almost fell beneath the damn thing.'

Shit!' Hall grunted and thumped the steering wheel hard.

Before they turned out of Mepham Street, an ambulance swept pass from nearby St. Thomas's Hospital. Garvan glanced anxiously over his shoulder as it pulled to a halt, Spencer put his foot down, and they hurtled off into York Road.

Chapter 17

It must have been the sheer surge of adrenaline that enabled Maggie Hamilton to leap onto the tram as it rattled along York Road. Having run the length of Mepham Street she had just enough of a head start on Hall's men to make it. Maggie heard them shouting at her to stop, to give herself up. They were gaining ground fast; it would be only a matter of time before they caught up.

As the tram approached it was a now or never split second decision - Maggie leapt toward the fast oncoming tram. It was an almost suicidal decision. Even Spencer's operatives pulled up sharp and looked on in horror convinced she'd end up mangled beneath the tram.

Propelled by an intense adrenaline rush, she knew there was just the one chance to make it, and lunged forward in a bid to grab hold of the hand rail on the rear platform. In reaching out Maggie stumbled and almost fell. Somehow she just managed to retain her grasp, but caught her foot on the lower step, and the momentum shot her headlong into the carriage, where she crashed to the floor in a dishevelled heap.

Maggie hauled herself up onto the nearest seat gasping for breath. Her lungs felt as if they were burning up after having run so hard. She still clung tenaciously to her shoulder bag as if her very life depended on it. Resting the bag on her knees, she slumped forward trying to regain her breath. Spencer's agents had been within a hair's breadth of grabbing hold of her. She sat up and glanced nervously through the rear window. For now, at least, they'd lost contact with her and had faded into the pitch darkness of York Road. She'd twisted her left wrist badly but otherwise had managed to survive pretty well unscathed apart from the odd scratch and bruise. Maggie had bought herself a little time, a small amount of breathing space, but nothing more.

Sitting on the tram, it began crossing her mind that she ought to have given herself up in Mepham Street. Why hadn't she? Probably through a mixture of panic and fear, she simply wasn't thinking straight. Maggie closed her eyes re-living the moment Mackenzie had stepped into her line of fire. For pity's sake, she'd never intended him any harm, far from it. On the other hand, she had meant to kill Joyce Leader, it was a shame he'd taken the bullet for her. Maggie had never warmed to the woman, had never liked her right from the off; she was arrogant, self-opinionated and a worthless social gadfly. If she was going down for the murder of Sarah Davis, then it had occurred to Maggie then there was nothing to lose by adding Joyce Leader to the tally. As she began to cry, she was oblivious to the tram's conductress who was making her way steadily along the length of the vehicle.

'What yer doing darling, we're not in service,' she called out clinging to a grab rail.

Hearing her voice, Maggie almost leapt out of her skin. 'I – I'm sorry,' she stuttered looking up at the woman, 'what did you say?'

'We're not in service luv.' The conductress gestured over her shoulder. 'And you could 'ave got yourself killed back there.' She sat down beside her on the long back seat. 'What's wrong darling?'

Maggie blew her nose.

'Me driver said it looked like a couple of blokes were chasing you across York Road, is that right, were they?'

'Yes - yes they were.'

'We'll call the police when we get to the station.'

'No, it's very kind of you, but there's no need I'll be fine.' As the tram turned and started to rattle its way through the entrance of the tramway tunnel beneath Waterloo Bridge,

Maggie looked startled. 'Where are we going?' she asked, nervously.

'To the Kingsway Underpass near Holborn to the tramway Station, we're going off duty luv, I told you we're not in service.'

The tram lurched underground swaying even more violently and noisily than it had at Street level. Once free from the Blackout the internal lights flickered into life. Maggie blinked against the sudden brightness and found herself face to face with the conductress, who turned out to be a plump, middle-aged woman with grey hair swept back into a neat bun.

'Take this,' she said, offering Hamilton a clean handkerchief, 'you look as if you need a fresh one. Are you sure we can't call the police for you up at the Station?'

Maggie accepted the handkerchief and shook her head. 'Thank you, but no, I only live a short distance from the Station.'

'So why were they chasing you?'

'If you must know we'd had an argument, nothing serious, it just got a bit out of hand that's all,' she lied.

'If you ask me, darling it was more than just a bit out of hand, we thought you were a goner back there. How you managed to cling on to the grab rail and not kill yourself God only knows.'

The conductress remained at her side aimlessly chatting until they covered the short distance to the tramway Station. Maggie thanked the woman and stepped out of the tram onto the platform, then followed the signs to the connecting passageway to Holborn Tube Station.

On reaching the concourse, she stopped dead in her tracks. The place was heaving with people still heading down to the platforms to shelter for the night. Knowing Spencer's operatives' would never risk a confrontation in such a crowded place it crossed Maggie's mind that perhaps she ought to remain inside until morning. They knew she was armed, and the last thing MI5 wanted was to have a shooting match on a busy platform.

Maggie took a sharp intake of breath, a little uncertain what to do next. Even if she decided to stay the night, what then, at some point in the morning she'd still have to leave and break cover? Remaining at the station was only delaying the inevitable. The reality was, there was nowhere left to hide, her situation was futile.

People jostled past her carrying bundles of bedding stuffed under their arms. They were all heading in one direction, down into the bowels of Holborn to escape the Blitz. The tunnels were among the deepest on the entire network and had long proved a magnet for Londoners seeking refuge. There was a huge demand for spaces. Literally hundreds of people would spend each night on the platforms. Since the outbreak of war, London Underground had helpfully put up signs directing people toward the designated Air Raid Shelters.

Even the terrible disaster at Balham Tube Station still hadn't stopped people seeking refuge in the London Underground. The catastrophe had occurred when a semi-armour piercing bomb managed to penetrate almost 32 feet below ground. The bomb exploded just above a cross passage between two platforms. It was rumoured there'd been about five hundred people sheltering at the time. Inside the station, rescuers discovered a terrible scene of panic and carnage. Most of the fatalities were caused by drowning when the blast tore apart watertight doors. The explosion fractured water and sewerage mains, causing a terrifying gush of water. To begin with the Government tried suppressing the news fearing a knock-on effect on public morale, but, in the end, word of mouth had made their well-meaning attempts entirely futile.

The Balham tragedy had little lasting effect, though. Every Tube Station on the network still remained filled to capacity. In comparison to other public shelters, the Tube still provided the safest haven from the bombing.

Maggie was still trying to make up her mind what to do when she caught sight of a familiar face. Wing Commander Hugh Dickinson had already spotted her. He was a tall, striking man, with a sleek mop of dark hair, and an equally dark moustache, a remnant of his RAF career before his secondment to the Double Cross team. She recalled meeting him once at the Ritz. He'd been accompanied by Tar Robertson for some meeting or other. Maggie braced herself, half expecting him to take her to one side, but for some reason, he kept his distance and allowed Maggie to leave the station unhindered.

Outside the main entrance, she hung back, taking the time to scan the crowds, but apart from Hugh Dickinson, she didn't recognise anyone else. Should she return to her flat? She wasn't quite sure. But the longer Maggie stood outside the station, the more she resigned herself to the fact, there wasn't any point in trying to evade them, there was nowhere left to hide.

Setting off down High Holborn, Dickinson followed her, again keeping a respectful distance. They must be under orders, Maggie decided, Spencer's orders not to intercept her. She crossed the road over to Red Lion Square. A colleague had now joined him. Maggie smiled to herself; it didn't matter how many agents were tracking her, she was simply too tired, and too exhausted to carry on.

Spencer drove towards Waterloo Bridge. 'There's the radio transmitter,' he said sharply, gesturing in a stabbing motion toward the middle consul. 'Just pick it up. The phone's linked directly to St. James's.'

Garvan hesitated. 'Do I have to press anything?'

'It gets straight through, just pick the damn thing up. Ask the office if they know where she is.'

Garvan picked up the receiver. It crackled into life; a woman answered, told him Maggie had escaped by clambering aboard an out of service tram that had terminated at the Holborn tramway underpass in Kingsway. By all accounts, she was lucky not to have been killed.

'Holborn?' Spencer repeated questioningly, as he drove toward the Aldwych.

Garvan replaced the receiver. 'What the hell is she playing at do you know?'

Hall put his foot down hard on the accelerator. 'I guess she's heading for her flat, she lives in Red Lion Square.'

'Perhaps she's finally realised there's no point prolonging the agony. It's a pity she didn't think that way earlier.'

'Maggie's always been slow on the uptake,' Spencer grunted, trying to concentrate on the pitch black road ahead.

As they hurtled over Waterloo Bridge, Garvan found himself automatically gripping the sides of his seat. With their headlamps adjusted to shine feebly down on the road, it was practically impossible to see anything travelling in the opposite direction until it was almost too late. Any pedestrian stepping out into their path wouldn't have had a cat in hell's chance of them stopping in time. Even at the best of times driving through the Blackout brought its own peculiar risks. It wasn't unknown for vehicles to plummet down unseen bomb craters. Clutching onto the passenger seat for grim death Garvan's growing sense of unease almost validated itself when Spencer was forced to swerve, and only narrowly missed an oncoming car in The Strand. Hall hardly flinched and rammed the accelerator pedal back to the floor.

'Christ almighty that was close,' Garvan gasped.

'Their fault, they were the wrong side of the fucking road!' Spencer grunted.

'Are you sure?'

'Course I am!'

They turned down Kingsway past the tramway terminus, and then took a hard right into High Holborn, and then drove the short distance to Red Lion Square.

They drew up outside what had once been a rather grand Georgian house. It was now converted into flats over five floors. Waiting for them at the bottom of the building's shallow steps was Hugh Dickinson. As he leaned forward, Spencer wound down the window.

'What's happened?'

'Sir,' he said, brusquely, 'it was lucky the tram was terminating at Kingsway. We spotted her on the concourse of Holborn Station. Fortunately, by the time she arrived London Underground had turned the rails off for the night so she couldn't give us the slip by jumping on a tube. I kept my distance as I didn't want to spook her again.'

'Did she see you?'

'Almost immediately,' he admitted.

'Where is she now?'

Dickinson gestured up toward the window on the first floor. 'In her flat.'

'Is she alone?'

'Yes sir, Eldridge is in the corridor just in case she decides to do another runner.'

'Stay here Hugh.' He looked to Garvan. 'Come on let's get this over and done with.'

Up on the first floor, Captain John Eldridge was loitering outside the flat. Spencer nodded briefly at him, and then knocked on the door. He waited for an answer, but none was forthcoming. He reached into his coat pocket and retrieved a bunch of keys.

'You came prepared,' Garvan remarked.

'We always have duplicate keys,' he explained and let himself into the flat.

Garvan had half expected to find Maggie had topped herself rather than face the consequences. But as Hall opened the door, to his surprise Maggie was sitting on a window seat overlooking the square, nervously sipping a ridiculously large glass of brandy.

Spencer quietly closed the door. She didn't acknowledge their presence. Her gaze remained fixed on the street below. The radio was blaring, the room vibrating to the strains of a dance band. Maggie slowly swivelled around to face them, her cheeks red and blotchy. There was a sullen confrontational scowl on her face. Spencer turned the music down.

'Disappointed?' she snapped at him, 'were you hoping I'd save you the trouble and kill myself?'

Garvan wondered how many brandies she'd managed to sink since she got home.

'Disappointed? Why should I be?' Hall said, in a deadpan voice. He removed his gloves and threw them down on a mahogany bureau, his gaze locked onto Maggie's. 'I just want an explanation. I just want to know why you did it. Along the way you ended up destroying so many lives, here and in France.'

Her grip tightened around the glass. She lowered her gaze searching for the right words. 'I don't expect for one second you'll believe me, but as God is my witness, I never set out for any of this to happen. I panicked, I - I just didn't think it through,' she stammered.

Spencer calmly removed a gun from the pocket of his jacket and put it beside his gloves on the bureau. He wasn't about to take any chances. The move was made with studied deliberation.

'Colonel Robertson has asked the SOE to investigate how many agents were arrested as a result of your treachery.' He stared at her. 'When things started to go wrong in France, and you began to get out of your depth, why on earth didn't you come to either me or Sarah for help? We might have managed to salvage something.'

Maggie looked genuinely horrified. 'What do you mean?' she cried. 'Admit I'd slept with Hugo Bleicher, and become a triple agent?' She let out a nervous, fractious laugh. 'Christ almighty you'd have shot me on the spot!'

Hall couldn't deny the thought wouldn't have crossed his mind, in fact, it had never been far from his mind, but Robertson and Sarah had always held him back. They would have tried to salvage something out of the mess she'd made for herself. His reply, when it came, was measured, and under control.

'At the very least we might have helped a few Interallie agents go to ground and avoid being arrested and tortured.'

She eyed him warily before taking another gulp of brandy. 'By that time, I was already dead on my feet as far as you were concerned. I'd dug myself into a hole and was still digging. When I came back from France it crossed my mind whether I ought to own up, confess what had happened with Bleicher.' She closed her eyes and shook her head. 'You have to understand,' she said, pleadingly, 'I just couldn't bear to face either of you or the Colonel. To put it bluntly, I was too fucking afraid and ashamed of what had happened in

Paris to own up. With every day that passed I was sinking further and further into the shit, and as far as I was concerned there was simply no escape, no excuse for what had happened.'

'Personally Maggie, I think you were more concerned about saving your own neck!'

She didn't respond.

Hall perched himself on the arm of the couch beside the bureau. He crossed his legs and lit a cigarette. 'What actually happened Maggie?' he asked her, his tone was softer now, 'It wasn't as if you didn't understand what you were doing.' He sucked heavily on the cigarette. 'When Patreaus recruited you back in 1938, I'll give you the benefit of the doubt that you were at best naive. But what in God's name possessed you to bed, Hugo Bleicher?'

'I told you, I panicked!' she sobbed at him, 'I was scared rigid the Gestapo would discover the truth, discover I was working for British Intelligence.' Maggie steeled herself to meet his questioning gaze; her face arranged in a tight, perfunctory smile. She claimed unconvincingly that Ritter had dropped various hints the Abwehr were already dubious about her commitment to the Reich.

Spencer raised his hand to silence her. 'Please don't insult me with that crap!' he said, dismissively. 'Ritter has never once questioned the quality of your transmissions. We know for a fact that almost every single one was passed to Berlin. That's all the validation we needed to know they were falling for your transmissions hook, line and sinker.'

Maggie lowered her gaze and traced her index finger around the rim of her brandy glass. 'Bleicher singled me out straight away,' she said. 'He seemed wary of Joyce. She probably frightened the life out of him.'

Spencer shot a look at Garvan. 'He's not alone there then, is he? I can't think of many men who'd be brave enough to take that one on.'

Garvan smiled lamely in response to Hall's barbed comment.

'I'll be honest with you,' Maggie said.

'Well, that'll be a novelty!' Hall snapped.

'If you must know I was flattered by Bleicher's interest.'

Spencer smirked at her. 'What's the saying, power tends to corrupt, and absolute power corrupts absolutely.'

She stared through him and breathed deeply before focusing her attention on Garvan. 'Bleicher and I got on well right from the start, but there certainly wasn't any great master plan on my part that we should become lovers.'

'So how did it all go so disastrously wrong?' Garvan asked her.

'As you know our brief was to get close to Ritter. I think we're all agreed it paid off,' she said, shooting a questioning look at Spencer.

He stared through her without responding.

'And Hugo Bleicher,' Garvan queried, 'there's getting close, and there's getting close, and you went way beyond your instructions from London.'

'It's true we hadn't seriously factored him into the equation. I think even Spencer would agree, that in the grand scheme of things, he was considered important but certainly not in the same league as Ritter.'

Hall still didn't respond.

'I thought London would be pleased,' she said, lamely, 'that I'd managed to gain his confidence.'

Hall folded his arms and pulled a face. 'But sleeping with Bleicher and betraying the Interallie network wasn't in the equation, it certainly wasn't in your brief. Why don't you just face up to the fact you screwed up Maggie and screwed up big time?'

'You don't have to tell me that!' she snapped at him angrily. 'I never went to Paris with the intention of betraying either British Intelligence or the Interallie, far from it. As I said things simply got out of hand with Bleicher, I just got carried away.'

'Carried away, is that what you call it, you ended up responsible for the arrests of at least six Interallie agents, and the death of Sarah!'

She drained the brandy. Garvan picked up a cut glass decanter from the sideboard and without thinking poured her another.

'Let's face it,' she said, defensively, 'British Intelligence sanctioned our mission to France, it was St. James's who wanted us to play along with Ritter's instructions, rather than run the risk of the Germans finding out we'd already become double agents.'

'So it's my fault now, is it? I never denied the plan wasn't risky, it was a huge gamble,' Spencer said honestly, 'but the long term benefits far outweighed the short-term risks, and if you hadn't gone rogue in Paris, then the mission would have been a complete success.'

Her grip tightened around the glass, but his accusation wouldn't draw her.

'You were spoon fed information about the Interallie, and deliberately kept on the periphery of the network. The only trouble was you made it your business to dig deeper, to pass on every snippet of intelligence you gained to Bleicher. You won't believe me, but I do understand why you were afraid of being thrown into the lion's den in France. I accept there was an outside chance that your cover might have been blown, but you are forgetting one important thing Maggie - both of you were sitting pretty. Outwardly, you were trusted Abwehr agents operating on Ritter's personal orders to try and infiltrate the French Resistance.' He reached for an ashtray. 'Neither Bleicher or Ritter had any reason whatsoever to distrust either of you.' He waited for a reaction from her, but there was none. 'Fear alone,' he said, 'didn't send you into the bed of Hugo Bleicher. There were other reasons.'

'Like what?' she demanded with a scowl.

'Your fascism, your political beliefs? Wasn't that the real reason you jumped ship again, risking everything, even your own life?

He'd suddenly hit a raw nerve. Rather than deny the accusation, Maggie suddenly launched into a passionate defence of her father's political beliefs.

'Back in the thirties, my father and I fought for peace, for appeasement. Tell me Major; was that such a very wrong thing to do?'

'You fought to appease a totalitarian state where all opposition is crushed ruthlessly. In Germany and its satellites, there's no such thing as freedom of speech, is that what you really want for Britain? Is that what your father wants for Britain?'

'The Nazi Government brought their country back from the brink,' Maggie countered, 'restored prosperity to the country, brought an end to mass unemployment. Don't you understand they gave the people hope!' she cried, passionately.

'I don't deny any of that. But while your father and his pals in the Right Club were supposedly fighting for peace in the thirties, their friend Hitler was rearming Germany. He wasn't exactly planning some bloody picnic party but world domination. Do you still not understand that?'

Maggie lowered her gaze from him, either unable or unwilling to answer.

'And what about Sarah, when did you decide to kill her?' Spencer demanded angrily, 'where did she fit into your master plan?'

Maggie twisted round on the window seat, moved the net curtain aside and watched two more vehicles draw up outside. She turned back and said quietly. 'When the Abwehr intercepted Durand's message, you know full well what happened next. They ordered me to kill Sarah and keep a low profile until the dust settled.'

Maggie leaned forward and shakily placed her half-empty brandy glass on the floor. She met Hall's direct, uncompromising gaze. She had to admit, there was a quality about him that was hard to pinpoint. His light blue eyes were watchful but never wary, not quite cold but unwavering. It was apparent to Maggie he wanted her dead, and she'd always known that he'd been unconvinced by her ability and commitment as a Double Cross agent. Maggie recalled having once overheard him talking to Colonel Robertson. "How did she get through the assessment at Latchmere?" he'd argued, "old 'Tin Eye' usually manages to sniff out the basket cases, he must have had an off day."

Maggie always assumed Spencer had been talking about her. Right from the very start, he'd unnerved her whereas Joyce relished the verbal confrontations and the constant sparring with him. Maggie had always longed to melt seamlessly into the background, desperately trying to steer clear of his watchful attention. She sensed that he could read her like a book, had seen right through her, and had known all along that her heart and her loyalties lay elsewhere. Sarah's death had now made it even more personal from the moment Maggie had pulled the trigger. She knew Spencer would seek retribution, would track her down and destroy her.

'While I was still in France, the Abwehr,' she said, 'told me we couldn't run the risk of Sarah talking, of taking the matter further with MI5. We didn't know how much of Durand's message had managed to get through, but either way, we knew enough had reached London to jeopardise my safety. To be perfectly honest I wasn't sure if she hadn't already spoken to you or the Colonel about Durand's message. But I had a hunch she might hang back a bit, at least until there was proof of my identity, Nicolette's identity.' Maggie hesitated, nervously meeting Spencer's steady, watchful gaze.

A flicker of irritation crossed his face. 'Let's face it, you pulled the trigger to save your sodding neck, it's as simple as that, isn't it!'

Her thoughts tumbled back to the night of the murder, the moment she'd squeezed the trigger and the moment Sarah had died. It kept playing over and over in her mind like a bad recurring dream.

Garvan steeled himself seeing Spencer glance down at his gun. Christ, he thought, was he going to shoot her there and then? It must be running through his mind.

Hall stared at her long and hard, his expression at best described as chilling. 'Is that why you decided to take a few shots at me, in case I knew the contents of Durand's message?'

She nodded and picked up her glass from the floor.

'You know how it works with the Colonel,' Spencer said to her, 'there aren't any half measures within our organisation. We can't afford the luxury of carrying passengers especially ones capable of betraying and killing their colleagues. You must have realised long before you killed Sarah that it was only a matter of time before we'd catch up with you.'

'Without your tracking down Louis Durand, I always had a fighting chance of slipping through the net.' She stared at Hall, her eyes narrowing as she added. 'The trouble is, you really can't take any of us for granted, can you? There's always going to be the risk that one of us will become a triple agent.'

'It comes with the territory,' he said with a dismissive shrug. 'I guess there's no harm in telling you now, there isn't a single Abwehr agent in Britain who's managed to escape our notice. Some were obviously easier to spot than others, but even those like Joyce, who managed to successfully embed herself into society by creating an entirely false background for herself couldn't slip the net.' He looked at Hamilton, almost pityingly. 'I believe Lt. Col Stephens told you that MI5 intercepted your radio transmissions.'

She nodded.

'Well it wasn't just yours Maggie British Intelligence has cracked the entire German Enigma encryption.' It wasn't without a sense of satisfaction he noticed the last vestige of colour drain from her face. 'I'm not saying you didn't jeopardize the Double Cross system, you did, but there was only ever one certainty, only ever one outcome that we'd eventually track you down. We just needed to limit the damage to our network.' He drew on his cigarette. 'I understand that when you were in Paris, you wrote to Bleicher. The letter was addressed to him personally at his office.'

She looked genuinely surprised. 'How did you know that?'

'Espionage my dear isn't just a one-way street.'

Maggie took a sharp intake of breath wondering how they'd managed to infiltrate the secret military police HQ. At the time, she'd been so worried about being spotted by members of the Interallie that Bleicher had decided they should correspond by letter. Perhaps naively, she hadn't even considered that Bleicher's HQ was infiltrated as well.

'It seems that right from the start you were completely out of your depth.' Garvan said. Maggie rounded on him angrily, and in a sudden fit of rage hurled her brandy glass across the room. It hit the wall and smashed. 'What the hell would you know what it's like being in my position?' Garvan noticed her hands were shaking.

She swallowed hard. 'For Christ's sake Chief Inspector I thought I could handle it, but the longer it went on, I was more and more -,' her words faltered, she started to well up.

'Everyone has a breaking point,' Hall said, coolly with the briefest of smiles, 'you were in a difficult situation, we all know that. But you ended up compounding everything by making a Faustian pact with Bleicher.' Spencer's fleeting but deadly smile had sent a shiver down her spine. 'There's no disguising you've left a trail of destruction and misery in your wake from here to France.'

Garvan asked her to go over the details of Sarah's murder, how she discovered the safe house, how she came to squeeze the trigger. Unlike Spencer, he was an unknown quantity. He'd always struck her as being professionally slick and unfailingly polite. Maggie guessed the slickness was probably nothing more than a thin veneer; her gut instinct was that he was a man not to be crossed. His gaze was almost snake-like, challenging, with a no-nonsense attitude. If push came to shove, she decided there was probably very little to choose between either of them.

Maggie appeared reluctant at first to go into detail about Sarah's murder and sat nervously biting her lower lip as she listened to Garvan. Slowly, she began to recall the earlier attempts on Sarah's life, the first outside her flat in

Westminster, and the second when she was leaving a Mayfair bar. On the first attempt, Maggie explained that by the time she got a chance to take aim the light was fading. It hadn't been an easy shot. She accepted that she hadn't planned the attack properly, and it was a rushed job. The bullet had ricocheted off a doorway but had apparently only narrowly missed hitting Sarah.

The second attempt came about by sheer chance. Having had a few drinks with friends, Maggie was on the way back to pick up her car, when she spotted Sarah walking down Orange Street in the West End. She kept her distance and trailed Sarah to the Beouf sur le Toit Club. From Maggie's viewpoint, it had seemed too good an opportunity to pass up. She positioned herself in the pub opposite the club and kept a close eye on the comings and goings. About an hour later Sarah had emerged from the club with a girlfriend. They were giggling and chatting so animatedly it was easy enough for Maggie to slip out of the pub unnoticed. She got to her car then drove back into Orange Street, pushing the accelerator hard to the floor. She mounted the pavement and drove straight at them. They'd dived out the way, and in doing so, both women lost their footing and fell heavily onto the pavement. It had all happened so quickly, and with the Blackout in full force, neither of them had been able to identify the driver.

Spencer silently shook his head and gave her a rueful smile. But she wasn't quite sure why was he smiling - was it pity or reproach?

Maggie explained to Garvan that after the failed attempts on Sarah's life their meetings had become increasingly sporadic. Whenever she'd asked about Sarah there were always excuses, illness, family bereavement; it was a different excuse every time. It was none of her business, of course, she hadn't the right to know Sarah's whereabouts, but she'd decided to test the waters, to see what excuses the team would come up with next.

Maggie confessed she hadn't a clue where Sarah was living, hadn't the faintest idea about the safe house in South London, why would she, it was hardly information the XX was likely to share with one of their agents. She discovered Sarah's whereabouts by chance when she met up with Henryk Nowak in the so-called Pink Sink at the Ritz Hotel. Maggie had arranged to meet up with a friend, but they were running late, so she decided to order a drink and wait.

'So what happened?' Garvan asked.

'Henryk was already there. He saw me and came over.'

'Pissed was he?' Spencer grunted.

'He'd had a few. He was on the champagne and asked me what I was doing at the Sink. I explained I was waiting for a friend, so Henryk decided to keep me company until they arrived. We got talking about Latchmere. It was just general chit chat really. Sarah's name came up in conversation, and Nowak let slip that he'd seen her two days previously in South London. It wasn't his regular stamping ground, but he'd been to visit an old friend, a bit part actor living in theatrical lodgings along the Lambeth Road. Seeing Sarah curiosity got the better of him, and he'd followed her to Monkton Drive, number 17.' She shot Spencer a wary look. 'In fairness to him, Henryk didn't give seeing Sarah much thought, other than wonder what she was doing there. I felt sorry for him.'

'Why?' Hall demanded.

'He hadn't the slightest notion of what he'd just done, why would he?'

'He handed Sarah to you on a plate!' Hall snapped.

'You could say that.'

'So what did you do?' Garvan quizzed her.

'I couldn't afford another slip-up, so the following day I checked out the address, and planned how best to make my approach. I spent time getting to know the area.'

'Weren't you on an evening shift at the BBC the night she was murdered?' Spencer asked.

'Yes, I was.'

'So how did you slip out undetected? We've accounted for your movements until 21.30 when your shift finished.'

'It wasn't that difficult I was helping prepare the German translations for the evening's broadcast. Once the programme airs, you're meant to stay until it finishes, but in reality, it's very rare for the translators to be needed during a transmission. So I took the chance and nipped out, and was back at Bush House within the hour. Fortunately, no-one missed me, there was plenty of time in hand, and the broadcast was still on air.'

'What time did you arrive in Monkton Drive?' Garvan pressed her.

'It was early evening,' she told him, 'to be honest with you, I can't remember the exact time, maybe 6.30, perhaps a little later the bombing raid hadn't long started.'

'Your timing was perfect.'

She seemed almost pleased and took Garvan's comment as a compliment. 'As I walked along the Kennington Road, there were a few people about but not many, I guess they were heading to the shelter in the park or the one in East Square.' Maggie shot Spencer a wary glance. 'I was wearing trousers, a raincoat. You know how it is, people tend to see what they want to see, witnesses never quite seeing exactly what's in front of them. It happens all the time, at least, it does in the movies.'

Maggie hesitated, she'd sounded flippant, but that hadn't been her intention. She looked tearful - Spencer was right, she could do it at will.

Spencer was struggling to keep a grip on his temper; he wanted to end this nonsense, to finish her sobs, her whining, and the feeble excuses but knew he had to hold back and allow Garvan to carry on with the formalities.

'Weren't you taking a bit of a chance turning up at Monkton Drive? Did you know she was alone?' Garvan asked.

'I wasn't sure, I didn't know what the security arrangements were, but I thought it was a risk worth taking.'

'It sounds like a pretty foolhardy thing to do,' he suggested.

'As I said Chief Inspector, it was a risk I was willing to take. I knew I was already living on borrowed time and needed to make a move.' Maggie again looked to Spencer trying to gauge his mood. Though his expression remained outwardly impassive, his eyes betrayed the loathing that he felt for her.

'So when Sarah opened the front door she was taken aback?'

'If she were, you wouldn't have known, but it must have dawned on her right away that I was her -.'

'Rogue Agent,' Spencer supplied.

'I'll give Sarah her due she played it pretty cool. Letting me in probably seemed the lesser of the two evils. I guess in hindsight Sarah thought she could handle the situation.'

'So what happened after she let you in,' Garvan asked.

Maggie shut her eyes tight for a moment. 'I couldn't take the risk of leaving things as they were, at least not any longer. I'd messed up twice already,' she continued, 'I guessed Hamburg was probably getting impatient that I hadn't managed to eliminate Sarah. Ultimately, it was either her or me; it was as simple as that.'

'Taking another life,' Garvan cut through, 'is rarely that simple.'

'I assure you it was,' she said coldly. 'Sarah was angry with me and let rip straightaway, it became heated, we argued.'

'And then?'

'She was obviously expecting me to make a move. You could say I struck lucky and took her by surprise, she was off guard, and didn't have a chance to respond.'

'And after you shot her, did you leave the house straight away?'

'Put it this way, I didn't want to hang around.'

'The trouble is,' Garvan said smoothly, 'your account doesn't quite hold together.'

'What do you mean?'

'Scotland Yard's forensic team reported that the killer had gone to a great deal of trouble to clean up any trace of fingerprints from the murder scene. There was also a minor abrasion and bruising on the left side of Sarah's face. In the pathologist's opinion, it was probably caused by a slap of the hand, the skin was broken slightly, probably the result of a finger nail. So things not only got heated, but there was a physical fight?'

'Of course, it was heated!' Maggie snapped back at him, 'Sarah was mad at me.'

Maggie started struggling to recount exactly what had happened. There had been an argument; she repeated, raised voices, and a scuffle had broken out. Sarah had freed herself from Maggie's grasp and had somehow managed to run upstairs in a desperate bid to retrieve her revolver from the master bedroom.

'I followed her into the bedroom.'

'And then what happened?' Garvan said.

'I called her name,' she said, matter of factly, 'Sarah spun around to face me, and didn't have time to react.'

'We never found Sarah's Smith and Wesson at the house, what did you do with it?'

'I thought about leaving it, but there didn't seem to be much point, so I decided to take it with me.'

Maggie clasped her hands together, not wishing them to see that she was shaking. She looked pleadingly at Garvan and begged.

'Are you going to arrest me Chief Inspector? I was half expecting a Black Maria outside to take me into custody.'

The prospect of spending a night or even a year in prison was preferable to being left entirely alone with Spencer Hall.

'That's really out of my hands Maggie.'

'Why is it?' she cried and instinctively turned to Spencer, waiting for what seemed like an eternity for him to respond.

'You have to understand a public trial,' he said, quietly, 'would be deemed an embarrassment for His Majesty's Government. Think of the consequences Maggie. Your family would be hounded, castigated in the national press. Is that what you want to happen?'

'I might still be of use,' she pleaded, 'think of it, my relationship with Hugo Bleicher, he trusts me.'

'It'd be a cold day in hell before I'd trust you, and that's what matters, and quite frankly I always knew you were a train crash waiting to happen.' He stubbed his cigarette out in an ashtray. 'For the time being you'll be taken into custody and held at Latchmere House.'

Folding her arms defensively, she stood up from the window seat. 'So what's to become of me?' Looking at the expression on Hall's face, she raised the flat of her hand toward him. 'You don't have to answer that one.'

Her thoughts started spiralling out of control. Deep down, she hadn't believed it would come to this. In her mind, there had always been just a small glimmer of hope that somehow she'd turn the tables to her advantage. Maggie knew only too well after Latchmere there'd be a closed court hearing; she'd be found guilty and sentenced to death. As a German spy, she'd either be condemned to hang at Wandsworth Prison, or face a firing squad. Her life was all but over, fading away like the flickering light of a dying candle. The game was indeed up. Spencer remained perched on the arm of the couch, waiting, biding his time, allowing Maggie to make the next move. He wasn't in any particular hurry to take her back to Latchmere. He knew she was unbalanced enough to make one last frantic, dramatic gesture. Better it happened up here in the confines of her flat rather than outside in Red Lion Square. Spencer's stillness, his calmness only served to aggravate her even more.

'Perhaps we should be thinking about taking Maggie into custody,' Garvan suggested.

Maggie glanced at him, nodded and reached down behind an armchair to retrieve her handbag. But when she stood up it wasn't the handbag she was holding but Sarah's Smith and Wesson.

Before Maggie had a chance to squeeze the trigger, Spencer had grasped his revolver off the bureau and fired, not once but twice. It was a standard practice just to ensure there were no mistakes and no chance of survival.

For a split second her expression registered something approaching surprise before crumpling down to her knees, one hand desperately trying to cling to the arm of the chair. The gun slipped from her grasp as a dark red crimson stain seeped from a chest wound hideously staining her pale blue silk blouse. Her body suddenly went into a convulsive spasm, then slumped sideways, and by the time she hit the floor she was already dead.

Hearing the sound of gunfire John Eldridge, who was still standing guard outside the flat flung the door open, and in his hurry tripped over the doormat. He stopped dead in his tracks, took in the scene and puffed out his cheeks in relief. Spencer opened the window and leaned out, and shouted down to his men to stay where they were. He closed the window and then realised the radio was still on.

'Turn that bloody thing off!' he ordered Eldridge.

Staring down at Maggie's body, Garvan felt strangely disconnected. The shooting had happened so quickly that he was still trying to take it all in. He couldn't understand why she hadn't preferred to take her own life, rather than risk the long drop at Wandsworth Prison. He'd attended one or two executions in his time, and given the choice he'd much rather have taken matters into his own hands. At the end of the day, she'd been nothing more than a frightened, bewildered young woman caught up in a deceitful spiral of destruction and betrayal, not only against the French Resistance and Sarah Davis but ultimately in a sense, circumstance as well.

Spencer calmly replaced his gun back down on the bureau. He glanced at Hamilton's body and felt a sense of satisfaction, coupled with the sweet taste of revenge. It had been a simple case of kill or be killed.

He became aware that Garvan was watching him. 'I owed it to Sarah,' he said, bluntly. He gestured at Eldridge to leave them alone. As the door closed, he added. 'Do you have any idea Chief Inspector what it's like to fail? I don't just mean failure at work, but to know that your mistakes, your personal mistakes have cost the life of another human being? I failed Sarah, and she paid the ultimate price for my mistakes. After the first botched attempt on her life she came to me for protection, and when she needed me most, I wasn't there, I wasn't there for her.' His voice was edged with anger, anger at himself.

'You weren't to know who the traitor was, not even Sarah knew that.'

'But Sarah might still be alive if I'd kept a closer watch on things. I took my eye off the ball. I should have played it differently, followed standard practice, and shouldn't have left her out on a limb.'

'From my understanding,' Garvan interrupted, 'Sarah was aware of the risks. Didn't I read somewhere it was her idea to live at the safe house in Monkton Drive?'

Spencer gave a slight shrug of his shoulders. 'The first part of the plan worked well enough, but up until the night of the murder, Sarah hadn't spent a night alone at the house. I always made sure she was covered by a small group of operatives. The duty cover was assigned that night, but during the afternoon there had been a flap at St. James's, we couldn't spare anyone, and as long as she kept calling in as arranged then I knew there wasn't a problem. But then she missed the deadline.' Spencer hesitated, remembering the phone call telling him that Sarah was dead. 'I had to think on my feet. We'd failed to find the traitor. Things were rapidly getting out of hand. A triple agent in our midst was endangering the entire operation. I needed time. I needed space to take a step back, so I suggested we had no other option than to call in Scotland Yard right away. You'd already been earmarked if things went belly up. We knew it was perhaps our only real chance of flushing the killer into the open. By the time Sarah was murdered, we'd run out of options.'

'Realistically Major, I doubt whether you could have saved Sarah,' Garvan suggested. 'You know damn well Maggie was out of control, she was little more than a ticking time bomb on a one-way path to self-destruction.'

'Yes,' Spencer said, thoughtfully, 'I just wish we'd been able to prevent her from destroying so many lives along the way.' He took one more long hard look at Maggie's lifeless body, before calling John Eldridge back into the flat. He ordered him to contact St. James's and tell them Maggie was dead.

'Do you want me to arrange the removal of the body? It probably won't be until the morning now,' Garvan offered.

Spencer accepted. 'Colonel Robertson will probably give Dr Menzies a call tonight and ask him to carry out the inquest. We use Menzies a lot. He's a personal friend of Tar's.' He turned to leave and gestured to Garvan. 'Come on, let's get out of here, I'll drop you off at the hospital.'

'I hope to God he pulls through.'

'So do I Chief Inspector.' Pulling on his gloves, he added. 'I'm sorry about this evening.'

'Sorry?'

'I didn't have a choice, I couldn't have moved against her in the club, and risk her injuring innocent bystanders.'

'I know.'

Chapter 18

Spencer pulled up outside the main entrance of St. Thomas's Hospital in Lambeth Palace Road.

'Are you coming in?' Garvan asked him.

'No, I'll drop by tomorrow, I've some unfinished business I need to sort out first.'

'Tonight?' Getting a bit late isn't it?'

'I'm sorry, it really can't wait. I just need to tie up a few loose ends.'

Garvan nodded and went to open the passenger door, but Spencer tapped him on the arm.

'By the way, I'm going to ask the Home Office to give Sir Philip Game a courtesy call first thing in the morning, just to let him know the case is closed officially.'

'And what about the body, do you still want the Yard to take care of it?'

'Better keep it all above board. By the way, if you're plagued by too many questions from on high don't forget to mention that you're bound by the Official Secrets Act, National Security, or whatever, just take your pick. It should help stave off Charles Harmer snooping about too much and making things difficult for you.'

'And if it doesn't?'

'You know my number.'

Garvan got out of the car, closed the door and watched Spencer do a tight U-turn in the middle of the road, and drive off in the direction of Westminster Bridge. He couldn't help thinking that Hall's unfinished business was connected to Henryk Nowak. Not only had he become a regular irritant to Hall, but, more importantly, he was now a proven liability to the entire Twenty Committee.

As Garvan entered the main entrance of the hospital, he was struck by the all-pervading odour of carbolic antiseptic. It always happened, the smell once more transporting him back to his childhood, and to the time of his mother's death at the local infirmary. He felt a growing knot in the pit of his stomach, and an overwhelming sense of dread. It was strange that even after all these years, his childhood memories still managed to retain such a tight grip on his emotions.

He walked along a green and cream corridor following the signs to Reception, where he was then directed upstairs to Sebastopol Ward and told a member of staff would meet him shortly to discuss Sergeant Mackenzie's condition. Garvan headed off as directed, climbed two flights of stairs, down yet another corridor and through endless heavy brown coloured swing doors.

He came across Joyce Leader and Jack Charteris sitting together on a long wooden bench outside the ward.

Jack came to his feet, ramrod straight. 'Sir, are you all right?' he barked, 'did you manage to track Miss Hamilton down?'

'Yes, we caught up with her,' he answered, hesitantly.

Joyce looked drained; her clothes still splattered with Mackenzie's dried blood.

'Where's Mac, is he doing okay?' Garvan asked, tentatively.

'He's in the operating theatre,' Joyce explained. She checked her watch. 'They took him down about an hour ago to try to remove the bullet. The x-ray showed he had a pretty lucky escape; it was a hair's breadth away from a main artery.'

'Did either of you get a chance to speak with Mac before he went down to theatre?'

'No sir,' Jack said, 'when we arrived in Casualty all hell had broken loose. It was pandemonium downstairs, doctors and nurses flying about every which way.'

Garvan turned to Joyce. 'There was no need for you to stay as well, not with Jack being here.'

She smiled. 'It wasn't exactly a chore, I think you forget your Sergeant Mackenzie saved my life this evening; if he hadn't intervened, I wouldn't be here.'

'I think you're probably right.'

'Where's Major Hall?' she asked.

'He dropped me off outside the hospital. He needs to sort out some unfinished business.'

'And where's Maggie?'

'We caught up with her in Red Lion Square.'

Joyce looked at him, her eyes narrowing. 'You mean at her flat?'

Garvan nodded.

'It doesn't make sense, after all, that's happened why she didn't just give herself up!'

'I guess she panicked,' Garvan mused.

Leader shook her head and snorted. 'Silly little bitch.'

'So is Miss Hamilton under arrest?' Charteris queried.

He puffed out his cheeks. 'Not exactly Jack. Major Hall shot her dead.'

'Dead!' Jack blustered in disbelief.

'Yes dead. Maggie managed to grab a tram in York Road; it terminated at the Kingsway Underpass, so she headed into Holborn Tube Station. She might well have given us the slip, but she was spotted on the concourse by one of Spencer's team. I imagine at that point, even she realised it was a fait accompli.'

'So what happened when you arrived at her flat?' Leader enquired.

'Spencer's men were waiting for us outside. We found her downing a large brandy.'

'Pity she didn't top herself,' Joyce said bristling.

Garvan pulled a face. 'You only commit suicide if you really want to die. Personally, I think Maggie wanted to explain her reasons for what happened in France.'

'Well, she was never going to be able to justify killing Sarah to Spencer, was she? What a waste of fucking time!' Joyce was by now pacing the hospital corridor, arms folded. 'So what did she say about France?' she asked angrily.

'She tried justifying herself.'

'How in God's name, how did she try?' Joyce demanded of him.

'That she was scared rigid the Gestapo would discover she was working for British Intelligence.'

'That's a downright lie!' Joyce scoffed coming to a halt in front of Garvan. 'And how did she try explaining away sleeping with Bleicher?'

'That she hadn't set out to become his lover, things had just got out of hand.'

Leader shook her head in disbelief. 'That's one way of putting it,' she smirked. 'I suppose Maggie just reverted to kind.'

'I think this evening was in part, at least, almost a cry for help.'

Joyce rolled her eyes. 'For Christ's sake Chief Inspector, however, addled her brain might have been, surely to God even she must have realised it was pointless trying to justify her reasons for murdering Sarah Davis to Spence.'

'She wanted someone to listen,' he said evenly.

'Well, let's face it; it doesn't seem to have helped her much, does it?'

'It might have,' he suggested, 'if she hadn't taken it into her head to pull a gun on Major Hall.'

Joyce looked genuinely amused. 'Bet that pleased him, no end.'

'It also didn't help matters that she tried shooting him with Sarah's Smith and Wesson revolver.'

Joyce pursed her lips together and whistled silently. 'Did she, by God? I don't care what you say she obviously did have a death wish. Why else would you risk pulling a gun on Spencer and not expect to end up dead? Unless of course,' Joyce conceded, thoughtfully, 'she really had lost the plot.'

'Rather than take her life, perhaps she found it easier for someone else to pull the trigger. Put yourself in her position, what would you have done?

'Give myself up,' Joyce said without the slightest hesitation.

'But Maggie's was a difficult position. The National Press castigated her entire family. They were already social pariahs after her father's fascist rants. At least, what passed this evening will never make it into the newspapers.'

'But if she'd given herself up outside the Union Jack Club, what difference would it have made? Her crimes would still never have been made public; you know that.'

'But that's what I'm trying to explain to you. Maggie was on the verge of a mental breakdown, she wasn't thinking straight, and I guess having killed Sarah Davis already it didn't much matter if she finished you off as well this evening. They can only hang you once.'

'It's a pity Spence wasn't able to finish her off weeks ago,' Joyce said coldly. 'Since our return from France things were getting increasingly tricky. Up until now I've been very lucky.'

'In what way?'

'The success of my transmissions to Hamburg and my standing with Ritter has afforded me a degree of personal freedom with the Double Cross. But since Sarah's death, there was an understandable tightening of the leash. However useful I might be to Colonel Robertson and his committee, I'm under no illusion that had you failed to flush Maggie Hamilton out into the open a decision would have eventually been made to liquidate both of us just to be on the safe side. They needed to protect the Double Cross, and ultimately nothing else mattered. That's why I don't share your compassion for the woman!'

He smiled thinly. 'Did you ever get along?'

'I can't say that we ever did. Right from day one we never once saw eye to eye, we always managed to rub each other up the wrong way. I guess one way or another we were both at fault.'

'It's getting late, why don't you let Sergeant Charteris take you home?'

'I did offer Miss Leader, a lift home sir, but she refused point blank,' Jack explained.

'I just want to stay until Sergeant Mackenzie is out of the operating theatre.' She looked thoughtfully at Garvan. His face looked drawn, almost grey. It probably wasn't surprising given the strain he'd been under over the last few weeks. The collapse of his marriage had also probably taken its toll. It must have been a shock discovering his wife had left him for another woman. 'You look very tired.' she said, kindly.

'I'm fine,' he said, brusquely and checked his watch. 'Sorry, I need to make a call to Scotland Yard, forgive me I'll be back in a minute.'

Joyce watched him re-trace his steps along the dimly-lit corridor. She heard the swing doors clank behind him, and she slowly sank back onto the hard wooden bench, her eyes occasionally closing as tiredness took an increasing hold. It had been a long night, and it was likely to be some hours yet before Mackenzie was wheeled out of the operating theatre.

*

Spencer pulled up outside the Ritz Hotel in Piccadilly, to be greeted by the imposing head hall porter Victor Legg. They'd met on numerous occasions, and passed a few pleasantries before he headed down into the basement world of the so-called Pink Sink. It was the leading place to be, and the best homosexual pick-up joint in town. The evening was already in full swing, and the bar was packed to the gunnels, filled with pulsating music, laughter and the sound of raised drunken voices. The air was a heady mixture of cigarette smoke and the pungent smell of alcohol.

Spencer stood at the entrance trying to take everything in. The lighting was subdued, and it was quite difficult to get a clear view. He scanned the heaving crowd and recognised a War Office high-up, and a Conservative MP, neither of whom interested him in the least. He eventually saw Nowak with his arm looped around a smartly dressed Royal Naval officer. Spencer pushed his way through the heaving mass and tapped Henryk on the shoulder.

Nowak spun round. A look of horror suddenly crossed his face. 'Major Hall,' he stammered, 'what brings you here tonight?'

'I want a word with you Henryk,' he shouted over the din.

Henryk reluctantly let go of his new friend. Even half sloshed he had enough sense to realise Hall was in no mood to mess around.

'What's wrong Major?' he cried, pleadingly.

'Get the fuck outside,' Spencer growled at him, and roughly grabbed hold of his arm.

Nowak's naval officer intervened and attempted to push Hall aside. 'Who the hell do you think you are coming in here ordering people about?'

Spencer let go of Henryk and faced up to his companion. 'Matey, for your own sake get out of my sodding way or I'll report you to the Admiralty,' he snarled.

'Georgie,' Nowak begged, 'please just do as he says!'

George Henderson was still in no mood to give way, at least not without a fight - the drink was talking. 'Just back off and leave us alone!' He shouted stabbing Hall's chest with his finger. He turned to Nowak and placed a protective arm around his shoulder. 'You don't have to put up with this, no matter what's happened between you and this Major of yours!' he said, dismissively.

'Oh my God Georgie, it's not what it seems, just leave it be, I don't want you getting involved, it's not worth it!'

Spencer angrily brushed Henderson aside and caught hold of Nowak, and propelled him roughly toward the exit of the Pink Sink. Once outside the bar area, he dragged Henryk up the stairs toward the main foyer. By the time they reached the second landing Nowak was already struggling for breath, and slumped against the wall gasping for air.

Henryk was shaken. Why in God's name he asked himself had the Major hauled him out of the bar? Spencer had never really seemed that interested in him before now.

There'd been confrontations of course, but nothing like this. Something was seriously wrong.

'Why are you here?' he begged again, 'what's wrong Major, for Christ's sake just tell me what's happened,' he sobbed sliding to the floor. 'Honestly, I've been here all evening; I haven't done anything wrong.'

'You're fucking pissed!' Spencer snarled at him.

'No, I've had a few drinks, but I'm not drunk.' Nowak pleaded. 'But this isn't just about me drinking one cocktail too many. You'd have picked me up months ago Major if it was just about me getting pissed.'

Spencer grabbed him by the scruff of the neck, hauled Henryk to his feet, and rammed him against the wall. There were scores to settle, and he was running out of time.

'Before Sarah was murdered you met up with one of your lovers, some bit-part bloody actor who lives in the Lambeth Road.'

Nowak recoiled from him and squirmed. 'Please don't hurt me, Major!'

Hall dragged him up another flight of stairs and into the toilet. Fortunately, it was empty.

'This isn't some sodding game Nowak. You caught sight of Sarah when you came out of his digs, didn't you?'

'I did.' he stammered, 'she was walking along Lambeth Road.'

'And for whatever reason you decided to follow her.'

'Yes,' he murmured feebly. Where on earth was Spencer going with this? He was scared out of his mind.

'You followed her to Monkton Drive. Why?'

'I'm not sure,' he sobbed truthfully, 'I guess curiosity got the better of me as simple as that, the Lambeth Road was the last place on earth I'd have expected to see her.

I know it was wrong of me, but I couldn't help myself. I kept my distance until Sarah turned into Monkton Drive.'

'But you didn't leave it there, did you?'

'What do you mean Major?'

'You followed her to No17.'

He nodded his head mutely.

'And a few days later you met up with Maggie Hamilton, here at the Pink Sink.'

Nowak was still none the wiser, Why was meeting up with Maggie so important? 'Yes I did, her friend was late arriving, and we had a couple of drinks together.'

'And you let slip that you'd seen Sarah in Lambeth and that you'd followed her to Monkton Drive.'

Nowak's thoughts were all over the place. He was frightened and still didn't quite understand what it was all about. Why had Spencer dragged him out of the bar, what was going on? Admittedly, Henryk accepted he shouldn't have followed Sarah, and shouldn't have gossiped with Maggie, but that didn't explain why he'd been hauled physically out of the Pink Sink. Beads of sweat began to glisten on his forehead.

'A few days later you met up again with Maggie at the Red Lion, only, this time, you blabbed to her that you'd seen me hand over Sarah's notebook to Chief Inspector Garvan.'

'Did I?' he sobbed shaking his head, 'I really can't remember.'

'No, you were probably too bloody pissed to remember!'

'Please Major, what's this all about?' he cried.

'I'll tell you what it's about Henryk. Maggie Hamilton was a triple agent.'

Nowak placed his hands over his mouth. 'I swear to God I didn't know Major!' he begged, 'I swear to God!'

'I'm sure you didn't, but your tendency for verbal diarrhoea ended up costing Sarah her life.'

Henryk was paralysed to the spot, the consequences of his idle, seemingly innocuous gossip, finally dawned on him. 'I had no idea Major, no idea at all! Have you arrested her?' he asked.

'Not exactly.'

'What's happened?'

'I shot her, I shot her dead,' came the cool reply.

'Shot her!' Nowak cupped his hands over his face and slunk back to the floor in an almost foetal position. 'What have I done, I didn't know, how could I have known!' he cried, as much to himself as Spencer.

Henryk's feelings were immaterial. Hall really didn't have the time to mess around. He grabbed hold of him and hauled Nowak out of the Gents' and up the last flight of stairs and pushed through the swing doors into the main foyer.

'Right, stand up straight and stop bloody snivelling. Walk through the foyer and keep your fucking mouth shut!' Spencer growled at him.

Tightening his grip on Nowak's arm, he propelled him through the foyer, briefly pausing to pass the time of day again with the Head Porter. With the niceties out of the way, Spencer escorted Henryk outside to his car, and then set off down Piccadilly. Nowak sat in the passenger seat, arms crossed. He felt vulnerable, anxious, not quite sure what was going to happen next. As they drove along Piccadilly, Spencer told him about Mepham Street, how Maggie had ended up shooting Mac.

'After leaving Maggie's flat I called St. James's', Spencer said to him, 'and asked them to re-check your radio transmissions over the last three months to Hamburg.'

Nowak didn't respond.

'Your drinking is getting way out of hand. They've started to become sloppy, too many unforced errors. Even your Abwehr handlers have begun to feel uneasy about you.'

Nowak stared unseeingly through the windscreen. 'What errors?'

'You've simply been too pissed to take the information we've given you on board. Hamburg has detected a change in the quality of your transmissions; it's subtle enough for them to become wary, to question what's going on and whether MI5 have rumbled you.' Spencer looked at him. 'You're simply not thinking straight Henryk, are you?' he said sharply. 'You spend every fucking day and night pissed out of your tiny brain.'

'Where are you taking me?' Nowak queried, choosing to ignore Spencer's accusation.

'I'm passing you over to Special Branch. They've been instructed to drive you down to Latchmere. You can re-acquaint yourself with Lieutenant Colonel Stephens.'

'Stephens,' he repeated in horror.

'We're closing you down Henryk; you've become too much of a liability.'

'You're-you're not going to shoot me, are you?' he stammered uncertainly.

'Good God no, why would I waste the ammunition!' Spencer snorted derisively at him.

Nowak bowed his head and sobbed into his hands. There was no going back now. The war for him was over. The best case scenario was that the authorities might decide to detain him in prison as an active enemy agent, or in an internment camp for the duration. The only other alternative was that he'd face trial. Once convicted of espionage, there'd be only one possible outcome: execution by the hangman's noose.

At St. Thomas's Hospital, Joyce nudged Garvan awake. He awoke with a start, not quite sure where he was. He blearily opened his eyes to see Mac being wheeled past on a trolley. He was fresh out of surgery. Trailing a short distance behind the trolley was a short rather tubby figure wearing thick dark-rimmed glasses, and dressed entirely from head to foot in a green surgical gown. As the trolley was wheeled through the doors of the ward, the surgeon stopped, and removed his cap to reveal, a sparse receding hairline.

'Chief Inspector Garvan?' he asked, quizzically, in a broad Glaswegian accent. Garvan stood up and shook the surgeon's hand. 'I'm Robert Short,' he said by way of introduction.

'How is he?'

'Your sergeant had a very lucky escape this evening; a fraction, either way, would have been a different matter altogether.

'Will he pull through?'

'God willing yes. All things considered, the operation went very well.' He screwed up his surgical cap in his hands and said. 'May I suggest you all go home, there's no point staying here any longer, at least not tonight. At the moment, he's very heavily sedated and won't be coming round until morning. If there's any change in his condition, we'll, of course, give you a call. And I really wouldn't want him to be having too many visitors tomorrow, it'll take some time before he feels up to it.'

'Thank you, I'll check to see whether he's up to visitors in the morning.'

Good idea,' Short answered, before heading off into Sebastopol Ward after his patient.

Chapter 19

It seemed as if he'd hardly closed his eyes when he was woken up by the persistent ringing of his bedside telephone. Garvan put his head under the covers hoping that whoever was phoning would ring off, but then he suddenly remembered Mac. He stretched across the bed and fumbled for the receiver.

'Did I wake you up?' he heard Spencer say.

'Don't you ever sleep Major?'

'I don't have the time Chief Inspector, at least not right now.'

'Good God what time is it?' Garvan grunted, with one eye desperately trying to focus on the alarm clock.

'It's 9.30.'

'I didn't get to bed until after four.'

'Nor me.'

'I don't have your stamina, Major. Has something happened to Mac?'

'No, I haven't heard from the hospital. But I've had a whisper from Special Branch that Harmer has taken it into his head to visit Red Lion Square.'

'When?'

'He's just left the Yard.'

Garvan tossed back the bed covers. 'What in God's name is he playing at?'

'I haven't a clue. First thing this morning the Home Office let Sir Philip Game know we'd solved Sarah's murder. I guess Game took it into his head to brief Harmer on a need to know basis.'

'Harmer can't be going to Hamilton's flat with Game's blessing.'

'Hardly.'

'I'll get myself down there right away.'

'Good, I'll see you there.'

Garvan perched himself on the edge of the bed and re-checked the time. 'I should be there by about ten.'

He thumped the receiver down then dialled Scotland Yard and ordered a vehicle. Not bothering to wash or shave, he threw on his clothes from the night before and hurried downstairs into the lobby to await the arrival of his transport.

In Red Lion Square, Charles Harmer stepped out of his black chauffeured Wolsey. He half expected to be greeted by a token presence from the local police. To his surprise, there wasn't a single Metropolitan police officer in sight. Instead, the doorway was guarded by four imposing uniformed military policemen. He strode up to the entrance of the house and introduced himself.

They snapped to attention, and Harmer demanded that he be taken up to Hamilton's flat where he met Spencer's agent, Hugh Dickinson. With the introductions over Harmer demanded access.

'Sorry Sir,' Hugh said, with a self-deprecating smile, 'I'm under strict instructions not to allow anyone inside, at least not without the permission of Major Hall or Detective Chief Inspector Garvan.'

'But I'm the Assistant Commissioner!' he blustered, his face reddening as he spoke.

'Of course, you are sir,' Dickinson said, 'but you of all people must understand I can't countermand a direct order.'

Harmer hesitated. 'I understand there were a number of calls to the local police station last night.'

'Calls?' Dickinson repeated, blankly.

'From the other residents man, who else!'

'Yes sir, there were.'

'They reported hearing shots from the flat.'

'Yes, Sir, two shots to be precise.'

'And Holborn Police Station dispatched two detectives to Miss Hamilton's address.'

'There were three actually.'

'So why aren't my men on duty outside the building?' Harmer snapped at him.

'Orders,' Dickinson replied, smoothly.

'Whose orders?' Harmer demanded

Dickinson knew the Home Secretary had briefed Sir Philip, but for whatever reason he'd chosen not to share the intelligence.

'The Home Secretary's orders,' Dickinson said, with a degree of satisfaction of seeing Harmer's obvious irritation. 'Special Branch stood down the local coppers until they were relieved by the Military Police. I'm surprised, sir, Special Branch didn't inform you earlier.'

The fact hadn't been lost on Harmer either, but he wasn't particularly surprised. He'd never seen eye to eye with Norman Kendall, the head of Special Branch.

'Was Chief Inspector Garvan here last night?'

'Yes sir, with Major Hall.'

Hearing the sound of footsteps approaching the corridor, Harmer and Dickinson looked round. It was Garvan. He was tired, unkempt and in no mood to be dealing with his boss.

'You look like you've been dragged through a bloody hedge backwards. 'Harmer snapped at him.

Garvan wasn't in the mood. His temper was always on a short fuse, and Harmer wasn't helping. 'It's been a long fucking night.'

'Has it?'

His response wasn't helping. 'How often do you end up having a Detective Sergeant nursing a bullet wound?' I left a message with your office!' Garvan was by now face to face with his senior officer. 'I was expecting a call!'

'I only picked the message up this morning.' Harmer was rattled and blustered. 'I asked my secretary, Martha to make a call to the hospital.'

Garvan knew he was lying, Martha hadn't made the call. 'Does Sir Philip know you're here?'

'No,' came, the unexpectedly blunt response.

'Then with respect sir, what are you doing turning up here?'

'Wheels within wheels Garvan,' he said, vaguely with a flourish of his hand, 'I'd like to take a look round the flat.' Harmer locked his eyes on Garvan's, 'or are you going to deny me access, Chief Inspector?' His voice had a challenging edge to it.

It was a loaded question, but at the end of the day, Garvan had nothing to lose. It was Harmer who'd have to explain himself to the Commissioner. It was the AC's neck on the line, not his.

Garvan turned to Dickinson. 'Is the flat unlocked?'

'Yes, sir.'

'When Major Hall gets here let him know we're inside.'

'Very good Sir.'

Garvan opened the door to the flat and stood back to allow Harmer to enter. Maggie Hamilton's body was still sprawled lifelessly across the living room. It wasn't a pleasant sight, but until Sam Menzies arrived to carry out an initial examination the body couldn't be removed.

'What happened here last night?' Harmer demanded of him.

Garvan politely told him the Official Secrets Act bound him and, therefore, couldn't divulge any information regarding the murder investigation.

'So who shot the poor woman?' the AC asked.

'It was suicide, Sir.'

Harmer looked up at him and smirked. 'It's the queerest ruddy suicide I've ever seen Garvan.'

Garvan's expression didn't falter; he didn't have to justify himself.

'Look at her,' Harmer said, gesturing to Hamilton's body. 'Either the girl had exceptionally long arms or someone else helped send her into the next world! Whatever you may think I'm not a bloody fool Garvan and nor are you, even a rooky still wet behind their fucking ears would know this wasn't some bloody suicide. Look at the damn clues man, look at em!' He pointed in a stabbing motion at Maggie's body.

Garvan didn't respond. There was no need, he didn't have to explain, Harmer was a spent force, but it didn't make it any easier to deal with. Even if he'd wanted to explain, which he didn't, his hands were well and truly tied. It was evident Harmer felt side-lined, irritated at being left out of the loop that all his old demons and insecurities were beginning to re-surface. The Commissioner had failed to fully take him into his confidence, and here was Garvan, a mere Detective Chief Inspector, who was entrusted with not only a case of national security but had been drawn into the inner sanctum of British Intelligence.

Since the start of the investigation, Harmer had begun wondering whether his increasing exclusion was in some measure a thinly veiled sign that he was already out of the running to make Met Commissioner. In the cold light of day, his spur of the moment decision to visit Red Lion Square was something of an own goal. He'd stepped way too far out of line, but he'd been desperate to retain a grip, to re-establish his authority at Scotland Yard. I should have known better, he thought to himself, I ought to have played it differently, have accepted the status quo, and pretended not to care, but he simply hadn't been able to let go.

It hadn't helped that Garvan was obviously the Yard's man of the future, and very much Sir Philip's blue-eyed boy. Since the outset of the Davis murder inquiry, Garvan had been welcomed into the heart of British Intelligence, whereas Harmer had found himself increasingly out on a limb, and increasingly envious of his junior officer. He'd always been more at home driving a desk at the Yard rather than roughing it out on the Streets like Garvan. He wondered whether it was pity in his Chief Inspector's expression or downright contempt, he wasn't entirely sure which.

'When is forensics due?' Harmer said stiltedly; he didn't quite know what else to say.

Garvan looked at his watch. 'The pathologist should be here in about an hour's time. As for forensics …' his words faltered hearing the familiar Welsh tones of Spencer Hall outside in the corridor.

Spencer bestowed a fleeting if rather a forced smile on the AC. 'Ah gentleman, I'm so sorry I should have been here earlier,' he apologised, quietly closing the door, and nodding in greeting toward Garvan. He fixed Harmer with a cold, almost dismissively hard stare; it was intense, challenging. 'I couldn't help overhearing you mention the forensics team.'

'That's right,' Harmer said solemnly. 'I was just saying to the Chief Inspector here -.'

Spencer cut across him. 'Without his professionalism we'd never have solved Sarah's murder so quickly, God alone knows we tried.' He pointed toward Maggie's body. 'We'd rather Miss Hamilton had stood trial for murder of course,' Spencer lied, 'but, at least, we've brought some small measure of closure for Sarah's family.'

Instinctively, Harmer glanced down at Hamilton's body. 'So why did she kill Sarah Davis?'

'You of all people will appreciate I can't go into specifics,' Hall said, slowly unbuttoning his overcoat.

It was another barbed comment that Harmer found wounding, and yet another affirmation that he'd been left out of the loop.

'By the way, I took the liberty of phoning Sir Philip before I came here,' he added with seemingly off-handed casualness.

The AC's head shot up like a bolt, saying uneasily, 'I beg your pardon, Major!'

'I just wanted to check Sir Philip thoroughly understood there were certain restraints and security issues regarding the investigation that had to be kept under wraps.' Spencer removed his overcoat and slung it over the back of an armchair. 'I hope you understand the last thing we wanted was for the Met to feel out of the loop, I assure you it was never our intention. For the sake of national security we had to be, how shall I say, economical with the truth?' He allowed his words to sink in; he had the upper hand. Harmer looked through him with barely concealed annoyance. 'But what I can tell you is, if we hadn't tracked down Miss Davis's killer, our continuing fight against Nazi Germany would have been severely impaired, if not destroyed altogether.'

Spencer lit a cigarette and deftly snapped shut the lighter, and then played with it thoughtfully between his fingers, before slipping it back into his trouser pocket. He was in no mood to mess around, to waste time playing cat and mouse with Charles Harmer, but there again Garvan thought, he never did. He remained outwardly cordial, but the AC's arrival at Maggie's flat meant this was now getting personal, not to mention highly unprofessional. Since his arrival, it was increasingly apparent that Harmer was feeling distinctly awkward, if not a little embarrassed, wondering what had passed between Sir Philip and Spencer over the phone. He was rattled, and it showed.

'Sir Philip,' Spencer said, coolly, 'told me that after the Home Office briefed him, he then spoke to you at some length about the case.' Spencer pushed back the curtains in the hope of getting some more light into the oppressively dark living room. 'With respect sir, can you tell me why you've come here this morning without the Commissioner's permission? It's highly irregular; I really can't understand what were you hoping to achieve?'

Harmer deflected the question. 'Can you just let me know one thing, Major Hall?'

'Fire away.'

'Who told you I was picking up my car from Scotland Yard to come here this morning?

'Does it really matter?'

'Well, it does to me, man!'

'I'm not at liberty to divulge my sources', Hall said smoothly.

'Was it Special Branch? Was it their head, Norman Kendall who contacted you?'

'Let's just say I was tipped off.' Spencer's smile lacked expression; he looked right through Harmer. 'You have to understand sir that the governance of this murder investigation right from the very start was taken at the very highest levels of the Government.'

'I'm curious Major Hall.'

'About what exactly?'

'Did you ever have any intention of Miss Davis's murderer standing trial?'

'My only remit was to track the killer down. Any decision regarding what happened to the accused after their arrest was always going to be a decision taken way above my head.'

'Am I expected to believe you, Major?'

'You can believe whatever you like, sir, it doesn't matter to me one way or the other.'

In the early stages of the investigation, Harmer had initially been flattered to be liaising with the Security Services. He enjoyed the sense of being taken into their confidence, or, at least, it had seemed that way to him. Unfortunately, the novelty of assisting British Intelligence had soon worn thin. Within the first couple of weeks, he'd found himself almost entirely frozen out, and kept at a firm distance from the inquiry. Garvan had been ordered to report directly to St. James's rather than to Scotland Yard, and had thereby cancelled out the Met's normal reporting chain. To all intents and purposes, Garvan's investigation had been controlled entirely by Hall, Colonel Robertson and the mysterious Twenty Committee. He'd heard the name of the committee, but, in reality, had no concept of either its role or place within the Security Services.

'I really ought to get going,' Harmer said, making to leave.

'One moment sir,' Spencer said to him, 'I think I do owe you an explanation. I think you should be aware that throughout the entire investigation, Sir Philip was involved at all levels of discussion. When his diary permitted, he also attended meetings at the Home Office and St. James's.'

He paused as if for dramatic effect, and then let slip the real reason behind Harmer's exclusion from the weekly meetings.

'Under normal circumstances you would have been included of course, but I'm sorry to have to tell you, Sir, you don't currently hold the relevant level of security clearance.'

Spencer's bombshell hit him with deadly accuracy. It also took Garvan by surprise. Hall had told him the news so casually, seemingly at least, without the slightest hint of rancour or malice, but it had struck home like a dagger to the AC's heart. It was in effect a death knell to his entire career. Harmer's world had suddenly imploded. Where had it all gone so very wrong? He asked himself. His mind was in turmoil, his thoughts began to race wildly; wondering whether he'd lost his clearance because of his wife's well-known drink problem, or had her gambling finally got out of hand? Or perhaps he'd somehow managed to blot his own copy book at Scotland Yard. There was simply no way of telling, but something had made him a potential security risk in the eyes of MI5.

Turning up unannounced at Hamilton's flat, without the Commissioner's permission, was he knew, the final nail in the coffin. Without the right level of clearance he'd never receive the endorsement of the Home Secretary, wouldn't even be placed on the shortlist of candidates for the Commissioners' job when Sir Philip finally retired and left office. Beneath Spencer's thinly veiled charm Harmer sensed all the deadly charm of a laconic assassin. Meeting his cold hard gaze, he felt unequal or able to initially challenge him.

Spencer hadn't drawn breath and carried on seamlessly. 'The pathology report will state the cause of death as suicide.'

Harmer had lost the battle; he knew his career was over, and though he wanted the ground to swallow him whole, he didn't immediately budge.

'We are all aware Major,' he said, resignedly, 'that whatever happened here last night Miss Hamilton didn't commit suicide. I know my opinion counts for very little here, but that's the way I see it.'

'It's a moot point.' Spencer observed. 'Shall we just say a verdict of suicide ties up a few loose ends? Colonel Robertson needs to draw a line under all of this; there's more at stake here than a mere murder investigation.'

'But this girl was murdered,' Harmer persisted.

'Murder?' Spencer queried and pulled a face. 'You might call it murder sir; others might call it justice. She was the cause of many deaths both here and abroad. She wasn't just responsible for the murder of Sarah Davis. It goes far deeper than that.'

The AC wasn't quite sure how to respond. He was intrigued and desperately wanted to know more about the woman lying dead on the floor, and about Sarah Davis. Where did she fit into the equation? Suddenly it didn't seem to matter anymore. Why had he even bothered turning up at Red Lion Square? He'd done nothing more than make a fool of himself. More to the point, he was gripped by an overriding feeling of envy, the envy of Garvan, who'd read the Intelligence reports, while he, the Met's Assistant Commissioner, was excluded, and now thanks to Major Hall he knew precisely why. As hard as he tried, the exclusion rankled, and his lack of a high-level security clearance meant he was nothing more than an also-ran in Scotland Yard's top hierarchy.

His career might be over, but he needed to know, to satisfy his curiosity who shot Maggie Hamilton dead. He simply couldn't help himself. He posed the question and wasn't surprised by the answer.

I shot her,' Spencer said matter-of-factly. 'If you must know it was self-defence, but even if it hadn't been, I'd still have squeezed the fucking trigger!'

For Garvan, everything was starting to fall into place, the cut-throat in-fighting, and the politics; the growing antagonism against Harmer at Scotland Yard. His enemies had been circling like vultures for months now. Even before Sarah's murder investigation, there'd been numerous times when Harmer hadn't appeared to be well briefed. He now realised it simply hadn't been a case of the old man losing his grip; there'd been other factors involved, including a lack of trust after the downgrading of his security clearance. No wonder Special Branch had so ruthlessly sidelined him.

Garvan guessed there was a huge power struggle going on at the Yard. With Harmer out of the running, there was a vacuum to fill, leaving senior officers jostling for position. Sir Philip Game, as Commissioner, would have been above the pettiness. He was a stickler for the rules and always played by the book, but those around him were quite another matter. It was dog eat dog.

Promotion up to the rank of Inspector and Chief Inspector level was conducted strictly on merit; it was a given. But beyond that level, it became a whole different ball game. Merit alone was often perceived as a secondary issue, and the appointment boards became somewhat more convoluted. They were more personality based, often coming down to a particular member's personal preference. A personality clash with the wrong high ranking officer, or with someone from the Home Office could destroy a career overnight. Had his wife blotted his copy book? It was more than possible. At Harmer's level there really wasn't much room for leverage. There was also the possibility that he'd upset the Commissioner, or perhaps the Home Secretary.

Harmer looked, and was, a broken man, suddenly uncomfortable in his own skin. Almost said as an aside he mentioned something about stopping by St. Thomas's later in the afternoon to check on Mac's progress. He made to leave the flat and opened the door but turned hesitantly to address Hall once more.

'I do hope to God Major there isn't a reason for our paths to cross again.' It was a quite unnecessary remark, but as always he couldn't help himself, he was in a deep hole and still digging.

Spencer smiled broadly. Harmer had no doubt meant it as an insult, but his words fell wide of the mark.

'Trust me, sir, there's no chance of that ever happening again.' Harmer knew what he meant. They'd never work together again by dint of his lack of security clearance.

'To be perfectly honest Major Hall,' he said, at length, 'I never quite know where I stand with you.' He paused thoughtfully, before adding. 'What I find rather ironic is that I've known serial killers who I'd consider far less dangerous than you are! It's just an observation of course, but it comes from many years' of experience.'

Garvan felt a little uneasy with the ACs' character assassination. Spencer for his part was completely unperturbed. If anything, it seemed to amuse him no end. Harmer still hadn't got the message, still didn't know where to draw the line. Perhaps, Garvan decided, he ought to add a lack of diplomacy to the list of reasons why he had a problem with his security vetting.

He still hadn't finished and carried on regardless. 'In peacetime Major, you'd have been arrested by now, and found yourself on a murder charge.' He then took it into his head to round on Garvan. 'And I'm surprised by you playing along with this squalid little mess.'

It was Hall who replied in a calculated, deceptively calm voice.

'War can be fought on many levels sir; my war just happens to be fought at the shittiest level of all.' Spotting an ashtray on the sideboard he stubbed out his cigarette butt. 'Sometimes there's a need to bloody our hands. Just remember that some poor bastard is risking life and limb on your behalf so that you can go home safely every night to your nice little house in the suburbs. So don't be too hasty in either prejudging or condemning my actions. Each of us in our different way has a role to play, mine maybe not to your liking, but while we're at war, it's a necessary evil. War doesn't determine who are right - only those who are left. '

Harmer looked on the verge of answering but stalked out without another word. As he slammed the door behind him, Garvan breathed a sigh of relief.

'I must apologise for that.'

'There's no need to apologise the poor old boy's obviously lost the plot.'

'You probably didn't help matters mentioning the problem with his vetting. In one fell swoop, you blew all hope of his making Commissioner right out of the water.'

'He'd crossed the line, gone too far, and needed a reality check to put him back into his box.' Spencer looked at his watch. 'It's about time we were making a move before Dr Menzies arrives to examine the body. I don't want to get under his feet, and the sooner he and his assistant complete their preliminary work, the sooner they'll remove the body to the morgue.' Spencer headed toward the door, paused, and then swung back around to face Garvan. 'Did you get the impression your Assistant Commissioner doesn't' particularly like me?' he grinned.

Garvan couldn't help but laugh. 'I think it's a pretty safe bet you're not on his Christmas card list. But I still can't fathom what possessed him to turn up here in the first place?'

'God only knows.'

'Did you tell Sir Philip that Harmer was heading here?'

'Yes, of course, I did, but by the time I called the Commissioner, Special Branch had already tipped him off.'

'There's no love lost between him and Kendall from Special Branch I really wouldn't want to be in his shoes when he gets back to the Yard.'

Spencer gave a shrug. 'He's brought it all on himself; he'll get a bollocking from Sir Philip and no doubt a dressing down from the Home Office. You know the way it works. My guess is that his position at the Yard will eventually become completely untenable. If he's got half a brain, he'll tender his resignation and retire quietly to the suburbs, tend his garden and live out his life on a comfortable police pension.'

'He certainly won't enjoy his retirement.'

'Why ever not?'

'His old woman has been hankering after him getting a knighthood for years.' I guess she thought Lady Harmer had a rather nice ring to it.'

Spencer smiled at him. 'Then she's in for a rude awakening. I don't know about you, but I need a drink. We need to have a chat.

Chapter 20

Outside Maggie's flat the autumnal sunshine was beginning to break through the leaden skies, but there was still a sharp biting chill in the air. The strong gusting breeze caused the knarled branches of the trees in the square to sway creakily, like so many upturned knotted skeletal fingers reaching up toward the clearing sky. The last few remaining leaves fluttered to the ground and tumbled across the grass onto the damp, slippery pavements.

Garvan and Spencer walked in silence to the nearby pub of the same name as the garden square. The pub was well known locally for keeping irregular hours, and was therefore hugely popular, a magnet for workers and the local community alike. Many a drunk had been allowed to sleep off their hangover sprawled across the saloon floor. The publican neatly side-stepped the licensing laws because the Red Lion enjoyed the enthusiastic patronage of the nearby Holborn police station, whose coppers after their shifts had ended turned a blind eye to the publican's so-called lock-ins after normal opening hours. Spencer bought the first round; carrying two pint glasses across the small threadbare saloon, he joined Garvan at a table nestled in an alcove.

'It's Stout, is that okay?'

'Yes, thanks.'

Hall sat opposite Garvan, and reached into his jacket pocket and took out a pack of cigarettes. Garvan declined. Having lit a cigarette, Spencer began absent-mindedly tossing and turning his ornate silver lighter endlessly in his right hand, occasionally flicking the flame on and off as he spoke. Hall didn't encourage the trivial, and his voice had an almost mesmerising quality to it. Garvan found himself thinking that Hall wouldn't have been entirely out of place as a stage actor. The voice, the aura that he generated commanded attention, and in his case respect. He'd played the chameleon for so long as a member of the SOE; he could probably change character as easily as other people put on a comfortable old overcoat.

'Do you remember the first time you met Colonel Robertson at St. James's?' Spencer reminisced over his pint.

'Of course, I do. When I first knew him years ago, he was an interesting enough character, but now - well let's just say that meeting at St. James's was like a baptism of fire. If I'm completely honest with you Major, I wondered what the hell I'd got myself into.'

Hall's mouth twitched with the barest hint of a smile. 'He explained the reasons why he wanted you to head up the murder inquiry.'

Garvan nodded.

'After that second attack on Sarah, it was obvious to all of us we were chasing our tails and getting nowhere fast. I started pushing for help, help from Scotland Yard. To begin with the Twenty Committee were none too enthusiastic, far from it in fact, but with Tar's support the chairman, John Masterman came on side.'

'But why wasn't I called in until after Sarah was murdered?'

'Tar couldn't convince the committee to accept you were the right man for the job. They still thought we should use one of our Special Branch contacts. You can't fault their logic. Other than Tar no-one knew you from Adam.'

'So how did I get lumbered?'

'The committee requested a short list from Sir Philip, three from Special Branch of course, and just your name from the murder squad.'

'Did Sir Philip pluck my name out of the blue or did Robertson ask for me to be included?'

'Tar had an informal meeting with him and dropped your name into the conversation.' Hall looked at him long and hard, trying to gauge his expression.

'Did he take much persuading?'

'No,' Spencer said, 'quite the reverse in fact. Game had already considered throwing your name into the mix. When the list landed on the committee's desks, Robertson apparently mentioned how you'd impressed him during the Baillie-Stewart investigation, and was adamant that he wanted you right from the off, in fact, owned up that with the Commissioner's agreement, he'd personally asked for your name to be included. But it was the Commissioner's write-up of you that actually won the day, in his opinion you had the experience, the right profile to help track down Sarah's murderer. You ran a tight ship and that even when the odds were stacked up against you; you still had the ability to see a case through to the end. Quite simply he described you as the most talented Detective in your peer group.'

Garvan's expression remained unreadable, but deep down he was surprised. His relationship with Sir Philip had always been relatively distant, and it hadn't seriously crossed his mind that the old boy had thought so highly of him. Unlike Harmer, their worlds had never seriously collided, he only ever saw him at case meetings or to pass the time of day in the corridor. Game was old school, standoffish, a stickler for rules. When he became Commissioner, there'd been considerable discontent over some of the changes made by his predecessor. He'd dealt effectively with the problems and overtime had steadily improved the Met's morale.

'So Sir Philip didn't object to my name being added to the List?' was all he said.

'Far from it, he thought Tar's choice was inspired.' Hall smiled at him. 'His words not mine. From the Colonel's point of view,' Spencer explained, 'you played a straight bat.

The Commissioner confirmed you had a reputation for being a tough bastard. Ruthless, in fact, is how Sir Philip described you, but perhaps more importantly to us incorruptible. Robertson always keeps people in mind when they've made an impression on him; he stores them up, a bit like mental reference cards.'

Hall didn't quite hesitate but waited, wanting to gauge Garvan's reaction to what he was saying. He should have been a poker player; Spencer decided; he was still giving nothing away, but there again he hadn't expected him to. 'Sir Philip,' he continued, 'was quite open about some of your Met colleagues who've been known to accept the odd bung or two from characters like Charlie Price - you must know him, doesn't he own the Chester Club?'

'And about half a dozen others dotted around the West End, yes, I know Charlie very well. As for the bungs, well, there's always going to be some bent copper or other on the take, it's human nature I suppose.' Garvan couldn't help wondering where the hell Spencer's conversation was heading.

Hall drew thoughtfully on his cigarette. 'You see we needed someone we could trust implicitly and yet as far removed from our setup at St. James's as was reasonably possible. We wanted a fresh pair of eyes, someone who wouldn't get bogged down sifting through complex Intelligence reports looking for clues.'

Garvan picked up his Stout. 'I was just wondering about my security vetting' he said.

'What about it?'

'I guess that even before I found out, you knew that my wife had left me for someone else.'

Spencer flicked on his lighter before snapping the lid shut. 'Yes of course we did, but it wasn't my, I mean our place to tell you she'd run off with a WAAF officer, it was entirely immaterial to our remit, we simply weren't that interested in her. Why would we be?'

'No, I guess not.' Garvan said, thoughtfully.

'You know how the system works.'

'Yes, of course, I do.'

'Robertson was more concerned that you'd kick up a fuss and turn the case down.'

'Just like you Major, I wasn't in a position to disobey a direct order. I didn't have a choice in the matter. I guess one way or another I made it pretty obvious that I wasn't happy. I viewed the Case as an unwelcome distraction from the day job. I already had a heavy workload, and didn't want to take anything else on board, and become side-tracked by some bloody Whitehall shenanigans. The final straw came when I was ordered to transfer my other casework to colleagues around the Yard. At the time, I just couldn't understand what was so bloody important about Sarah's murder. The only thing that crossed my mind was that I was probably caught up in some grand MI5 Machiavellian plan with me caught firmly in the middle; as far as I was concerned I'd drawn the short straw and was on a hiding to nothing.'

Spencer smiled at him. 'You now know it wasn't quite that simple.'

Changing the subject, Garvan asked: 'Has anyone been to see Maggie's family yet?'

'We have tried to make contact,' Spencer explained. 'Her father is currently on his way back from Scotland. He's been up there for a week or two staying with his brother on their estate. The local constabulary believe he's due back at King's Cross this afternoon. If you don't mind, Chief Inspector, I'd like to take you along when I visit her father at the family home in Cadogan Square.'

'Are you planning on breaking the news, then?' Garvan said, unable to disguise his surprise. 'What are you going to say to the old boy that you shot his daughter?'

'Hardly, you know you're not giving me enough credit here I can be diplomatic when the occasion demands.' Spencer stubbed out his cigarette. 'However, Tar believes it'll be better all-around if you break the news to him, you know, coming from the Police and all that. Hamilton would take exception if he were told by a member of MI5 if you understand my drift?'

'So why are you coming along for the ride then?'

'In their infinite wisdom, the Twenty Committee have come to a decision that old man Hamilton, needs to be made aware that indirectly his links with Fascism set his daughter on a path of self-destruction. I won't go into all the nitty gritty, just the broad brushstrokes of her activities with the Abwehr.'

'That still doesn't explain why they've chosen you to help deliver the news of his daughter's death. Isn't it a bit like having the grim reaper turning up on your doorstep?'

'That's as maybe, but the committee do have their reasons for my going along. What we need you to do is emphasise your part in heading up the murder investigation, and that you were on the verge of taking Maggie into custody for the murder of Sarah Davis when she resisted arrest and was killed.'

'It's not going to be an easy conversation, is it?'

'Precisely,' Spencer mused. 'I thought afterwards we could perhaps visit Sergeant Mackenzie in St. Thomas's.'

'Sounds like a good idea' Garvan said, leaning thoughtfully back into his chair. 'I was just wondering.'

'Wondering what exactly?

'Do you have a grain of sympathy for Maggie Hamilton? It's just that to my mind I can't help thinking that she should never have been recruited to the Double Cross in the first place.'

He knew it was a sore point for Spencer having fought against her inclusion after her interrogation at Latchmere House. But he'd been outnumbered, outvoted by those who thought they could make good use of her. In all fairness, even Spencer accepted that Maggie had operated very successfully as a double agent right until her mission to France. Garvan just couldn't help thinking that fear as much as anything else had sent her completely over the edge.

Hall set his lighter down on the table. 'I guess that if I were being charitable, I'd have to say she was nothing more than the unwitting product of her father's Nazi sympathies. Maggie was brought up in a household where the achievements of Hitler and the Third Reich were admired and looked up to. You could argue she was indoctrinated at a very young and impressionable age. But I think the root cause of her treachery goes way beyond mere political ideology. Maggie certainly wasn't a fool. She knew that once Britain declared war on Germany, there'd be no quarter given to traitors. She took a cold, calculated decision to volunteer her services to the Abwehr. Walter Patreaus didn't exactly have to force her hand to join the cause. When we eventually arrested Maggie, she was certainly left in no doubt whatsoever about the seriousness of her situation. You already know my thoughts on the matter, Chief Inspector; I entirely agree with you, she should never have been used by us. But I was overruled. We can all voice our opinions of course, but at the end of the day, it's down to Tar and the committee. As you know she got through 'Tin Eye's' interrogation process, admittedly not with flying colours, but enough for him to write her up as promising, but requiring a bit more work. She struck him as potentially quite a good prospect for the future.'

Spencer folded his arms. 'It's certainly no secret I thought the girl was unstable right from the very start, a bloody basket case, a train crash waiting to happen.' He leaned forward on the table hands clasped together. 'The rest, as they say, Chief Inspector is history.'

'Are you sure her father didn't know what she was up to with the Abwehr?'

'Yes, yes we're content he didn't know anything. Her controllers needed Maggie to run a tight ship, her recruitment to them, as it is with us, was strictly on a need to know basis. As you can imagine James Hamilton is very well known to them, but even so, they wouldn't have wanted to widen the circle unnecessarily.

'What do you think happened in France? Why did she become a triple agent?'

'Initially, I imagine she was genuinely scared there was a possibility the Germans might have discovered she was working for us, we'll never know for certain. The only certainty is that her decision to bed Hugo Bleicher didn't stem from any sense of fear or panic. By becoming his lover she placed herself even further into the lion's den, and all her subsequent actions were calculated. She knew what she was doing. As far as her feelings toward Sarah goes it was simply a matter of kill or be killed.' His expression hardened like granite. 'I have many regrets about the evening Sarah died.' He fell silent, searching for the right words. Garvan noticed that he was gripping the cigarette lighter so tightly that his knuckles had turned almost white. 'And as for me,' he said, his voice edged with emotion, 'the only saving grace is that Sarah taught me to understand what it means to love, to love without question.' Spencer shot him a long lingering gaze before venturing. 'You know, Chief Inspector, I'd willingly have given up my life for her.'

Garvan hadn't expected such openness, such candour from Hall. He'd always been such a closed book. 'I know from personal experience that it's never easy losing a colleague,' Garvan responded, sympathetically, 'but Sarah wasn't just a colleague, was she, right now you must be going through hell.'

'The loss is one thing the guilt is quite another thing to try to cope with, to get a grip of. It never leaves you - and I guess it never will. Maybe,' he added sweeping his hand in the air, 'at the end of the day in some ways we're all victims of the system.'

'You mean for accepting Maggie Hamilton into the Double Cross?'

He looked almost resigned. 'No system is ever going to be foolproof. We're meant to weed out the basket cases; you know those likely to crack under the pressure. On this occasion, our processes failed. Fortunately, it really doesn't happen too often.' Spencer reached for his pack of cigarettes and lit another. He wanted to change the subject, and not dwell on the rights or wrongs of Hamilton's recruitment to St. James's. 'One way or another your Sergeant Mackenzie,' he said blowing out a cloud of smoke, 'has had a pretty rough time of it lately as well, what with losing his family in a bombing raid, and now this bloody lot. One thing's for certain; he'll need a few months off to recuperate it takes a long time to get over something like that.'

Garvan looked at him searchingly. 'You sound as if you know what you're talking about.'

'I do,' he said thoughtfully, 'it happened to me last year when I was in France.'

'What do you mean?'

'I was shot.'

'Who in God's name shot you?'

Without the slightest hint of irony he responded. 'The French Resistance.'

'Was that meant to be some kind of a joke?' Garvan said, in disbelief.

'I only wish it were. In all fairness to them it wasn't entirely their fault they were simply doing their duty,' he paused a smile hovering about his mouth. 'Unfortunately for me, it may have been down to the fact that I was wearing a German uniform at the time.'

'What the hell were you doing that for?'

'Tar had allowed me to return to the SOE for a particular mission. I was infiltrating a large German Garrison in Northern France. We'd received intelligence from the Resistance secret armaments were being stored there. To begin with it worked out rather well, there were so many troops in transit it was relatively easy to slip into the Garrison without too much difficulty, one more German officer amongst a thousand troops who's going to notice?'

'So how did you end up getting shot?' Garvan asked, incredulously.

Spencer explained he had a look around the Garrison Camp, found enough evidence of the armaments he'd been tasked to locate, and then decided not to hang around any longer than was necessary. It was all going very smoothly. In hindsight, perhaps too smoothly - he even managed to relieve the Germans of a staff car.

'I wouldn't normally have taken the risk,' he explained to Garvan, 'but I was already running late for a rendezvous at a farm just on the outskirts of the local town.' He leaned back, his light blue eyes staring unseeingly into the distance, reliving his fateful journey through occupied France. 'Basically, it was an ambush, a random attack. I was just in the wrong place at the wrong time. Dressed as a German officer driving down a quiet country lane I was just too good a target to resist. I do remember seeing a group of men emerging from the bushes on either side of the road carrying sub-machine guns.' He grinned to himself. 'It does tend to focus your mind, and I guess they wanted to get in some target practice. I remember the windscreen shattered, and all hell broke loose. I don't recall too much about the shooting itself. I was hit and lost control of the car and shot off the road. I do remember hitting something or other, and then the car somersaulted until it flipped to the ground and landed upside down.' Spencer gave a shrug. 'I suppose I must have blacked out at that point.'

'Why didn't they finish you off?'

'They apparently took one look at me in the car and left me for dead. I've no idea how long I was there, either way, it's a miracle I'm here at all to tell the tale.'

Spencer recalled that his next recollection was waking up in a German military hospital. He'd feigned amnesia rather than risk trying to answer too many tricky questions. The one thing he feared more than anything was that he might become delirious, and start blabbing away in English. He realised that his SOE colleagues would have started searching for him by now, he'd missed the rendezvous by God knows how many hours. They'd be trying to check out if he'd been either captured or killed, but he knew full well it would be like looking for a needle in a haystack. Hall's chilling account of his experience was interspersed with self-deprecation as if he was recounting nothing more unusual than a shopping trip down Oxford Street. His stories were invariably touched with a certain dry humour, and his daring foray into the heart of the Wehrmacht was told very matter-of-factly. Garvan listened intently as the story unfolded, and couldn't help thinking that Hall's life must have consisted of moments of great bravery, coupled with moments of abject fear. The more windows Spencer opened on to his strange twilight existence as a spy, he felt a growing admiration for the man. It required an especially unique brand of courage to operate undercover behind enemy lines, a type of courage few people were blessed with.

Seeing the consternation on Garvan's face, Spencer seemed faintly amused. 'That's enough about me,' he said, brusquely, 'that's not why I invited you to the pub. I've something more important to discuss with you.'

Garvan wasn't ready to let the matter rest; he wanted to know more, to know how Spencer had extricated himself from the hospital. Reluctantly Hall gave in and told him that as he'd grown stronger, he'd found himself rapidly running out of options. At some point, it was inevitable that he'd be unable to answer all the medical staffs' questions about his Wehrmacht unit. Unbeknown to him the same group from the local Resistance who'd shot him up on the road were now tasked with helping the SOE track him down.

'It was a stroke of luck really,' he grinned broadly.

Even now, Spencer explained to Garvan; he still wasn't quite sure how they managed to track him down in the end. The first he knew of his rescue came in the early hours of one Sunday morning when he was woken up by a French woman dressed as a German military nurse. So that he did not give the game away, she'd placed her hand over his mouth, and had whispered in his ear that Auntie had come to rescue him.

'Auntie,' Garvan repeated blankly.

'Auntie was the Codename for my SOE contact in France.'

'How did she to get you out of the hospital?'

'The nursing staff had a shift change, so there was no-one on the main ward at the time, they were in the Sister's office. My saviour placed me in a wheelchair and pushed me out of the ward to a rear loading bay, where I was hauled out of the wheelchair, and deposited into the back of an ambulance. At first, it crossed my mind she was a plant, which was a ruse by the Germans to get me out of hospital and cart me off to prison. It was when I was in the ambulance, and I heard a familiar voice that I knew I was in safe hands, thank God' he smirked. 'It was Hugh Dickinson.'

'Don't tell me he was Auntie?'

Spencer allowed a wry smile to cross his face. 'Not quite. I knew that I was in safe hands, and that's all that mattered.'

'How long did you stay in France?'

'Only a matter of days. The RAF airlifted me, and I was moved to the secure ward at the Cambridge Military Hospital in Aldershot.' His expression softened as he recalled Sarah visiting him. 'She'd been told I'd had a serious car accident, not that I'd been shot.' Spencer smiled almost to himself as much as to Garvan. 'In the end, I suppose the doctor was right once I'd been shot, and I let go of the steering wheel and crashed the bloody car.'

Garvan couldn't stop himself laughing. 'But there's something I don't understand?'

'What's that?'

'If you and Hugh Dickinson were members of the SOE, how is it that you've both ended up working for the Twenty Committee? I thought the SOE and Robertson were locked into some kind of turf war?'

'Well spotted,' Spencer relaxed and smiled. 'You're right. Dickinson and I were seconded to St. James's in much the same way as you were. We were doing our old colleagues a favour checking out the ammunition dump; there'd been a trade in information, so Robertson agreed to the mission. But in the past, we'd both made an impression on Robertson and were filed away on his mental reference cards, to be used, as and when he needed.'

'But how did Robertson manage to second you from the SOE?'

'In another life, another time, Tar would have made a great politician. He played the SOE for all they were worth, and in the end, both he and the Twenty Committee outgunned them with their Whitehall contacts.' Hall rested his elbows on the table adding, quietly. 'When Churchill's signature appears on a posting order, it's quite difficult to countermand.'

Garvan grinned at him. 'I guess that stymied the SOE just a little, even I'm impressed!'

'That's what makes Tar such a deadly adversary; he's so self-effacing, and so charming that sometimes, he's completely underestimated.'

'At least, we have something in common.'

'Do we?'

'Well, it seems that we've both been adopted by Tar Robertson for starters, and neither of us exactly had any say in the matter, did we?'

'You have a point, Chief Inspector.'

'Will you ever return to the SOE?'

Spencer met his gaze thoughtfully, and absentmindedly smoothed back his hair. 'There were a number of reasons why Tar asked me to help him out. To be honest, I was only too glad to re-join him at St. James's, it allowed me some breathing space after my convalescence.' He suddenly chuckled. 'Maybe he saw me coming. It hasn't proved much of a rest so far!! Put it this way if there's an overriding operational requirement for me to be pulled out of Robertson's setup, and then I'll go wherever it's decided, that decision is entirely out of my control. At the end of the day my fluency in German has created a particular demand for my services,' he smirked. 'I work hard and play even harder. I know old habits die hard Garvan, but enough of this grilling. Let's just give it a rest, shall we?'

It was still obvious that Garvan was on a mission, and wasn't in any particular mood to be steamrollered by Hall. He needed to know what had happened to Henryk Nowak. Spencer was happy enough for him to take the lead, it was actually playing into his hands, he needed time to tread carefully with Garvan, didn't want to press him too hard with Robertson's instructions.

'After you dropped me off at St. Thomas's,' Garvan queried, 'my gut instinct is that you were going off to find Henryk Nowak.'

'You're spot on again, Garvan.'

'Where did you find him?'

'It wasn't exactly difficult, he spends most evenings at the Pink Sink,' Spencer explained.

'I've heard of the place of course, but I've never been there.'

'I'm surprised you haven't.'

'Unless there's been a murder there recently then take it as a no.'

'You should go; it's quite a place.'

Garvan looked dubious. 'I'm getting a bit long in the tooth for clubs like that.'

'Don't knock it until you've been there, I guarantee you'd love the place, they make the best cocktails in all London. '

'So what happened when you met up with Nowak?'

'Let's just say he won't be troubling us anymore,' came, the deadly response.

It crossed Garvan's mind whether Spencer had taken it into his head to eliminate two agents in one evening, or whether he'd held back and handed him over to Special Branch.

'So where is he now?' he asked, tentatively.

Hall gave him a rueful smile. 'Not on a morgue slab if that's what you're thinking! I've merely closed his file.'

'So what does that mean?'

'In his case, it means he'll be placed in an internment camp. He's currently in custody. They'll probably send him to the camp on the Isle of Man, near Douglas. We keep quite a few of our failures there safely under lock and key.'

'But how are you going to explain away his absence to the Abwehr?'

'It's all in hand. Joyce Leader has already been instructed to send a message to Ritter, to tell him Nowak is currently under arrest for being drunk and disorderly. That his drinking is now out of control, and the booze has started not only affect his health but to jeopardise the entire Abwehr network in Britain. We'll wait for a response of course, but we already know that Ritter will want him to be closed down. He simply won't want to take the chance of Nowak cutting up rough, getting drunk and spilling the beans to the police. In his position, we'd do the same thing.'

'And then what?'

'We'll get Leader to ask Hamburg what she should do about Nowak's radio transmitter, and so it'll go on from there, bit by bit.'

'But couldn't someone else step into his shoes and take over his radio transmissions?' It's not as if your people don't write the stuff in the first place. Why not just carry on regardless?'

'It's not that easy,' Spencer told him, 'it'd be pointless trying to replicate Henryk's messages', at least, without him being physically present. To the trained ear, Morse code transmissions are as distinctive as handwriting. Whoever taught the agent in the first place at the Abwehr's

Hamburg training school, would detect any bogus messages from a different operator, a different hand. We had problems with him a few months ago. His communications had been tapped out so erratically through his drinking that Ritter believed British Intelligence had forged his messages. At the time, they'd wanted to close him down immediately. It was a close shave.'

'So why didn't you close him down there and then, wasn't it the perfect excuse?'

'The timing didn't quite fit in with Robertson's plans. We were still caught up in the investigation into Sarah's murder. In the short term, it might have saved us a great deal of trouble, but the Twenty Committee wanted all their agents to remain in situ until Sarah's killer had been tracked down.'

'So how did you stop Hamburg from closing him down?'

'One of our double agents was tasked to inform Ritter, that Henryk was developing a serious drink problem, which had accounted for his increasingly erratic messages.'

'And was that enough to stop Ritter from pulling the plug on him? If I was Ritter, I don't think I'd have taken the chance.'

Spencer was pleased with Garvan's analysis. 'Tar always knew it was only going to be a temporary fix, but we managed to spin it just enough to give us a little extra time. As far as Ritter was concerned Henryk was still a high risk and living on borrowed time; but Robertson ordered that we upgrade the quality of his transmissions to Hamburg, it gave us a hook to keep Ritter from pulling the plug.'

'So won't Ritter question why "Agent Nicolette" has suddenly stopped all contact?

'We've sorted it out.'

'I rather thought you might have, but how?'

'We're going to get Joyce Leader again to send a message; it'll be blunt and to the point. There's probably a grain of truth in it.' Spencer reached inside the pocket of his jacket and produced a folded piece of A4 paper. 'Read it,' he said bluntly, passing it across the table.

Garvan opened it. The note was headed, Prost. He looked up questioningly. 'Why Prost?'

'Prost as in a toast to someone, it's a password only used by Leader to highlight an important message for Ritter's attention. Maggie had a similar one it was slàinte because of her Scottish blood.'

Garvan nodded and read Hall's handwritten note. Joyce was to say that Maggie has been arrested outside the Union Jack Club. "Impossible for her to carry on. Will contact you again at 18.00hrs for any further updates or instructions."

'Is this classified?'

'Well, it will be once I've placed it on file. Give me a chance Chief Inspector I've not long written the damn thing.'

'And eventually, you'll let them know she's dead?'

'All in good time, maybe by the end of the week. The timing is up to Tar. As I understand it, we'll let Hamburg know she died resisting arrest having been charged with the murder of Sarah Davis.' His eyes met Garvan's. 'I guess that should put the wind up them for a while.'

Garvan handed back the paper. 'So why are you using Joyce for all this stuff? You must have others who could do it.'

'Think of it. Ritter will have in effect lost two of his agents in a single week. It really won't go down too well with his masters in Berlin. He needs to produce results to prove constantly he's providing valuable intelligence. In that respect, he's no different from Tar or the Twenty Committee.

We're all under constant pressure to deliver the goods on a daily basis. With the removal of Nowak and Hamilton from the scene, Leader's standing with Ritter will now be even higher than it was before. From his perspective, she's sound, reliable and consistently provides high-quality information. And from our point of view, she's also one of our most trusted double agents.'

'I see,' Garvan said, thoughtfully.

'For all her faults and God knows there are many, our main concern was that it was Joyce who'd turned. She's always been far more valuable to us than Maggie Hamilton ever was. With Maggie and Nowak out of the equation, she'll prove to be even more important in helping us shape the German High Command strategy. With double agents of her calibre, we're able to pull strings in Berlin, and even influence their thinking, their decisions. Joyce Leader is certainly tough enough, and bright enough to help carry it through.'

Garvan was still learning, still trying to get a grip on Spencer's work with the Double Cross.

'I think it's time we got down to serious business.' Hall started rolling his cigarette between his fingers. 'Since the beginning of the inquiry into Sarah's death, John Masterman, the chairman of the committee has been impressed by your support and handling of the investigation.'

'I've never met Masterman.'

'He's an academic,' Spencer told him flourishing the cigarette in the air. 'After being interned in Rubleben detention camp during 1914, he polished up his German. I guess there wasn't much else to do.'

'What was he doing there?'

'He was an exchange lecturer at the University of Freiburg.'

Garvan raised his brows, 'Was he well treated?'

'He had enough books to keep him occupied. In a perverse kind of way, he enjoyed himself.' Spencer sucked hard on his cigarette. 'Masterman intends putting something formally in writing to the Commissioner about your involvement with the murder investigation.'

Garvan's face registered surprise. He'd always felt that his role had been somewhat limited, constrained by the difficulties surrounding the case, that he hadn't contributed very much in helping track down Maggie Hamilton.

'I don't' understand.'

'We have a bit of a problem.'

'What problem?' Garvan repeated blankly.

'I should explain it's probably not so much of a problem as a proposal, only how shall I say, it's a little complicated.'

Garvan looked nonplussed. 'You've lost me, but not for the first time, everything's ruddy complicated where you're concerned.'

'You have a point, but to put it bluntly, you have two job offers on the table one, from the Commissioner and one from Colonel Robertson.'

Garvan's eyes narrowed questioningly; he was curious, if not a little on edge, what were they offering?

'Tomorrow,' Hall continued, 'Sir Philip Game is going to offer you an appointment with Special Branch.'

'Special Branch, really?' He was genuinely surprised by the offer.

'You can't fault his reasoning can you, after working alongside MI5 it's a logical progression. I know you did a stint with them as a junior officer, but let's face it you've got even more to offer them now. My understanding and I could have got it wrong,' Spencer said raising his hand, 'is that initially, you'd be slightly more desk-bound than you're accustomed to, but I guess things would change rapidly once you'd got there.'

'Are you sure about this?'

'Let's just say I've made it my business to find out.'

Garvan didn't doubt that he had. He found himself almost reluctant to ask about Robertson's job offer.

'And what about the Colonel's offer?'

'Having visited my office you probably noticed the team's made up of a rather strange mix of people. All of us in our own way have a particular talent or skill.' A slow ironic smile crossed Spencer's face. 'I can almost hear the cogs starting to turn over in your mind wondering what particular talents I have to offer.'

Garvan relaxed and smiled. 'Am I that transparent?'

'But this isn't about me it's about you Garvan, we need someone with your experience, someone with your ability to scrutinise complex documents, to extract information, which to the untrained eye might be overlooked. And who better than a professional Detective to interview German spies, after all, it'll be no more than bread and butter stuff for you.' Spencer coolly met his gaze. 'I'll be perfectly frank with you St. James's lacks someone with your experience and your expertise.'

'But there's any number of Special Branch officers' who'd fit the bill.'

'That's as maybe; you probably know the two Special Branch officers MI5 has already seconded to good effect.'

Garvan began shaking his head. 'I do know them, but with due respect Major, I don't think I'm the right man for the job.'

'Why ever not?' Spencer asked him bluntly.

He breathed deeply, leaned back in his seat, and momentarily raised his gaze heavenward at the badly cracked plastered ceiling. 'Take yesterday for example,' he said, resting his arms on the table.

'What about yesterday?'

'I don't have a problem working undercover, it's a given, that's not the issue, but you're missing something here, or I am, I'm just not cut out for the role of some bloody would-be assassin.'

Spencer raised his brows; he appeared amused by Garvan's response. 'It's something of an acquired skill.'

'Well, if you don't mind it's one I'd rather not acquire.'

'Good God, Garvan I'm not asking you to. Why do you think the committee employed Sarah Davis? She wasn't exactly cut out to be an assassin either.'

'I know that,' he conceded.

'If I wanted someone for that line of work, I'd look to one of my own operatives, and not an ex-Met officer. All I, all we want is for you to sit in on the occasional interview of Abwehr agents at Latchmere, to work alongside 'Tin Eye' Stephens, but report directly back to St. James's', and provide your input, your thoughts. The rest of the time you'd be scrutinising paperwork, analysing incoming intelligence, and writing up reports.' Spencer rested his cigarette on the ashtray. 'Chief Inspector, I'm not asking for strong-arm tactics that's really more my department than yours, you know that.'

A posting to re-join Special Branch at this stage of his career would be considered a damned good move; there'd be no delays in being appointed as he already held the proper levels of security clearance. There'd be countless high profile cases, some doubtless relating to national security.

On the other hand, superficially, at least, Hall's proposal sounded pretty sedentary, but try as he might, Garvan couldn't quite bring himself to believe that any offer from Spencer Hall would ever prove to be that straightforward. His instinct was to play it safe, to remain at Scotland Yard and accept Sir Philip's coveted job offer with Special Branch.

But a voice inside his head was still telling him to take his time and weigh up both offers. If he decided to accept Hall's proposition, it was a huge step, a gamble, and completely outside his comfort zone. It could quite literally alter his life forever or very possibly shorten it. All the while Spencer continued to spin his line with disarming clarity. Garvan listened and found himself almost being swept along by his infectious enthusiasm for what lay ahead if he joined St. James's. Try as he might, he still couldn't quite dislodge the thought of staring down the barrel of Maggie Hamilton's revolver in Mepham Street, or how, a few weeks earlier he had been knocked senseless in his own flat.

Garvan suddenly realised Hall had stopped talking. The hard sell was over; he was sitting back and picking up his cigarette. He inhaled heavily as if in dire need of a sudden nicotine fix.

'I distinctly remember you saying,' Garvan said to him, 'that we'd be completely safe at the Union Jack Club. But it didn't quite pan out that way, did it?'

Spencer's expression was quite unreadable.

'Mac ended up lying in hospital nursing a gunshot wound, and by all accounts was fucking lucky to have escaped with his life.'

'I can't deny it was unfortunate,' Hall responded, with his usual understatement. 'But I think that you forget that Maggie Hamilton was totally out of control, and on the verge of a complete mental breakdown, it was just bad luck Mackenzie ended up getting in the way of a bullet meant for Joyce Leader.'

Garvan drained his beer, God he thought, I'm getting nowhere here he's got a fucking answer for everything. The trouble was he was right.

'You're not a man of violence Chief Inspector,' Hall carried on seamlessly, 'I'm not even asking you to carry a gun. There aren't any hidden agendas or catches, I promise.'

A silence fell between the two men, a silence Spencer was in no rush to break. He was far too astute to press the matter further. He took himself over to the bar and ordered a fresh round of drinks, and then headed off to the Gents. When he emerged, he lingered at the bar chatting to the publican. It was a shrewd move on his part allowing Garvan enough time to weigh up some of the pros and cons of joining Tar Robertson's team of unconventional misfits.

He still felt uneasy at the prospect of joining St. James's. He was well aware that Robertson already had a file on him, held a record of his entire life history, his every success, and every single mistake he'd ever made since leaving school. Even to where he bought his clothes, his bank details, right down to the last penny he owed to the corner shop. Apart from the obvious intrusion into his personal life, which he accepted as being part of the status quo, Garvan was firmly convinced that if he accepted Robertson's offer, Spencer would end up leading him on a crazy roller coaster ride of extreme highs alternated with the lows of abject bloody fear. The trouble was if he turned the offer down he'd probably end up living the rest of his life regretting the decision. Equally, the prospect of working for Special Branch again was a golden opportunity to further his career, and the fact that Sir Philip Game had proposed him for the role was recommendation enough. As with Robertson's offer, it had come as a bolt out of the blue, completely unexpected.

To give Hall credit, he hadn't disguised the fact that it was a lot to ask at such a pivotal stage in his career, perhaps a step too far, to walk away from Scotland Yard and the world he knew so well. Hall wasn't certain what Garvan's answer would be, and he certainly didn't want to put any additional pressure on him, and as he suspected correctly, it wouldn't have worked anyway.

Spencer returned to their table carrying two fresh pints. 'Sorry to have sprung this on you like this,' he apologised placing them down. 'But if you do jump ship I don't think it'll do your career at Scotland Yard any harm, quite the reverse in fact. You've nothing to lose.'

'What about my life?' Garvan said setting his eyes on Hall.

'That's crap, and you know it!' Spencer said.

'Is it?'

Hall raised his beer and said. 'At the end of the day I can't force your hand, either way, it's entirely your decision, it has to be. Take as much time as you need, it's a big commitment to make over a couple of pints in a pub. I won't deny Special Branch is an excellent opportunity for you, high profile, interesting, and a tick in the right box for promotion. Rumour has it your already earmarked for greater things at the Yard.'

Garvan smirked. 'Bloody typical I'm always the last to know. The last few months with Harmer at the helm have been a fucking nightmare!'

'Ah well he's out of the equation now,' Hall said, dismissively. 'It's an enormous decision for you to join MI5, I know that, and I'll understand if you turn us down. But as I've already said, a tour with us might not do your prospects any harm at all. For starters, you'll certainly come to the attention of the great and good at the Home Office. At the end of your secondment, you'd end up being a prime candidate for Special Branch again. Only this time round armed with an array of Intelligence contacts your colleagues could only ever dream of.'

Spencer couldn't have been fairer, he'd laid down the facts, and it was now up to Garvan to make a decision.

Hall took a cigarette out of the packet; he met Garvan's steady, unblinking gaze.

'I know. I smoke too much.'

'I guess things with Sarah haven't helped.'

'That's just an excuse, but I'll always find a reason, at least until the war's over,' he added, almost wistfully. 'I might be wrong Garvan, but you don't strike me as a man who relishes the Yard's internal politics and the petty jealousies any more than I would,' he said. 'I guess it happens in every large organisation. The Army certainly isn't without its internal bickering and struggles. Personally speaking, I've found working alongside Tar has allowed me a certain amount of freedom, you know, away from the constraints of the SOE.' He absent-mindedly began tracing his index finger around the rim of his glass. 'It hasn't always been easy with the SOE, at least not in the early days. As you can imagine, there were quite a few teething problems, but like everything else, with experience, their methods have become far more sophisticated. I'd like to return one day, but that decision rests solely with Tar.'

'I can't imagine him releasing you anytime soon.'

'You may well be right Garvan,' he answered, in a measured tone. 'I can't exactly offer you sanctuary with the Double Cross, far from it, but I can offer you a degree of freedom that you've never enjoyed at Scotland Yard.'

Spencer had done his homework well Garvan thought he knew exactly which buttons to press. He'd hit on the in-fighting, the jockeying for position, in fact, every bugbear that constantly irritated him. There was always the chance a stint with the Double Cross might well hinder his future career prospects; there were certainly no guarantees. On the other hand, as Hall had pointed out Special Branch would certainly welcome him back with open arms. His insider knowledge and the gravitas of dealing with Government Ministers would make him an invaluable asset to the Yard.

'I may have misjudged the situation,' Spencer continued, turning on the charm, 'I just saw it as an opportunity which might appeal to you.' He sank his beer in one go and unexpectedly reached for his coat. 'As I said, you don't have to make a decision right now, just think of it, you know where to find me.' He stood up and slipped on the coat. 'If I don't hear from you by the end of the week I'll give you a call.'

'You don't have to wait until the end of the week Major you can have my answer right now.'

It was Spencer's turn to register surprise. 'Are you sure you don't need more time, it's a big decision?'

'No, my mind's made up.'

Hall's eyes narrowed questioningly.

'You can tell Colonel Robertson I'll accept his offer.'

'Good God man, I thought you were going to blow us right out of the water!'

Garvan smiled. 'I may, of course, live to regret joining the Double Cross. I'm taking a chance, a big chance.'

'But are you sure?' Spencer asked, still shaken by Garvan agreeing so soon. 'Tar dragged me kicking, and screaming from the SOE, I still give him gyp at times, keep reminding him that I'm a square peg in a round hole.'

'And what does he say?'

Hall chuckled. 'He reckons I'm a work in progress and that once he's got rid of my rough edges, I'll fit in just fine. But tell me, Garvan, what about Special Branch, are you sure?'

'I guess as you pointed out there'll be other opportunities in the future.'

Hall reached out to shake his hand. 'Do you know that the difference between a good and bad joke. It's all about the timing - in your case, the timing couldn't be better. At least not only for Tar and myself but think of it, a year or two down the line when you return to the Yard and get your appointment with Special Branch, you'll be streets ahead of your peer group. Welcome aboard Chief Inspector.' Spencer sounded genuinely pleased.

'I think I probably need my head testing, but at the end of the day I suppose I can always blame you if it all goes tits up!'

Spencer laughed. 'We'll contact the Commissioner later today, and then let the shit hit the fan when he tells Charles Harmer. I'd love to see the expression on the old buggers' face.' He buttoned his coat. 'I think it's time we made a move and headed off to Cadogan Square and break the news to Maggie's father.'

On the way to the Tube Station, they passed a pile of rubble, where once a row of terraced houses had stood until the Luftwaffe decided to do a little demolition work of their own. The rescue services were out in force; Air Raid Wardens, firemen, police and the Home Guard were searching through the rubble looking for signs of life beneath the collapsed buildings. They'd formed a human chain, and despite the obvious dangers were determined to carry on until there was no possible hope of finding anyone else alive.

In the midst of the debris they saw an old man sitting on a wooden crate, a policeman crouched down at his side handing him a mug of tea. Garvan noticed the old boy's hands were shaking so uncontrollably; he had difficulty trying to get a grip on the mug. Beside him sat a small white dog as dirty and dusty as his owner. It kept whimpering, its eyes wide with fear, and locked onto the old man's face. He was clearly as bewildered and shaken as his master. They huddled together both of them trembling with shock. Occasionally the old man would reach down, to reassure his pet. In turn, the dog would half-heartedly wag its tail almost as if it too was trying to reassure the old man.

Only ten minutes earlier they'd been trapped beneath the collapsed wooden beams of their home. Those same beams had helped to save their lives as the remainder of the house crashed around them. Beneath the rubble, the old man had wrapped his arms around the dog in a desperate effort to protect his pet fearing for their both lives, until the auxiliary services had finally hauled them to safety.

A fireman, poised precariously on top of the debris shouted for silence. Garvan and Hall stopped dead in their tracks. The man leaned forward anxiously listening for what he thought had been a cry for help. An uneasy silence fell, the atmosphere taut. Everyone hoped they'd found someone else alive. Until now they'd only managed to pull a handful of people from the debris.

Garvan's eyes narrowed, locking onto a mound of bricks and mortar spread across the road. At first, he hadn't quite managed to work out what it was he could see sticking through the debris until it dawned on him, that it was an arm, a child's arm, reaching up toward the autumn sky at a strangely distorted angle. He said a silent prayer. The child was past all hope before they'd even had a chance to live. Looking around at the desolation, he found himself thinking how on earth the auxiliary services could do this stuff day in and day out, how in hell's name did they cope with the prospect of digging some poor dead kid out of the rubble?

They were all still waiting, still listening, and straining for the slightest murmur or sound. The fireman leaned up, and shook his head to his colleagues; he was mistaken, he said or had perhaps been simply too late to help. Garvan looked round and watched Spencer dart off across the road, he lit a cigarette and gently handed it to the old man sitting on the crate, his eyes still stricken with shock, but even so, he managed to nod his thanks. Hall rested his hand on the old boy's shoulder, leant down and said something before heading back across the road.

'Poor bugger,' Spencer said to Garvan, 'he couldn't have known what bloody hit him.'

'But at least, he's alive.'

Hall nodded.

'Did you see the child's arm sticking out of the rubble?'

'Couldn't sodding miss it, could you?' Spencer grunted staring straight ahead.

They hadn't even reached the end of the road before they heard the same fireman call out again. 'Over here,' he shouted pointing down. The rescuers descended as one toward a faint tapping sound. Garvan and Hall halted, waiting just long enough to see a woman dug out of the rubble. She was scarcely alive and covered in blood, but it was a victory of sorts.

'We'd better get going, there's nothing we can do to help them out,' Spencer suggested.

'I guess not.' Garvan agreed, albeit reluctantly.

Outside Holborn Tube Station, a newspaper vendor was setting up his pitch. The headline emblazoned on the placard read "Heavy Luftwaffe losses last night." It was the usual fare of propaganda aimed at boosting public morale. It was perfectly understandable of course, but having just seen the old boy and his dog sitting forlornly in the middle of the street he had difficulty believing the Luftwaffe might not just have the upper hand.

Chapter 21

Spencer rang the doorbell of a large red bricked house in Cadogan Square. The property had belonged to the Hamilton family since the late 19th century. Maggie's father had inherited the place on his father's death back in 1929. The black front door clicked open. Garvan and Hall were greeted by rather a small, grey-haired man, in rolled up shirt sleeves. He was no more than about five feet in height, his eyes at once wary, and judging by his appearance he'd just emerged from somewhere in the basement as his hands and shirt were smudged with a black oily grease. Garvan presented his warrant card to him and asked to see Mr Hamilton on an urgent matter relating to his daughter, Maggie.

The man's eyes suddenly darted toward Spencer in wary recognition. 'Major,' he said, with a slight inclination of his head.

'Perrodow, it's been a while since we last met.'

'Yes sir,' he said, opening the door wider. 'Come in gentlemen,'

He escorted them across the imposing black and white chequered floored hallway and into a large room on the right of the hall. Once inside Garvan stopped dead in his tracks, as he tried to take stock of what had once been, at least in its heyday an elegant Georgian dining room.

His eyes were drawn to the large dining table in the centre of the room, which must have been capable of seating, at least, twenty people comfortably. It was submerged completely under a raft of papers strewn across its entire surface. He then began to realise that every single available space in the dining room was piled high with an assortment of old files, letters and dust-covered books. This was hoarding on a grand and disorganised scale, clutter beyond belief. There were countless stacks of discoloured newspapers dotted randomly about the floor. It was as if James Hamilton was completely unwilling to discard or able to throw anything away. Even the faded green walls were in urgent need of a fresh lick of paint, and the ceiling was stained a disgusting brownish yellow through years of endless cigar and cigarette smoke.

As the door closed on them, Garvan turned to Hall. 'What the hell's going on here, what's the old boy think he's playing at? How can he live like this?'

Spencer grinned at him but wasn't surprised by the chaos. 'Fucking mess isn't it.'

'Everything's covered in dust, and it smells like a musty old library gone wrong,' Garvan said, still trying to take in the mess around them. 'What about the rest of the house, is it the same as this?'

'God yes, I've been here a few times before. Remember, he's been under surveillance for a while now.' Spencer glanced around the room. 'He's lived like this for years, calls it his office. Since the war started the only member of staff left is the old boy who answered the door. Poor old Perrodow does all the odd jobs around the house, and a few more besides like looking after Marianne, Hamilton's wife when she's had one too many to drink. The poor sod's bedroom is a converted store cupboard. I think he stayed on to help Maggie and her sister Vivian out when they were younger. They treated him well enough, but since they've moved on things can't be any too easy for him.'

Garvan still hadn't quite managed to get over his shock at the state of the room; Spencer looked on amused at the expression of horror on his face.

'Tar thinks he's just a little eccentric; I just think the old bastard's barking mad. He was lucky not to end up spending the war under lock and key; he's fared a lot better than many of his Right Club cronies.'

At the beginning of the war, Hall explained, Hamilton was arrested under Defence Regulation 18B, which in effect allowed the authorities to imprison people suspected of being Nazi sympathisers. He was held for six months; then it was decided he didn't pose a realistic threat to national security. Hamilton had apparently felt vindicated, almost as if he'd beaten the system. While other leading members of the Right Club remained incarcerated, MI5 continued to monitor Hamilton's activities as a means of gauging how much of an on-going problem the extreme right wing in Britain still posed. He was in effect out on license until such time as MI5 decided to rein him in again.

The dining room door opened, and James Hamilton entered. Garvan instantly recognised him from pictures in the daily newspapers and the Picture Post. At the time, Hamilton had struck him as being something of an imposing figure, but in reality, he was smaller and much older than he expected. He was slim to the point of being wiry and had a neat grey moustache with a mop of silky white hair. The suit, like the dining room, had seen better days. It was covered in a combination of cigarette and cigar ash. There was also the odd cigarette burn on the jacket.

So here was the famous firebrand of British right-wing politics, a close friend of Oswald Mosley, the leader of the British Union of Fascists, and of Archibald Ramsay, the Tory MP who'd founded the Right Club.

There must have been some defining quality that had brought Hamilton so notoriously to political prominence, but right now, Garvan thought, he just seemed like a rather grey, nondescript figure with a permanent scowl etched across his forehead. Hamilton quietly closed the door, his eyes locked instantly on Spencer, with what can only be described as a disdainful look up and down. His expression said it all.

'Major Hall, I didn't know you were here as well.' He made a point of turning to Garvan. 'Perrodow mentioned there was a Chief Inspector Garvan from Scotland Yard to see me. I take it that's you?' He asked condescendingly.

Choosing not to answer Garvan merely inclined his head slightly. Hamilton's voice carried loudly through the room, the Oxbridge accent sharp, rather peremptory, and he came across to Garvan as being overbearingly arrogant. He guessed the old boy probably viewed all policemen, however senior, as little more than publically funded hired help. He started to sympathise with Spencer's understandable antipathy toward the cantankerous old sod.

'My man told me you needed to see me urgently.'

'That's correct.'

'So what is it that brings you to my home, Chief Inspector?'

'Unfortunately Sir, I've come here about your daughter.'

'Which one, Vivian or Maggie?' he barked.

'It's about Maggie.'

For a moment, he allowed his expression to register surprise. His odd job man, Perrodow, hadn't mentioned Maggie nor had he told him that Major Hall was with the Chief Inspector. As a result, Hamilton had naturally assumed their call was connected to the Right Club.

'This obviously isn't some social visit,' he snorted looking directly at Spencer. 'I really can't imagine the Major here would turn up on my doorstep unannounced without good cause. So tell me,' he said addressing Garvan, 'what brings you here, what has my daughter to do with either of you?'

'There's no easy way of telling you this Sir, but your daughter died last night.'

'Maggie,' James said, blankly.

'Yes, sir.'

'I'm - I'm sorry Chief Inspector,' he stammered trying desperately to take the news on board.

'We did try contacting you earlier in Scotland at your brother's estate.'

'Did you,' he said vaguely.

'We placed a call to the local police, but unfortunately, we'd just missed you, you were already on the train to King's Cross. I apologise for the delay.'

Hamilton wasn't surprised the local police knew of his exact whereabouts, he was under constant surveillance by the authorities both north and south of the border. It didn't matter where he travelled, it had become an irritant in his life, but he'd learned to live with the constant attention, the interminable snooping. But he was shocked at the news of Maggie's death, it had hit him hard, and he didn't quite know how to respond or what to say. For once in his life, he was quite lost for words. He moved over to the sideboard and poured himself a large whisky. Standing with his back to them, only a slight tremor in his hand gave away any hint of his grief.

He turned back to face them and asked abruptly, 'How did my daughter die Chief Inspector tell me?' Gripping the glass close to his chest, his eyes glistened with tears. 'Please tell me,' he begged, 'what in God name's happened to her?'

As a father, Garvan empathised with Hamilton's loss, clearly for all his many faults, he was distraught and had loved his daughter deeply. Dispassionately Garvan explained that they had been on the point of arresting Maggie for murder, but that she'd suddenly pulled a gun on him and his colleague. Visibly shaken, Hamilton sat himself down at the head of the deeply cluttered dining table. Taking a sharp intake of breath, he gripped the whisky glass tightly in his hands. He was clearly struggling.

'Murder charges you say?' he said, in disbelief. His eyes met Garvan's. They were wary, questioning. 'Maggie was always such a gentle, loving girl.' He downed a large shot of whisky. 'It can't be right, it can't be right,' he repeated shaking his head, 'there must surely be some mistake.'

'I can assure you there's no mistake sir.'

'But how did she come to have possession of a gun?'

'We're still investigating the matter,' Garvan explained to him. 'I know this must have come as a terrible shock to you Mr Hamilton, but your daughter's action's last night ended up with a Detective Sergeant shot, and lying critically ill in hospital. It's only by the grace of God he's pulled through.'

Hamilton was clearly wrong-footed and wasn't quite sure how he should respond. What could he say that would make any difference? He seemed almost to brace himself before asking. 'How - how did my daughter die?'

'She was shot dead in self-defence, sir.'

'Self-defence?' he repeated, in a measured tone. 'In defending your sergeant, is that what you mean, Chief Inspector?

'Yes, she was,' Garvan lied, giving Spencer a meaningful look.

'But murder charges,' Hamilton said, distractedly, 'who exactly is my daughter accused of murdering?'

'A woman called Sarah Davis.'

He shook his head. 'I've never heard of the girl.'

'There's no reason you would have sir. They weren't exactly friends. Theirs was a strictly working relationship.'

Hamilton bowed his head. 'I don't' understand, Chief Inspector, please tell me?' He looked at Garvan pleadingly. 'I don't understand why my daughter would wish to take this woman's life?' He looked totally bewildered, completely broken. 'Was she a colleague of Maggie's from the BBC?' he suggested, hoping to find an answer.

'No, Miss Davis didn't work for the BBC.'

'Then forgive me Chief Inspector, please explain what connection there was between them, and why you believe Maggie murdered this poor woman?'

'We had a cast iron case against your daughter.'

Hamilton visibly steeled himself as Garvan began explaining the background to the murder inquiry, firstly, how the Abwehr had recruited his daughter by a young man called, Walter Patreaus during their last annual family holiday to France before the outbreak of the war.

Hamilton suddenly looked shell-shocked and placed his hands together as if in prayer. He cast his mind back, and remembered meeting Patreaus in London, when he'd been an exchange student, but couldn't recall seeing him again in France. If memory served him, Walter hadn't appeared to have a single political bone in his entire body. But since then, of course, the world, life itself had changed out of all recognition. He then heard Garvan say that Maggie had seemed a natural choice, an ideal candidate for the Abwehr given his highly publicised Nazi sympathies.

Hamilton took a sharp intake of breath. It was difficult enough to discover his daughter was dead, let alone that she'd somehow become embroiled in the grubby world of espionage as a result of his political activities. He stared straight ahead with unseeing eyes, lost in thought as he listened as his daughter's story unfolded.

'Twelve weeks to the day,' Garvan explained, 'after Walter Patreaus recruited your daughter during the family's holiday in France, she travelled to Germany. She was quite within her rights to do so of course, war hadn't been declared, and there were no limitations on travel then.' He met Hamilton's eyes coolly. 'Were you aware of your daughter's visit to Germany?'

'No Chief Inspector I was not,' he said, stiffly.

'Everything was arranged for her by the Abwehr. Maggie stayed at Wohlsdorf, a suburb of Hamburg. It was where she learned how to operate a short-wave radio transmitter. At a later date, her radio was shipped over to Southampton, and deposited at the left luggage for her to pick up the following day.'

Hamilton closed his eyes briefly, before shooting Spencer a long, cold hard look. 'At least, I now understand why you've brought Major Hall along with you Chief Inspector, it explains everything!' He then looked back at Garvan and said. 'You still haven't explained how Miss Davis fits into this whole sorry saga?'

Garvan didn't respond. He glanced at Spencer. This was Twenty Committee territory, not his. Hamilton noted the exchange between the two men and waited, dreading what Hall might have to say as he took up the story.

Hall's manner was clipped, and to the point as he began rattling off how MI5 had intercepted Maggie's transmissions to her German handlers. As a result, she'd been arrested at her flat in London, interrogated by British Intelligence, and eventually agreed to become a double agent working for MI5.

Hamilton hadn't thought things could get any worse, but by now his thoughts were in free fall. He desperately wanted to end it all, to silence Hall and tell them to leave. There was simply too much to take on board all at once. It was bad enough learning of his daughter's death, let alone discovering she was working for the Abwehr and had then somehow ended up killing someone before injuring a Scotland Yard Detective.

How in God's name Hamilton began thinking to himself was he going to break all of this to his wife? The shock alone might end up killing her. He couldn't help but imagine she'd end up blaming him for Maggie's death, blame him for brainwashing their daughter with his fascist principles. His eyes narrowed. Did he hear correctly, had Spencer Hall mentioned that Maggie was sent to France, there'd been a high ranking Abwehr lover, she'd betrayed members of the French Resistance? Hall's words were rattled out like machine gun fire. Once Maggie was back in England, Hamilton heard him say, fearing her duplicity would be discovered she murdered Sarah Davis, her London MI5 controller in cold blood.'

He took a moment to speak. 'Will any of this be made public?' he asked, tentatively.

'You have my word, sir it will not,' Spencer assured him. 'I think we're all agreed that it's for the best if your daughter's activities were left out of the headlines.'

'I see,' Hamilton said thoughtfully, before meeting Hall's eyes. 'I presume my daughter would be deemed something of an embarrassment to His Majesty's Government.'

'That's one way of looking at it,' Spencer said flatly, 'but I'd have thought you might also be grateful your daughter's name wasn't splashed all across the headlines.'

He gave Hall a long hard stare but didn't respond.

'Just picture them,' Hall said with a flourish, 'the Right Wing Fascist, James Hamilton's daughter arrested on espionage charges!'

Hamilton could see his point. 'I think you have to remember Major Hall that I never wanted the Germans to win this war, I just wanted peace, and I still do before Britain finds itself on its knees and ready to surrender.'

'That's as maybe, but you know damn well the Press would have had a field day with you and your family. Be honest, would you really want reporters lining up on your doorstep again? I remember Maggie telling me that it was a pretty unpleasant experience for all the family. Let's face it, Mr Hamilton since war was declared you haven't exactly had an easy ride in the newspapers, have you?'

'You may well be right Major.' James drained his whisky glass. 'But to be perfectly honest.' he added, 'the only thing I need to know right now is when you expect the authorities will release my daughter's body?'

'My understanding,' Garvan interjected, 'is that it'll probably be sometime next week. The Coroner's office will be in touch with you shortly and let you have all the necessary details.'

'Thank you, Chief Inspector.' Hamilton stood up, his emotions now in check. He placed his empty glass down on the sideboard and adjusted his jacket. 'Now if you don't mind gentleman I must ask you to leave. You'll understand that I need to break the news of my darling Maggie's death to my wife.'

Stepping out of the house back into Cadogan Square, Garvan breathed a huge sigh of relief. 'I'm glad that's over and done with.'

Spencer pulled up his collar. There was a decided chill in the air. 'He's as tough as old boots that one.'

'I wasn't sure you'd be quite so open about her spying for the Abwehr, and what happened in France. Aren't you worried he might talk things through with his right wing cronies?' he asked.

'No,' Spencer replied bluntly. 'The Twenty Committee made a conscious decision to be entirely open. Even if he does decide to confide in his friends, it really won't make any tangible difference. But my gut feeling is that Hamilton will keep his head down now.' Spencer walked slightly ahead before turning to wait for Garvan to catch up. 'You know, you really mustn't be fooled by the old boy. If Hamilton ever got half a chance, we'd both be interned as enemies of the State.

Garvan looked at him questioningly.

'Make no mistake, he might seem like some mild old eccentric codger to you, but the man's a dangerous maverick. Heaven forbid if we lose this war. Hamilton and his cronies will be right up at the front there helping Adolf rule this country. Not a pleasant thought is it?'

'Not really.'

'The Twenty Committee knows Hamilton has seen a copy of the Sonderfahndungsliste GB.

'What in God's name is that?' Garvan queried.

'It's an arrest list drawn up on Himmler's orders. It consists mainly of prominent, or from a Nazi point of view undesirable personalities living in Britain. It's quite an interesting mix. Some of the names were to be expected, others less so.'

'So what would happen to those on the list?

'They'd be in the first wave of arrests' after the invasion.'

'And Hamilton, what would they expect of him?'

'That he'd become a member of a quasi-political Government.'

'Meaning what exactly?'

'Berlin would pull the strings. They'd be the puppet masters for the likes of Hamilton while Hitler and his cohorts made all the real decisions.' Hall smirked at him. 'After our little visit today I reckon we'll both be topping the list in the first wave of arrests.'

Garvan pulled a face. 'I'll bear that in mind!'

From Sloane Square, they caught a train to Waterloo and walked the short distance to St. Thomas's Hospital. On Sebastopol Ward at the nurses' station the duty matron met them. She checked her notes and said Mackenzie was still a little groggy from last night's anaesthetic, but that overall the doctors seemed quite pleased with his progress. She asked them to keep their visit short as he needed plenty of rest.

'Mind you Chief Inspector I'd be surprised if he wasn't worn out already his last visitor has just left.' Matron sniffed disapprovingly.

'Did the visitor leave a name?' Hall asked.

'Joyce Leader,' she said, sniffily. 'She was quite a persistent young woman. I told her that only next of kin or colleagues from Scotland Yard were allowed visiting rights.' She looked at them questioningly. 'Miss Leader mentioned Sergeant Mackenzie lost his family in a bombing raid recently?'

Garvan nodded. 'Yes, he did.'

'She also told me that he saved her life last night?'

'Yes all true,' he confirmed.

'The poor man,' she said sympathetically.

They found Mackenzie propped up on his pillows staring bleary-eyed across the ward, watching the curtains being pulled round the bed of the patient opposite. There wasn't much else to do. He caught movement out of the corner of his eye and smiled at them lamely. Matron fussed about the bed, pumping the pillows, straightening the covers.

'Not too long mind,' she said, wagging her finger at his visitors before heading back to her desk.

Garvan sat down in the chair beside the bed and gently touched Mac's shoulder. 'You look fucking awful mate.'

'I feel terrible.' Mac murmured. 'Did you see Joyce Leader?'

'No we didn't,' Hall said.

'She was here a few minutes ago. You must have just missed her. She said you caught up with Maggie Hamilton last night.'

Garvan nodded. 'At her flat in Red Lion Square.'

'Joyce said she was dead, is it true?'

'Maggie was about to get trigger happy again,' Garvan told him, 'so Major Hall here shot her. We've just broken the news to her father.'

'Blimey that can't have been easy.'

'It never is,' Garvan said flatly, 'but, at least, we set him straight, he now knows his daughter was on the point of arrest for murder.'

'And what about the other business in France?'

'He knows about that as well,' Spencer intervened, 'the committee decided it was better to clear the air once and for all. Otherwise, the old bugger would only have started conjuring up conspiracy theories.'

'What do you mean?' Mac asked.

'You know the type of thing that we'd killed his daughter just to get back at him. Complete nonsense of course, but from past experience, it's the kind of twisted theory he was likely to come up with.'

Mac met Hall's eyes. 'I just to wish God you'd managed to shoot the bloody woman down before she managed to get a chance of killing me!'

'It wasn't for the want of trying, but I simply couldn't get a clear enough shot of her. So what have the doctors told you?' he asked, lifting the clipboard from the end of the bed with Mac's medical notes.

'That I was lucky, a fraction of an inch to the left and I'd have been pushing up daisies.'

'Have they said anything else?' Spencer quizzed him, rifling through the notes.

'Not really other than they expect me to be in here for several weeks it all depends on how the next few days go. The surgeon came round this afternoon and checked me over, nice enough little bloke, told me everything was fine and breezed off along the ward with his junior doctors trailing after him.'

'Do you need anything?' Garvan asked.

'Pyjamas mate, I can't have me arse hanging out of this gown when they start getting me out of bed. And I need my shaving kit.'

'Are you in much pain?'

'They've dosed me up with so many painkillers I feel as high as a sodding kite can't feel a bloody thing. Matron over there reckons they're going to start getting me out of bed tomorrow.'

'They have to,' Spencer cut across him 'it's all to do with the circulation if you're bed bound for too long you increase the risk of developing a blood clot.'

Mac raised his eyebrows. 'Blimey Major you some sort of medic or what?'

Spencer laughed. 'Me, Christ no, it's just that I took a bullet myself last year, well actually, more than a couple.'

'Really,' Mac said trying to prop himself up on his pillows. 'What happened?'

'It's a very long story Sergeant, I was shot up by the French Resistance, but I've bored your Chief Inspector with my story already. I'll maybe tell you another time, perhaps when you're feeling a bit better.'

Mac seemed disappointed.

'Trust me,' Spencer assured him, 'I'll visit you again, say next week and give you the whole gory story. We don't want to go upsetting Matron now, do we, besides she looks as if she'd be quite a handful?'

Mac glanced toward her desk. 'She's kind enough, but you're right. I wouldn't fancy getting on the wrong side of that one!'

Hall re-attached the clipboard to the end of the metal framed bed. 'If it's any consolation you're doing a whole heap better than I was after surgery.'

'Thanks for that,' he answered wearily.

It didn't take too long before Mac began drifting off to sleep. Garvan and Hall thanked the Matron and made their way out. On arriving back at Waterloo tube station, they saw Joyce Leader standing at the ticket office.

'Hello,' Spencer called out to her.

She swung round from the booth ticket in hand. 'Have you just come from the hospital?'

'Yes, we have.'

'All things considered, don't you think he's doing pretty well? I know its early days, but even so I thought he'd be at death's door.'

'It was kind of you to visit him, he'd have appreciated it,' Garvan said to her.

'He saved my life Chief Inspector,' came the simple response, 'it's the very least I could do'.

'Where are you going?' Hall asked her.

'Time's getting on,' she said checking her watch, 'I thought I'd head off to the Savoy and meet up with some friends.'

'Are you going to Crockford's Casino afterwards?'

'Not tonight.'

Joyce followed them through the barrier and onto the wooden escalator. Garvan and Hall needed to catch a train to Embankment Station, and then change onto the Circle line to St. James's.

On reaching the platform, Joyce said to Garvan. 'I guess Chief Inspector you'll be only too happy to get us out of your hair.'

'Actually, it's not going to be quite that easy,' he tried explaining.

Spencer wandered off along the platform by himself, hands stuffed into his overcoat pockets.

'Why ever not?' she asked Garvan.

'The Colonel has offered me a secondment to St. James's.'

'A secondment?' Joyce repeated sceptically.

'Yes. I've accepted.'

She pulled a face.

'You look surprised.'

'You could say that.'

He couldn't tell if she was pleased, or perhaps thought he was completely out of his senses to accept the poison chalice of working for Robertson.

Spencer wandered back along the platform just in time to hear the end of their conversation.

'Actually Jo,' he said, 'amongst the Chief Inspector's many duties will be assisting me in keeping you in check. So God help us both.'

'Are you seriously leaving Scotland Yard?' she turned back to Garvan. 'This isn't some kind of sick joke, is it?'

'It's not a joke,' he assured her. 'It's a secondment for a year or maybe two.'

Leader shook her head and looked at him almost pityingly. 'You just don't understand Chief Inspector, do you?

'Understand what exactly?'

'Once they get their claws into you'll never break free from their clutches, never. Will he Spence?' Joyce shot at him.

Hall shrugged indifferently. 'Don't drag me into this.'

'He'll tell you,' she added, pointing at Hall.'

Spencer was still non-committal as Garvan looked at him searchingly.

'They even told Spence he'd only be seconded from the SOE for six months! Robertson lied, they all lie! Just walk away while you can. Whether you like it or not,' Joyce continued in full flight, 'MI5 will always be breathing down your neck. Your life is going to change Chief Inspector in so many different ways, ways you would never have imagined.'

Joyce reached out and touched Garvan's arm. 'You really should have run for cover once you had the chance, once this caper was over. I guarantee you Scotland Yard will seem like a picnic in comparison with what Spencer has in store for you.'

Hall rolled his eyes. 'I think what Joyce is trying to say is that compared to me, you're simply too good a bloke for the Double Cross.' He stopped and looked at her quizzically. 'Or is it that he's too nice a bloke to work for me? Which is it?'

'Take your pick!' she snapped at him.

'Your new boss,' she said to Garvan, 'is a hard operator. I guess the Colonel doesn't only need intellectuals like Sarah, but others like Spence,' she admitted. 'If someone steps out of line it's always Spence who's assigned to their case, to knock them back into shape.' She let out a giggle. 'Believe me, that's normally enough punishment in itself.'

'Thank you, Ma'am,' Hall grinned at her.

'For Maggie and me it was a slightly different scenario. We weren't particularly alarmed that Spencer had been brought in to take control, to be honest; we hadn't expected anything else after Sarah's death.' Joyce reached out and gently patted Hall's shoulder before turning to Garvan. 'Tell me, as an experienced copper, once this war is done and dusted, don't you think the Major here has all the makings of a successful criminal or perhaps,' she hesitated, 'a hired assassin?'

Spencer smiled in spite of himself. 'Don't' answer her Garvan. For your information Jo, the Chief Inspector's role at St. James's is going to be strictly desk bound.'

Joyce held his gaze but didn't respond. Beneath the cool expression, there was something obviously on her mind. Was it part amusement, part mistrust that Spencer was being economical with the truth, Joyce decided to keep her thoughts very much to herself. After all, it wasn't her place to question the Major's intentions or anyone else's for that matter.

After the harrowing events of last night, Joyce knew she'd be allowed a little more leeway again and also that she was now one of St. James's most valued agents. As a result, the pressures would increase even more; the Twenty Committee would undoubtedly raise the stakes. The quality of her transmissions, always high grade, would now be moved up a notch or two, and with Maggie Hamilton out of the equation life would soon settle down to its usual endless merry-go-round of messages, concocted intelligence, and ever more demands from both Ritter and Robertson. And so it would continue, this endless cycle of bluff and counter bluff.

Joyce was worn out and mentally exhausted by the never-ending spiral of subterfuge. Standing on the platform sandwiched between Hall and Garvan, she closed her eyes briefly. If only there were some way of turning back time. She should have walked away from Ritter, have refused his offer of becoming an Abwehr agent, but she had genuinely feared for the safety of her family back in Austria. It had all been so difficult, and now there was simply no way out, no place left to hide.

The West End cocktail parties and the clubs, the high life, still couldn't entirely compensate for being trapped in a deadly gilded cage. Was that the reason Joyce asked herself, why she sometimes partied a little too hard, to blank out the despair of her circumstances, the constant lies about her life in Britain, and the misinformation to her handlers in Germany? She fully accepted it was a situation of her own making, but one she now deeply regretted.

Her memories started to tumble back to her very first meeting with Sarah Davis. She hadn't been overly impressed by her newly appointed London controller to the point where she was virtually dismissive of anything she said to her. In hindsight, Joyce realised now Sarah's stunning beauty had clouded her opinions. If she was entirely honest with herself, there was probably an element of jealousy involved, and she'd mistakenly assumed Sarah was just some blonde, air-headed secretary who had probably made good by sleeping her way around Whitehall.

It hadn't taken Joyce very long to realise she'd been utterly wrong. The old saying that you should never judge a book by its cover was never more appropriate than in Sarah's case. She ended up proving her worth time and again. She'd possessed a fierce, almost frightening intellect, coupled with profound insight into German politics and its culture. Perhaps more importantly, she had a deep understanding, far greater than Joyce, of the Third Reich's leadership many of whom she'd met personally during her father's stint as a diplomat.

Sarah had frequently briefed Joyce in her faultless High German rattling off orders, and complex transcripts for the transmissions with a clear-sighted, no-nonsense briskness. In so many ways, it was still difficult to accept Sarah was dead. For Joyce, at least, it still didn't seem quite real.

By the time Spencer had stepped into the breach after Sarah's death, his life was in turmoil, but he'd never once allowed his emotions to interfere with his work with either of them. He was quite simply an extraordinary force. Every German agent in the Double Cross both admired and feared him in equal measure. By his own admission, he'd never been Sarah's intellectual equal, but anyone who saw them instinctively knew they were a couple, deeply in love with one another.

Joyce recalled overhearing Spencer say to Hugh Dickinson that Sarah had saved his soul, but what had he meant by that she wondered. Joyce was intrigued, and also a little envious. She'd never yet experienced either that depth or intensity of feeling for another person.

Tears began to burn her eyes. God, she needed to get a grip, the last thing she needed right now was for either them to see her cry, to break down. She didn't do vulnerability, or so she wanted them to believe. She hurriedly wiped the tears with the back of her hand hoping neither of them had noticed.

Spencer checked his watch. He was always checking that fucking watch she thought to herself, there was always some deadline or meeting to attend, yet another transmission to analyse, another script to help draft with the policy makers. Each of them in their own way she decided was trapped in the same cycle of deceit and subterfuge.

Hall looked up from his watch and glanced toward the darkened tunnel waiting expectantly for the first flutter of warm breeze from the approaching tube train. His thoughts flittered back to Red Lion Square, to the moment Maggie had aimed Sarah's pistol at him. It had been mercifully quick he thought, Maggie had barely known what hit her. He found himself praying to God that Sarah's last moments in Monkton Drive had ended as swiftly. Haunted still by his decision to remain at his desk on that fateful evening he kept asking himself if it had been the right one. He should have done more to ensure Sarah's safety, and perhaps, more importantly, never have agreed in the first place to her becoming the bait in the hope of flushing out their rogue agent. The pain, the grief of losing Sarah was a constant, grinding torment. The guilt of not being there for her repeatedly kept playing over in his mind. He suddenly became aware that both Joyce and Garvan were watching him. His tight expression relaxed into a smile, and he gave Garvan a sidelong glance.

'The one thing I can tell you with any degree of certainty is that working with me at St. James's isn't going to be an easy ride.'

'I never really thought it would be.'

'Do you know what I think your greatest challenge will be?'

Garvan shrugged.

'It'll probably be trying to keep Jo under control. If you don't watch your back, she'll be all over you like a fucking rash.'

Joyce didn't rise to the bait. Her hair suddenly blew in the warm breeze as the tube train started its approach through the tunnel, and at that moment; Luke realised Spencer was only half joking. The train noisily rattled into the station; the doors opened smoothly. As they boarded the carriage, Garvan found himself wondering again if he'd made the right decision.

Spencer had once said to him that war wasn't about who was right or wrong; ultimately it was about who was left standing. The Double Cross was a means to that end, and without the ability of the Intelligence services to maintain the upper hand against the Third Reich, it was very unlikely that Britain would ever be the one left standing.

The sensible, the safe decision, would have been to turn down Hall's proposition, to have gone back to the relative safety of Scotland Yard, to the world he knew so well. St. James's was an unknown quantity, but one where he could make a difference. Spencer had given him a window onto a world of intrigue, of fear, of national importance. Surely he thought you'd have to be a fool to ignore such an offer, such a tantalising nugget of hope, of opportunity. It had certainly proved a challenge he'd felt unable to refuse.

Seated on the tube, Spencer turned to Joyce and said. 'Colonel Robertson always predicted our Chief Inspector would end up working alongside us.'

She smiled, an enigmatic smile hiding a myriad of mixed emotions. A silence fell between them as the train rattled off through the dark tunnel, each of them separated by their own thoughts, their own feelings.

For Garvan, it was just the start of an adrenalin fuelled roller-coaster ride into the unknown.

*If you liked this book you might also wish to read the other books by the same author; they are all Free on Kindle Unlimited – **FIVE STAR RATED REVIEWS ON AMAZON AND GOODREADS***

Mission Lisbon the V-1 Double Cross
Review from Amazon UK

This is a very well researched wartime novel with believable characters and a twisting storyline. It is a gripping story of espionage during World War II, and I hope there will be another book in the series as it leaves the reader on a cliff-hanger.

Dead Man Walking - A Spy Amongst Us
Review from Amazon.com

Fans of British WWII espionage intrigue will love Dead Man Walking, A Spy Amongst Us by Toby Oliver. A British cabinet member is murdered, and the evidence points to infamous double agent, Toniolo, as the perpetrator. The author is a master at weaving deception and conspiracy at every turn of the page. It is a fascinating backstage look at the relationship between England, Germany, and the Soviet Union during the war. The author blends meticulously researched fact with fiction and will keep your interest until the very end. Buy this book if you love spy novels, and you won't be disappointed.

The Downing Street Plot – An Agent's Revenge
Review from Goodreads

This was the first book I've read by this author Toby Oliver, but I certainly hope it's not the last. He has a gift for writing descriptive and life-like scenes that make us feel like we are really there inside the story, as opposed to it all just being "told" to us, as so many authors make the mistake of doing. I like that this book didn't feel stale or derivative of every other thriller/spy book out there, but instead like a new niche of political action and suspense that serves well to help diversify a somewhat cookie-cutter genre (in my opinion). Spencer and Jack were great, and I also really liked Virginia and Taylor (yes, I know…). But they were interesting characters that kept me hooked. It was fast paced and creepy and shocking at times, but overall the entire novel was one that I thought was well-crafted and delivered an emotional win in the end. Recommend

Printed in Great Britain
by Amazon